The Other Black Girl

The Other Black Girl

— A Novel —

ZAKIYA DALILA HARRIS

ATRIA BOOKS
New York London Toronto Sydney New Delhi

ATRIA BOOKS

An Imprint of Simon & Schuster, Inc.
1230 Avenue of the Americas
New York, NY 10020

This book is a work of fiction. Any references to historical events, real people, or real places are used fictitiously. Other names, characters, places, and events are products of the author's imagination, and any resemblance to actual events or places or persons, living or dead, is entirely coincidental.

This Atria Books hardcover edition June 2021

ATRIA BOOKS and colophon are trademarks of Simon & Schuster, Inc.

Interior design by Jill Putorti

Manufactured in the United States of America

1 3 5 7 9 10 8 6 4 2

Library of Congress Cataloging-in-Publication Data

Names: Harris, Zakiya Dalila, author.
Title: The other black girl : a novel / Zakiya Dalila Harris.
Description: First Atria Books hardcover edition. | New York : Atria Books, 2021.
Identifiers: LCCN 2020048720 (print) | LCCN 2020048721 (ebook) |
ISBN 9781982160135 (hardcover) | ISBN 9781982160159 (ebook)
Subjects: GSAFD: Suspense fiction.
Classification: LCC PS3608.A783293 O85 2021 (print) |
LCC PS3608.A783293 (ebook) | DDC 813/.6—dc23
LC record available at https://lccn.loc.gov/2020048720
LC ebook record available at https://lccn.loc.gov/2020048721

ISBN 978-1-9821-8718-7
ISBN 978-1-9821-6015-9 (ebook)

For my family—present and past

Black history is Black horror.

—Tananarive Due, *Horror Noire: A History of Black Horror*

Prologue

December 1983
Grand Central Terminal
Midtown, Manhattan

Stop fussing at it, now. Leave it alone.

But my nails found my scalp anyway, running from front to back to front again. My reward was a moment of sweet relief, followed by a familiar flood of dry, searing pain.

Stop it. Stop it.

I'd already learned that the more I scratched, the more it'd resemble the burn of a bad perm—a bad perm that had been stung by fifty wasps and then soused with moonshine. My small opportunity for reprieve would come only after the train started moving, when I could finally close my eyes and take comfort in the growing distance between me and New York City. Still, I continued to scrape at the itch incessantly, my attention shifting to another startling concern: We weren't moving yet.

My eyes darted to the strip of train platform visible through the open doors, my mind moving faster than I'd moved through Grand Central Terminal just minutes earlier. *What if someone followed me here?*

Slowly, carefully, I raised myself up to check. On the left side of the car were a young brunette mother and her baby, clad in matching itchy-looking red winter coats with black velvet lapels. On the right was a gray-haired, greasy-looking man with his forehead smashed against the glass window, snoring so loudly that I could almost feel the train car shake. We were still the same four we'd been when I'd ducked into this car five minutes earlier.

Good.

I exhaled and sat back down on my hands, willing the wave of mild relief that had washed over my brain to wash over my heart, too. But the latter organ hadn't gotten the memo yet, and a sudden flash of a shadow passing by the open door set my brain off again.

Did anyone see me get into the cab?

What the hell am I doing?

What the hell are they *doing?*

I shook my head and crossed my legs, my nylons scraping against one another like two black pieces of sandpaper, the round toe of my too-tight heels rubbing the bottom of the seat in front of me. I hated these tights and these shoes and this peacoat I'd thrown on in the dark; I hated how stiff my entire body felt—cold, numb, like it had been dipped in a tank full of ice water.

But I could fix all that later. What concerned me more were the things I couldn't name. The things that were causing me to buzz and burn and want to flee not just my home, but the tightening constraints of my skin itself.

There was the sound of a bell, followed by a calling voice. A male voice. It took me a moment to realize that the shadow I'd seen passing by the door belonged to the conductor. He was in the back of my car now, working his way up to the front. "Sir," he was saying, in a polite attempt to wake the snoring man for his ticket. "Sir."

I fumbled nervously for my shoulder bag. I knew I had enough money on me; before sneaking out of my apartment, I'd made sure to grab the savings from that torn pair of polka-dotted panties I kept hidden in the bottom of my sock drawer. But now I was here, about to get going, and I still didn't know where I was get going *to*. I'd meant to make small chat with the brother driving the taxi—flash him some teeth in the rearview mirror the way I used to do before everyone knew my name, see if he knew any parts of upstate New York that were particularly cordial to our kind of people—but my mind had been too fixated on what had sent me running in the first place. What I'd overheard her say to him on the phone.

Imani says it's not supposed to burn.

I uncrossed my legs as I considered how long I could stay missing. Judging by how hard my name was being dragged through the papers, it wouldn't be difficult for anyone to believe I'd want to "take a break" from the spotlight. But how long would they leave me alone? How long would they be kind to Trace before demanding answers? They weren't going to let me off the hook *that* easily. Not after what I had done.

All those careers, jeopardized. A note, slipped under my door in the dead of the night by a Black writer I'd idolized for much of my youth: *You couldn't just let things be?*

More burning. More searing pain. I was scratching at my neck again, grateful for any kind of distraction from those words, when a hand gripped my shoulder. I let out a small shriek and batted it away, only to realize it belonged to the equally frightened-looking conductor.

Never had I been so excited to see a white male stranger in my entire life.

"I didn't mean to startle you," he said, "but I'm going to need to see your ticket, ma'am."

"Oh." I pulled out a crisp twenty from my wallet. When I looked back up at him, he was leaning against the seat across the row from mine, waiting patiently with a small smile. He appeared to be in his mid-twenties, at most five years younger than me, and he had a kind enough face when he asked where I was headed.

"Good question," I said, just as the snoring started back up again a few rows behind me. "What's the most northern stop on this train?"

The conductor's smile widened with curiosity as he moved to accept the bill. "Poughkeepsie, ma'am," he said. "About two hours north, and it'll be four seventy-five to get there."

"Okay. Actually, hold on—I might have seventy-five . . ." I reached for my wallet again to unearth a few quarters. Only after he handed me my ticket and my change did he punch the air in front of him and say, eyes flickering, "Right! I've got it. I know where I've seen you before."

I swallowed, shook my head once. *No, no, no.*

"I was just reading about you this morning," he said, pointing at something in his back pocket. A rolled-up newspaper. The twinkle in his eyes went out, and when he spoke again, his words came slowly, like he was deciding if I was worth wasting them on. "I was a big fan of yours. So I was *really* surprised to learn how you *really* feel."

Look away. That was what I told my eyes to do. But instead of averting my eyes, instead of telling this man, *Leave me alone, I don't know what you're talking about*, I did something that surprised him, and surprised myself even more.

I looked him in the face. And I smiled.

"Oh, heavens—you mean that witchy lady from the news, right?" I crowed. "Why, that happened to me on the way here. My taxi driver made the *same* mistake. Can you imagine that? Twice in one day! I reckon it's a good thing I'm leaving the city now, ain't it?"

When the last of the shrill, inhuman sound escaped my lips—laughter, it was supposed to be—some of that early twinkle returned to the conductor's eyes.

He moved closer, sizing me up a little too long. But I kept my smile big and bold and harmless, just like Grandma Jo did every morning she traveled across town to clean white folks' houses.

"Ah. I see it now. The eyes," the conductor decided, finally. "You look far too young to be her." He turned to leave. "Well, you have a good day, ma'am. And I'm real sorry about that."

As he made his way to the next car, I heard him chuckle. "Witch indeed," he muttered.

I breathed out a tiny poof of air. That was easy—*too* easy. But I couldn't sit with it for too long. There was another bell; a moment later, the train doors slid shut.

Relieved, I cast one more glance toward the door, the sudden movement causing me to shrink from the pain. The itchiness hadn't just returned; it was all-consuming. Unyielding. I reached up again to scratch—*stop it, stop it*—but the itch simply moved to a new site, and I had to bite my lip to keep from screaming. One scratch would always lead to another, then another. I'd be scratching until the end of the line. And once I got to the end of the line, that wouldn't be it. I'd still be scratching. And I'd probably still be running, too.

I groaned and slid over in my seat to rest my head against the window. It was as warm and sweaty as the skin beneath my collar, but as the train sped up, each swath of tunnel passing seamlessly into the next, I closed my eyes anyway. I could pretend, at least for this train ride, that everything was okay. That it wasn't too late.

Part I

1

July 23, 2018
Wagner Books
Midtown, Manhattan

The first sign was the smell of cocoa butter.

When it initially crept around the wall of her cubicle, Nella was too busy filing a stack of pages at her desk, aligning each and every one so that the manuscript was perfectly flush. She was so intent on completing this task—Vera Parini needed everything to be flush, always—that she had the nerve to ignore the smell. Only when it inched up her nostrils and latched onto a deep part of her brain did she stop what she was doing and lift her head with sudden interest.

It wasn't the scent alone that gave her pause. Nella Rogers was used to all kinds of uninvited smells creeping into her cubicle—usually terrible ones. Since she was merely an editorial assistant at Wagner Books, she had no private office, and therefore no walls or windows. She and the other open-space assistants were at the mercy of a hard-boiled egg or the passing of gas; they were often left to suffer the consequences for what felt like an hour afterward.

Adjusting to such close proximity had been so difficult for Nella during her first few weeks at Wagner that she'd practiced breathing through her mouth even when it wasn't called for, like when she was deciding between granolas at the grocery store, or when she was having sex with her boyfriend, Owen. After about three months of failed self-training, she had broken down and purchased a lavender reed diffuser that had the words JUST BREATHE scrawled across its front in gold cursive letters. Its home was the far corner of her desk, where it sat just beneath the first edition of *Kindred* that Owen had given her shortly after they started dating.

Nella eyed the gold foil letters and frowned. Could it have been the lavender diffuser she smelled? She inhaled again, craning her neck upward so that all she could see were the gray and white tiles that lined the ceiling. No. She'd been correct—that was cocoa butter, alright. And it wasn't just *any* cocoa butter. It was Brown Buttah, her favorite brand of hair grease.

Nella looked around. Once she was sure the coast was clear, she stuck her hand into her thick black hair and pulled a piece of it as close to her nose as she could. She'd been proudly growing an afro over the last three years, but the strand still landed unsatisfyingly between her nose and her cheek. Nonetheless, it fell close enough to tell her that the Brown Buttah smell wasn't coming from her own hair. What she was smelling was fresh, a coat applied within the last hour or so, she guessed.

This meant one of two things: One of her white colleagues had started using Brown Buttah. Or—more likely, since she was pretty sure none of them had accidentally stumbled into the natural hair care aisle—*there was another Black girl on the thirteenth floor.*

Nella's heart fluttered as she felt something she supposed resembled a hot flash. Had it finally happened? Had all of her campaigning for more diversity at Wagner finally paid off?

Her thoughts were cut short by the loud, familiar cackle of Maisy Glendower, a squirrelly editor who appreciated modulation only when someone else was practicing it. Nella combed through the bray, listening hard for the hushed voice that had made Maisy laugh. Did it belong to a person of a darker hue?

"Hay-girl-*hay*!"

Startled, Nella looked up from her desk. But it was just Sophie standing above her, arms wrapped snugly around the side of her cubicle wall, eyes as wide and green as cucumbers.

Nella groaned inwardly and clenched a fist beneath her desk. "Sophie," she mumbled, "hi."

"Haaaay! What's up? How are you? How's your Tuesday going?"

"I'm fine," Nella said, keeping her voice low in case any more audible clues floated her way. Sophie had tamed her eyes down a bit, thank goodness, but she was still staring at Nella as though there was something she wanted to say, but couldn't.

This wasn't unusual for a Cubicle Floater like Sophie. As Cubicle Floaters went, she wasn't the worst. She didn't play favorites, which meant that your chances of seeing her more than once a week were slim. She was usually too busy hovering beside the cubicle of another assistant, her lazy smile reminding you of how good you didn't have it. By the luck of the draw, Sophie worked for Kimberly, an editor who'd been at Wagner Books for forty-one years. Kimberly had edited her first and last bestseller in 1986, but because this bestseller had not been just a bestseller—it had been adapted into a television show, a blockbuster film, a graphic novel, an adult film, a musical, a podcast, a miniseries, and another blockbuster film (in 4DX)—she was granted a pass on every non-bestseller that followed. Royalties were nothing to laugh at.

Now nearing the end of her long career, Kimberly spent most of her time out of the office, and Nella suspected Sophie spent most of her time waiting for Kimberly to kindly retire already so that she could take her place. In a year, maybe less, it would dawn on Sophie that her boss wasn't going anywhere unless someone told her to, and no one ever would. But for now, Sophie hung on naively, just as every single one of her predecessors had.

"Kim's still out," Sophie explained, even though Nella hadn't asked. "She sounded *awful* on the phone yesterday."

"Which procedure is she getting done *this* time?"

Sophie grabbed the taut bit of flesh between her chin and her clavicle and wiggled it around.

"Ah. The crucial one."

Sophie rolled her eyes. "Yep. She probably dropped more on that than we make here in a month. By the way, did you see . . . ?" She cocked her head in the direction of Maisy's voice.

"Did I see what?"

"I think Maisy's got another potential candidate in." Sophie tossed her head again, this time adding in a suggestive, wiggling eyebrow. "And I don't know for certain, but she seems like she might be . . . you know."

Nella tried to keep from grinning. "No, I don't," she said innocently. "Might be what?"

Sophie lowered her voice. "I think she's . . . *Black*."

"You don't have to whisper the word 'Black,'" Nella chided, even though she knew why Sophie did: Sounds, like smells, carried over cubicle walls. "Last time I checked, that was a socially acceptable word to use. *I* even use it sometimes."

Sophie either ignored her joke or didn't feel comfortable laughing at it. She leaned over and whispered, "This is so great for you, right? Another Black girl at Wagner? You must be so excited!"

Nella withheld eye contact, turned off by the girl's intensity. Yes, it *would* be great to have another Black girl working at Wagner, but she was hesitant to do a celebratory Electric Slide sequence just yet. She'd only believe that the higher-ups at Wagner had finally considered interviewing more diverse people when she saw it. Over the last two years, the only people who'd been interviewed or hired were Very Specific People who came from a Very Specific Box.

Nella looked up from her desktop at Sophie, who happened to be one of these Very Specific People, and who was still chattering on. Over the course of just a few minutes, Sophie'd managed to talk herself onto a train of social awareness, and it was clear she had no intention of getting off anytime soon. "It reminds me of that anonymous op-ed *BookCenter* article I sent you last week—the one I swore you *had* to have written, because it just sounded so *you*—about being Black in a white workplace. Remember that piece?"

"Yeah, I do . . . and for the tenth time, I definitely didn't write that article," Nella reminded her, "even though I can obviously relate to a lot of the stuff that was in it."

"Maybe Richard saw it and decided to do something about the lack of diversity here? I mean, that would be something. Remember how hard it was just to get people talking about diversity in one place? Those meetings were painful."

To call them meetings seemed gratuitous, but Nella wasn't in the mood to go down that slippery slope. She had more important things to pursue. Like how to get rid of Sophie.

Nella reached for her phone, let out a small groan, and said, "Whoa! Is it already ten fifteen? I actually need to make a very important phone call."

"Aw. Darn." Sophie looked visibly disappointed. "Okay."

"Sorry. But I'll report back!"

Nella would not report back, but she'd learned that punctuating too-long interactions with this promise made parting much easier.

Sophie smiled. "No prob. Later, girl!" she said, and off she went, as quickly as she'd come.

Nella sighed and looked around aimlessly, her eyes skipping over the stack of papers she still hadn't delivered to her boss. In the grand scheme of things, the speed with which one could bring something from point A to point B should have zero effect upon whether that person deserved to be an assistant editor—especially since she'd worked for Vera, one of Wagner's most exalted editors, for two years now. But things between them lately had been, for the lack of a better word, *weird*. Their anniversary check-in a few days earlier had ended on a less-than-savory note. When Nella had asked for a promotion, Vera had listed at least a dozen surprise grievances she'd had with Nella's performance as her assistant, the last being the most unsettling of all: "I wish you'd put half the effort you put into those extracurricular diversity meetings into working on the core requirements."

The word "extracurricular" had hit Nella hard and fast in the eye, like a piece of shrapnel. The company basketball team, the paper-making club—*those* were extracurriculars. Her endeavors to develop a diversity committee were not. But she'd smiled and said *thank you* to her boss, who'd started working at Wagner years before Nella was even born, and tucked this piece of information into her back pocket for safekeeping. That was where she believed any dreams of letting her Black Girl Flag fly free would have to remain.

But now the smell of Brown Buttah was hitting her nose again, and this time, there were telltale sounds: First, Maisy's practiced joke about Wagner's zany floor plan ("It makes about as much sense as the science in *Back to the Future*"); then, a laugh—deep, a bit husky around the edges, but still cocoa butter smooth at its core. Genuine, Nella could tell, as brief as it was.

". . . impossible. I swear, once you find where one person sits, you'll never find them a second time!" Maisy cackled again, her voice growing louder as she led her companion closer to her office.

Realizing that they would have to walk by her own cube to get there, Nella looked up. Through the small crack in her partition, she spotted the swath of dark locs, the flash of a brown hand.

There *was* another Black person on her floor. And given Maisy's spiel, this Black person was here for an interview.

Which meant in the next few weeks, a Black person could quite possibly be sitting in the cube directly across from Nella. Breathing the same air. Helping her fend off all the Sophies of the Wagner office.

Nella wanted to put a victorious fist in the air, 1968 Olympics–style. Instead, she made a mental note to text Malaika this latest Wagner update the earliest chance she got.

"I hope your trip wasn't too long," Maisy was saying. "You took the train from Harlem, right?"

"Actually, I'm living in Clinton Hill right now," the Black girl responded, "but I was born and raised on One Thirty-Fifth and ACP for a while."

Nella sat up straighter. The girl's words, which sounded warmer and huskier than the laugh that had fallen easily from her mouth, evoked a sense of Harlem cool that Nella had always wished she possessed. She also noted—with reverence and not a little bit of envy—how confident the girl sounded, especially when Nella recalled her own anxiety-inducing interview with Vera.

The footsteps were only inches away now. Nella realized she'd be able to get a good glimpse at the newcomer if she slid over to the far right of her cube, so she did exactly that, pretending to leaf through the manuscript Vera was waiting on while keeping one eye trained on the strip of hallway that led to Maisy's office. Almost instantly, Maisy and her prospective dreadlocked assistant made their way into her periphery, and the full picture came into view.

The girl had a wide, symmetrical face, and two almond-colored eyes perfectly spaced between a Lena Horne nose and a generous forehead. Her skin was a shade or two darker than Nella's chestnut complexion, falling somewhere between hickory and umber. And her locs—every one as thick as a bubble-tea straw and longer than her arms—started out as a deep brown, then turned honey-blonde as they continued past her ears. She'd gathered a bunch and piled them on top of her head in a bun; the locs that hadn't made it hung loosely around the nape of her neck.

And then there was the girl's pantsuit: a smart-looking ensemble composed of a single-button marigold jacket and a matching pair of oversized slacks that hit a couple of inches above the ankle. Below that, a pair of red patent leather high-heeled ankle boots that Nella would have broken her neck just trying to get into.

It was all very Erykah-meets-Issa, another detail Nella was filing away for Malaika, when she heard Maisy ask the girl to explain what "ACP" meant. And it was a good thing she had, because Nella hadn't known, either.

"Oh, sorry—that's Adam Clayton Powell Jr. Boulevard," the girl said, "but that's kind of a mouthful."

"Oh! Of course. A mouthful indeed. Harlem is such a great neighborhood. Its history is just so rich. Wagner held an event at the Schomburg earlier this year—February I think it was—for one of our authors. It was very well received."

Nella fought back a snort. Maisy hadn't attended this aforementioned event; what's more, Nella was willing to bet her middle name that the Museum of Natural History was as far north as Maisy had ever traveled in Manhattan. Maisy was a kind enough woman—she made bathroom small talk as well as the next senior-level employee—but she was fairly limited in her sense of what "the city" entailed. Just the mention of Williamsburg, despite its Apple Store, Whole Foods, and devastating selection of designer boutiques, caused Maisy to recoil as though someone had just asked to see the inside of her vagina. *Surely* this dreadlocked girl could sense that Maisy had no true sense of Harlem's "culture."

Nella wished she could see the look on the Black girl's face, but they'd already started to enter Maisy's office, so she had to settle for a chuckle in its place. It was subtle, but in the milliseconds that passed before Maisy shut her door, Nella was able to detect amusement at the end of that chuckle—an exasperated kind of amusement that asked, without asking, *You don't spend time with Black people often, do you?*

Nella crossed her fingers. The girl probably didn't need it, but she wished her luck, anyway.

2

August 6, 2018

Nella cleared her throat and ran her left thumb down the edge of the manuscript, then across its bottom. She knew that she might cut herself deep enough to bleed if she moved her finger any faster, but she also knew that with this risk came the possibility of a reward—an excuse to flee and win a few precious minutes of stall time—and such a possibility was tempting.

"Well?" Vera placed both elbows on her desk and craned her head forward, too, a tic that justified her biweekly appointments with her chiropractor. "Tell me what you thought about it."

"Well . . . there's a lot to talk about. Where do I begin?"

It was a question Nella had spent an unreasonable amount of time trying to answer. There was no way she could begin with the truth: that it had been difficult for her to finish *Needles and Pins* without stomping across the kitchen floor in her socked feet, opening a window, and throwing the pages out onto Fourth Avenue so they could be chomped into bits by oncoming traffic. That at around midnight, she'd taken a break to jot down a list of all of the things she'd hated about it, then torn the list up before feeding the pieces of paper to a Yankee candle. How she'd taken a ten-second video of the burned bits and sent it to Malaika, who texted back, in all caps, *GREAT. NOW GO TO BED, WEIRDO.*

Nella might have deserved this scolding a *tiny* bit. The book wasn't altogether terrible. It did a nice job conveying the bleakness of the countrywide opioid epidemic, and it contained a few particularly moving scenes rife with moving dialogue. A family of ten finally confronted long-buried secrets; a baby escaped a precarious situation unscathed. The book's heart appeared to be in the right place.

It was just that one of its characters was not: Shartricia Daniels.

Nella would never be able to confirm it, but she sensed that Colin Franklin's first draft had been written exclusively about frustrated white characters living frustratingly white lives in a frustratingly white suburban town. After reading this draft, someone—a friend or an agent or maybe even Vera herself—must've suggested he throw some color in there.

Now, Nella was no fool. She understood that characters of color were en vogue, as was maintaining vigilance when it came to calling out anything that lacked proper representation. Nella wasn't the one doing the calling out, but she closely monitored social media so she could support whoever did. She read think pieces by day and retweeted that the Oscars were indeed too white by night, and following the infamous Black-boy-in-a-monkey-hoodie incident, she took a six-month-long break from shopping at H&M—a big deal for someone who loved buying cheap basics in the summertime. She could see the common thread of perceived subhumanity that ran between the cultural faux pas of major corporations and the continuous police killings of Black people.

And of course, she wasn't alone. She could always count on the Internet to cry foul on the latest trend. Perhaps the loudest voice of all was Jesse Watson, a nationally known, outspoken blacktivist whom Nella and Malaika and over a million other people followed on YouTube. The mere mention of his name, which rested quite comfortably on the more extreme side of the social activism spectrum, often tinted dinner table atmospheres faster than Cheetos-stained fingertips, and his supercharged manner of speaking suggested that this was exactly what he wanted.

Sometimes, Nella felt Jesse went just a tad *too* far in his YouTube videos, like the time he made a ninety-minute video on why all Black people should abandon CP Time. But in other instances, he made so much sense that it hurt, like his post on why "well-meaning white folks" were sometimes far worse than white folks who wore their racist hearts on their sleeves. So, as Nella considered why she distrusted *Needles and Pins* so much, she also considered what Jesse had said about white people who went out of their way to present "diversity": "With heightened awareness of cultural sensitivity comes great responsibility. If we're not careful, 'diversity' might become an item people start checking off a list and nothing more—a shallow, shadowy thing with but one dimension."

Shartricia was less than one-dimensional. She came off flatter than the pages she appeared on. Her white male creator had rendered her nineteen and pregnant with her fifth child, with a baby daddy who was either a man named LaDarnell or a man named DeMontraine (Shartricia could not confirm which because both men had fled town as soon as they'd heard). She cussed and moaned in just about all of her scenes, isolating herself from the reader just as much as she isolated herself from her family and non-opioid-addicted friends (of which she had few). Then, there was the kicker: Her name, "Shartricia," was her uneducated crack addict mother's attempt to honor the color of the bright green dress she'd been wearing at the club when her water broke.

Okay, so maybe Nella had found this last detail both vexing *and* endearing. But everything else about Shartricia's character felt icky—especially her voice, which read as a cross between that of a freed slave and a Tyler Perry character down on her luck. Still, even with all these thoughts swirling in her head, Nella didn't know how exactly to express any of them to the white woman who was sitting in front of her, asking what she thought. The white woman who just happened to be her boss *and* Colin's editor.

"I think this book is very . . . timely," Nella said, opting for the buzzword that everyone at Wagner liked to hear. "Timely" meant coverage on NPR and *Good Morning America.* It meant "adding something new to the conversation," which was what Colin Franklin always sought to achieve in his long list of ripped-from-the-headlines books that included a murderous sister wife, a deadly school shooting, and a sexy serial killer.

Vera nodded eagerly, her light brown bangs undulating above gleaming gray eyes. "Timely. You're right. He refuses to shy away from the hardest parts of the opioid epidemic." She jotted down one or two words on the yellow notepad that sat just beneath her elbows and then tapped her pen on her cheek the way Nella had seen her do in countless meetings. "And do you feel like anything in the novel didn't particularly land the way it should have?"

Nella examined Vera's expression carefully, searching for what Vera wanted her to say. The last time Nella had critiqued a book that her boss favored—six months earlier—Vera had dipped her head and told her that her feedback had been spot-on. But then, when it came time for Nella to overnight the marked-up pages along to the author, she happened to notice her comments on the last few pages hadn't made it in. She flipped through the first chapter and hadn't seen any of her comments on those pages, either.

It hadn't bothered Nella too much at the time. She'd planned to bring it up at their check-in. But that talk had failed, and now Nella was left wondering what her true purpose as Vera's assistant *was.* If Vera didn't trust her opinion, then Nella would never be more than just an "assistant"; if she didn't become more than just an "assistant," she'd never become an editor. It was a dream she'd been nursing for ten years, ever since she decided to join the newspaper staff during her junior year of high school. She loved sliding words and paragraphs around in a game of literary Tetris. The act of editing soothed her, and while she'd be the first to admit she had an inclination toward Black writers yearning for a space to tell Black stories, she'd happily edit just about anything thrown her way. She was excited by the prospect of being able to make a living off editing, and the idea of having a say in what people were reading and perhaps—in the future—what people would write? That was monumental.

Not too long after Vera called the diversity meetings "extracurricular," dashing Nella's hopes for a promotion anytime soon, Nella met up with Malaika at their favorite Mexican spot. Enchiladas usually salved her wounds, but Nella spent a good minute and a half staring at her plate before finally positing the question that she and Malaika always asked one another when they'd been slighted: "Do we think it's a race thing? This no-promotion thing?"

"Maybe." Malaika had swept up the near-empty bottle of habanero hot sauce and shaken it all over her plate for the third time, smacking the bottom to get every last drop into her side of guac. Then, unsatisfied, she'd leaned over and swiped a bottle from the table next to them. The white couple sitting there looked befuddled, but said nothing—they hadn't been using it, anyway—and they even offered a cheerful *you're welcome* when she thanked them and handed it back.

Such a gesture more or less summed up this brazen person whom Nella had come to befriend a few summers earlier at a karaoke bar in the Village. The two had first met when she asked Malaika to jump on a mic at the last minute to help her rap through "Shoop," since Nella's original Pepa had been sick from one too many Bloody Marys at brunch. They'd been best friends ever since, constantly comparing notes on online dating disappointments and homegrown hair care regimens (like Nella, Malaika's curls were also 4C, although she'd been natural since day one, and therefore had a fro-mane that rivaled Pam Grier in her heyday).

Their most vital notes of all, though, came from comparing Black Female Experiences. They had remarkably different backgrounds—Nella had been raised in a mostly white suburb of New Haven, while Malaika had grown up in Atlanta around a whole mess of Black people. But they'd had zero problems finding common ground. Nella believed this had something to do with the fact that they'd both been raised on Black '90s sitcoms and smooth jams from a very young age.

Malaika had also been her own kind of Oreo for much of her life, which was why she'd taken a bite out of her torta and said, in her best

Dr. Phil twang, "Maybe Vera also sees you as competition. Maybe she feels that fully accepting you will somehow validate the secret fear she has that every woman under the age of thirty is out to get her job. Maybe . . . she's jealous."

At this, Nella had given her a skeptical look. "You obviously haven't met this woman. Or me. I wear Keds to work. *Keds.* Not even the fancy kind. The basics."

Malaika had swatted this away. "Well, that's your own fault, but hey—lemme ask you this. Do you see any other white assistants getting promoted that have been there for less time than you?"

"No," Nella had admitted, "I guess pretty much every editor has been stingy about upward mobility—even for the white assistants."

"Well, there you go."

"So . . . we *don't* think it's a race thing?" Nella still wasn't convinced.

"Hell, yeah. That's a factor, too. She's protecting what's hers for as long as she can . . . you know, the way some white people insist on only reproducing with other white people because they want to preclude the population of mixed-race babies that's obviously gonna rule the country by 2045. But here's what I say to myself whenever Igor gives me shit at work about little things that don't *really* matter, like his Twitter bio. Girl—I'm saying this to *you* now, Nell, not me—*you* are a double threat. You understand me? You're not just Black, you're Black *and* you're young. And if she's smart—and she must be, since she's been doing this for what, thirty years?" Malaika paused, continuing only after Nella confirmed this with a nod. "If she's smart, she knows that girls like you . . ." She smiled a small, silly smile. "And *me* . . . are the future."

Nella had appreciated this sentiment enough to laugh and clink her glass with Malaika's as she had many times before. There in that indistinguishable restaurant, tucked away beneath the less-trafficked folds of the Lower East Side, the talk had felt like a warm, fuzzy Snuggie. But now, in the bright light of Vera's large office, one window glaring out onto Central Park—hours after Nella had struggled to read a white man's bizarre depiction of a pregnant Black opioid addict—she was beginning to feel a chill. And the source of it seemed to be her boss.

"Did anything land the way it shouldn't have?" Nella repeated. "Well, um, the characters were pretty solid. But there were one or two that didn't quite work for me."

"Okay. Say more," Vera pressed, knitting her eyebrows more tightly together.

Nella didn't want to say more, but if there was one thing Vera didn't like, it was people who were afraid to say more. Especially women. It was partly why she'd hired Nella, Vera once told her at a holiday party, after partaking in a little too much nog. She had found Nella's literary tastes "raw and bold and unique" when they'd first met. Which was pretty funny, since after meeting Vera for the first time, Nella had been sure she'd blown the interview entirely.

Nerves . . . Nella had had many of them. They'd hovered around logistics, like potential MTA mishaps and navigational failures and the worry that the inch-long run in the crotch of her stockings wouldn't make it through another wear. But she'd also worried that she and Vera would have zero chemistry. She'd never really worked a proper Manhattan office job. She didn't know what to expect, save for what she'd seen in television shows and movies, and a part of her deeply worried that all of the things she'd seen—severe hierarchy, homogeneity, and rigidity—were true. Nella had grown accustomed to working behind bars and coffee counters, which spoiled her with exposure to all kinds of people with all kinds of occupations. Such jobs had also allowed her to wear whatever she wanted, whereas she didn't think she could have shown up to her interview with Vera wearing a Black Lives Matter shirt.

So, the morning of her interview, Nella erred on the side of caution: Twenty-dollar no-frills flats from Payless that, if necessary, would enable her to chase after a stray train. On her deep-brown legs she'd worn her favorite pair of old black stockings underneath her most conservative blue dress; on her shoulder, a tote bag she'd snagged from the *Nation*'s booth at the Brooklyn Book Festival the year before—just for a little touch of personality.

Thankfully, the MTA gods were good to her. Her train arrived exactly when the sign said it would, and as it whisked her out of Bay Ridge into Manhattan, she felt comfortable enough to lose herself in an editorial assistant blog she'd been following for years. Forty minutes later, she found herself on the street, just one block away from Wagner. She was waiting for a light to change, mentally patting herself on the back for being almost fifteen minutes early and just all-around interview-ready, when she looked down and nearly screamed. The run in the crotch of her stockings had traversed the length of her leg, all the way down to her ankle.

That had done it. Any confidence she'd felt from the sunshine and the perfectly timed train dispersed. *You gotta be twice as good, remember?* she'd chided herself. She couldn't remember who'd said it to her first, or if it had ever been said directly to her at all, but that didn't stop her from telling herself over and over again that her brown skin meant she needed to be twice as good as the girl with white skin, and that this giant run would do her in.

The *twice as good* mantra did not go away—not when she reached the front desk and completely blanked on Vera's last name; not when she went for a hug and Vera went for a handshake at the door; and certainly not when she used the word "literally" three times in two sentences. Therefore, when Vera called a week later to say that she believed Nella would be the perfect addition to Wagner's editorial team, she'd been stunned. There *had* to have been another candidate with wholly intact stockings and a firm grasp of the word "literally." Or, surely, a white Ivy League grad who seemed like he or she had potential to do great things.

But Wagner wanted *Nella*, and this had delighted her so much that she'd done her finest pajama-twerk as soon as she'd hung up. Then, she'd quit her three food-service jobs in Brooklyn in rapid succession; fewer than two weeks later, she had a new boss, a new desk, and appointments set up for an eye exam, a physical exam, and a much-needed dental cleaning. Goodbye, self-medication of monthlong colds with Emergen-C and Flintstones vitamins. Hello, health insurance.

Now, Nella studied the little zen garden that sat on Vera's desk just below the window. Her boss never let anyone else touch it, but sometimes, when Nella was having a particularly hard day, she'd sneak in and push the rocks around for a minute or two. Thinking of this brought her peace of mind, as did the memory of her pajama-twerk celebration after she got Vera's call. To Nella, it hadn't seemed *that* "raw and bold and unique" to stan Amiri Baraka or Diana Gordon, but it had apparently worked on Vera then, back when she'd been nothing more than a stranger with a run in her stockings and a Public Ivy on her résumé. Why not try leaning into it again? Why not bring out that "raw and bold" (and Black) person from her interview?

Besides . . . if *she* didn't say anything about Shartricia, who else at Wagner would?

"I'd love to know which specific characters you think need more work," Vera said, her eyes flicking toward the door, then back again. "I saw some things here and there, too."

Nella sat up straighter in her chair. "Great! Okay. So, here's my main issue." She took a breath. "To be completely honest, I think . . ."

But any steam she'd gained from the start was deterred when Vera's eyes flashed to the door a second time. They remained there the third time, glowing with interest. This was enough to quell Nella's mumbling. She turned, too.

Maisy's tiny fist was poised mid-knock on Vera's doorframe. "Sorry, ladies," she said, even though she didn't look sorry. "There's someone I'd like you both to meet." She stepped all the way into Vera's office, smoothing her hands up and down her maroon pencil skirt. Nella brightened as she watched the Black girl she'd clocked two weeks earlier, in all her dreadlocked glory, take Maisy's place in the doorway. "This is Hazel-May McCall, my brilliant new assistant."

"My parents were pretty ambitious," the new girl said warmly. "Y'all can just call me Hazel. No, please—y'all don't need to stand!"

she added, rushing in vain to meet Vera before she could take one more step away from her wooden desk. She found Nella's hand next, pumping it so hard that both girls' pairs of dangly earrings shook violently back and forth.

Face-to-face, Nella could see Hazel had one inch, maybe two, on her. Today, her locs were free of any constraints, sprouting spiritedly from her scalp and pouring down the back of her baby-blue blazer. Nella grew suddenly aware of her own wrinkled gray V-neck T-shirt underneath an even more wrinkled gray sweater. Of her Keds, dirty and basic.

"Welcome to Wagner! I've heard such marvelous things about you!" Vera nodded in Maisy's direction. "You're working for a great one here."

Maisy batted a hand in a gesture of *Oh, stop it.*

"Yes, I know," said Hazel. "Thank you! I'm so honored to be here at Wagner. I almost can't believe it's happening."

"And we're excited to *have* you. Where are you coming from?"

Nella cringed ever so slightly, embarrassed for her boss, and worried that Hazel would be scared away so soon. *That* question. Oh, how publishing people *loved* that question. She'd first been asked this by Josh, Wagner's sales director, at the Keurig. Nella hadn't known what he'd meant, so she'd mentioned her Connecticut hometown, telling him pretty much everything about it just short of its geographical coordinates. She only understood when Josh said to her, a bit impatiently, "Ah. Interesting. And where in publishing did you last work?"

Nella had looked down at Zora Neale Hurston's face, printed on the side of a coffee mug her mother had gifted her, and said, *Nowhere.* "I was in food service," she'd clarified, and that had been the end of questioning.

But Hazel provided the appropriate prerequisite: a small magazine in Boston. "I lived there for two years and decided to come back here a few months ago. I like New York too much, and I wanted to return to the nonprofit that I started up in Harlem back in the day."

Maisy nodded with noticeable pride. Nella, in the meantime, marveled at Hazel's omission of what she presumed was another reason why she'd left Boston: because it was such a shitty, racist city.

"Boston! Such a great college town," remarked Vera.

"I know," Hazel said. "But even so, it's a lot quieter. And *cold.* I really missed New York's energy."

She furrowed her brow, as though a particularly unpleasant corporate memory were washing over her in that very moment. Nella watched her curiously, spotting a small gold stud above Hazel's left eyebrow, so tiny that it could only be discerned with particular facial expressions such as this one. Had Hazel received nasty emails from her old job's HR department about her locs? *People are starting to complain about the* odor *coming from your cube,* the note might have said. Or maybe something about eyebrow piercings being too unprofessional. Nella had been to Boston only a handful of times, but she'd read enough to know that Hazel probably hadn't had an easy time.

She could already see Hazel telling her all about it after work, dishing stories over gin and juice, when Vera chimed in, "Yes, it really is quite cold. We think we get snow here. But up *there* it's a different animal entirely. Maisy knows all about that. Don't you, Maze?"

"Ah, that's right!" said Hazel good-naturedly. She didn't seem bothered that her use of the word "cold" had been misunderstood. "Weren't you telling me that you were born and raised in Boston?"

"From diapers to my dissertation," Maisy chirped. "And my first job was in Boston, too. It'll always be my home"—she placed a hand on her heart—"but it's definitely not for everybody. The food scene is dreadful. Ver, do you remember that awful awards dinner up in Cambridge?" And with the introduction of this memory, she and Vera were off for about three minutes, going back and forth about every course, sparing not one extravagant detail.

Nella stretched her face into as little of a smile as she could get away with, prepared to exchange a knowing glance with Hazel as they waited for the conversation to circle back. But when she tried to meet the girl's eye, Hazel didn't look bored. She was actually smiling and tutting and *Ohmygod*ing right along with Vera and Maisy. At one point, she contributed a joke of her own and even nudged Maisy with her elbow.

Nella frowned, a little bummed that her glance hadn't been reciprocated. She was a little surprised, too. She couldn't remember when she'd first ventured to touch her boss, but it certainly wasn't her first day, probably not even her first month.

"Anyway, what was I saying?" Maisy said finally. "Hazel, Nella here will be an *amazing* resource for all of your questions. You should totally pick her brain."

"We call her the author whisperer," Vera added, even though Nella had never been called this a single day in her life. "Whenever a diva is freaking out, Nella just lays on that charm of hers and it's all good."

"Aw, nah." Nella chuckled. Fake-humble was the MO at Wagner, after all. "I don't know about all that. But yes, ask me anything. I'll be just right across the aisle."

Hazel flicked her locs over her shoulder, a cheeky smile spreading across her face. "Careful what you say! I'll probably be bothering you all the time. I know magazines, but books are a complete mystery to me."

Had the new girl really just admitted that in front of her boss? *That's pretty ballsy of her,* Nella thought, remembering how much she'd downplayed her own inexperience in publishing when she first started. But an explanation for this came to her almost immediately: *Entry-level assistants are liked way more when their bosses think they're blank slates.* "It'll be no bother at all," she said. "Really!"

Hazel's head tilted to the side just so, like it was being gently tugged by an invisible string, like she was just *so* happy to know Nella was in her corner that she couldn't keep her head straight. "I'm *so* glad to hear that."

Maisy bowed her head in gratitude. "Great! And Vera, before we go: Do you know if Bridget is here today? I would love to swing by her office and introduce Hazel before we grab lunch."

"I heard Stevie playing through the wall earlier, so . . ."

Both women made faces at one another. "Ah. I'll take my chances. We'll let you get back to it. So sorry, again, for interrupting!"

"Oh my god, Maze, don't even worry about it!" Vera waved her off and sat back down in her chair, her hands already returning to the couple of scrawled notes on Colin Franklin's latest novel. "And Hazel—again, it's *so* nice to meet you. We're thrilled to have you on board."

"Yes! Welcome!" Nella added cheerily, and after a few half waves, four became two again.

Nella sat back down, feeling readier than ever to delve into her Shartricia feedback. Meeting Hazel had poofed away her apprehension, renewed her sense of purpose. But when she started to speak, she noticed something disconcerting had come over her boss's face. After a few wordless seconds, Vera put her pen down and said, a bit grumpily, "Jeez Louise. I'm always ready to take a break from work after I talk to Maisy. She's *that* exhausting."

Nella shrugged. It was startling whenever her boss treated her like a confidante.

"Now, where were we?"

"Colin Franklin. *Needles and Pins.*"

"Yes. Yes, so you were saying—"

Vera was interrupted again, this time by Stevie Nicks. Bridget, an associate editor with an affinity for the singer, was definitely in the office that day, and had apparently been in a good enough mood to open her office door when Maisy knocked. Nella and Vera listened as Maisy shouted out the name of her new assistant, and then as Hazel shouted it even louder. Nella was shutting Vera's door when Maisy yelled Hazel's name a third time, adding, rather helpfully, "Like the nut!"

Vera sighed. "Thank you. Ugh. Someone really needs to do something about that," she complained, even though they both knew very well that the last person who'd asked Bridget to turn down her music had suffered a rough couple of months with HR, because Bridget happened to be the granddaughter of one of Wagner's first authors—who in turn happened to be a golf buddy of Richard's. This explained why she'd scored her own office at such a relatively junior level, a decision of Richard's that had uniquely pissed off both upper- and lower-level employees.

Nella eased back into her chair and squared her shoulders. She waited an appropriate amount of time before saying, firmly, "So. *Needles and Pins*. I'm going be candid here: One of the characters *really* didn't—"

"Listen, Nella . . ." Vera rubbed her temples and exhaled. "I think Colin will be coming into the office soon, maybe next week. How about you just share your thoughts with both of us then? That way we can take his response to your critique into account when we prepare our offer for *Needles and Pins*."

Nella wasn't sure what made her queasier, the fact that she'd have to speak with Colin in person about her feelings without flying them by Vera first, or the fact that Vera already seemed so set on buying this book. "Um . . . okay. I just wonder if maybe you and I should talk about it, um, first—just maybe the—um—weaknesses, or . . ."

"Yeah, yeah, we'll just tell Colin in person," Vera said, now fully closing her eyes. "It's just, I can't focus now with . . . with this." She gestured at the wall through which the fiery riff of "Edge of Seventeen" was blaring.

"Good god, this place sometimes," Vera continued. "Is it me, or are they putting something weird in our water?"

Vera was right. There *was* something in the water at Wagner. But Vera had had a hand in that. She and pretty much all of the higher-ups at Wagner who earned livable incomes—they were all messing with the water, making it difficult and sometimes impossible for smaller fish like Nella to survive. Lurking beneath many of the friendly seeming meetings was an environment of pettiness and power plays; cold shoulders and closed-door conversations.

The most fascinating part was that they all thought everyone *else* was crazy. At least, that's what Yang, the girl who'd been assisting Maisy when Nella had first started at Wagner, had intimated to her. Yang had taken on the noble task of not only training her on editorial procedures, but also giving her the scoop about all of her new coworkers—whom to watch out for at holiday parties, whom to avoid in the elevator, whom to get coffee with. All the important intel.

Yang had been an incredibly helpful guide, and as a first-generation Chinese American, she'd also been the only other POC Nella had ever gotten to work with at Wagner. Together, they made cracks about how hard it must be for everyone to tell them apart and rolled their eyes at the higher-ups constantly walking outsiders through their side of the office—purposely, they half-joked, to showcase the company's diversity.

It all came to an end six months later, when Yang quit to go get her PhD. Three days after Yang's last day at Wagner, another shooting of yet another unarmed Black man—this time, an elderly one—went viral. He had been pulled over by a white police officer hours before sunrise in rural North Carolina. Minutes later, he was dead, and hours later, the world was on fire. Numerous reports said he'd been reaching to turn up his hearing aid. One day after Nella watched Jesse Watson's livid response to the shooting blow up on Twitter, Richard Wagner sent out a company-wide email announcing an upcoming series of Diversity Town Halls.

Very rarely did the editor in chief of Wagner Books send emails to his employees; he either popped into your office unexpectedly or sent you a note handwritten in impeccable cursive. The very existence of this email was thrilling, and its contents were so promising that Nella had printed out the email and thumbtacked it up in her cube. The news of the shooting had outraged the country and it had particularly outraged her, too—not only because the man had been hard of hearing and in his seventies, but also because he'd borne a subtle resemblance to a grandfather she'd never met. It was comforting to know, then, that all Wagner employees had received a directive to start talking to each other about the major elephant in the room.

But there was just one problem: No one really knew what the elephant was. Or where the elephant was. Or if there was even an elephant at all. The definition of "diversity at Wagner" managed to mystify all of Nella's colleagues, and Natalie from HR and the British moderator she'd brought in as a "neutral party" spent the first hour of the first town hall trying to pinpoint what they were really supposed to be talking about. "Do we mean diverse *employees* or diverse *books*?" asked Alexander, one of Wagner's most literal editors. "Or do we mean diverse *authors*?" "Didn't we publish this book by that Black writer just last year?" others asked. And so on.

Their confusion was understandable enough, and Nella did her best to rein everyone back in toward the task at hand with her own small "objective" observations. But she couldn't bring herself to say that maybe higher-level employees shouldn't primarily hire people with Ivy League degrees or personal connections, because her own résumé had been boosted by an editor friend of one of her professors at the University of Virginia. And the zinger she *really* wanted to deliver—*Yes, we just published "that Black writer" last year, but that writer, along with the last six Black people we've published here at Wagner, was not a Black American, he was from an African country, and while that's definitely an example of diversity, it's also really not*—wouldn't work, either. It would only unleash a whole new slew of gradations that Nella didn't even feel comfortable grappling with on her own yet, let alone with her white employers.

The second hour of the "meeting" was filled with clumsy role play and even clumsier word association games, and naturally things got worse. When Nella offered up the acronym "BIPOC" as a term she associated with "diversity," her coworkers *ooh-yeah*ed . . . and then offered their own examples of "diversity": "left-handedness," "nearsightedness," and "dyslexia." Only when someone volunteered the word "non-millennial" did Nella realize that a return to her own concern about the treatment of Black people both inside and outside of the literary sphere would be highly unlikely. And just like that, faster than it took to utter the words, "what about ageism?" the moderator was bowing her head and lauding everyone—the one hundred or so people in the room, all white save for Nella—for being so *open*.

Relieved at the prospect of watercooler debriefings, her colleagues had hustled out of the conference room faster than they'd exited any sexual harassment education seminar. And everybody had seemed far more perplexed leaving the town hall than they'd been going in.

Nella was, too. But for different reasons. Her coworkers could publish books about Bitcoin and Middle Eastern conflicts and black holes, but most of them couldn't understand why it was so important to have a more diverse publishing house. It didn't surprise Nella, then, that the next non-mandatory Diversity Town Hall had half as many attendees as the first. The following, even fewer. By the time the fourth meeting rolled around, its attendees were just Nella and a blue-eyed publicity assistant whose name Nella no longer remembered, because she was no longer with the company. Even Natalie in HR had stopped attending due to "scheduling conflicts."

"Maybe we should offer donuts or something, to get more people to come?" the blue-eyed assistant had meekly suggested, and in an uncharacteristically public gesture of frustration, Nella had ripped up the latest think piece she'd planned to share with everybody and stormed out of the room.

Heat still brushed Nella's cheeks whenever she remembered this public display of weakness. Being the only Black girl in the room wasn't so hard a gig most of the time. She'd slowly befriended every other individual at Wagner who worked as an assistant in any capacity, and the other people of color who worked at the front desk and in the mailroom knew her by name. But it wasn't the same as having a "work wife" who *really* understood her. She craved the ability to walk across the hallway, vomit out all of her feelings about a racially insensitive fictional character, and return to her desk, good as new.

Nella had grabbed one of Colin Franklin's twenty-page contracts from the printer and was flipping through it, thinking about just how many feelings were churning around her insides, when she walked straight into her newest cube neighbor.

"Sorry!" She held out an arm to steady Hazel, even though she was the one who needed steadying.

Hazel raised her eyebrows in either bemusement or judgment—it wasn't quite clear which. She placed a hand on her hip. "Dang, girl, where you rushing off to so fast?"

Yes, Nella realized from the twitch that tugged at the left side of Hazel's mouth, curling it up into a smirk—it was indeed judgment.

"It's hard not to run around here like a bat out of hell a lot of the time," Nella said, even though such an arcane saying had never left her lips before. She looked at her watch in an effort to recover from it. "So, um, how was lunch with Maisy? You guys were gone for what—two hours?"

"Was it really that long?" Hazel asked, staring in the direction from which she'd come. "Lunch was pretty great. *Maisy's* great. We went to a Taiwanese spot."

"Nice. Lu Wan?"

"Yep. On Ninth."

"Yeah, that's a favorite around here."

"*So* yummy. Anyway, I was just happy she made the time," Hazel said, stopping next to Nella's cube. "Now that I'm back, do you think I could ask you about this one email?"

"Oh, sure!" Nella dropped the contracts on top of the stack of Colin Franklin books Vera had asked her to wrangle from Wagner's library in preparation for the offer. She hadn't been asked to get the sales numbers from Josh for *Three-Ring Bullet* and *The Terrorist Next Door* yet, but Nella was quite positive that request would be coming by the end of the week. Which meant that in the next two weeks, Wagner would most likely be making a deal on Colin's next book—baby mama Shartricia, five and a half children, six figures and all.

Nella shuddered at this last very painful straw. She felt her soul, which often sounded a lot like Angela Davis, cry out a little bit—but she put on her best smile anyway. Then, she walked over to Hazel's cube to take a look at the email that filled her screen. Seeing that the text was in red Papyrus font was enough for Nella to say, without even reading it, "It's Dee over in production. Yikes."

"Honestly . . . I'm not sure what any of this means."

Nella couldn't blame her—the email subject line read *Simpson?* and the email read, simply, *WHERE IS THIS*?

"Just a second. I think Erin left me a note about this before she left . . ." Nella flipped through the master packet that she hadn't touched since Erin, Maisy's last assistant, had gone back to working at her father's law firm in the Upper West Side four weeks earlier. "They pay us shit here," the girl had said, packing up her third box of books. "How you can afford to live in *this* city on *this* salary, I have no clue."

The irony of this comment coming from a girl with such a convenient exit strategy was not lost upon Nella. But, like all of the other people under the age of thirty-five who eventually left Wagner for similar reasons, Erin had a point. The pay was shit, and it would be shit for the next five years at least, depending on how close you could get to *the* Richard Wagner in that time. If you were able to snag his attention, you were set for the rest of your publishing career, but if you couldn't—if you weren't a legacy hire, like Bridget, or if you worked for someone he wasn't particularly keen on—you were pretty much screwed. You could work at Wagner as long as you wanted, but you were still going to make twentysomething an hour.

Nella traced a finger down the second page of Maisy's assistant packet, careful to avoid the large grease stain in the top right corner. She wondered which of Maisy's assistants had left that mark—definitely not Yang, who never ate anything at her desk except green grapes and red pears, and not Emily, whom Nella had never seen eat anything at all. Heather, the one who'd just graduated from King's College London and was always quick to drop a "bloody" here and a "loo" there, had hardly been at Wagner long enough to get her name on her cube. Nella supposed the perpetrator had been Erin herself. All those bags of Lay's. All that noisy crunching.

"It says here in Maisy's master packet that Simpson usually takes at least a week longer than he's given to get his edits back," Nella read, "and it looks like he's three weeks late. Do you see anything in your inbox from him?"

Hazel scrolled through her emails, tapping her long, French-manicured thumbnail on the mouse as she went along. "Nope, *nothing*."

"Alright. Well, what you're going to do is tell Dee that Maisy will have a chat with Simpson. And then you're going to write to Simpson yourself. Introduce yourself, gush about his last book on cumulus clouds, and then in the last line mention that you *think*—never say anything like it's fact—that he might be . . ." Nella scanned the packet once more. "A week or so late."

"He's *three* weeks late, though."

"Right. But it'll be better if you pretend he isn't. Good to tread lightly when you first start working here; then, over time, you can ramp it up. Once he likes you."

"But wouldn't it make more sense to just . . . I don't know . . . start out by telling Simpson how late he actually *is*? Hold him accountable? He's a grown man."

That's debatable, Nella thought. "Maybe it would. But this is just how it's always been done."

"*Al*right," said Hazel, although she still sounded doubtful. She craned her neck to get her own look at the master packet. "And all of *that* is in there?"

The gracious smile Nella had plastered on her face for this how-to demonstration was starting to feel like work. She hadn't asked *this* many questions when she took over for Katie, had she? "No, it's not *all* in there. Well, just the bit about his cloud series, and about using kid gloves on him. A few years back, someone got sick of figuring out which types Maisy's authors were, so whoever that was compiled an entire spreadsheet of quirks, which are in the back. Here." Nella handed over the packet.

Hazel accepted it uncertainly, her perfectly arched eyebrow raised at a perfectly alarmed angle. "This looks like it should really be laminated. And alphabetized."

Nella sucked some air through her teeth on her way back to her desk. "Yeah, well. You're not wrong about that."

"Mm-hmm." They sat in silence for a moment as Hazel took in the pages. "Hey, girl—thanks for this."

"No problem. I'm here if anything else comes up." A sudden email on Nella's screen distracted her from saying anything else. *Can you print the very best reviews for Colin's last three books?* Vera asked. *I've got a phone call with his agent in thirty.*

"That's really great of you," said Hazel, who had turned her chair to face Nella. "I'm so glad I have you here."

"Hey, it's nothing." Nella tried to put on her best smile again, but the thought of spending the rest of the afternoon compiling praise for Colin Franklin made it difficult.

"You'll let me know if I'm too extra with my questions—right?"

"Please, don't worry about it. Another assistant trained me. It's the Circle of Life. That's how assistants operate. On goodwill."

Hazel flipped through the packet, humming at different pointers, shaking her head at others. "You've helped a lot of Maisy's assistants, I'm guessing."

"At least four since I started here two years ago. Maybe more."

"Wow." Hazel lowered the packet at the same time she lowered her voice so she had a clear view of Nella's face. "That's a *lot* of turnover. Is there anything I should know about Maisy? Or anything about Wagner in general?"

Nella considered this. Assistants were supposed to pass on the gossip to a new assistant, but the general consensus was to let her believe, at least for the first few weeks, that her boss was a fairly normal human being. Wagner was the hardest publishing house to get into. Every interviewee—Nella included—underwent four back-to-back interviews with various higher-ups, the last one culminating in a high-intensity tea with the editor in chief and founder of Wagner Books himself. The last thing any new hire wanted to hear after finally climbing over these esteemed walls was that an insane boss had been waiting on the other side.

But this felt different. Who was Nella *not* to tell Hazel the truth?

She looked up at her cubicle wall and cast a bit of side-eye to the empty space where that Diversity Town Hall email had once hung, a story her father had told her about his very first job floating back to her. He'd walked into a Burger King and seen a brother sweeping the floor, and a brother at the register, too. Behind the register, there was a brother preparing the orders.

"No white people in charge? Looks like a pretty good gig you guys have going on here," Bill Rogers had said to the Black guy behind the register, who turned out to be the brother—the actual brother—of her father's classmate, Gerald Hubbard.

Gerald's brother had smiled and handed her father a job application. "We practically make our own hours," he said, "and you know what—you've come just in time. There's going to be an opening."

Five days later, he found himself on the register. He made it an entire two shifts without screwing anything up. It wasn't until his third shift that a white man in a sharp suit and tie walked in and introduced himself as the owner. On its own, this would have been fine—Bill hadn't forgotten that the owner was white, and he could handle white people as well as any Black person in those days. But the owner had ended up being a modern-day Simon Legree. And as it turned out, Gerald's brother had been finishing his very last shift at Burger King when he told Bill a position was opening up.

Nella's father continued to work there for three weeks, which was how long it took him to decide that if a boss had to call him "boy," he might as well be making more money for it. A few weeks later he started working as an attendant at a fancy hotel on the other side of town.

Years later, at a neighborhood picnic, her father asked Gerald's brother why he hadn't warned him. "I don't know," he'd said, nibbling on the gristle of a rib somebody's mama had spent all morning cooking. "Same thing happened to me when I applied."

Nella had heard this story several times, and she always felt the same way when her father reached the end. She always swore that if she ever found herself in a similar situation, she wouldn't behave as selfishly as Gerald Hubbard's brother had. And now, here she was, finally in a position where she could be transparent with someone other than Malaika about what it was like to be a Black person working in an all-white office.

As though she sensed Nella was about to break, Hazel sucked her teeth. She was still staring at Nella, except now her eyes were cool, serene. "C'mon, sis," she said quietly. "You can be real with me."

The diminutive washed over Nella like balm on a tight knot in her neck. Nella felt her joints loosen as she released a tiny whoosh of air from her lips. "Honestly . . . your boss is so good at what she does. Everyone who knows her respects her, especially since she's willing to edit all the science books nobody else wants to touch. But." She lowered her whisper to lip-read-only level. "She's a little high-strung. Like, for real."

Hazel didn't flinch. She just nodded. "I kind of had a feeling," she said after a moment. "And tell me: How do they feel about Black people in these parts?"

Nella looked around to make sure no one happened to be lingering nearby. "I'll just put it this way," she said, widening her eyes dramatically. "They don't 'see' color here at Wagner."

Hazel didn't respond. For a moment, it was unclear she'd caught the playfulness in Nella's voice. Maybe she hadn't even heard her at all.

But then that coolness in her eyes turned up, and a knowing grin overtook Hazel's face. "Yeah, that's the vibe I got. It's always good to know what you're working with, right?" She smiled a little, all lip but no teeth, before turning back to her desk and starting to type.

Nella turned her chair back to face her monitor and grinned to herself. *Sis, indeed.*

Hours later, Nella dabbed at the layer of condensation that had gathered at the bottom of her glass with her pinky nail, then deposited the water onto her already-saturated napkin. "Did I tell you she lived in Boston for a few years? *Boston.*"

Malaika shook her head. "No shit!" she shouted as the opening notes of "Juicy" started to flow through the speakers above their heads. Tonight's spot was 2Big, a Bed-Stuy bar that exclusively played songs by Tupac and Biggie in a rather belated attempt to, as their website stated, *Bring Two Coasts Together.*

"And Maisy and Vera just kept going on and on about Boston like they always do whenever they get on a roll. Building it up like it was this magical kind of city, or whatever."

Malaika shrugged and took a sip of her rum and Coke. "Magical for some folks, maybe. What is it Jesse Watson calls it? 'The White Man's Mecca'?"

Nella assented, remembering the segment Jesse had done on the city just a few months earlier, after attending his first—and last—Celtics game.

"God, I'm gonna miss that man. With Jesse on his weird hiatus, how will I be able to tell the difference between a microaggression and a sheet with holes in it?" Malaika joked wistfully. "By the way, is Vera resting easy now that he's gone forever?"

Last year, Nella had suggested they invite Jesse to contribute to Wagner's *Forty Under Forty* anthology, but Vera had tutted at the thought. Literally, and quite loudly, at that. "Between you and me," she had whispered, "some people see him as an emotional terrorist—and I can't say I don't agree with them."

Nella winced now as she'd winced then. "Not sure how tuned in she is to Black Twitter," she said, "but that doesn't matter, anyway. There's no way Jesse's *actually* 'gone forever.' He likes the spotlight too much."

"True."

"Besides, I bet he made that announcement about going offline so that when he returns with his big Beyoncé-sized creative drop, it'll be that much bigger. People like him do that all the time." Nella stated this like she didn't care one way or the other, although Jesse's announcement about taking a break from social media—especially his reason of wanting "to work on some things"—had fascinated her, too. Vera might have said no to Nella's *Forty Under Forty* suggestion, but she hadn't said no to a book written by Jesse and Jesse alone. If Nella found a way to contact him, maybe she could get him to write an outline so irresistible Richard and Vera would have no choice but to sign him on the spot.

She had meant to fly this idea by Malaika earlier, maybe even spitball what kind of projects he'd come back from hiatus with—A memoir? A doc? A gospel album? But the Jesse news had gotten lost in the Hazel shuffle.

"Anyway, going back to this new Black girl," said Malaika, reading her mind. "White Man's Mecca or not, the important question I have for you is: Do you think you'll be friends with her?"

"For sure!" said Nella. "Mal, you *know* how long I've been waiting for this moment! And Hazel seems cool. Probably way too cool for me, actually."

"Impossible."

"She's from Harlem. She's natural—long locs. Ombré."

The ombré locs invoked an *ooooh*, followed by a raising of Malaika's glass. "Okay, maybe she's a little bit cooler than you. But now," she said, pulling away when Nella tried to flick her arm in protest, "a toast: to no longer being the Only One."

"I'll drink to that." Nella clinked her almost empty beer with Malaika's drink. Then she threw back the second-to-last sip and put her glass down, surveying the other people who had decided to grab a drink on a Wednesday evening. For the most part, pairs of twenty- and thirtysomething-year-old women dotted the high barstools, sipping and laughing and shaking their heads with unabashed delight. She felt a warming touch of solidarity as she took in the dozen or so women in their business casual ensembles, mouths full of gin and juice and post-work exasperations.

Nella thought about the gripes she'd planned to bounce off Malaika, mostly about her anxiety toward having to address the Shartricia thing. It just didn't seem fair. Only a few months earlier, Colin had finally stopped misspelling her name in his emails; weeks earlier, they'd even had a brief bonding moment over growing up in

Connecticut. The two of them weren't ride-or-dies by any means, but Nella did feel as though they'd made quite a bit of progress in their author-assistant relationship. And now, she had to look him in the eye—Colin Franklin, an award-winning author who was on a first-name basis with Reese Witherspoon—and tell him that she had issues with his book?

She'd been saving this Colin thing for last as she listened attentively to her friend kvetch about Igor Ivanov, the fitness guru she'd personally assisted for the last eight years. Nella didn't want to hog too much of the conversation, especially given how much time she'd spent complaining to Malaika about Shartricia already. So instead of pivoting to Colin when Malaika finished recounting Igor's latest tirade about her calves, Nella raised her glass again. "I'd like to propose another cheers: to not being confused with the new Black girl. Thank *god* she has locs," Nella joked.

Malaika snorted. "Oh, I can drink to *that.*" She finished the last of her rum and Coke, plopping it down on the table harder than necessary. She had that *real talk* look on her face that Nella knew so well, her big brown eyes unblinking and opened wider than usual. "Locs or no locs, though . . . you *know* one of your coworkers is gonna mix you and the new Black girl up at least once. I *promise* you."

3

August 20, 2018

Nella yawned and wrapped her arms around her shoulders, a feeble attempt to stop herself from grabbing at the coffee before the machine finished spurting. The thing had been dying for about a week or so, which meant Jocelyn—Wagner's business manager and the only employee who knew how to coax sweet nectar from the snarling kitchen Keurig—was visiting family in Germany.

Nella needed her back. Now. Her head was pounding something awful, thanks to the fact that Owen had ended up joining her and Malaika at 2Big the night before. They'd left the bar at an hour far too late for three people who knew they had to get up early the following morning.

Nella was trying to remember what time she and Owen had finally slipped into bed when a new smell disrupted the scent of her coffee and, subsequently, her thoughts. She sniffed the Keurig curiously, unable to name the sweet culprit until she looked over her shoulder. Hazel had breezed into the kitchen, coffee mug in one hand, Tupperware container in the other. She was wearing a bright yellow scarf heavy enough to hinder the aggressive air-conditioning of the subway, but light enough to stick in her bag while enduring the sweatiness of the platform, and a pair of those big white movie-star sunglasses that looked like the ones Nella had tried on the last time she'd gone shopping. With her own small, round face and lack of ample chin, she'd looked like a Chihuahua playing dress-up in the convention center glow of the Herald Square H&M. But Hazel's bright red lipstick and oversized silver hoops managed to tip the scales in her favor.

"Morning, Nell! What's going on?" Hazel set her mug down on the big glass table fixed in the middle of the kitchen. Nella had already learned that this was how Hazel initiated most conversations, no matter how obvious the answer was, and no matter how much it stumped Maisy. Which was, Nella observed, every time.

"Just waiting on my morning fix." The Keurig eked out another wet sound—louder than it had two days earlier—as though it, too, were desperate to contribute to the conversation. Jocelyn needed to return from her vacation, stat, before everyone at Wagner turned on one another with box cutters and loose staples out of caffeine deprivation.

"I still haven't figured that thing out. Is it any good?"

"Eh. You'd be better off siphoning water from the Gowanus Canal and pouring it over coffee beans that you've stepped on with your dirtiest pair of shoes. But it's free, so . . ."

"Shit, 'free' is my favorite flavor." Hazel laughed as she stuffed her lunch in the fridge and closed the door. She reached into her jacket pocket and pulled out a pouch filled with herbs. The flurry of movement sent another wave of sweetness toward Nella's nose that she had to fight not to recoil from. Although she and Hazel had been cubemates for two weeks, she still hadn't gotten entirely used to her new neighbor's hair grease. Or perfume. Whatever it was, Nella was sure it wasn't Brown Buttah. Brown Buttah didn't smell *that* strong.

"My boyfriend works at a tea salon. I get 'free-flavored' tea all the time."

"Nice." Nella considered asking her about this tea salon, but her coffee had finally finished brewing, and a new author of Vera's was supposed to call her in fewer than five minutes to talk about the copyediting process. "Gotta run."

"Okay! See you in, like, three seconds."

"Yeah! See you." Nella grabbed her mug from the Keurig. As she turned to leave, Hazel said, more excitedly than Nella had heard her say anything before, "Ohmygod, wait! I *love* your mug!"

"Thanks! It was a gift from my mom."

Hazel took a couple of steps toward the table and picked up her own mug. Painted on its side in swirls of purple and blue and orange was an unmistakable drawing of Zora Neale Hurston, tilted hat and all.

Nella wasn't sure how she hadn't noticed it before; it was so stunning. "Mug twins! Except your Zora is even prettier. That artwork is beautiful."

"Thank you! It's kind of my pride and joy," Hazel squealed, walking over to the hot water tower.

"Where did you get it?"

"My boyfriend, actually. He painted the art. Then he had a friend of his who works in ceramics do this up for me for our five-year anniversary. He customized the handle just for me, too. Ain't it dope?"

Nella peered closer at the small, finger-spaced grooves in the handle, unable to not notice that Hazel had mentioned having a boyfriend not once, but twice over the course of a very short interaction. It amused her, this double-mention, because it was the kind of detail that meant nothing—until, of course, it was combined with enough other nothings to turn into a something.

In Nella's eyes, this "something" was a lack of self-reliance. She felt a little bit of pride at not having mentioned Owen's name even once to her new cubemate. Hell, she even felt just a tiny bit smug. *Her* boyfriend didn't define her.

Then again, Owen *had* forgotten all three of their anniversaries.

Nella offered up one more laudatory phrase regarding the mug and, as Hazel turned to doctor her tea, a brief goodbye. She needed every second of the remaining three minutes to prepare for her phone call.

She'd started to make a subtle run for it when she heard Hazel say something else.

Nella paused mid-step, considering her options. She was far enough away to pretend that she hadn't heard Hazel speak. But she *had*. Two words, in fact: *Burning Heart*. Black Kryptonite against her steeled workaholic heart.

Her parents had gifted her Diana Gordon's first book for her fourteenth birthday, the summer before she started high school. It had captured her from the epigraph. She loved reading about headstrong Evie, a young, Black teenager who runs away from her conservative parents in a small New England town, and the rough-and-tough Black Panther Party member she falls in love with along the way.

Nella saw bits of herself in Evie. Her own parents had never been the turn-the-other-cheek kind of folks—they'd raised her to speak up when something wasn't right, and to never let anyone treat her like she was less than. But Nella had never really needed to wield these tools as a teenager. And so, she could relate to Evie's desperation to really *experience* life, and her desire to take a bite out of the unknown world that existed just beyond her grasp.

Nella hadn't been able to put *Burning Heart* down for the entire month of August, and even though it rounded out at a whopping five hundred pages, she'd read it three times in rapid succession. She wrote about it for a freshman summer reading project in September, and nearly eight years later, it provided the backbone for a senior thesis that she'd never managed to publish. Since *Burning Heart* had been both written and edited by Black women, she placed its societal impact front and center, along with two other books that were edited and written by individuals of the same race—a rare feat, Nella had come to learn.

This was all, however, too much to explain when she was in a rush, so Nella scurried back into the kitchen, let out a small sigh, and said, "Sorry—did you say something about *Burning Heart*?"

Hazel looked over her shoulder. "Oh, I was just wondering if you're into Diana Gordon. I stumbled across an old piece on her by Joan Circatella last night, and it made me want to reread *Burning Heart*, like, *right* now."

"Joan Circatella? That's amazing! I relied pretty heavily on her work for my thesis in college." Seeing what seemed to be curiosity unravel across her companion's face, Nella added, "'For Us, by Us: The Effect of Black Eyes on Black Ideas.'"

"*Girl.*" Hazel's eyes widened as she put her mug down so she could clap for emphasis. "That. Sounds. So. Dope. Look at you, being all modest. You should *own* that thesis."

"Thanks!" Nella smiled. Worried she might be coming off as just a hair pretentious, she added—even though Hazel hadn't asked—"I'd always been really into the fact that *Burning Heart* was both written and edited by Black women, and that inspired me to put that element into conversation with its societal impact. And I compared two other books that were also written by Black editor-writer pairs."

Hazel clapped again. "That's *bril*liant! I could see something like that running in *Salon* or someplace. *Please* tell me you've done something with it, sis. I'm *begging* you."

"Well—it's been kind of hard, you know . . . with Kendra Rae Phillips, and all . . ." Nella shrugged.

"What do you mean? Wait, oh my god—does she still work here?!" Hazel's locs slapped her cheeks as she glanced excitedly around the kitchen.

"No, definitely not," Nella said, lowering her voice. "That's the thing. She's been MIA for years."

"Oh, right. Yeah, I imagine that leaves an annoying hole in your work." Hazel picked up her mug once more. "It's too bad she left. This business needs more Black editors, more Black mentors . . . more Black *every*thing."

"I know, and—" Nella shook her head, feeling frazzled. This was a conversation she wanted desperately to have, just not right now. "God, I am *so* sorry. I'm going to miss this phone call."

She thought she'd said it softly enough. She'd spent so much time on the *so*, and had indicated how little control she had of the whole situation. Nevertheless, there was a shift in Hazel's disposition. Her shoulders were slumping, as though a weight had been tied to each one. Even her hold on her mug was different—rather than letting it sit in the palm of her hand, Hazel was pinching the handle with almost all of her fingers, using the last one to tap the side with her long nail.

"I'm sorry!" Nella said again. "It's not a personal thing. The call, I mean. It's an author thing. For work."

Hazel shrugged, her eyes narrowed. "I get it. I'll be doing that, too, at some point. I guess."

"You'll be doing it a lot. Maisy doesn't like talking on the phone to anyone but Tony."

"Her husband?"

"Her therapist."

That got a smile out of Hazel. "So many things I need to learn!"

Feeling confident she'd smoothed things over well enough, Nella tried once more to leave the kitchen. Hazel followed after her this time, keeping pace.

Nella cast her a quick, awkward smile. "Hey, how about we do lunch sometime this week, now that you're a little bit settled?" She looked around to see if any of their coworkers were ambling through the halls, even though most upper-level employees didn't float in until ten or so. "I can fill you in on everything. Off the record, of course."

"For sure. I would *love* that."

"Great. Let's plan for tomorrow?"

"Tomorrow's *perfect*."

They'd finally reached their desks. Nella moved a stack of papers that had been snowballing over the last couple of weeks in order to make room for her practically untouched coffee and took a look at her desk phone. There were two missed calls: one from Vera, and another from Colin Franklin, presumably confirming his meeting with her and Vera next week.

She groaned.

"What's up?" Hazel asked. "Shit, did you miss that call you were waiting on? My bad, girl."

When Nella looked up, Hazel was by her side, her mouth formed in a perfect *O*.

"Um. No. No, I didn't miss it. I'm—I just have a lot of things going on right now. Author stuff, you know."

"Aww, you poor thing. Well, hey, just know this: I'm here. To talk about Diana, Zora, Maya, literally *any* Literary Black Queen . . . I can go on and on. But I'm also here for *you*. To spill the tea, complain, anything." Hazel dabbed Nella's shoulder. "I didn't have any Black coworkers in Boston, and I didn't think I would have one here. So, this is . . . pretty awesome."

A warmth Nella hadn't felt for any other cube neighbor since Yang flooded her senses. She smiled, her eyes welling up with . . . were those tears? What the hell? "I feel the same way, Hazel," she said. "Thank you."

"Of *course*!"

Nella turned to reach for her phone, rejuvenated and raring to get to work. But something stopped her.

It was Hazel, whom she could still feel lingering above her.

"So, you're good, then? Everything's okay?" Hazel's voice had dipped a couple of octaves, hovering at a register usually reserved for a mother comforting her child. Her eyes seemed vacant, void of anything other than a needy emptiness.

Nella stared up at Hazel, disconcerted. She was still cradling the phone in the crook of her neck, but the dial tone was doing that beep-beep-beep thing it did when you left it off the hook for too long. "Yes. I'm good. We'll talk more at lunch," she whispered, motioning around at their surroundings with her chin. "Wandering ears, you know?"

Hazel nodded and grinned, her vacant expression disappearing with the wink of an eye. "Oh, I know."

4

August 21, 2018

Lunch with Hazel was at Nico's, an independent hole-in-the-wall café that served Au Bon Pain–quality food with a side of Pret A Manger ambiance. It wasn't a particularly nice spot, but Nella often chose it because it was cheap, and the higher-ups who actually did set foot inside always took their food to go. And since higher-ups certainly didn't take agents or authors to Nico's—waitstaff was an absolute must while wining and dining clientele—the café afforded Nella what she wanted and needed most: a lunch spot of her own, since her cube at the office was everyone else's battleground as much it was hers.

Hazel finished paying first and, to Nella's delight, chose a sunbathed table next to a large window that looked out onto busy, bustling Seventh Avenue. Nella joined her, setting down her sandwich and juice as she stuffed her wallet into her worn-out Wagner Books tote.

"I thought it'd be nice to sit in some sunlight. This is cool, right?"

"Definitely. Good to get some vitamin D."

"So true." Hazel removed the plastic lid from her salad and poked at a walnut with her finger. "I'm so glad we're finally doing this. I've been meaning to ask if you wanted to get a coffee, but shit, man. This learning curve is hard. I feel like I've been drowning the last couple of weeks and I haven't found any time."

Nella nodded. "Yeah, I remember how hard the first few months were. But you've been doing great! Really, you'd know if you weren't. I mean it."

Hazel let the compliment roll off her shoulders and into the small tub of salad dressing that she was having trouble peeling open. She picked up her fork and stabbed at it. "So, Maisy mentioned that Vera has some pretty big books in the works right now," she said. "You must be really excited about that."

Nella grimaced as the sound of Colin Franklin's voice reading with a downtrodden Black woman affect echoed in her ears. "Yeah, you could say that Vera has some pretty big-name authors."

"Sam Lewis, right? Evelyn Kay. And . . . Colin Franklin?"

"Mm-hmm."

"And what's he like?" asked Hazel, her eyes widening. "He must be interesting."

"Interesting is . . . a good way to describe him."

Hazel grinned, leaning in. "Why do I get the feeling there's more you're not saying?"

"Well . . . he's not an easy man to work for. Although he *has* mellowed out some."

"Yeah, but, like—where did he start off, right?"

"Right. *Exactly*. But the thing is . . ." Nella looked around Nico's to see if she recognized anyone within earshot. "I try not to talk about Vera's authors with anybody else, really. It's a good rule of thumb—some editors see it as airing out their dirty laundry."

"I get that."

"And I hate complaining . . . because really, it was so hard to get a job at Wagner in the first place. I should be thankful."

Hazel put her fork down. "Sheesh. What is it? You can tell me. I don't really have a horse in this race."

Nella angled her neck, her eyes full of questions.

"Not yet, anyway. Hey, I'm not even sure I want to *be* a book editor," Hazel added. "I'm still feeling this whole thing out."

"Oh." Still, Nella wasn't convinced. "You promise you'll keep this between us?"

"C'mon. You and I both know we gotta stick together here. And who knows, maybe my outside perspective'll help."

Nella couldn't argue with that. And so, she told Hazel everything about Shartricia in *Needles and Pins.* Her disgust, her reservations—she dumped everything she'd been sifting through in her mind right there on the table between them.

By the time she finished, Hazel had eaten her entire lunch while Nella still had a whole sandwich in front of her. "Sorry," she said, peeling back the plastic so she could take another bite. "It's just that every time I talk about it, I get even more frustrated. And I wonder, am I just crazy? Am I overreacting?"

"*Sheey*it. From what you've told me about Shartricia, it sounds like you're right to feel the way you do. I read one of Franklin's novels for a book club in high school. *Illegally Yours*, I think it was? The portrayal of the Mexican woman in that is so problematic. I can already imagine your pain."

Nella made a face. "I know. Thankfully I wasn't here when he was writing that one."

"And what kind of name is Shartricia, anyway? Sweet lord. Shaniqua wasn't good enough for the stereotypical Black girl name? Of all places, *that* was where he really felt the need to get creative?"

"Girl, preach," Nella said, snapping her fingers. This was exactly what she needed to hear. "I'm with you on that. But that's why it really sucks—because I can't call him out on it."

"Why not?"

"Because he's just going to think I'm calling him a racist. You know how white people get when they think you're calling them racists." Nella sighed, remembering how, shortly after the bout of Diversity Town Halls, she'd overheard a couple of Wagner employees in the kitchen chatting about the idea of being forced to hire nonwhite people. "Let's just go and do exactly that," Kevin in digital marketing had said indignantly. "*Exactly* that. And then let's watch what Richard does when we start hiring unqualified people here, and things start getting screwed up. I'm sure he'll change his song then."

Kevin's back had been to Nella, as had been the back of the other unidentifiable white guy he'd been talking to. But even if they *had* seen her, Nella sensed that neither would have said anything differently. Her colleagues, strangely, had made it clear very early on that they didn't really see her as a young Black woman, but as a young woman who just happened to be Black—as though her college degree had washed all of the melanin away. In their eyes, *she* was the exception. She was "qualified." An Obama of publishing, so to speak.

Sometimes, she saw this as a blessing. They never really bothered asking her for sensitivity reads, and they rarely asked her about "Black issues"—either because they didn't want to offend her by doing so, or because they simply didn't care enough to ask. But other times, she found it almost demeaning, as though accepting Wagner's job offer had also meant giving up her Black identity.

"Girl, you're speaking my *truth*," Hazel said, tapping her plate with her fork. "Even when you just subtly *imply* that a white person is racist—especially a white *man*—they think it's the biggest slap in the face ever. They'd rather be called anything other than a racist. They're ready to fight you on it, tooth and nail."

"It's basically their version of the n-word," Nella agreed.

"Which is hilarious, because Black people have been called niggers for *years*, and they've always just had to keep it moving. Always had to just stay walking down the street without complaining. For *centuries*," Hazel said, hitting the table with her fist, "we've been called niggers, man. And for maybe thirty years, we've been calling white people racists—I mean, the word didn't really mean shit in our English vocabulary until fairly recently, and even *now* some people still don't count it as a disqualifier. But suddenly, it's the end of the fucking world for these people."

Nella sat stock-still, taken aback. Everything Hazel said rang true with what she and Malaika bemoaned after hearing the latest newsflash that yet another politician had been caught doing or saying something racist, but Nella hadn't expected Hazel to get *this* passionate. She'd done so well keeping up with Maisy and Vera's Boston chatter that time they first met, seemed so good at keeping her cool.

The well-dressed Korean couple sitting at the table beside theirs hadn't seen the outburst coming, either. Nella noticed they'd stopped speaking to one another and were curiously looking over at them between bites of food.

Hazel seemed to register the change at the nearby table, too. She unclenched her fingers and breathed out a small *sorry*.

"No. It's fine. Actually, it's really refreshing," said Nella. "So . . . thank you."

"My parents are pretty big in their community for social activism," Hazel added quietly, "and my grandparents were, too. My grandfather actually died in a protest. It's in my blood, I guess."

Nella gasped. "Oh, wow! Hazel, I'm so sorry. When?"

"1961. He was protesting one of the new busing bills. 'Excessive police force.'" Hazel used air quotes for these last few words.

Nella's hands found her cheeks. An amalgamation of Civil Rights Movement footage flashed through her brain in black-and-white, complete with an angry rush of police batons and a soundtrack of somber Negro spirituals. "Wow," she repeated, at a loss for a better word, even though there were many. She settled on an added "I'm sorry."

Hazel shrugged. "Thanks. But I'm here, ain't I? I don't think *he'd* be too sorry about that."

Nella nodded and chewed her food. The two women sat in thoughtful silence long enough for the Korean couple to get up and be replaced by a slightly older, vaguely European-looking pair. Meanwhile, the ghost of Hazel's grandfather hung over their table, daring Nella to say something that carried as much reverence as the words his granddaughter had just said.

Finally, she swallowed her last bit of sandwich and said, "Maybe I *should* say something about this book to Colin and Vera. Harder sacrifices have been made, right?"

Hazel looked up at her. She nodded once, solemnly.

"The question is, how, without jeopardizing my relationship with Vera? I don't think either of them would really get it. A Black girl telling one of Wagner's bestselling authors that his Black character is written a tiny bit racist? C'mon, now. I could get *fired.*"

"You think?" Hazel asked, considering it. "Well, maybe. But Vera seems way smarter than that."

"She's smart, but I'm not sure Vera is *that* . . . 'enlightened.'"

"Really?"

"She came from money," Nella said.

"So did you, right?"

Nella cocked her head, wondering how Hazel had guessed that. She often prided herself on how different she was from her Ivy League, upper-middle-class colleagues—not just in her appearance, but in the ways she moved about the world. Still, Nella knew she had it pretty good, too. Her parents hadn't been wealthy, but as a child, she hadn't wanted for anything. They'd lived in a nice house; they'd taken semiannual vacations. She'd attended nice public schools, and it had always been a given that she would attend college. It had also been a given that, if Nella ever really *needed* financial help, her parents would provide it.

"My parents were pretty well-off when they had me, I guess. If being middle class counts as well-off. But it's not the same thing as coming from real money. *Generational* money. At least, I don't think so."

"Sorry, I didn't mean to offend you . . ." Hazel held up a hand. "I just figured since you work at Wagner and the pay is pretty shitty, you must have a little bit of a cushion holding you up some. That's all."

"Not really. I have college debt that I have to pay back on my own," Nella said, unable to mask the defensiveness that was creeping into her voice and causing her to cross and recross her legs under the table. "And my parents don't give me money for rent. Not unless it's an emergency or something."

"Right. I'm sorry," Hazel repeated. "Anyway, all of that is beside the point. What I was getting at is, do you think that just because Vera has money she's automatically incapable of having any kind of empathy for Black people?"

Nella stared at the girl, wondering where her lunch companion's Black Panther spirit had gone. She'd moved from channeling her inner Baraka to her inner Barack—from confrontational to compassionate—in less than sixty seconds. The change was befuddling, and suddenly Nella wasn't certain which Hazel she was talking to. "Maybe Vera's not incapable," she admitted, "but I do imagine the privilege of money plus the privilege of white skin makes it far less likely."

Hazel shrugged. "I don't know. I know I'm new, but of all of them, Vera just seems so . . . I don't know. Approachable? At least, she seems way more down than Maisy."

"Eh. Maybe. Still feels like there are some pretty obvious boundaries keeping us from having a straight-up conversation most of the time."

"The fact that she's your boss . . . yeah. That's a given. I'd just thought maybe Vera was one of the good ones. I don't know, maybe that's crazy to say."

One of the good ones. One of the most dangerous phrases to ever exist in the English language, Nella's mother always liked to say, and Nella had grown to agree with her. She could accept the idea of allies—people who "got it." She'd decided Owen was one of these people a couple of weeks after they'd met online and started dating. Nothing in particular had moved her in this direction. It wasn't really because he "didn't see race" or that he knew all the lyrics to Al Green's "Love and Happiness," because, respectively, he did and he didn't (although he did a pretty great imitation of Al Green's ad-libs). But she refused to call even her boyfriend "one of the good ones," because such consistency, such innocence, was quite nearly impossible from one human.

Nella had expected her new cube neighbor, who hailed from one of the country's greatest and richest Black meccas, to feel the same way.

Hadn't Hazel spent her last few years working with white people in Boston?

But then, she considered how warm of a welcome Vera had given Hazel on her first day. And how kind Vera could be one-on-one—when she was willing to let her guard down; when she was willing to let herself wilt just a tiny bit. There was a chance, Nella realized, that she *was* being a bit too hard on her boss. Perhaps, for Hazel's sake, she should ease up a little.

"You're right, though," she conceded. "Vera's no Maisy."

The two Black girls sat in silence again, staring outside the window at the passersby milling around Midtown. It was a particularly warm day, and it was clear that many tourists who were out and about didn't know what to do with the ninety-five degrees they'd been given. Nella herself regretted not looking at the forecast before putting on a high-collared blouse that morning, noting the little bit of moisture that still remained between her armpits from their three-block walk forty minutes earlier.

Hazel, on the other hand, had looked completely at ease in the sunshine. She'd dressed smartly in a blush-pink halter top, which she'd revealed only after they'd taken their first steps away from the office and she felt comfortable removing her modest button-up sweater.

Nella fanned herself a few times in anticipation of going back out in the heat.

"We should probably head back," she said at last, crumpling up her garbage with one hand.

"Probably a good idea. Given all the things I've already screwed up so far for Maisy, I'm not sure I've earned the right to have full hour-long lunches yet," Hazel joked. "Hey, one last thing, though."

"What?" Nella was already poised to walk over to the trash can, her bag looped over her shoulder.

"My two cents, for what it's worth: Whether Vera's down or not, I think you should say something to her. She'll thank you for it. And isn't it better to give her a chance to fix it now, rather than be that one person of color who just let it slip right by, under her nose? Remember how much flak that Kendall Jenner Pepsi commercial got because no one spoke up?"

Nella did, of course. She and Malaika had text-dissected it to death immediately after they'd each seen it, wondering about the Black people who'd played a part in making the commercial happen. It was highly likely that there weren't any Black decision-makers at Pepsi, which explained its inception. But what about the Black people who hadn't been in the drawing room, but had been a part of getting the commercial made? That chance Black person who'd maybe helped find the shooting site, or held a camera, or styled some hair? Surely *some* Black people had to have been nearby; some might have even watched the ad bloom from a germ of an idea into a full-fledged campaign. Had something felt a bit wrong, a bit off to the hypothetical Black camera guy as he watched Kendall Jenner rip off her wig through the lens? Or had he been pummeled so frequently by the industry that he hadn't seen anything wrong with it?

Nella and Malaika couldn't decide which was worse: knowing and not acting on it, or not knowing at all. But Malaika's own position was that she would have kept quiet. If the pay was good enough—and it was—she didn't see the point in blowing up her own spot. It was the twenty-first century, after all. If white people couldn't navigate politically correct waters on their own, that was their own problem.

Nella had sent a row of side-eye emojis to Malaika in response to this, and nothing more. She hadn't yet found herself in such a situation at Wagner, one in which she had to choose between going along with the machine or sticking a foot in its gears.

Not until now.

Hazel was carefully studying Nella, clearly trying to decipher whether she would voice the apprehension that was written all over her face. When she didn't, Hazel slowly eased up out of her seat. But before she went to dispose of her trash, she leaned forward and placed a fist on the table between them. She didn't bang on it as she had before, but the agita from earlier had returned to her timbre. "I *know* it's scary. But remember your thesis? Just think about it. *You* know as well as I do how hard it is for a Black female writer to find a Black female editor in this industry. And how *special* it is when it happens. How else are we going to make that happen again? We *have* to make it easier for Black people who decide they want to work in publishing after us, right?

"Right?" she repeated when Nella didn't part her lips soon enough.

Nella nodded fervently. "Yes! Yes. Right."

"We need to break down some of these barriers for them," Hazel declared.

Nella stood. She felt energized; she felt liberated. She felt ready to go to a rally—or, ready, at least, to grow some Black-bone. "You're *so* right, Hazel!"

"Damn straight! That's what I like to hear, sis." Hazel gave Nella a hug no longer than the length of a dap before grabbing her things. "Hey, this was so fun! Can we do this again soon?"

Nella nodded, prepared to joke that if they got lunch too many times, their white coworkers might start to worry. But Hazel was already several feet ahead of her, too far away to hear her joke, so she swallowed it whole.

5

August 28, 2018

Nella held the cup up to the light for the third time and turned it around. It didn't feel quite right, so she set it down and added a pinch more Sugar in the Raw before shaking in two and a half drops of almond milk.

She was contemplating whether that half drop was suitable when Shannon from publicity entered the kitchen, an empty Pyrex container in hand. She eyed Nella with the same wariness Nella was using on the cup.

"You're working entirely too hard for this time of the summer," Shannon observed on her way to the sink. "You don't have an author coming in now, do you?"

"I do."

"Rude. It's the last week of August! Doesn't Vera normally go to her vacation home in—where is it?"

"Nantucket," Nella said, unflappably focused. "But she drove back to the city last night. Cut her trip short."

Shannon let out a low whistle. "Vera did *that*? Wait," she said suddenly, seeming to finally notice that Nella hadn't once looked up from her task. "Are those *ice* cubes in there?"

"They are indeed."

"Which means that drink is for . . . ?"

"Yep. It's for Colin Franklin."

The sound of glass striking metal finally broke Nella's intense concentration. Shannon had blanched and she was peering in the direction of the elevator bank as though Colin himself might suddenly appear. "Oh. Shoot. *Today* is Tuesday," she whispered, turning on her heel and walking in the other direction. "I completely forgot he was coming in. Seriously, who comes in the last week of August?! If he asks—"

"You're in meetings all day."

"You're the best."

"You're welcome," said Nella, envious she couldn't proffer the same excuse. With a sigh, she opened the Ziploc bag Colin had asked her to hold on to at the beginning of the year and poured its mysterious contents on top of the coffee. She needed to keep her spirits up, but it was hard as she watched the black powder dissolve into the liquid, turning everything an unseemly shade of gray. Colin was due any moment now, and she could already feel Shartricia's presence lurking nearby, watching, waiting to see if Nella was going to save her.

Colin and Vera were giggling at something on Vera's phone when Nella entered Vera's office five minutes later. She set the coffee down in front of Colin, hand-crushed ice cubes and all.

"And she just drags the paintbrush all over the carpet," Vera said, dabbing at a tear in her heavily mascaraed eye. "It's just the cutest thing!"

"What a precious pooch!" Colin put his hands together once, then kept them there. For today's meeting, he had worn his multi-fabric page boy cap, the one made up of spirals of denim, leather, satin, khaki, and lace fabric. It was the cap he always wore when he wanted to get the writing gears "a-turning," which was a piece of information he'd shared with Nella the first day they'd met; he'd also shared it with his couple of million online followers. Once, for kicks, she had looked it up to buy for Owen as a gag gift. She quickly changed her mind when she discovered it would cost her seven hundred dollars. No laugh was worth that much—not on an editorial assistant's salary.

Nella hadn't seen Colin wear the cap since she'd made this discovery; now, she peered at the designer accessory suspiciously, as though it might get up off his bald head and slap her in the face. But even if it had, it wouldn't have made a difference, because neither he nor Vera seemed to see her sit down in the only empty chair left in the room, hands folded in her lap.

After a few moments Nella coughed and said, brightly, "Fun! What's our boy Brenner up to now?"

"Oh, Nella! Thank you for this." Colin picked up his coffee and took an indulgent sip. He munched on one or two of the bite-sized ice cubes before winking at her. "Perfect, as usual."

"I was just showing him Brenner's latest video. They're finally painting the addition to our kitchen in Nantucket—*fi*nally!—and Brenner of course saw this as an opportunity to be viral." Nella tried not to flinch at how clunky those last two words sounded as Vera exited out of Instagram and placed her phone aside. "Now. Time to talk about *Needles and Pins*."

"Yes! At last!" Colin stood up and whipped out a small, green spiral notepad. "I really can't wait to hear what you two think. I've kept my wife up the past few nights talking out all the things that might be wrong with it."

"Aw, Colin . . . well, we love it!" Vera gushed, bringing a fist down onto the pages. "It's topical, it's direct. It's the perfect thing to get people talking about the nasty opioid epidemic that's sweeping across our country."

Nella bobbed her head up and down in agreement, mouth sealed shut. One of the things that Nella loved about working for Vera was that even though she didn't necessarily take all of her opinions, she did give Nella as many opportunities as she could by bringing her to every meeting and telling her when an agent was and was not being an asshole. She treated Nella like she was competent, which was more than what many other assistants could say of their bosses.

But what Nella appreciated most of all—what she most respected and internalized—was her boss's knack for speaking to authors about their writing. Vera had a way with phrasing; she could still make you think the second half of your book deserved a Pulitzer even after she told you that the first half needed to be completely rewritten.

"And the cast of characters is just so great," Vera continued. "You really implemented my suggestions on your first draft about bringing out the diversity of this community, and I think that will have your book speaking to a lot of people."

Nella stiffened, but kept her pen to paper.

"Perfect! That's exactly what I was going for." Colin jotted down a few notes that Nella couldn't make out. But given Colin's eager-to-please complex, she was willing to guess it said something along the lines of *They like it! Thank fucking god.*

Vera and Colin traded compliments for another couple of minutes. When that portion of the meeting was finished, and the actual criticism part of the meeting was supposed to begin, Colin unexpectedly turned to Nella, readjusted his cap, and said, "Now, I'd really love to hear what *you* think. Vera mentioned there were one or two things you felt need fixing."

Nella froze. Critiquing the book *after* her boss had lavished him with praise wasn't a part of the script. She looked over at Vera, but her boss was stone-faced, not an eye spasm in sight.

She faced Colin once again. "Well, I think it's a great read. Like Vera said, it's *so* important."

"Thanks!"

"And there's just such a *wonderful* driving force pushing this story," Nella continued. "The consciousness of the voice of this town is just so . . . so powerful. And it gets louder and louder until . . . suddenly the town is just *screaming*, you know? And by the end of the book you're just, like, *Wow, how is the rest of the world not seeing this?* How is this town hanging by a thread and yet meanwhile, hundreds of miles away, people are sitting all comfy-cozy in their own homes, worrying about coffee and parking spaces and playground bullies? Like we are right now. I mean, not the bullies. Although, maybe we *are* worried about the office bullies around here."

Vera chuckled.

Nella put a fist to her chest. "And that chapter that takes place at the dinner table? Just . . . wow."

"Thanks," Colin said, smiling. "That bit was so fun to write. The kid who grew up next door to me in Connecticut had a family like that. His older brother, mother, and father were drunk out of their skulls all the time. It's not opioids, but still. And I swear to god, they'd just throw food at each other whenever they got tired of hearing someone else speak. *Hot* food. Too much politics? Womp, spaghetti and meatballs. Sick of talking about money? Boom, sausage in your eye."

"That's wild!" Vera's eyes danced as she put her hands up in her hair to scrunch her bob. "Why'd you keep going over there?"

"Because they had MTV!"

The room dissolved into a fit of cheerful laughter, even though the cause of it had been a highly dysfunctional family whose fate did not seem particularly promising. "We'll have to tell the publicity team that story," Vera said, looking over at Nella pointedly. Nella nodded once, then jotted down *flying spaghetti*. "Maybe that can be part of an interview or something. Like, the backstory of where this all came from."

"Certainly. I could certainly work on that." Colin gazed out the window for a moment, already imagining himself beneath a sea of lights at McNally Jackson, retelling this story. "But, c'mon, seriously—I can take some criticism, Nella. I've been around the block enough to know that even the best writers can keep refining, keep pushing."

"Always! Here, Nella—I'm handing the metaphorical microphone over to you now," Vera said, pretending to zip her lips shut.

Nella would rather knock herself unconscious with an actual microphone than proceed.

"Wow, thank you, Vera! But I'd be happy to let you take the lead—and *then* I'll chime in?" She had hoped that tangent about Colin's inspiration had let her off the hook, just as she'd been let off the hook last week, when Maisy had brought Hazel into Vera's office and foiled The Shartricia Conversation. She kicked herself for not bringing up her concerns with Vera before this moment. There'd been times when she'd seen an opening, but a stray phone call or something else "urgent" had swatted the ball out of her hand before she could properly position herself to just do it. She had even tried a Hail Mary just the evening before, when Vera was packing up her things, but then her *own* phone had started to ring.

It was as though the gods were trying to tell Nella something. And now, days later—when she found herself being stared down by two very influential white people—she convinced herself this something was, *It's time, Queen. Tell it now.*

Colin gnawed on his ice expectantly, the crunching noise still audible through his closed lips. Above his head, she saw a headline for an imaginary Buzzfeed article: "COLIN FRANKLIN'S WELFARE QUEEN: WHERE WAS THE SENSITIVITY READ?"

"Alright," Nella said, her voice deepening, "there *was* this . . . *one* thing . . . that I do think could use some work."

"Hit me with it!" he said spiritedly, although his hunched back and his fingers, white from being clamped too tightly at the knuckles, implied that he was thoroughly prepared to be hit by a sharp, blunt object rather than her honest thoughts.

"Shartricia Daniels."

Colin nodded, picked up his pen again. "Okay! Great! Let's talk about her."

"Great idea," Vera chimed in, although she didn't quite look ready to hear what Nella had to say. "You were mentioning to me the other day that something about her didn't quite work for you?"

"Yes," Nella said. It took everything she could find deep within not to lose steam, even though she knew that at this point, it was all or nothing. "I'm not sure we really finished that conversation. But yeah."

Don't look in your lap, said her inner Angela Davis, and then another Davis spoke up. Viola. *You is kind. You is smart. You is important.*

Nella met Colin's eye. "So . . . I do think it's super important that she's in this. Because it's good to show how people of color have been ravaged by the epidemic."

"That's what my thinking was when I suggested he add some more diversity in his second draft," Vera jumped in. "Especially because the media overlooks their plight so often. And the media ignored their plight in the past, especially with crack in the 1990s, even though all kinds of diverse people are affected by drugs." She looked pointedly at Nella. "Right? That's what you mean?"

"Yes. Exactly that. So . . . it *is* great that there is representation here of a Black person going through this."

"It's *so* great, Colin," Vera added.

Nella regarded her boss more sharply. Vera's face looked like it had been pinched at its edges—particularly at her temples, where her skin was slightly purple.

Colin's eyes went over to Vera, too, although they cut back to Nella in a flash. "I agree. I really wanted a Shartricia kind of character to be in this. Once we got to talking about diversifying this book and its cast of characters, it seemed vital that I go beyond my comfort zone a bit."

"To show *all* diverse sides of the experience," Vera clarified.

"Right!" Nella said, trying to ignore how many times the d-word had been dropped in the last few moments. "But, Shartricia . . . I have to say . . . she feels a bit off to me. She didn't quite strike me as particularly . . . authentic."

"Oh. *Oh.* Could you give Colin some specifics?" Vera commanded.

"Yes," Colin said, as though she'd just told him she'd accidentally thrown his page boy cap onto the train tracks. "Please, do say more."

"Well . . . to be honest, it seemed like she was based off an idea of what a Black person suffering due to an opioid epidemic in Ohio would be like. She felt like a collection of tropes . . . all of the unflattering ones . . . and by the time we get to the end of the novel, she never becomes a redeemable character at all. She's still stuck."

Vera put down her pen and crossed her arms as if to say *You're on your own on this one.*

Colin's pen was down, too, and he was frowning and no longer chewing his ice. He took his cap off, then put it in his lap and crossed his legs. It was an act that sent his pen falling to the rug, precisely halfway between his chair and Nella's chair. He didn't move to grab it.

Nella reached up and gave a nervous tug on one of her curls as she reached for buzzwords that were less critical and more meaningful. "I didn't quite connect with her. She felt a bit flat, I think. One-dimensional. Like one generalized experience—a particular swath of experience—that didn't feel entirely genuine to me. She read more like a caricature than an actual living and breathing character, and I think a lot of Black readers will find her unsatisfying.

"And, I mean, the chartreuse thing felt too much like a joke. It felt like her mother was being mocked for not knowing how to spell, and I know that's not—"

"I really don't know what you're talking about," Colin interjected. He looked worriedly at Vera, gesturing for his manuscript. "Is that in there? Did I put that in there?"

Vera shook her head, handing the pages to Nella instead. "I'm not sure what she's talking about, either. Nella, could you please point out a specific scene where you think Colin is mocking Shartricia?"

A few seconds ago, saying the word "unsatisfying" to Colin had felt really, really satisfying. Now, Nella wasn't so sure. "Um . . . I can't remember exactly *what* page the name thing appears on. I'm not even sure there's something specifically *said* to point out. It's just a feeling."

"A *feeling*."

"Yes. And 'LaDarnell'? 'DeMontraine'? That just read like caricature to me, too. And did she really *need* to have seven children?" Nella added, realizing how unhinged she was starting to sound. But she couldn't stop. *Rip off the Band-Aid!* Angela commanded angrily. She was on a roll and didn't feel like getting off it until she'd said everything she needed to say.

"I mean, isn't that exactly what we'd *expect* from a Black woman who's addicted to heroin? You couldn't be a *little* more creative with your *one* Black protagonist?"

Colin was still paging through his book, a half-crazed, feverish blaze in his eye.

"Um, Nella," Vera said, cocking her head diplomatically, "just to play devil's advocate—couldn't one say that's just a tad bit racist of *you* to say?"

"I *do* kind of feel like she's calling *me* a racist," Colin agreed. "Or perhaps she just *feels* like I'm racist." He wiggled his fingers around in the air, insinuating that the feeling of racist tendencies was akin to voodoo. His eyes never left Vera the entire time, as though it were just the two of them in the room now.

And that was exactly how Nella felt—like she'd slipped and somehow gotten lost beneath the hideous wall-to-wall carpeting. This wasn't what she'd wanted. She hadn't expected Colin to massage her calloused feet and apologize for all the sins of his ancestors, but she had thought he'd be somewhat grateful to have her take on his Black character. How many other writers published by Wagner had the benefit of a sensitivity read they didn't have to seek out on their own?

"Colin, I'm sorry," said Nella. "That's not what I meant to—"

"I chose *one* particular depiction of a Black woman having a hard time. That was *her* hard time. Not an *actual person's* hard time," Colin said, each new word louder than the one before until Nella was sure, without a doubt, that people outside Vera's office could hear the chaos. She wondered if Hazel was listening to everything from her desk, unsure whether it would be better or worse if she was. "*I'm* the writer. Jesus. I'm not a *racist.* Do I need to make her hair curlier, too? Or make her skin a little bit darker? Should I make her speak like . . . like Sidney Poitier, instead of a Black girl who grew up in rural Ohio without a father? Whose book is this, anyway?"

Vera finally found her voice. "Now, Colin, I wouldn't—"

"No, Vera. No. Just a moment." He pressed his multi-fabric cap with his fingers and closed his eyes, taking three or four deep yoga breaths. After the fourth, he stood up and plopped his pages on Vera's desk.

Then, to Nella and Vera's horror, he walked out.

Nella swallowed, unable to tear her gaze away from the wide-open door. A reprimand was coming; she was sure of it.

She waited. And waited. When nothing came, she retrieved the ballpoint pen Colin had dropped on the floor earlier and placed it on Vera's desk.

Vera remained silent. She was still staring down at Colin's pages.

And suddenly, it's the end of the fucking world for these people.

"Vera," Nella started after a few more seconds of gut-checking silence. "I didn't mean to—"

"Not now, Nella," Vera hissed. She wouldn't look up at her. "Please. Not now."

Part II

Kendra Rae

September 1983
Antonio's
Financial District, Manhattan

"'Indian descent' or not," I said with a yawn, "My point is, if you saw Ben Kingsley walking down the street, you wouldn't think, 'There goes an Indian man.' You would think, 'There goes a white man.'"

"But, what was Kingsley *supposed* to say? 'No thanks, Sir Richard Attenborough, but I don't have brown enough skin to play one of the greatest leaders of the free world?' Kingsley was nothing before, I promise you, and taking that role was the smartest choice he could've ever made."

Rather than eye the glob of melted cheese that had been stuck in Ward's bushy mustache for the majority of our debate, I glanced down at my depleted drink, disappointed that I hadn't ordered a double but happy about my extra olive. I plucked the wet fruit up with my fingers and shoved it into my mouth, pretending to work through a thought as I chewed.

Only when Ward seemed convinced he had won did I say, food still in my mouth, "Sure. But what if Billy Dee Williams—"

"*Who?*" Ward interrupted.

"*Star Wars*. Lando."

The confusion left his face. I'd been right in thinking he'd seen it—maybe more than once. "Ah. Go on."

"Let's say Billy Dee Williams is going to be Mozart in that new film that's coming out next year. Would you be okay with *that*? Would *that* sit well with you?"

The speed with which Ward's face twisted back upon itself was so satisfying that I paused before grabbing the last glorious olive to take it in. I'd seen that face at Harvard many times before, from professors to thesis group colleagues to my thesis adviser himself. But that didn't lessen the effect of such incredulity upon my ego.

It fueled me.

"*Well?*" I asked.

"Now, that's different. Billy Dee Williams isn't . . . well, it's just not . . . that would be utterly—"

"Ridiculous," I finished for him. "Yes. Yes, I thought so, too."

Ward loosened his tie, an angry red blush blooming from his collar as he tried to decide whether I was being sarcastic or not. "Now. If you'll excuse me, I'm going to go check on my wife."

I glanced over his shoulder. His wife, Paula, hands down the most attractive editor at Wagner, was currently surrounded by four different men, two of whom I'd never seen before. The other two—editors who'd barely spoken to me since I'd started at Wagner—flanked her, touching her back far more than anyone should during a polite conversation. "Yes. Sure does *look* like she needs your help."

My sarcasm was loud and clear this time. Ward hurried off, a reckless sense of urgency infecting his stride. I was turning, too, ready for more olives and more alcohol, when a warm hand burned through the silk of my cap sleeve.

"Hmm. Let me guess—you scared another spouse away."

I didn't have to look back to know it was Diana who had stopped me, but I did, anyway. She had a lopsided grin on her face and a hand on her hip.

"Guilty as charged," I murmured. "And yeah, I know, I know, *Be on your best behavior*, *It's only a few hours*, but dammit, Di, they're all just so . . . draining. And so damn easy to scare. Every single one of them." I gestured at the fifty or so people who were milling around the dim lighting of Antonio's under the guise of celebrating my and Diana's accomplishment: our first week with a number one *New York Times* bestseller.

Diana tousled the wavy bangs of what I called, only in private so as not to embarrass her, her "Donna Summer wig." Scanning the room, too, she said, "You may be right about that, girl. But can we just take in this view for a minute? I mean, damn! If having all these white people here in this room doesn't mean we've made it, I don't know what does."

I let Diana link her arm in mine and tried to see what she was seeing: the expensive centerpieces overflowing with white roses; the plates of expensive, plump scallops being distributed by waiters who resembled shaving cream models. A smooth jazz quartet in one corner that had started playing "I'm Every Woman" the moment we'd first walked in. An enormous fish tank filled with sapphire-colored water and jewel-colored creatures a few feet away.

I didn't really care about the fish tank; I could take or leave the fancy seafood. If I'd had my way—and I never would—I would've picked a different venue for this. A different neighborhood, really. Anywhere but the Financial District, a frigid, bloodless neighborhood that held one of the country's biggest slave markets, once upon a time.

Whether I thought the party décor was tacky or not, though, Diana was right. *We* were the women of the evening—the women of the year, people were starting to say, even though *Burning Heart* had barely been out for a week. We, two Black unknowns, had managed to turn what many predicted would be a minor blip into a book that had the entire country buzzing. The buzz had gotten so loud that we were booked solid with interviews for the next three months. A big weekly magazine had even mentioned they were "strongly considering" putting the two of us on their cover.

We had a bestseller on our hands, and nobody—not even some random husband who saw no problems with Ben Kingsley winning an Oscar for playing an Indian man—could take that away from me.

Still.

"Yes, everything here is incredible. But . . . I . . ." I shrugged, trying to find a way to push the words out. "I still haven't forgotten how so many of these white folks doubted me about *Burning Heart*."

I turned to Diana. The movement broke our arm-chain link, but what I was about to say needed to be said. "Why else do you think Richard let me edit your book instead of him? And gave us so little money to work with? And that measly two-week author tour publicity gave us . . . every single one of those moves were calculated, Di. They did all that in case it turned out to be a flop. That's why *I* had to fight him every step of the way."

I wished I could take back the word "flop" immediately. Something strange played out in Diana's eyes as she studied me, her lips tightly pressed together. Only then did I notice that her burnt-orange lipstick was smudged. I motioned for her to fix it, prepared to ask her if she and Elroy had snuck a little one-on-one time in the coat closet, but Diana spoke again. "Hey—all of that is in the past now. What matters is the book got made, and we're *here*.

"Besides," she added, pulling a compact mirror from a clutch as white as her white asymmetrical minidress, "you know how it goes. A dozen nos before you get one yes, and that yes is the only one that matters. Everyone else can take their nos and shove them up their perfectly perfumed assholes."

That made me smile. Very rarely did Diana talk about shoving anything anywhere. When all the girls in middle school started calling her "High-Yellow Di"—not really because of her skin, but because of her good grades, her perfect diction, and her love of *I Love Lucy* reruns—it was *me*, not Diana, who'd told them to go fuck themselves. For the most part, everyone had listened; granted, I was pretty sure my punching Geoffrey Harrison out in the fourth grade during a field trip to the Montclair Art Museum had something to do with that.

I eyed my friend, who was having a hard time standing in one place for more than a few moments. Clearly, she'd helped herself to more than a couple of glasses of wine, which explained the messy lipstick, the "perfumed assholes," and the fact that she was again linking her arm in mine—this time, more forcefully. "I can't believe *I'm* the one telling *you* this," she said, "but Kendra Rae Phillips, you need to chill the hell out and take a deep fucking breath."

"You know how I hate breathing."

"I do. But humor me. C'mon, now. *Innnn* . . ."

I pouted, but did as I was told.

"Now, out. See? Don't that feel good? See!" She patted me on the back without waiting for my response. "Hey," she said, sniffing the air, her naturally turned-up nose twitching like that of a puppy on the prowl. "You smell that?"

I frowned. "No. What am I supposed to be smelling?"

Diana beamed. "Money, honey. Not just white folks' money, neither. You wanna know what I did with the first check I got from Wagner?"

"I'm guessing the answer isn't 'deposited it in the bank.'"

"You guessed right. No, I just put it down on the kitchen table and stared at it for a good long while. Forty minutes, maybe an hour. I kid you not. And when Elroy got home from work and tried to pick up the check and see it, would you believe what I did? I *barked* at him, honey. I've never done that in my life."

It was all just too much. We both howled. I mean, *really* howled. And that was all it took to bring us back to back in the day. We were high schoolers again, getting ready to go roller-skating at the Eight Skate in downtown Newark with the rest of the girls. We were drinking red juice and whatever liquor Imani could sneak from her parents' stash. Singing *Drums keep pounding a rhythm to the brain* while either Ola or I pressed Diana's hair—her *real* hair—and I was usually the one doing the pressing, because unlike Ola, I knew to quit grooving when I had someone else's head and a hot piece of metal in my hand. Half-knowing that soon more than just our outfits would have to change.

We would be splitting up—Diana and Imani would be off to Howard; Ola to Oaxaca, where she would meet a man and start a family and a nonprofit, all in the span of one year. And I'd be off to Harvard, where I . . . what exactly *would* I do there? Pick up a man here, drop him off there. I'd miss New Jersey; try—and fail—to love Boston. I'd be pulled deeper into books.

And I'd be pushed further away from white people.

This recollection, although not a new one by any means, was sobering enough to chase away any joy a Chaka Khan–playing jazz quartet could bring me. At the same time, I detected a white couple nearby that seemed noticeably concerned by our laughing fit. When I met the man's eye, they hastily feigned interest in one of the many literary awards that Richard had requested be temporarily affixed to a wall for this swanky affair.

I didn't let them off the hook, though. I gave each of them a disdainful up-down, my eyes remaining transfixed upon the string of diamonds around the woman's fine porcelain neck. Five seconds later, they wandered over to the far side of the room for air.

"Oh, for God's sake. *Girl.*" Diana's words had no semblance of softness this time, and when she finished rolling her eyes, I knew she was going to say what she'd been trying not to say for quite some time. *You're beyond saving*. Or, maybe, *You're bringing me down*.

Instead, she pointed at my drink and ordered me to get another. "Then, once you've finished it, meet Richard and me over by the fish tank in five."

Hearing my boss's name killed my buzz for an instant. "Ah, is *that* it? Richard sent you to summon me? I already said hello when we got here, and I'll say goodbye and thank you when it's time to go home. I don't think I should have to—"

Diana shook her head. "No, stupid. There's a guy from the *Times* here who's doing a write-up on this and he wants to take a photo of the three of us. Seriously, girl—why do you hate Richard so much? It's getting kind of old, you know."

My eyes caught her lipstick, newly reapplied. "Where's Elroy?" I asked pointedly. "Is he here yet?"

But Diana pretended not to hear. "So, he's a yuppie who was born with a silver spoon in his mouth. Okay, fine. So, he took some convincing. But he is *not* representative of every single white man you've ever met. I mean, come *on*. Have you ever seen another white man do all of *this* for a couple of Black women nobody has ever heard of?

"Plus, remember what I've always said," Diana added, trying unsuccessfully to whisper in my ear. "We use them until we don't need to use them no longer. Plain and simple."

Plain and simple. Of course she'd say that. How many white men, *really*, had Diana been forced to stomach in her everyday life? She'd gotten her bachelor's at Howard, her PhD at Howard, and she had stayed there to teach. The white gatekeepers hadn't been shoved in her face nearly as much as they'd been shoved in mine. At a historically Black college, Diana had been granted the blessed gift of tunnel vision. She'd been blessed with the ability to forget white people existed, if only for a little while.

I had been blessed with being smothered by them.

Diana never understood that, though, and there was no way I could ever tell her this. Not point-blank. Because it would mean telling her she'd been right when we were sitting on my stoop in '68, holding all of our acceptance letters in our hands. That attending any place that wasn't Howard or Hampton was a mistake. That I hadn't been as strong as I'd thought I would be.

No, Diana would never stop trying to convince me to lay off on trying to sabotage this night. So I put on a happy face and backed away toward the bar. "I'll have *two* more drinks," I said, "and I'll meet you guys in ten."

"With a smile?"

I held up my empty glass. "With a big fucking smile."

6

August 29, 2018

It was no surprise Nella's day ended on a bad note. After all, it started off on one.

To be fair, that was Nella's fault. Anybody with half the will to be employed knew that stepping on the toes and fingers of one of Wagner's bestselling authors, then showing up to work forty-five minutes late the following day, was downright reckless.

Nevertheless—out of fear, mostly—Nella spent too much of the morning trying to convince herself to get out of bed, and even more of the morning allowing Owen to convince her that no, her decision to be upfront with Vera and Colin had not been a bad one.

In fact, he found the whole situation hilarious.

"The image of him dabbing his eyes with that soggy, expensive-ass hat . . . it's just . . . it's just too good," he said, laughing.

Nella finally slid out of bed and started rifling through her drawers for something to wear. "But you should have seen their *faces*, baby."

"I didn't need to. I've seen white guilt enough to know what it looks like."

Nella couldn't help herself. "In the bathroom mirror, you mean?"

"After we watched *Twelve Years a Slave*, I mean," said Owen, without missing a beat. "It only lasted a few seconds, though, and then it went down the drain with the hand soap."

Nella jumped up and down in order to get her freshly lotioned leg into her favorite pair of jeans. "That was fast! Remind me to make you watch the entire *Roots* miniseries next February," she teased, nearly teetering headfirst into her dresser.

Owen had groaned and rolled over on his side, even though they both knew he had no qualms about watching *Roots*—or reading it, for that matter, if that proposition had also been on the table. He was more than happy to be inundated with "Black Thangs," as Nella called them, either through the Black literature and film canons, or straight from Nella herself as she recapped her day-to-day feelings—which was the case on the morning after the Colin Incident. Owen was always ready to discuss the latest hot-button issue circulating on Twitter: blackface, underrepresentation, police shootings of unarmed Black men and women. But it was because he was never *too* eager—he didn't feel the need to call all of the things racist *all* of the time, like a few of the white men she'd dated and known before him—that made Nella trust him the most. He had nothing to prove; he was perfectly content that his worldview, established thirty years earlier by a lesbian couple in Denver and glued in place by a daily viewing of *Democracy Now!*, had set him on the right course.

Such bedrock had also enabled Owen to blaze a path of his own—one that allowed him to be his own boss at a startup company called App-terschool Learning. Nella knew little about this startup, besides that it had to do with mentorship and connecting underprivileged teens. She also knew that it permitted Owen to leave their Bay Ridge apartment whenever he felt like it and work from home when he didn't—a luxury she wished she had more often than not.

"But seriously, Nell," Owen said, still lying on his side, his voice muffled by the bedding. "You're going to be fine. It's all going to be fine. This will all blow over in, like, five days."

"That's easy for *you* to say." Nella paused, her stick of deodorant poised mid-application, and waited for Owen to flip over and look back at her. She hadn't intended for her words to come out as loaded as they did, but they had, and now it was too late to deny what was weighing them down: the fact that Owen was a white cis male who would never have many of the conversations she did, unless they ended up having children one day. What she'd really been trying to say, simply, was that he would never be able to understand the bizarre world of publishing the way she did. The gang of characters at Wagner was incredibly peculiar, but on the whole, their actions and subtle microaggressions seemed harmless to an outsider. *Shucks, I've seen worse behavior in other office environments,* Owen would more or less say, then cite a disgruntled employee of his own who'd peed in several Disney character thermoses and left them in an old boss's office overnight.

Nella's colleagues at Wagner weren't sociopaths. They all knew where one was and was not supposed to pee. But that didn't make being around them any less stressful. Once you were in close quarters with them each day—once you'd spent more than a year making catatonic small talk around sputtering Keurigs and mottled bathroom sinks and Printer Row, grinning and bearing it while you learned about their new summer homes and their latest European vacations and wondered why you were still making fewer than twenty dollars an hour; once you got used to the fact that almost every time you came into contact with an unknown Black person in your place of work, this person was most likely going to ask you to sign for a package, or offer to fix your computer—it started to grate on you. So much so that, at least once a month, you got up from your desk, sauntered over to the ladies' room, shut yourself in a stall, and asked yourself, *Why am I still here?*

At last, after twenty minutes of dragging her feet, Nella finally finished getting ready. Owen kissed her lightly from his side of the bed and told her everything was going to be fine. But the effect of his words lasted as long as the sensation from his lips, and as Nella got on the Manhattan-bound R train, she had a feeling it was going to be a breakdown-in-the-bathroom-stall kind of day.

The feeling intensified nearly an hour later, as she took a deep breath and waited for the revolving doors to spill her out into the lobby, wavering only when she waved a quick hello to India, the cheery, mocha-skinned receptionist who'd sat at the front desk from six to eleven every weekday morning ever since Nella had first started at Wagner. "Loving that scarf today, India," she said as brightly as she could manage, pulling out her Wagner identification card.

India reached up and touched the silky blue and gold scarf, as if to remind herself which one she'd worn that day. "Thanks, girl!" she said, her smile genuine, even though Nella almost always said the same thing about her scarves or earrings or newest hairstyle. Nella's compliments, of course, were always grounded in truth; today, the fabric, a striking collage of blue and gold geometric shapes, was arranged almost too stunningly for an office in Midtown, wrapped ceremoniously and tied up in two equal-sized bows that sat on the top of India's head. But Nella also made sure that her one-liners took exactly the right amount of time to get her from the lobby to the elevator bank without having to slow her step. It was part of her morning routine, the same way she fixed grits in the morning, or made her way down two-thirds of the train platform so that she wouldn't have to walk far once she got off at her stop in Manhattan.

"It *is* a great scarf, isn't it?"

Nella turned around to hear who'd agreed with her. It was Hazel, of course, who was suddenly right behind her, a stack of manuscript pages in her right hand. The inaugural navy-blue Wagner tote bag she'd been given on her first day dangled from her wrist, swinging precariously back and forth.

"What's going on, ladies? By the way, India," said Hazel, reaching into her tote for what Nella presumed was her ID but was actually a brown paper bag, "I went to that African fabric store in Queens I was telling you about last week. And . . . look!"

India reached across her desk to accept Hazel's offering, a vulnerable, almost greedy vigor in her movements. Nella hadn't seen the woman betray this much emotion in the two years she'd known her.

"It's beautiful, Hazel!" India marveled, waving around a long satin scarf the color of the inside of a juicy pink grapefruit.

"Whoa. That's gorgeous," Nella agreed. She was egregiously late for work, but Hazel didn't seem concerned about the time. Besides, Nella felt like she had some sort of unspoken stake in this exchange. Her feet remained planted as other employees piled in, clamoring for the next elevator like passengers rushing for lifeboats on the *Titanic*.

"Isn't the pink great? I saw it and naturally thought of you, India. I know you mentioned that the pinks and the oranges sell out so quickly at the store you go to in the Bronx."

"It's for *me*?" India fingered the fabric. Her big almond eyes were heavy with near-spilled tears.

"Of *course* that scarf is for you!" She lowered her voice slyly as she gave India a single pat on the arm. "Happy birthday, girlfriend."

"Oh!" Nella said awkwardly. "I'm sorry. I didn't realize . . . happy birthday, India!"

But India's eyes were still on Hazel. "Really?" she stammered. "I can't . . . I'm sorry, it's just . . . just, no one here has ever done anything like this for me before. And I've been here for almost ten years . . ." India's tears were falling now; the woman seemed to have forgotten where she was. She put the scarf down and stepped away from her desk so she could come around and fold Hazel into a tight hug. A few feet away, a lost-looking visitor who'd come close to asking India for admission upstairs feigned sudden interest in something that had gotten stuck on her shoe.

"Hazel, thank you! But . . . how did you know?"

"I have my ways. And there are plenty of other hair goodies where this came from, too. You know I got the hookup." Hazel winked. "Don't you work too hard today, okay? Remember to treat yo'self. Bye, girl!"

And she was off before India could finish mouthing another emphatic *thank you*. Nella scurried to keep up, cutting off a tall, unamused man who most likely worked at the software company on the floor below Wagner's. "That really is a gorgeous scarf," Nella repeated as she and Hazel squeezed into a crowded elevator that couldn't possibly fit them both. It did, but it didn't fit the software company man, and he had no qualms about expressing his frustration as the doors shut in front of his cherry-red face.

"Isn't it great? Normally I'd get something like that from Curl Central."

"Curl Central?"

"Yeah. It's this dope hair café in Bed-Stuy," Hazel said in a low voice, a sudden swell of cocoa butter nipping at Nella's nose. "A *Black* hair café."

"Ah."

"Yeah. So I was gonna find something for India at Curl Central. But then Manny told me he'd forgotten he made plans for us to meet some friends for a happy hour in Queens, so it just made more sense to go to the African fabric store."

"Manny?"

"Sorry. Emmanuel. Manny. My boyfriend."

"Oh, right. Manny."

"Do you have a boyfriend?"

"I do," Nella replied. "He's . . . he's pretty great."

"Aw, look at you—smiling all big."

Nella nodded and shrugged, waiting for Hazel to ask her boyfriend's name, or how she'd met him, and then wondering—when she didn't ask—if she should say anything more about Owen.

Instead, she lowered her voice and said, "You know, I've always wanted to wear scarves like the ones India wears. It's just, I'm shit at YouTube tutorials. Most of them." Nella had spent countless hours trying to learn how to French-braid her own hair, turning the speed down on the video and then rewinding it back, because she always seemed to miss a crucial part. The process made her arms ache badly enough for her to give up until her hair grew longer and she could try again. "I can't even do flat twists. And my braids usually come out looking pretty rough."

As she finished speaking the doors opened, and the majority of riders got off on the fourth floor. Free to move her head around without getting a mouthful of someone else's hair, Nella looked over at Hazel, seconds away from asking her if she had any YouTube tutorial suggestions of her own. But the girl was staring at Nella like she'd just proclaimed she'd never seen *The Color Purple.*

"So . . . you can't tie scarves, *or* do flat twists?" Hazel was visibly taken aback.

"I . . ." Nella reached for the strap of her bag instead of reaching for one of her curls. Hazel hadn't asked, *How have you made it this far without knowing how to style Black hair?* But she didn't need to. Nella asked herself this often.

Usually, her answer was her parents. They were the ones who'd raised her in a predominantly white Connecticut neighborhood and sent her to predominantly white public schools. To keep Nella grounded, they established a Black force field of sorts around her, encouraging her to be Black and proud. They gave her their own Black history assignments all year round; they bought her Black dolls and refused to buy her white ones. But like the world's best-built force fields, there were cracks, and the adoration of fine, straight hair slipped right on through. What could her parents do? Nella saw it everywhere she went: at school, at sleepovers. On her Black Barbies. It was even in her own home. Her mother had been relaxing her hair since the mid-nineties, ever since she became a dean at a small private university in Fairfield, which could have been why when nine-year-old Nella said she wanted to start doing it, too, neither parent batted an eye. They probably saw her wish as inevitable. A rite of passage, even.

Her mother started taking Nella along on her trips to the hair salon in New Haven shortly after she started sixth grade. Together they would sit, their scalps plastered with creamy crack, their hands holding year-old issues of *Essence* and Terry McMillan novels. They continued this ritual together every six weeks until Nella passed her driving test, and, thanks to her editor position on her high school newspaper, started to cultivate something of a busy social life. The secondhand Subaru Legacy her uncle gave her for her sixteenth birthday granted her the ability to come and go as she pleased.

And it was a good thing she had somewhere to go, because life as she knew it at home was deteriorating. With each passing month, her parents seemed to care less and less about pretending to enjoy being married to one another. Dinners that had once been dotted by one or two heated back-and-forths were besmeared with all-out spiteful volleys. Nella, an only child, would play referee, but with little success. Hard as Nella tried, she couldn't prevent her parents from divorcing, as they finally would the week after she received her high school diploma. But she could keep up the facade that despite all of it, she was Good, and if you looked at her senior photo—all white teeth and makeup and shiny black straight hair that curled up just a little bit at her shoulders—you believed it. That girl was going to an exceptional university miles away from home, where she'd make some Black friends and fall in love with a Good Black Man and get an exceptional degree in English literature. If she liked UVA enough, she'd stay and get a second degree, get a teaching job at some university, marry that Black man, travel to all the continents with him, and when they were finally ready, they'd have a couple of kids.

Nella got that first degree. But the other things that had been planned for that girl in the photo never panned out for her. She went to a couple of Black sorority parties her freshman year and they just hadn't been Nella's thing. She wasn't willing to jump through all of the burning hoops that would get her picked, didn't feel like investing all of that time (not to mention money) in acquiring a new, not entirely organic sisterhood.

Should she have tried harder in college? Sometimes, when Nella cared to look back on those days—usually when Malaika reflected upon her time at Emory, but especially now, as Hazel looked at her with bewilderment at her inability to do flat twists—she ventured to blame the person whom she felt was even more responsible than her parents: herself. She should have kept up with the Black Student Alliance meetings and ventured out of her comfort zone more often. She should have made her first close Black friend sooner. Then, she would have learned about the wonders of natural hair far earlier before the mainstream world embraced it. Maybe Nella would have started her own literary organization for young Black women in New Haven, or spent more time marching through the streets rather than wading her way through Black Twitter for something to share.

The list of hypotheticals, longer than each of Nella's brown arms and legs all put together, went on to include not just hair, but love interests. If she'd had Black friends as a child, maybe she'd have gone on more than just one date with Marlon, a Black UVA classmate who'd asked her out in baggage claim after they met on a plane one holiday season. Maybe she'd feel less self-conscious about holding Owen's hand on various subway platforms, because then, at least she'd know—even if that Black teenager across the way who was giving her side-eye didn't—that she'd been courted and bedded by a man with the same ancestral lineage as her own at least once.

It wasn't until she started a new life in New York City—after so many Black people had been wrongfully killed by the police; after wrapping herself up in the writings of Huey Newton and Malcolm X and Frantz Fanon for hours on end; after seeing how extensive a Brooklyn Target's natural Black hair-care aisle could be—that she decided to chop all her relaxed hair off and see what happened. Turned out, she liked what was underneath. What she didn't like was how long it took her to learn this about herself.

Nella searched for a way to tell Hazel all of this before they got to the thirteenth floor. "I know, it's weird. Hair's never been something I've been good at. It's—"

"It's something you get better at as your hair gets longer," Hazel advised with a half smile. "And I can show you some tricks. I resisted braids for a while. Scarves, too. But once I started locking my hair, they just made sense. Especially when it gets so hot . . ."

Whatever judgment Nella thought she'd seen in Hazel was gone, and those painful memories of burning her scalp for beauty wafted out of the shaft. She relaxed as a few more people exited the elevator. "How long have you been locking your hair for?"

"God, it must be like . . . eight years now. Best decision I've ever made."

"Really?"

"Hell, yeah. *Very* low-maintenance."

"I bet. Yeah, sometimes I'm just too tired to twist my hair up every night, you know? But this 4C hair . . . you can't just go to sleep on it all loose without expecting the next morning to be a struggle."

"Oh, I remember that struggle. Trust," said Hazel. "I'm type 4B mostly, but my kitchen is 4C."

Nella smiled. What a thrill it was to be having this conversation in broad daylight in a Midtown building. Only one woman remained with them in the elevator, still squeezed into the far back corner even though there was no need for that anymore. A Wagner tote bag hung on her shoulder, too, although her model was from 2012. She was on the digital marketing team—Elena, Nella believed her name was, although she might've been confusing her with another brown-haired woman in marketing.

Nella watched maybe-Elena thumb through her phone, seemingly deep in concentration. There were no headphones in her ears, so she'd probably heard their entire conversation, Nella realized. She closely eyed maybe-Elena's plain, light brown bob and wondered how much Black hair talk she had ever been exposed to. Was she Googling "twisting" and "4B" and "kitchen"? Or was she altogether unmoved? Did she know this conversation had nothing to give her, and was therefore too apathetic to engage?

The elevator doors opened on the thirteenth floor. Maybe-Elena took a left, still lost in her phone. But instead of following her, Hazel pointed right. "Okay if we stop by the kitchen first? I wanna throw my lunch in the fridge."

"Oh. Um . . ." Lord, she was *so* late. But being forty-five minutes late rather than forty-four couldn't make *that* big of a difference, could it?

No, it couldn't. Nella decided to follow.

"Anyway, next time you find yourself in Clinton Hill, let me know," said Hazel, her gait a little too leisurely for Nella's liking. "You live in Brooklyn, too, right?"

"Yep. Bay Ridge."

"Bay Ridge, huh? Must be weird to live out there, no? It's pretty . . ." The rest of her sentence went limp as a senior production editor clicked by with a stack of pages in her arms, seemingly ready to give somebody—a careless editorial assistant, perhaps—a proper talking-to.

"Pretty white, right?" Nella finished once it was just the two of them again. "Kinda, yeah—it's not my favorite. But it's pretty much all we can afford right now."

"Ooh. '*We*'?" Hazel raised her eyebrows as they entered the kitchen. "Let me see . . . just judging from your tone, I gather that this is a . . . *special* roommate?"

"Ha! Well, yeah. I guess you could call him that. He's my—"

"Aw, you live with your boo, don't you? Cute! So, I'm guessing Bay Ridge was *his* idea, then? 'Cause, like, there are plenty of other places in Brooklyn that aren't crazy expensive. Or crazy white. And there's Queens . . ."

"He's pretty obsessed with Bay Ridge," Nella said. "He has this weird nostalgic love for *Saturday Night Fever*, even though it came out way before he was born."

Hazel, who'd been poking around the refrigerator, stuck her head out from behind the door long enough to say, "Ah, so he must be *Italian*," then disappeared again.

"A whopping twenty-five percent," Nella said slyly, "although that's not really—"

"He knows where *twenty-five percent* of him comes from? Lucky him," Hazel remarked once she'd finally found a home for her salad. They started walking toward their desks. "White boyfriends are *always* such a trip."

Nella perked up. Was Hazel speaking from firsthand experience, or just assuming? "If you don't mind me asking," she started, "is Manny w—?"

"Ah! *There* you are, Nella. *Finally.*"

Vera was standing above Nella's desk with a manic gleam in her eye, cheeks flushed, hands planted firmly on her hips. Her terse smile suggested that she was trying not to lose it, and had been trying for quite some time. "Hi, Hazel."

Hazel slipped into her desk chair and murmured a soft hello.

"I'm sorry I'm late," Nella said, searching for an excuse that she couldn't find.

"Yes. Next time, please send me an email, a text, a smoke signal . . . something. Just so I know. Okay? Thanks. I mean, the morning has been *insane.*"

Nella was speechless. Yes, she *could* have sent her an email. But she had been late to the office a handful of times in the two years she'd worked at Wagner—both reasonably and unreasonably—and none of these prior infractions had ever warranted such a showy confrontation. Sure, Nella had realized she was going to be about twenty minutes late when she got on the train, and when she got off the train, and when she stopped in the lobby to chat with Hazel and India. She'd again noticed it in the elevator, somewhere between the second and third floor. But Vera usually spent the early part of the morning inside of her office with her door closed, taking advantage of that time to accomplish the things she never could once everyone began to float in and out of her office for all sorts of reasons—to ask for editorial advice or opinions on a new cover design; to introduce new hires; to shoot the shit.

That morning, however—for Colin-related reasons, Nella suspected—Vera's door was wide open. And as far as she was concerned, the opinions she had aired out during the Shartricia conversation were still very much alive and dancing in the air between them like little hell-bent demons.

Perhaps sensing the demons, too, Hazel—in that same respectful whisper she'd used for her *hello*—volunteered a complaint about New York City's muddled subway system. "We were just talking about how we both had problems this morning—someone threw themselves on the tracks, I think. My train was stuck underground for twenty minutes, easily."

Nella stole a quick glance at Maisy's darkened office. The only person who would call Hazel out for being so late wasn't even in the office yet, but Hazel had helped Nella out anyway. She made a note to thank her later and added, "Mine took twenty-five. In the tunnel."

"In the tunnel," Vera repeated.

"Y-yes. In the tunnel." Nella's temperature rose a few degrees, a byproduct of either the lie she'd just told or Vera's *I don't believe you* stare. She suddenly remembered that her sweater was still on, so she slipped it off and dropped her stuff on top of her chair.

Vera bit her lip before breaking the silence. "All good." All was not good, but she moved on to briskly ask Nella if she'd print out two copies of *Needles and Pins*. Then she disappeared into her office and closed the door.

Nella looked over at Hazel's desk. Hazel looked back at her.

"Oof. What was *that* about?"

So, she hadn't heard. Fine. Nella cast a glance at Vera's closed door to make sure it was completely shut. Then she rolled over to Hazel's desk.

"Colin *flipped*," she whispered. "He went batshit."

"*What?* Why?"

"I was real with him about Shartricia. I decided to be honest, like we talked about at Nico's. He said I called him a racist. Just like I thought he would."

"Well, *did* you?"

"Of fucking *course* I didn't call him a racist," Nella said, offended Hazel could think she'd make such a heinous mistake. "But he got the *impression* that I did, and I can't undo that. It wasn't my finest moment, but I apologized when he finally came back from the bathroom."

Colin had returned to Vera's office about twenty minutes later, his cap restored, his jaw squared, and his eyes more than a little bit red. *I'm sorry that you thought I was calling you a racist,* Nella had conceded, trying her best to move her mouth without vomiting. The words had felt flat on her tongue, like she was apologizing to a man for pulling out her pepper spray on him after he'd followed too closely behind her on an empty street. But she'd said it. Because at the end of the day, she *was* sorry—just for slightly different reasons.

"He was gone from Vera's office for a while, right?" Hazel asked. "Like, twenty minutes? Such a long time."

"I guess that makes two of us who were counting," Nella murmured. "God, I'm so mortified."

Hazel shrugged her shoulders. "I felt the chill from my chair the moment he opened her office door. I'm so sorry, girl. From what *I* heard—"

"Wait." Nella paused. "So you *did* hear what happened?"

Hazel shook her head. "Bits and pieces, but not all of it. I was in my own world, handling some stuff for Maisy. But the more *important* thing here—judging by what I *did* happen to hear—is you did everything right. Don't let anybody tell you otherwise."

Before Nella could bask in these words a moment too long, Vera's door swung open again. "Nella, are you logged on?"

"I—"

"I sent you something that needed to be addressed immediately half an hour ago, and resent it again just now. Could you please take care of that? Now? Thanks."

Nella wheeled back over to her own desk as quickly as she could, but her shoelace betrayed her at exactly the same moment, inserting itself into one of the wheels and causing it to stick. The chair was moving at a painful crawl, and Vera was watching, one eyebrow arched. But she didn't say anything. She simply exhaled and sauntered back into her office, slamming her door louder than she did before.

The rest of the day passed exactly this way: excruciatingly, soaked with subtext that neither editor nor assistant had the resolve to acknowledge. The "urgent matter" Vera had asked Nella to handle was asking the managing editor if there was still time to include an author's middle initial in the jacket's flap copy before the book went to print. The managing editor's office was a mere ten-second walk away from Vera's desk.

This, Nella could handle. But for whatever reason, despite her best efforts, every other small thing she did went horribly wrong in some fashion: She forgot to cc the agent on an email to an author; she'd accidentally cut off the important part of a scanned document for Vera.

Nothing she did was right. Or, at least, it didn't *feel* right. Was it all in her head—Vera's frustrations, these tensions, these Colin Franklin demons? Occasionally, she paused her apologizing to wonder if she was simply projecting her own shame. But then Vera would conclude an exchange with *all good*, her eyes even frostier than her tone, and Nella thought to herself that yes, something had definitely shifted between them.

Meanwhile, inversely, Nella's relationship with Hazel was beginning to flourish, as though they were two soldiers in the trenches. Hazel worked to keep Nella afloat by distracting her with non-Wagner related things. When Nella responded to one of Vera's complaints with "Did *I* do that?! I'm sorry," Hazel swiftly emailed Nella a Steve Urkel GIF. After lunch, she brought Nella a triple-fudge walnut cookie from the bakery across the street, which happened to be Nella's favorite. And a few hours later, around three p.m., she sent Nella a link to Curl Central, the "dope hair café" she'd told her about in the elevator.

Curl Central's home page claimed the store doubled as "an exhaustive mecca for all Black hair matters"—and it wasn't lying. Curl Central really *did* cover it all. Not only could you buy scarves there, you could take workshops that taught you how to wrap them in the most intricate of styles. There was even a hair therapist—"Miss Iesha B."—who, if you went between the hours of five and seven on Thursday evenings, would sit down with you for half an hour and discuss what was ailing your locs. For those who weren't fortunate enough to live in New York City, or preferred a more solitary hairapy experience, Miss Iesha B. had written a short book that was available online for $9.99.

Whoever owned this store had taken great care to provide smell and texture descriptions of all their hair products, and had found Black models with every kind of curl pattern to showcase the effectiveness of each. It all fascinated Nella, how much time and effort had clearly been put into this website, so she navigated to Curl Central's About Us page, curious. The café had been founded and owned by Juanita Morejón, an attractive, curvy woman who possessed 3C curls, a clear fondness for crop tops, and an abundance of love for the time she spent growing up in the Dominican Republic with her baby brother, Manny.

Nella paused. Manny? As in . . . Hazel's boyfriend?

She read Juanita's bio through to the end, then read it again. She felt uncertain, but she couldn't put her finger on why. It wasn't because Hazel hadn't told her Curl Central was her boyfriend's sister's shop, although for someone who seemed so open to sharing everything about her personal life, it was strange that Hazel had chosen to keep that part to herself.

Only after she'd clicked away from Curl Central's website could she identify the source of the feeling: It was the new knowledge that Hazel's boyfriend wasn't white. He was Dominican. *Dominican* Dominican. As in, he'd been born in the DR and had lived there for ten years before immigrating to New York.

Nella pondered this new piece of information about her new coworker. Even though Hazel dripped Harlem like Spike dripped Brooklyn, something about her had led Nella to presume she'd ended up with a white guy like Owen, too. Perhaps it was the mere fact that Hazel had lived and worked in Boston for a lengthy amount of time, which to Nella meant that she'd attended white-bright parties similar to ones she herself had attended back in high school and college. And now, here Hazel was at Wagner, surrounded by white people once again.

Then again . . . just because Hazel was *capable* of navigating white social spheres all the time didn't mean she *wanted* to. Nella could appreciate that.

"I'm leaving, Nella."

When she looked up, Vera was standing above her cubicle, all dressed up and ready to go home. The pinched expression she'd been wearing earlier had relaxed a bit, thankfully, but she still didn't look altogether forgiving. It was late, after seven p.m., and Nella's will to work had walked out the door with Hazel about an hour earlier; now, she was elbow-deep in a listicle titled "Ten Celebs You Didn't Know Were Afro-Dominican."

Nella clicked out of it with one hand, using the other to wave at her boss. "Is it time to go already? Wow! Have a great night!"

Vera called out a half-hearted *you, too,* and strode toward the elevators without another word.

Nella sighed for perhaps the thirtieth time that day—except this time, it was a sigh of real relief. *Finally*, she could leave and go meet Malaika for a drink. Finally, she could vent about the Shartricia explosion with her, and finally, she could relieve the tension she'd been swimming in for almost nine hours. She stood up and started to collect her things, tossing pages she didn't need the following day and stacking the ones she would.

That was when she saw the small, white envelope sitting in the far corner of her desk. Her name was written neatly across its front, glaring up at her in all caps.

Nella didn't move at first. She just stared down at it, confused, as something funny tugged at her earlobes. How long had it been sitting there? An hour? The entire day?

Was it a letter from Vera apologizing for today?

She brought the envelope up to her face to assess it more closely. Yes, that was Nella's name, alright—written in purple pen.

She rolled her shoulders twice, a nervous tic she didn't know she had. Her bag slithered off her arm onto the floor, but she didn't move to pick it up. Instead, she squinted at the mysterious thing in her hands once more. She wasn't sure she could face what was on the inside of the envelope. She felt even less sure she could go on not knowing.

To hell with it.

Nella ran her pinky under the seal, angling her finger to avoid any paper cuts. Inside was an index card no bigger than two-by-three inches, with three damning words typed up in, confusingly, Comic Sans font.

LEAVE WAGNER. NOW.

She counted to three, the numbers hard to hear beneath the sound of her heartbeat. Then she inhaled and cast a glance over the tops of the cubicles to see who hadn't gone home yet. She wasn't sure what she expected to see—someone running away in a pointy white hood, or a sadistic trespassing tween who actually thought Comic Sans was cool?—but she did see Donald, Richard's assistant. Donald, who was too shy to say hello unless he needed something; Donald, who was bobbing his head to music only he could hear, a pair of oversized Bose headphones connecting his round, close-shaven head to a Discman that rested by his left elbow. Donald, who still *used* a Discman.

There was no way Donald, whose emails were always in eight-point Times New Roman, would ever fuck with Comic Sans—not to intimidate, not even ironically. No one at Wagner would. It didn't add up.

Nella sank back down into her chair, a sudden chill threading itself down her throat and into her stomach, like she'd swallowed an unhealthy amount of helium. Again, she examined the piece of paper that was in her left hand; then the envelope in her right. She was so lost in thought as to how she could have missed its delivery that she didn't notice it was now almost eight p.m., and that the rushing air had shifted down from its usual loud hum to the gentle, power-saving whir of the afterhours.

Leave Wagner. Now.

She turned the notecard over, just in case she'd missed something. But that was all it said, so she read the words a second time.

And then, a third.

The fourth time she read them, a short, deep guffaw let loose from her belly. She couldn't help it. It wasn't one of those confident Olivia Pope laughs. By no means was she thinking, *Ha, I'm better than you, you small-minded anonymous racist stranger, you—because this isn't going to get to me; I'm going to rise from the ashes and write a think piece about this moment and you will rue the day you ever tried to fuck with me.*

No. The laugh was more of a simple, resigned chortle. A *Ha! Finally. I've always known this moment would come.* She thought of Colin Franklin with his crumpled cap; of the elderly Black man shot in North Carolina for reaching for his hearing aid. Of Jesse Watson's words about being seen as an equal to white colleagues: "You may think they're okay with you, and they'll make you think that they are. But they really aren't. They never will be. Your presence only makes them fear their own absence."

They. Yes, there had always been a *they* since she'd started working at Wagner, hadn't there?

Nella exhaled as she slid the note back into the envelope, intent on throwing the entire parcel into her recycling bin and forgetting she'd ever read it. But something stopped her—the cathartic desire to share its existence with someone else, and the inherent need to survive. She'd seen all the movies, watched all the videos about bullying and racism in health class. What Nella had in her clammy fingers, she knew, was evidence.

Shani

July 10, 2018
Joe's Barbershop
Harlem, New York

"Name."

I coughed into my fist, my throat suddenly dry although the night was humid as ever. "Shani. Shani Edmonds."

"Shani Edmonds. Okay. Hi, Shani."

The guy manning the door took a break from his phone so he could look me up and down. I didn't mind it so much. I'd done the same to him when I'd stumbled up to the entrance of Joe's Barbershop a few seconds earlier, studying as much of him as the shadows beneath the building's awning would allow. I got a decent look, and I'll say this: I'd never been to Harlem, but he looked exactly as I'd always imagined Black guys in Harlem would look: Tall, dark, and cute. The kind of Black guy that reminded me of one of the many debonair, coiffed men who speckled my grandfather's collection of army photos. Old school, 1940s, with skin the color of wet sand and a kind smile that suggested he'd much sooner call a woman "brown sugah" than "bitch."

He didn't call me either of these things, but he was smiling at what must have been a perplexed look on my face. "You don't gotta be nervous," he said, sticking his phone in his back pocket. "We ain't nothing but family here. The second you come inside . . . well, you'll see."

"'Family'?" About ten yards away, on the corner of 127th and Frederick Douglass, a car revved its engine in vain. I'd spent the forty-five-minute cab ride over here searching the Internet for information about "Lynn Johnson" and "the Resistance," and like every other time, I came up short. Yet here I was in the middle of the night in a strange new city at a barbershop that was supposed to be closed.

I shifted to my other foot and reshouldered my tote bag, trying to posture confidence I didn't feel. "That's cool and all, although I'm not sure what kind of family meets at three o'clock in the morning."

That got a laugh out of him. "You'll see exactly what kind in a little bit. Come on in, Shani," he said, offering a fist for me to dap. "Will."

I smiled, eager to enter and get into what I hoped was air-conditioning. But before I could set foot inside, a voice shouted at me to hold up. "Will!" a female voice shouted. "How many times have I told you, cuz: Ask the code question *first*, *before* you let anybody inside?"

Will groaned and turned to whisper something inaudible into the blackness behind him. I craned my neck, desperate to see who he was talking to, but the lights were completely off in Joe's.

"Shit," the voice said, after a moment. "She's seen your face, too. Knows your name. If she were an OBG this entire operation would be shut down. The Resistance would be made."

He sucked a stream of air between his perfect teeth. "'Made?' 'Code questions?' This all just feels so—"

"How many times do I have to tell you I don't care what it feels like to you? *I'm* in charge of making sure we're not found, asshole. So just ask her the code question so we can get this shit moving."

That put a wrench in Will's amusement. When he finally regarded me again, the softness in his eyes had given way to irritation. "An asteroid is spiraling toward Earth, threatening to destroy all Black folk except for one," he said flatly. "This lucky motherfucker is either Stacey Dash or Ben Carson. Who do you choose to save?"

Shit. *That* was the code question? I shook my head and yanked at my sweat-soaked bra strap. "How much time you got?"

"C'mon, just think. What's your gut saying?"

"My gut's saying you can't ask me that question when it's three—" I checked my watch, annoyed. I hadn't snuck out of my aunt's place in Queens in the middle of the night just to play secret clubhouse with a stranger; I didn't care how cute he was. "Three ten in the morning. I'm hot. Is that you, Lynn?" I called into the space behind him. "I'm here, just like we planned. I left Boston. Why are you making me do all this?"

The voice didn't reply. Just Will. "I wouldn't do all that. Probably better if you just answer the question."

"There are too many logistics for me to think about, though. I can't just—"

"You *see*?!" Will cried, his voice thick with vindication as he spun around to appeal to the person behind him. But when the voice didn't speak, he shrugged, readjusted his sock cap, and grumbled to me, "It's mandatory."

Sighing, I tried to weigh who was worse. It was hard to parse out an answer with that rusty car engine still sputtering on and on in the background, but after a moment, I was able to gather my thoughts.

"Ben," I finally said. "They're both awful—and he's said some pretty idiotic things—but at least he can save somebody's life. I guess."

"Fair." Will chuckled, once again chilled out. He turned. "Okay?"

There was a pause.

"Yeah," the voice said. "Okay."

My feet started to move forward before my heart had time to go back into flutter mode. "No lights until we're upstairs," I heard the woman say, this time louder, more relaxed. "But for now, you should be good with this."

A flashlight flickered on a few feet ahead of me. "Lynn?" I called again, blinking at the beam of light.

"We talk upstairs. Just c'mon. Follow me."

I shivered and did as I was told, even as I realized someone—Will, probably—had put his hands on my shoulders to guide me. Everything was dark, pitch-black dark, so I let him pull me forward, straining my eyes to detect chains hanging from the ceiling, or suspicious swaths of dried meat lining the baseboards—anything that would confirm that I was foolish to be there.

But I didn't need to see to know that. It was more than just foolish. It was *crazy*.

How did that saying go? Nobody looks for missing little Black girls?

"C'mon, Shani," Will whispered, his words interrupting my worries, the warmth of his breath in my ear reminding me that I was arm in arm with an attractive man in a strange, cold barbershop at three o'clock in the morning. A kind-lipped Harlemite who smelled heavily of Dial soap and Listerine.

I let him lead me slowly behind the shadow that was lighting our way. "By the way," he added, his tone suggesting he often took delight in saying what he was about to say, "the correct answer to my question was you don't save either of them. Use this asteroid as a chance to start over. But pretty much no one ever gets that right, so you're good."

7

August 30, 2018

Nella opened her eyes, glanced over at the alarm clock, and moaned. It was only five a.m.; her eyes had closed around one.

She turned to face Owen, noticed how rapt with sleep he was, and promptly returned to her other side, envious. But the flip just made her stomach feel worse. So did remembering how many drinks she'd had the night before . . . and the reason she'd drunk so much in the first place.

The words "Leave Wagner" worked their way up and down Nella's brain, stretching wider and wider and echoing louder and louder until her subconscious started playing them back to her in different genres: country, rap, polka, and then—perhaps the cruelest of all—big band. It got so bad that at about three minutes after five, she got out of bed so she could get herself as "together" as she possibly could.

She'd been hearing this tortuous song ever since she'd left Wagner fewer than twelve hours earlier. Throughout her entire train ride between Wagner and McKinley's, she'd been convinced everyone was looking at her. Was she being watched? Followed? Was that man who was standing by the doors looking at her because he wanted to knock her down and take her wallet, or because he didn't like the idea of Black people working at Wagner? Had his own son been denied internships at Wagner year after year, and he'd decided to take it out on the one person he thought nobody would miss?

Each new stranger made the note weigh heavier upon her shoulder, to the point that by the time she'd been carded by the McKinley's bouncer, waved hello to a familiar regular, and headed straight toward the bar, she had already unearthed the envelope from her bag. And as soon as she reached Malaika, she dropped it onto the table like a stick of dynamite she could hold no longer.

"What's *this*?" Malaika asked, picking up the envelope and holding it up to the dim bar lighting, as though that would make a difference.

Nella signaled for Rafael to make her the usual. "Didn't you read any of my texts? Jesus Christ."

"What? Oh, I'm sorry. I thought you understood that my hand is generally too far up Igor's ass for me to concern myself with the worries of my own people," Malaika said, eyebrows raised in mock amusement. "What is this? A wedding invitation or something?" She gasped suddenly, clutching her heart. "Is this *your* wedding invitation?"

Nella knitted her own eyebrows as she peered over at the bourbon cocktail Malaika was on the edge of finishing. "Mal, how many of those have you had?"

"This may or may not be my third. Igor let me go kind of early today because he wanted me to swing by the dry cleaners before they closed. So I figured, why the hell not?"

"*Oh*kay." For a moment, Nella wondered—and not for the first time, either—if perhaps she and Malaika should consider hanging out at an ice cream shop instead of a bar every once in a while. The moment passed fairly quickly, as it always did. "Just open it. Please."

Malaika picked up her drink and threw the last of it back long and slow, like a woman about to do something extremely dangerous. She set it down, swiped at the moisture above her lip that her previous act had left, and got to work on the envelope.

And strangely, it *was* work. The top flap had managed to re-glue itself shut, and to Nella's exasperation, it took Malaika much longer to open than it should have. But Malaika's reaction to what was inside was satisfying enough to make up for the delay: She threw the envelope on the ground as quickly as she would have thrown a used tampon.

"What the hell," she said once, and then again, as she retrieved the notecard from the floor. "Where did this come from?"

"I have no fucking clue." Nella thanked an apprehensive-looking Rafael for her Aperol spritz. It was clear that he wanted to stick around and hear what had garnered such a visceral reaction from Malaika, but another couple had just started to place their jackets on the barstools a few seats down. He gave Nella a modest bow, his sandy hair falling in his face, and ran over to greet them sunnily.

"It just . . . it just showed up on my desk today. At the very, very end of the day."

"And you have *no* clue who could have left it?"

"Nope."

"And no clue when someone could have dropped it off?"

"My desk is always covered with papers, so . . . no. It could have been any time of the day." Nella took a good, long sip of her drink, the shock of bitterness sobering her thoughts a bit.

"Hmmm." Malaika bit her lip. "Could it be a disgruntled author?"

The thought had flashed through her mind on her way over, but it had dissipated almost as quickly as it had come. There was no way that Colin's disdain for her feedback on his Black character had outweighed his desire to receive his next scheduled payment for *Needles and Pins*. The man might have been fragile, with a delicate sense of self-worth, but he wasn't stupid. "Funny you say that. A certain disgruntled author *did* cross my mind on the way over here . . . but there's no way."

"Who?!"

"Colin. He flipped *out* on me yesterday," Nella explained. "I told him my thoughts about Shar. But that's a story for my next drink."

Malaika furrowed her brow in concern. "Shit. Really?"

"Yeah. But there's no way he would even think about doing that to me. He's too obvious a culprit, especially since he has a history with harassment."

"Harassment?" Malaika scoffed. "Do you hear yourself right now?"

"It happened *years* ago, and Richard apparently put Colin through the ringer when the tabloids got ahold of it. Colin's been on his best behavior ever since. Kind of."

Malaika sighed. "Okay. Maybe not *him*. But what about Vera?"

Nella almost spilled her drink on herself. "You can't think—?"

"Well, you haven't told me anything yet, but I'd imagine Vera was pretty mad about the Colin thing."

"Yeah, but . . . it would be so *ob*vious if she did something like that. Vera's not *that* stupid, or petty."

Malaika delivered her favorite *Are you being for real* look. "I've watched Lifetime Movie Network. I know how power-hungry white women operate. They do whatever it takes to claw their way to the top, all sneaky and shit. And once they're at the top, you bet their asses they're gonna do anything they can to keep their place there. Steal a baby, cut up somebody's dog. *Sneaky* things."

"You mean *some* of them. Not all of them. Also," Nella added, even as an image of a distraught Vera standing above her with a box cutter and some packing tape flashed through her mind, "if Vera *really* wanted to fire me, she would have just fired me already. She's been at Wagner long enough to have the clout."

Malaika snorted. "You know and *I* know that it's not that simple." She picked up the envelope again and reread the note aloud the way she would have read a Dr. Seuss book. "'Leave Wagner. Now.' If this isn't a hate crime, I don't know what is."

"It would have been a hate crime if it had said, 'Leave Wagner now, *nigger*.'"

"Oh . . . but it's *there*."

Nella reached for the paper. "It is?"

"No, it's not *there*, literally. But it's *there*. Look, girl," she continued when Nella rolled her eyes. "You are *Black*. The fact that you're Black colors every single thing anyone ever says to you—pun intended," she added, before Nella could. "Whether they admit it or not."

"I know what you mean. And you're sort of right. But—"

"And with that anonymous article that was published last month—the one about the Black girl working in a white space—didn't you say that your BFF Sophie accused you of writing it?" Malaika gasped, clutching her chest. "What if they think you wrote it and they're trying to get you out?"

"I said they're pretty nuts. I didn't say they were the literary KGB."

"I mean . . . maybe not, but remember when Vera told you to chill out on all the *I'm Black and I'm Proud* ruckus you were starting?"

"Yeah. But that was different. And I plan on starting that ruckus back up again, by the way," Nella added, even though the thought of trying to resuscitate Wagner's Diversity Town Halls sounded just as appealing as sticking her hair into the nearest burning tea candle. "It's just . . . I've never had something like this happen before, you know? I know I'm definitely gonna sound like one of those crazy people in denial when I say this—"

"Yes, that is your usual style."

"—but during my time at Wagner, I've never had anyone be pointedly racist toward me. At least, nothing beyond, like, microaggressions. Trust me, you'd know by now."

Nella hadn't been just bullshitting to make herself feel better. It had been the truth. Ask her how much it pained her to be the only Black person in the room, and the answer varied depending on the day. It pained her to have to blacksplain cultural moments to people who didn't understand them, like the seriousness of Kanye's mental breakdown or the significance of seeing Black women wearing protective scarves in *Girls Trip*. And no, Nella had *not* read every Notable Black Book with gusto (she'd started *The Bluest Eye* at least five different times and had never gotten past the first chapter), so she could not speak to how this or that upcoming Black writer compared with Toni Morrison in her prime.

But Nella would be lying if she didn't admit that deep down, a small piece of her was proud of how utterly different, dare she say *radical,* her world viewpoint felt from the homogenous throes of Wagner Books. No, from *all* publishing. She may have been unsuccessful at getting her colleagues to hire people outside of their usual demographics, but she had at least gotten her foot in the door. She'd made people think about race, even if they didn't realize they were thinking about it, by simply being present at meetings, or being friendly in the kitchen.

And, even deeper down—thousands of feet past this last thought, swimming around in the depths of a place one might call "pride"—was Nella's suspicion that many of her coworkers at Wagner, Vera included, looked upon her with a sort of reverence. With awe. *Imagine how much harder she must've had to fight to get here,* she imagined them saying to one another behind closed doors when they considered the Ivy League names and publishing internships that were missing from her résumé. She didn't come from a long line of people in the book business. She'd had a much harder time elbowing her way into the fray than most; this went without saying.

"Even if it is true that nobody has ever committed any pointedly racist act against you there, *ever,*" said Malaika, cutting into Nella's thoughts, "let's talk facts. Fact one: You're Black. Fact two: You're *Black.* Fact three: How many white people do you think have gotten a note like this at Wagner? Or *ever*? These are facts, my friend. Straight-up facts."

Nella remained silent. She both loved and hated whenever Malaika got really tipsy and really real with her, which usually happened around nine p.m. and almost always happened after two drinks and no food.

"Oh-ho-ho-ho, but wait," Malaika squealed, nearly choking on an ice cube. "Fact four: You're no longer the only one! I forgot about that other Black girl. What's her name again?"

"Right. Hazel." Nella herself still sometimes forgot that Wagner wasn't all white anymore, perhaps because she and Hazel felt like extensions of one another, two sides of the same coin. "I should have checked her desk before I left to see if she got one, too." She searched for a memory of what her coworker had looked like when she left the office, trying to sift the day's events from all the others that had come before it, but all she could see were the many shades of agitated Vera: Vera tapping her black sensible shoe; Vera hovering at her desk; Vera frowning—always frowning. Hazel had to have slipped out without Nella noticing.

"Maybe . . ." Malaika's eyes widened. She was not so secretly loving this, Nella knew.

"Maybe what?"

"Maybe . . . it was *Hazel* who left it."

"What? That's crazy. She sent me a *Family Matters* GIF today. Why would you think that?"

Malaika considered this. "Nah," she finally said, "you're right. Homegirl wouldn't have been that subtle about wanting you to get gone. Plus, *you* did all the hard work. You broke in all those white people at Wagner. You've been preparing them not to say dumb shit in meetings for two whole years. She would never . . ."

Nella swatted away the thought. "She could *never*."

But the notion of Hazel planting the letter dug its claws into Nella's neck, sinking deeper as she finished her first drink and even deeper as she finished her second. On her third, when Malaika asked Nella if she'd Facebooked her new coworker, she'd practically flung her cell phone out of her purse, ecstatic at the thought of revisiting this topic once more. The fruitful topic they'd switched to previously—whether or not *Boyz n the Hood* could be turned into a stage musical—had been squeezed dry.

"Her name is Hazel McCall," Nella said, typing her name into the white search bar.

"I can't believe we haven't done this yet. How have we not done this yet?"

"I don't know. I was looking at her boyfriend's sister's hair café website earlier today, but I never got around to her because Vera was working me like a dog."

"Hair café?"

"I'll show it to you later, but we should definitely check it out." Nella pulled the screen down, frustrated. "Whoa, who knew there were so many Hazel McCalls!"

"Really? I find that surprising. Tabling this 'hair café' thing for the very near future, by the way."

"You know what?" Nella sucked down the rest of her drink, then tapped the screen a few times. "Her full name is something hyphenated. Something like Hazel-Anne, or Hazel-Sue . . . Hazel-May! That's what it was." She typed it in as Malaika grumbled something about how country Hazel's name sounded.

Only one person in the Brooklyn area popped up that time. Nella recognized her colleague immediately, even though her profile photo showed her decked out in an elegant jade-green gown, wearing a face model's amount of makeup.

"That dress!" Malaika cried. "And, that *man*! Hel*lo*. Who is this fella?"

Nella had hardly glanced at the sexy man in the forest-green tuxedo before the phone was taken away from her, but she knew Malaika was ogling Manny. Nella understood why. Normally, she thought that a tux in any color besides black or navy blue was tacky, but this green one complemented his terra-cotta complexion so strikingly that Nella couldn't deny how smart of a fashion choice it had been. His long, dark, wavy hair framed his face perfectly, and his smile was even more dazzling than Hazel's.

How good—no, how *bold* they both looked together, this young, beautiful couple donning nontraditional hues. Nella wondered what it would take to get Owen into a tux that sharp. Probably a lot. Probably too much.

"That's Manny. Her boyfriend. He's Dominican," Nella added, as though she'd actually met him, as though Malaika had asked. Malaika *ooh*ed in reply, like she'd just been granted a secret to the universe.

Nella continued to take a look around Hazel's Facebook, scanning her latest posts, peeking through photos that she'd recently been tagged in. Posted just three days earlier was a photo of Hazel surrounded by four Black girls. They were all wearing the same purple shirt, with a logo that was just too small for Nella to make out. Each looked to be maybe sixteen or seventeen and had their arms around Hazel, who stood dead center, smiling so hard that her pupils weren't visible.

Nella ignored the comments—she often got pulled into the most mundane of comment trails—and scrolled down to the next photo. This one was of Hazel staring straight at the camera, holding a large sign in her hands that said RESPECT BLACK WOMEN.

The last one she looked at was of Hazel bathed in soft pink lighting on a stage, a microphone in her hand, her locs piled high on her head. Nella vaguely remembered Hazel telling her she had gone to DC for a Black women's poetry retreat not long ago.

"Mentors young Black women . . . goes on poetry retreats . . . makes signs with all-caps letters . . . definitely suspicious," Malaika joked. "Hey, wait a second." She held up a hand. "You said her boyfriend's name is Manny?"

"Yeah." Nella was still looking at the picture of Hazel, comparing the all-caps letters in her sign with the all-caps letters on the mysterious envelope she'd received. "Why?"

Malaika reached for her phone again, nearly falling off her chair. "You are so freakin' familiar," she said, rapping on Manny's face with her thumb.

"He is? Rafael, when you have a second, could you please—" Nella gestured to their empty water glasses. Malaika's near-tumble reminded her that such drinking required hydration, especially on a weeknight.

"I got you two."

"You're my first, my last, my everything, bless you," Malaika called after him, not looking up from the photo. "I *know* I've seen this guy before, somewhere. Do you know what he does?"

"I think he's an artist or something? He painted this beautiful photo of Zora Neale Hurston and put it on a mug for Hazel for their anniversary."

Malaika banged the table with her palm. "I knew it! I saw him in *Melanin Monthly* last year, I think, on one of those 'artists to watch out for' lists. He's, like, the Andy Warhol of our generation. Warhol meets Basquiat. Their words, not mine, I promise." Malaika unlocked her phone and went into Instagram. Within five seconds she'd pulled up the mosaic of tiny square images that made up Manny's page. *Art + BK,* it read—a sparse and cool description, Nella noted, for a profile that had nearly one hundred thousand followers and more than three thousand postings.

She scrolled through the main page. Even as thumbnails, Nella could see that nearly every piece of artwork Manny had posted had been rendered in an understated, refreshing style similar to that of the Zora Neale Hurston artwork she'd seen, placed not only on mugs but on T-shirts and tote bags and pins and magnets.

There wasn't a single piece that Nella couldn't see herself buying either for herself or as a gift for someone else—each item was that special. Hazel might have been playing up the fact that she had a boyfriend, Nella observed, zooming in on an incredible impressionistic painting of a purple Althea Gibson, but she had definitely been playing down how impressive said boyfriend actually was.

What else was she hiding?

Nella scrolled through two or three more rows of posts, hoping to find more details about Hazel, then slid the phone back to her friend when she didn't. "Manny seems pretty cool."

Malaika left the phone where it was. "*Well?*"

"Well, what?"

"Do you still think Hazel left that note?"

Nella sighed. She didn't know what to say. She just knew what she felt: that it was unfair to point fingers at the only Black girl she worked with. The words "bad karma" entered her brain, followed by "crabs in a barrel," said not by Angela Davis but—this time—by her mother. It was a saying that her father despised, but her mother always held it close, the words as calming as a meditation chant and as practical as a house key. Typically, Nella sided with her father, erring somewhere between nonconfrontational and carefree.

But if there was one thing she was starting to comprehend, it was that these traits were of no use to her in the real world.

Nella kept her movements as catlike as possible once she finally crawled out of bed, found some pants, and threw on the first clean sweater she could find. She marched into the bathroom to finish the rest, the bright light bulbs above the mirror shocking her nerves into full wakefulness.

On any other day, what she saw in the mirror would have alarmed her: Her hair was all over the place, and not in the cute, *I'm too busy working on my career to care* way. She'd been so desperate to pass out the night before that she hadn't braided her curls or even put on a sleep scarf. But she wasted no time eyeing her hair's shrinkage as she pulled it all back into a small scrunchie, then brushed her teeth and washed her face. Nor did she bother brewing a coffee or preparing some grits. She simply put on her shoes, packed her tote bag, and stepped out into the sticky summer morning.

Something was pulling her toward her cubicle at Wagner. What that something was, she didn't exactly know. She just knew it had caused her to practically run over the small, confused woman who was taking too long to fish her MetroCard out of her wallet. And when the time came for her to walk through Wagner's lobby around a quarter to seven, far too early of an arrival for even the most diligent editors, it caused her to trip and nearly fall on her face.

Ever graceful, Nella fell on her hands instead. "Shit!" she spat, inhaling a rancid whiff of the ratty welcome rug before pushing her body up. How humiliating. But how lucky she was that no other Wagner employees had seen her fall or heard her swear so loudly.

Unless . . .

Nella spun around quickly. She checked for any conspicuous

strangers, ones with and without white sheets. Not a soul was in sight but India at the reception desk.

She continued on toward the elevators, fumbling breathlessly for her work ID, ready to explain why she was here so early. But as she drew closer, India's head didn't tilt up the way it normally did.

"India. Hey. How's it going? Did you enjoy the rest of your birthday yesterday?"

India's eyes darted up from her magazine. She appeared startled by the intrusion. Maybe even a little confused by it. "Oh. Hi, Nella," she said, with a touch of listlessness. "What'd you say?"

"I . . . I just asked if you had a good birthday."

"Oh. Yeah, I did. Thanks."

She looked back down at her magazine.

Nella felt her throat tighten. *That's it?* she wondered as she stepped into the elevator and pressed thirteen. The metal doors shut in front of her at an excruciatingly slow pace, granting her one last long look at the woman who had given her such an icy reception.

Floors came and went beneath her as she turned India's greeting over and over in her mind. Something had changed; the look she'd given Nella had matched the one she gave most of Nella's white colleagues.

Hazel *had* spent more time talking to India over the course of three weeks than Nella had in the last two years. Was it possible Hazel's kindness had caused India to group Nella in with everyone else? Had India and Hazel even concocted this note thing together in order to pull some kind of weird prank? India *did* have so many connections within the building. She knew where all the hidden entrances were . . . and probably had access to unlimited envelopes and purple pens.

But why?

Nella breathed out, then in. No. *No.* She *had* to be overthinking it. After all, her nerves from that scary note were still warping her perception of the world. *India was fine. You came into the office before everybody else, and she just hadn't expected to have to do her song-and-dance greeting so early. How would you feel if you had to smile at one thousand people a day?*

This logic only got Nella through a few floors. She was mulling it all over into a pulp, and by the time the doors opened on thirteen, the words *Oh hi, Nella* had tacked themselves onto the words *Leave Wagner,* and it was all playing in one nasty loop in her mind, a warning of she didn't know what.

Nella scrutinized every empty desk as she passed on the way to her own. She was glad to be free from the confines of the elevator, but she couldn't say she was happy to be back in the office. This was what she'd thought she wanted—to return to the scene of the crime; to explore the premises undisturbed. But everything about Wagner felt different now. The bright hospital-ward lighting felt more clinical than ever. And the AC didn't feel like it was on at all.

She dropped her things on her chair and booted up her computer before creeping over to Hazel's cubicle, startled by what she saw. Nella had never noticed how clear or organized her neighbor's desk was. Everything had its place: To the left of the keyboard were two piles; one labeled *To Do*, the other labeled *Check with Maisy*. Hazel's office supplies were lined along the back wall, jars of rubber bands and thumbtacks on one side, boxes of staples and paper clips on the other. And in the far corner sat a mason jar filled with highlighters, pencils, and pens.

Black pens. One red. Two blue. And zero purple.

Placated for the time being, Nella returned to her cubicle, sat down, and closed her eyes. Instead of darkness, she saw interactions from the day before. People. Everyone she'd come into contact with had been fine: the production team, the publicists, the other assistants. And Hazel—Hazel had been chummier than ever before with Nella. Sending her GIFs and a link to a cool Black hair mecca in Brooklyn. Trying to distract her from Vera's nitpicking.

Come to think of it, the only person in the office who'd had any kind of problem with Nella had been Vera. God, how stern she'd been. How unfair. Just because Nella had spoken her truth about Shartricia, and was absurdly late to work that one time . . . those things didn't make her a bad assistant. She knew what a bad assistant looked like. *Trust.* All anyone needed to do was look around the office when the other editors went out to lunch. The other assistants were easily distracted. Dispassionate. Neglectful.

Neglectful.

Nella's eyes popped wider than they had hours earlier in bed. She'd forgotten something. Not a hint as to where the note might have come from, but a task for Vera: tweak the online copy so that it spoke to a younger audience. Perhaps *that* was the real reason why she had felt pulled to work so early. It wouldn't be the first time her subconscious was more on it than she was.

Newly humbled, Nella rapped her fingers impatiently on her desk while she looked for the original Word file on her computer and hit Print. The printer on the other side of the wall spat out the page immediately. Nella glanced over toward the sound of the machine, caught by surprise. Usually, first thing in the morning, the machine took close to ninety seconds to warm up from sleep mode.

She grabbed the page and trudged back to her desk. It was only after she'd gotten to her chair, poised to sit down, that she realized she had two pages in her hand, not one. She placed her page on her chair, then headed back to the printer to leave the other sheet for its rightful owner.

It was common courtesy to do this. Nella preferred this method to trying to figure out whose it was by either reading the page's contents or by doing what Bridget always did, which was circle the office and wave the page high in the air like a pair of stray panties.

And yet, alone in the empty office, Nella broke etiquette and took an unabashed look at what she'd accidentally grabbed. What she saw made her stop in her tracks, just as she turned the corner.

It was a list. A spreadsheet, really. It looked official, like it had been drawn up using the software Wagner editors used to organize the books they were working on—except the titles in the left column weren't book titles at all.

Aaliyah H.
Ayanna P.
Camille P.
Ebonee J.
Jada A.
Jazmin S.
Kiara T.
Nia W.

Names. And across from the names, in the middle column, were dates. And across from the middle column, on the far right, was a list of cities. Well, mostly one city: New York, New York, New York, all the way down. Only Camille P. from Missoula dared to break the pattern.

Nella scanned the list once again. Missoula be damned; these names *had* to belong to Black women.

Bizarre.

And then, suddenly hopeful as she slipped it back onto the printer: *Could it be a list of candidates to hire?* She stood up on her tiptoes and confirmed that Richard's light was indeed on in his office.

"What you *doin'*, Nella?"

Nella started at the sound of her name. She'd expected to have the office to herself for at least another half an hour or so. "Hello? Who's there?"

The sound of laughter echoed from her desk. "Who you think?" the voice asked. "It's just me!"

Nella knew this voice. She made her way over to her cubicle to find C. J. standing next to her empty chair, his face stretched by a self-satisfied smirk, his arms crossed over the front of his too-small, navy-blue Wagner Mail short-sleeved button-up. Not long after she had started, maybe during her third or fourth week, he'd told her in his thick, buttery accent how he'd once made the mistake of putting it in a dryer for too long. It had shrunk down to a third of its original size, "just five minutes short of a crop top," he'd said, laughing. When she'd asked him why he hadn't just gotten another one, he told her that it would cost him more than fifty bucks to replace.

After that, they were buds.

"You fucking *terrified* me, Ceej." Nella punched his shoulder, even though she was so happy to see him that she thought she might cry. If she was sure about anything, it was that C. J. wasn't the perpetrator. "I'm so glad it's you."

C. J. raised his eyebrows. Apparently, he noticed that she was close to tears, too. "I should get surgery more often. It's been, like, what—six weeks? And you forgot I existed already?" His hearty laugh reverberated through the empty halls and through Nella's core, too, filling up her insides like a cup of gumbo on a January day.

"I didn't forget about you," Nella said. She felt like giving him a hug just to prove her point. Instead, she lowered herself back down at her desk. She didn't want him to get the wrong idea. Even though he'd apologized for that awkward DM he'd drunkenly sent her on Instagram a few months back, and they seemed to have gotten past it, Nella deemed it better to keep their relationship at a place that hovered somewhere around G-rated but meaningful.

"How's the knee?" she asked him.

"Oh, you know. Doin' what it should be. Hurts like hell, but I'm here."

"You didn't want to take a bit more time off?"

"Can't," C. J. said. "We only get so much time, you feel me?"

Nella nodded, although they both knew that his "we" didn't involve her, because he and the rest of the mail staff were given less paid time off than everyone else. Their situations outside of the office were vastly different, too. C. J. lived with his sister and his sister's kid in Ocean Hill and helped support them both, partly with his Wagner paychecks and partly with paychecks from his weekend job. She couldn't remember specifically which nightclub he was a bouncer at, but she vaguely remembered that it was nowhere near where he lived—in Hell's Kitchen, or maybe even somewhere up in Columbia territory. And it made sense. On Monday mornings, if she looked long enough, she might see him taking a break in between distributing packages, leaning against his mail crate to catch some rest.

Nella wasn't sure how he managed all of it at the age of twenty-two: the commute; the two jobs; supporting family that was his family but wasn't really *his* responsibility, not according to her own privileged rules, anyway. But somehow, he did. Usually with a smile.

Nella eyed his knee skeptically. "You could have at *least* come in a bit later, you know," she said quietly.

"Ha! Sherry texted me and told me the guy who was here in my place was doing a real shit job. I've been finding mail postmarked from more than a week ago that ain't been delivered yet. No good. It's like, how you gonna screw up this job? You know what I'm saying? It's so easy, my god."

Nella thought about the scrawny old mailman who'd come up from the software company below them to take C. J.'s spot. She chuckled as she remembered how he'd accidentally run Maisy over with his cart during the first week of his temporary residency at Wagner, of how Nella—of all of her colleagues—was the one person whose mail never got fudged. "I tried to help him out as best as I could when he first took over, but poor guy . . . he just couldn't get it together. I think he was overwhelmed by how many packages we get up here."

"You know what I think?" C. J. flexed his left bicep and kissed it. "I think he just ain't me. That's all it is."

Nella laughed. "I think you're probably right."

"So how have things been around here otherwise? Have you taken over the world yet? Bought the latest bestseller?"

"Hell, no. But . . . um . . . something strange happened yesterday. I got this really weird note."

"A weird note?"

"Yep."

"Who from?"

"That's what's really strange about it. I don't know. It was anonymous. But it was in this envelope with my name on it, and the note said 'Leave Wagner. Now.'"

"The hell? You're fucking with me."

"I wish I was, because I'm pretty freaked out. That's why I'm here so early."

"Why? So you can fight whoever left it for you by yourself?" C. J. joked, but the light air of humor he'd been reaching for hadn't quite reached his eyes. He looked straight-up concerned, reminding her why she *had* shown up so early: to search for clues that she might have missed the night before. To find a smoking gun—that damn purple pen—on Hazel's desk.

But while she trusted C. J., she wasn't ready to tell him that part yet, so she just shrugged. "I don't know what I thought I'd do, Ceej. I don't know."

C. J. nodded. "Have you thought long and hard about whether or not someone here's trying to mess with you?"

"I have. But why would they start now, after two years? The time to do that would have been when I first started, if we think it's some white supremacist kind of thing. Or when I was trying to do all that diversity stuff way back when."

"It's mostly you guys in the office this time of the summer, though, right? Assistants? So, if it *was* someone who worked here, that means . . ."

C. J. trailed off, but he was still giving her that scary, worried look. She was beginning to wish she hadn't said anything about it—not to him. Not before she'd overcome her hangover; not before she'd drummed up a likely narrative that *she* felt comfortable with.

"I don't know why you're so cool about this," he said finally. "This isn't something you can just ignore and then it'll just . . . go away. Have you told anyone here about it?"

"Not yet. I got it last night, after almost everyone had left."

"Almost?"

"Donald was still here, but as far as I know, that's it."

"Ah, Walk-Man," C. J. said. Nella could practically see the gears turning in his eyes as he considered Richard's assistant exactly the way she had twelve hours earlier. "And this note came through the mail?"

"No," said Nella, shaking her head. "Someone dropped it on my desk at some point."

"Anyone could have done that. Damn. Maybe you should talk to Natalie about it. She's real chill."

"Eh. If I get another one, I will. But I think I'm just going to ignore it for now. Too much going on." Nella paused. She thought about mentioning the Colin thing, but C. J.'s furrowed brow told her that probably wasn't a good idea.

"Just lemme know if you need anything, aight? I haven't broken up any Midtown office scrimmages yet, but I wouldn't mind being here when the staplers start flying."

Nella chuckled as he backed away slowly from her cube, throwing a few punches into the air above his head. "Thanks, Ceej."

"Anytime. Good seeing you, Nella."

"You, too. Actually, wait! I forgot one more thing." When C. J. reappeared, Nella pointed at Hazel's empty chair. "Maybe even bigger news: A Black girl started working here a few weeks ago!"

C. J.'s eyes lit up with recognition. "Oh, yeah! You know, I just met her. She seems pretty cool."

"You just met her? As in . . . today?"

"Yeah, she's floating around here somewhere. I ran into her in the copy room." He nodded at her cube. "Funny that you two happen to be together, ain't it? It's like we always have a way of finding one another. No matter where we are."

Nella looked over at Hazel's station again, speechless. She had to bend down to see it, but sure enough, there was Hazel's tote bag, stowed neatly under her desk like luggage on a plane. It was easy to miss unless you were checking for it. What wasn't easy to miss, not usually, was that sweet smell Hazel always carried around with her—although now that Nella thought about it, she couldn't remember the last time she *had* smelled it. Probably because she'd gotten so used to it. "I didn't realize she was here already."

"And they say we don't work hard. Shoot, look at you and her, both here at the crack of dawn."

It was a compliment, but Nella was too busy mourning the alone time she'd been hoping to have at her desk to appreciate it. "I wonder why she's here so early."

"She said something about wanting to get a jump on a manuscript she has to read? Or edit? I can't remember which."

"Hm. I'm not sure what she'd have to get a 'jump on' editing. She just started working here, like, a couple weeks ago." *And* I'm *not even editing yet,* she added, just to herself.

Nella had tried to keep her tone as neutral as possible, but the deep shrug of C. J.'s shoulders suggested she'd been unsuccessful. "No idea how it works here. I just keep the packages moving. I will say, though, that it seems like she's as hardworking as you."

"Well, we know how it goes: We gotta work twice as hard to get what we want." Nella recited the mantra, but realized the second it left her mouth that it was aggressively truer for C. J. than it was for Nella. Nella, whose mother had paid off half her student loans; Nella, who had no nieces or nephews to help with math homework when she got home from a long day of work.

C. J. simply nodded and started to walk away, this time with a bit more purpose. His voice drifted around the corner. "Hey—you know, Hazel got here around six or something. She might be working *three* times as hard. Better watch out."

Nella sat up. She wasn't sure if he'd really said those words, or if she'd just imagined them. "Huh? Watch out for what?"

But C. J.'s long legs had already taken him around the corner and down the hall, leaving her painfully alone with her thoughts.

Where was she?

Nella stole a glance across the aisle once more, this time letting her eyes rest on the place card affixed to the outside of Hazel's cube. Hazel's name, etched in an unassuming fourteen-point Arial font, directly faced her own name in a faint opposition of sorts. Nella stared at the bold-faced letters for a good long while, long enough for the letters to become one thick, indiscernible black block. Then she closed her eyes again, drew in a long, ragged breath, and sighed it out. She felt even more troubled than she had when she'd left the office the night before. She didn't like the way *better watch out* was still ringing in her ears—not unlike *Oh hi, Nella;* too much like *Leave Wagner, now*—and she *really* didn't like how big of a deal C. J. had made about that note. Maybe he'd been right.

And hadn't he been right, too, about Hazel? She belonged exactly where she'd been placed, of course: right outside of Maisy's office, which happened to be in Nella's corner of the office. But, *still*—it *was* funny. Funny that out of all the editors who would finally hire a Black assistant, that editor had been Maisy, rather than a different upper-level employee who worked on the opposite side of the office, where things could certainly use some spicing up. It was as though some sort of providence, in the shape of a five-foot-one HR employee named Natalie, had plucked Hazel up and dropped her there, right into Nella's—

"Hi, Nell! Great minds think alike, huh?"

They were words that no early-arriving employee desperate for privacy wanted to hear another employee say—especially when that other employee sounded as chipper as Hazel did. "Oh—hey, Hazel. Work was calling your name first thing this morning, too, huh?"

"Yeah, my eyes popped open at five a.m. and I just couldn't sleep. You know."

Nella did know; granted, her reasons for waking up early were likely much different than Hazel's. So, too, had been her morning routine. While Nella had swiped at a surprise crust of drool on her chin during her commute, realizing she hadn't looked closely enough at herself in a mirror, Hazel—fresh-faced and animated—had found time to put on mascara, eyeliner, and coral-tinted lip gloss.

"So," she said, shifting the huge stack of papers in her hands from one shoulder to the other, "what are you doing here so early?"

"I couldn't sleep, either. I had so much to do here that I couldn't finish last night so I . . . I figured I'd just pop in."

The words in her lie tumbled out of her like a mass of disgruntled passengers exiting out of a sluggish L train at rush hour.

"Crazy how that happened to both of us!" said Hazel, inching a bit closer to Nella's cubicle. "Maybe it's something in the air."

"Maybe. A low-pressure system, or something." Nella wiggled her fingers.

"Yeah. Speaking of pressure . . ." Hazel laughed nervously. "Can I ask you a dumb question? God, I don't know when I'm going to *ever* stop asking you dumb questions . . ."

"Aw, no. It's okay," Nella said, softening a teeny bit. "What's up?"

"I have this manuscript that I need to take a look at and give, like . . . 'editorial comments' on. I'm pretty sure I know what those are and how to do them—hell, they were part of the interview process! As you know. But I'm a bit worried I'm gonna screw it up."

Nella relaxed. "It's not a dumb question! I can email you a sample of what I send Vera when she asks me to read something. Although, it might be more helpful for you to look at that assistant guide for Maisy, since I'm pretty sure her editorial style is radically different from Vera's."

"Actually, whatever you send me might just do it. The letter is for Vera, not Maisy."

Nella's voice caught in her throat. "Vera?"

"Vera sent me a book that she'd like me to read. She wanted to get my opinion on it."

Nella froze. She still wasn't fully comprehending what Hazel was trying to tell her. After a moment, she said, "*Please* tell me it's not the Colin Franklin."

"Oh, no, no, no, thank God." Hazel laughed. "No, it's another one. *The Lie*. You've read it, right?"

Nella furrowed her brow. "No. What's that?" she asked, trying in vain to recall something with that title that had graced her inbox in the last few days.

"Oh, sorry—I thought you'd started it already. Leslie Howard's new book. She's one of Vera's authors, isn't she?"

"She is, yeah. Vera just . . . hasn't sent it to me yet."

"Weird. Maybe she sees how overwhelmed you've been, with all the Colin stuff . . ."

"When did she send it?" Nella interrupted, a band of sweat beginning to gather at her hairline. She scratched it away.

Hazel looked concerned. "Last night. I ran into her at the end of the day yesterday and I remembered how you told me it's good for me to ask other editors what they're reading, get to know their tastes, that kind of thing. I did that. Then she offered to send me a book that she got in yesterday afternoon. I thought that meant she'd send it today, but she sent it to me at eleven p.m. last night. Is she one of those editors who works twenty-four seven *and* on vacations, too? If so, I feel bad for her kids."

Nella ignored the part of Hazel's soliloquy that worried about Vera's kids, who were nonexistent, and zeroed in on the first part instead. "Yesterday afternoon" could mean anything, and if Vera had been shut in meetings all day, which wasn't atypical for her, Nella could see this slip being utterly insignificant. But she'd seen Vera multiple times, had spent at least one accumulative hour with her by the time she'd left the office for the day.

"Nella?" Hazel clicked Nella's cubicle wall with her pinky nail. "You okay?"

"Hm? Yeah. I just think she forgot to send that to me." Nella looked away from Hazel and moved her mouse to wake her computer. Once her screen lit up again, she found the strength to face Hazel once more and caught her staring off, a faraway, indiscernible look in her eyes. After a second or two, she snapped her eyes back on Nella.

"Sorry. I was just thinking . . . she sends you *every*thing her authors write?"

"Yep."

"Well . . . my first thought . . . and I could be wrong, but I can't help but think that she's still holding a grudge against you for that Colin thing."

"The thought crossed my mind, but—"

"And it's maybe not even a *conscious* grudge. Right? That would explain why she didn't forward the book to you. She's still feeling a way and she doesn't even realize—"

"I haven't checked my email since I left the office yesterday. I bet it's in there and I just haven't seen it."

Another lie. In reality, Nella checked her email compulsively. She *had* looked at her email on her way home from McKinley's, around midnight—just to see if the person who'd left her the note had also contacted her by email, too.

"Got it. In that case, I'm *sure* it's in there! I wouldn't worry about it."

"*Me?* Oh—I'm not worried."

Nella hadn't intended for her own voice to have such an edge to it, especially when Hazel had been so hopeful and reassuring. She didn't feel much like apologizing, though. Not now, and not when forty-five minutes passed without her cube neighbor speaking another word.

By then, the air had clicked on and other Wagner employees were finally starting to trickle in by ones and twos, swishing cups of coffee and grumbling about train delays and asking if you'd seen the latest review on this or that book. Office doors that had been closed for sixteen hours were creaking open; desk phones were whining for attention; the bassline of "Stand Back," Bridget's favorite morning song, could be heard near and far. The entire floor seemed more charged and far less scary than it had felt when Nella first arrived.

Vera ambled in at her usual time, her light blue raincoat speckled with raindrops, hood still pulled tightly over her hair. "Oh, great, you're here before me!" she exclaimed, looking at Nella with such astonishment that she wondered if she'd overlooked another smear of drool on her face.

But Nella didn't let the backhanded greeting get to her. "Good morning, Ver. Is it raining out now? It looked like it might a few hours ago."

"It's been raining the last hour or so, I think. Pretty nasty out."

"Yikes. That stinks. Oh, by the way—Gretchen called this morning, around eight."

Vera paused at her door. "My goodness. So early! What could be that important that an agent has to call *that* early?"

"She was calling to ask about the signing payment for—"

"For crying out loud, we *just* bought that book *last week*. Doesn't she have anything else to worry about? Like why Mickey's book isn't selling with people in the forty-to-fifty bracket?" With a dismissive flourish of her hand, she turned the doorknob to her office. "These agents! I swear. I know you meant well, but you *know* you don't have to answer the phone that early. Next time, just ignore it, okay?"

"You got it," Nella called, even though her boss was now in her office and therefore out of earshot. She chuckled in spite of herself. Now, *this* was the Vera she had grown to know and love. Perhaps their relationship hadn't been ruined, and Vera was trying to keep Nella free for some other big project.

Pleased and somewhat relieved, Nella strolled over to the kitchen and made herself her second coffee of the day. As she listened to the Keurig burble and groan, she thought about the various ways she might casually ask Vera about the new Leslie Howard. She could lead with it when they first sat down for their usual fifteen-minute morning meeting, casually, like it was something she worried she'd forget if she didn't. Or she could drop some jargon and ask Vera if there was anything she was reading that Nella should "move to the front of her pile."

She'd decided on the second approach as she made her way back from the kitchen, set on making a pit stop at Vera's doorway to ask if it was a good time to do their morning catch-up chat. But as she walked by Kimberly's office, then Maisy's, something gave her pause. This something was Hazel, who had popped up from her own desk, notepad in hand, determination in her raised shoulders.

She was making a beeline straight for Vera's office.

But before she officially set foot inside, Hazel paused and looked directly at Nella, who expected some kind of *What can I do? She called me in!* shrug. Some kind of apology.

There was nothing of the sort. Just a cold, hard look. And with that, Hazel swooped into Vera's office, her notepad held high like a successfully caught wedding bouquet. "Vera! *Girl.* This Leslie Howard book is so. Freaking. Good. I can't *wait* for you to read it."

Meanwhile, Nella's head hung lower than a defeated bridesmaid as she shuffled the few remaining feet back to her desk. "You're sure I'm not interrupting your work?" she heard Hazel say, her words thick with careful self-effacement. "I'd just love to chat with you for a few minutes or so."

Nella fell into her seat, dejected. She heard Vera's cheerful *come on in* loud and clear. She heard her eager, energetic tone—a tone that her boss hadn't used with her in she didn't know how long.

And then—finally—she heard the sound of a door closing.

Shani

August 14, 2018
Rise & Grind Café
Midtown, Manhattan

I didn't recognize her at first. Usually, on days like that one—days when I wondered how the hell I'd gone from working at one of the most respected magazines in media to sweeping straw papers off a café floor in Midtown—the sound of the front door meant nothing to me. The door scraped open, the door scraped closed; a few minutes later, this would happen again. The outcome was always the same: a smile; a nod. *Do you have WiFi? What's your bathroom password? Do you guys take cards?*

The day had started off like that. Carelessly, I'd glanced at her once—her striking hair; her high-collared tunic; her flashy gold hoops—and presumed she was yet another New York millennial doing far better at life than I was, and looked back down.

What can I say? She blended in so well. And I was pretty sure she would have continued to, had it not been for her voice—a little husky and a little too flirty with Christopher, my twenty-two-year-old boss. I didn't recognize the hair, but I recognized the way she flipped it so far back that she almost broke her neck. I recognized the way she giggled and pretended not to know the difference between a latte and a cold brew, even though I'd heard her speak so spiritedly about her knowledge of coffee with all the higher-ups at Cooper's magazine.

I practically dropped my broom. Yes, this girl looked more like a woman of the world than she did the last time I'd seen her in Boston—more Zara now than her J. Jill style then.

But it was her, alright.

My first instinct was to walk up to her and beat her with my broom. Anybody who did what she did deserved to be bludgeoned by a girl with a broom in a Midtown café.

But I didn't. Even after what happened in Boston, I still had *some* pride left. I also had new knowledge: She was frustratingly clever, with artful timing. If I didn't want to be bested in this new city, I knew I'd have to think three steps ahead. In Boston, my biggest mistake was being three steps behind.

What was it Lynn had said to me on the Red Line? *I saw you two last night, you know.* Something like that. Of course, I'd ignored her. At first. But she just wouldn't let up. "I know you don't know who I am. But I just want to tell you that you're fucked."

I'd glanced over at her just a little bit—the amount of glancing you need to do in order to confirm that someone is in fact talking to you, because she wasn't "Lynn" to me yet; she was just a weird stranger interrupting my morning commute. And when I saw that it was this Black lady who sort of looked like my aunt Krystal—if Aunt Krystal had been brave enough to rock a septum piercing, that is—I asked her to repeat whatever it was she'd just said instead of telling her to leave me the fuck alone.

"I said I saw you two last night. At Pepper's."

"How do you know I was at Pepper's?"

"And from what I overheard," she'd said, ignoring me, "well . . . it doesn't look good for you."

At that, I'd folded over the corner of the *New Yorker* story I'd been reading and said the first thing that came to my mind. "Sorry," I said, after I'd thought I'd gathered enough context clues to make a fair assumption, "but I don't understand. Are you two dating, or something? Because that's not what that was last night. We were just getting drinks, hanging out. We work together."

Lynn had stared at me for a moment. Then she'd laughed, a long, loud laugh that drew the looks of half of the commuters sitting nearby. I'd taken that time to actually give her a once-over, assessing the black headwrap she was wearing on her head and the sunglasses that covered up any hint of an expression.

Now? I'd say I was searching for some sort of confirmation that she was crazy, yet harmless. But at the time, I was also searching for some kind of sign that she was a woman scorned.

"Who are you?" I asked at last. "What do you want from me?"

"I want you to come join us."

"'Us'?" I looked at the jaundiced old man who was peeling a hard-boiled egg in the seat directly behind her. "Is he in your crew, too? Or do you have some more desirable imaginary friends here on the train who I don't know about?"

She hadn't found this funny. She'd just shaken her head. "You fucked up, girl. You said too much."

That was when she started rummaging around her small brown leather purse. It was this whole big production—or at least, it must have appeared as such, because a twentysomething white guy nearby who happened to be holding the same issue of the *New Yorker* I held was giving us his attention. I started to smile at him in solidarity, but before my lips could complete the motion, the mysterious girl cleared her throat, evidently displeased. And when I looked back at her, she was frowning at the white man—at least, that's what it seemed like she was doing beneath her sunglasses.

I felt the piece of paper tuck itself into my hand before I heard her say, "Take this."

"I'm flattered," I said, my face growing hot, "but I'm not into—"

"Shani," she had said, firmly. The sound of my name in a stranger's mouth loosened my grip on both the piece of paper and the magazine, which fell onto the dirty floor of the T. "You need to get over yourself. I'm *not* trying to fuck you, for fuck's sake. I'm just trying to *help*."

The train came to a slow stop. "I have to go back to Harlem tonight. But text me at this number after you leave work. You'll want to after today. Trust me."

She'd slipped off before I could get her name from her, leaving me no choice but to stoop down, feel around the pair of Sperry boots I'd bought upon discovering how unforgiving Boston winters really were, and retrieve the stained card.

Lynn Johnson resists, it read. Google told me even less when I searched for her on my work computer. I intended to let the incident go.

But it didn't take long for shit to hit the fan, just like Lynn had promised. The article was circulated. My boss went *in* on me in front of *every*body. I was fired . . . in front of *every*body. And that was it for me and Cooper's and that story I'd worked so hard to complete.

I texted Lynn on my way home from the office, finally ready to listen. There was no point in denying she knew something I didn't, and I ate every crumb she fed me from her home in New York: the lists, the charts, all compiled by Lynn and the rest of the Resistance over the last five years—and the promise that she'd tell me more once I got there. A bus ticket that came with an interview at a subpar café in Manhattan where I would be . . . sweeping floors.

I eased up on the handle of my broom. It had grown nearly as hot as my palms from my tight, anxious grip. *If you ever cross paths with an OBG out in the wild, blend in,* Lynn had told me. *You'll do a lot better knowing where she's at if she doesn't know where* you're *at.*

Had she seen me? Did she know I worked here?

I quickly went back to sweeping a far corner of the room, listening as she tried to convince Christopher that Maroon 5 had indeed gotten better with time. *Figures.* Back in Boston, she'd been willing to die on a hill for John Mayer.

The memory of this sent me over the edge. I pulled my phone out of my back pocket and snapped a photo as nonchalantly as I could. When it came out blurry, I snapped another one—then another, just in case. Taunting the bull, you could say, but I didn't care.

The third photo seemed to do it. Thanks to the angle at which she had suddenly flirtatiously tilted her head—she'd always been good at angles, I'll give her that—the late-afternoon sunlight creeping in from the dirty front windows of Rise & Grind clarified her deep brown skin and high cheekbones so well that Lynn could definitely compare the photo with the one in her own files.

Quickly, I stashed away the phone and went back to my sweeping. But it was no use. My broad, scattered strokes across the red tiled floor were doing more harm than good as I waited, anxious for the reply.

It came minutes later, after I'd moved into the bathroom to check soap levels.

Yep. It's her. It's Eva.

8

August 30, 2018

Nella couldn't get Hazel's cold, icy look out of her brain.

It wasn't normal for her to feel so possessive when it came to her boss. She'd never needed to be. None of the other assistants had any reason to curry favor with Vera. "You two seem well-suited for one another," Sophie had told her once, after showing up unannounced and reading one of their email exchanges over Nella's shoulder. "You're both perfectionists."

How someone who knew Nella so little could read her so well was beyond her. But Sophie'd had a point: For most of their time together, she and Vera had worked more like a team than any of the other editor-assistant pairings at Wagner.

Then the Colin thing happened.

Nella flinched. Was *that* what that list of assistants on the printer was about? Was the list of new hires for *Vera*?

She sat with this new possibility, listening for any tidbits of conversation she could get through Vera's closed door. She might have sat like this for the rest of the morning, but then she abruptly stood, refocused. It was obvious what Nella needed to do: talk to Richard. Sure, maybe she was sleep-deprived, and maybe she had no way of knowing if they really *were* potential hiring candidates—but sometime between seeing those names and being shut out of Vera's office, a feeling of deep uneasiness had planted itself in her gut. A feeling that her boss was going to kick her out and welcome someone else in. A new and improved *Black* someone, so nobody could give them shit for getting rid of her.

Nella was about as ready to give up publishing as she was to give up health insurance and paid vacations and Summer Fridays. She wasn't going out that easily. Plus, how would she explain to Eight Bar why she suddenly wanted to quarter limes and dry pint glasses again?

Her mind was set. She started toward Richard's corner office, even though she'd never done so unannounced. Ever. In fact, it had been two years since she'd had any kind of one-on-one time with Richard, and that time could hardly be called spontaneous. Once a new hire signed all of the paperwork, suffered through orientation, and shadowed another assistant, each was "required" to sit down and have tea with Richard Wagner before their first official day.

Hardly anything at Wagner was *seriously* required. Technically, you could wear a shirt with the words "I'm Rooting for Everybody Black" on it if you wanted to, because there was nothing about a dress code in the contract. Wagner held itself to a silently agreed upon "professional" standard, and when the occasional foolish intern broke this rule, employees showed them what time it was with the raise of an eyebrow or a chilly, withering stare.

Attending Richard's tea wasn't in your contract, either. But, as Nella had been fortunate enough to learn from her predecessor, Katie, you weren't doing your career any favors if you declined the invitation.

Richard Wagner was something of an enigma to anyone who knew him. He had so much money that it didn't show. He was the most "publishing" where it counted; he was on top of all the hot trends, or at least the ones that "mattered." He threw parties so exclusive that assistants would find reasons to snoop through their bosses' offices in the hopes of finding an invitation that had been carelessly left on a desk.

But what set Richard most apart from many other editors was that he was almost always in the office. He very rarely observed Summer Fridays, and the last week of August was as important to him as the first week of fall.

Some supposed this was because he was the first of the Wagners to venture into books rather than politics. Legend had it that when he decided in college that he didn't want to be a senator, his parents pretended he didn't exist for five years. A few years later, when he decided he wanted to open his own publishing house, a few notable literary heads agreed to help him—and by the time Wagner first opened its doors in 1972, the entire industry was scrambling to welcome him. His parents were, too.

More than four decades later, Richard was *the* Publishing Man to Please. A conversation with him forever marked you in his eyes, and one-on-one conversations with him were few and far between. So, it didn't just make *sense* to have tea with him—it was absolutely imperative.

"If you really want to be an editor," Katie had told Nella, "you have to be strategic about it."

Being strategic was what had led Nella to Wagner in the first place. It was no coincidence that she'd applied to the publishing house that had published her favorite book. She wanted to traipse the halls the two women she'd studied diligently in college had traipsed. She wanted to sit at the desk where Kendra Rae Phillips and Diana Gordon had sat when they talked over edits.

The morbid side of her, though, was particularly curious about what had happened to Kendra Rae. She'd disappeared from the spotlight the year after *Burning Heart* set the country on fire, following some kind of media spectacle, and hadn't been heard from since. Nella had had a hard time verifying the details of her disappearance, although Black Twitter had concocted some pretty believable theories. Except none of them held water. And that left Nella wondering: As Diana Gordon released book after book, year after year, what had happened to the Black woman who had been her editor? The Black woman who, according to Diana's acknowledgments, had had "an invaluable hand in crafting Evie into who she is?"

Naturally, this question nagged at her brain again as she and Owen rode a Midtown-bound R train together on her way to meet Richard for her new-hire tea two years ago. Owen had offered to take the ride up to the Wagner office with her, bless his sweet heart, since he'd figured he could run errands in the city while she sipped and supped with one of the most influential men in the publishing industry (according to *GQ*).

"So, I know we went over this, but . . . why *don't* you want to ask Richard if he knows what Kendra Rae is up to these days?" Owen asked Nella, their knees bumping one another as their train stopped at Prince, then 8th Street. "He might even still be in touch with her, and then he could put you guys in touch."

Nella shook her head. "That would just be poor manners. I can't go in there, guns blazing, asking him if he knows what happened to Kendra Rae Phillips. Then he'd think that I'm some kind of amateur stalker."

"But aren't you?" he asked. "I thought you wanted to be the next Kendra Rae. That's why you only wanted Wagner."

She bristled; he saw it. They rode without saying anything for a moment, until he spoke up again. "Can I ask another question now?"

"Do I have a choice?" Nella asked, trying to sound like she was kidding.

"No. Why are you meeting some old white publishing dude to drink tea in his empty office on a Sunday?"

Nella shrugged. "It's just . . . what you do."

Owen gave her a look.

"Baby, you just have to understand . . . it's tradition."

The words had been foreign to her tongue then, a mere mantra she'd already managed to pick up from three hours or so of shadowing Katie. They were especially foreign to Owen, who clearly didn't find this response particularly satisfying. But instead of pulling at a promising loose thread, he said, "So, are you excited to see the place where *Burning Heart* was created?"

Nella could've kissed him for changing the subject. "Hell, yeah. To know I'm going to be breathing the same air, it's insane."

"Maybe they'll even have a printer named after the two of them. Or a conference room."

"Maybe even Richard's office itself. Now, *that'd* be pretty sick."

Owen shifted uneasily.

"*Now* what's the matter?"

"I just—the idea of you being in this man's office alone, who you don't really know anything about. I'm sorry, Nell, I don't trust it. Maybe all that *This is just the way the industry is* talk would have worked ten years ago," he added, holding up a finger before Nella could interrupt him, "but in today's world, I'd be That Dumb Fool who has to tell people why I let you go to this thing with this old guy without asking any of the hard questions. And I'm not living the rest of my life like that."

Nella smiled. The "That Dumb Fool" label came from watching far too many true crime TV shows. The "dumb fool" in question was usually the interviewee who said things like *No, I never questioned why he had three different driver's licenses.*

Nella had watched too much television to get snuffed out in such an easy way, so she grabbed Owen's hand and told him it was all going to be fine.

But twenty minutes later, when it came time for him to let go of her hand so she could reach for the front door of the office building, he squeezed it once—a little harder than he normally did when he was merely trying to be cute.

"You sure about this, Nell?"

"Owen." She pulled her hand away from his as gingerly as she could, placing it on his cheek. He hadn't shaved in nearly four days, so his reddish-brown stubble scratched at the meat of her palm in that bristly way that she always liked. "He's pretty old. I'm not saying that pretty old men aren't capable of terrible things, but I am saying that I have some pepper spray in my purse. And you *know* I was raised by the streets." She beat her chest in mock emphasis.

"You were raised in the suburbs of Connecticut," Owen said drily.

"By a father from Chicago who did *not* fuck around."

"I thought he was from a suburb, too."

"Plus, remember, I've got—"

"A black belt," finished Owen, full-out grinning now. "Yeah, yeah, yeah. You always say that, but I'll believe it when I see it."

"See, I already *told* you—it got lost during the divorce." Nella kissed him on the lips, preventing any more words of protest. "I'll text you in an hour."

He pulled her toward him when she moved away. "If I don't hear from you after sixty-one minutes, I'm breaking down this door and finding you myself."

"There's no need to break anything down." She let him hold her for a moment before reaching for the door again. "See? This door opens. It's the doors *in*side, past security, that you'd have to—"

"Nella Rogers?"

Nella turned her head. Standing behind Owen was Richard Wagner himself: a tall, lanky man with a shock of white hair, wearing a beige jacket and navy-blue-and-kelly-green striped pants. It was an ensemble that wouldn't make sense for almost anyone else, but his tortoiseshell glasses and khaki-colored leather briefcase gave the impression that he was a smart man in media whose many accomplishments rendered any conflicting opinion of him irrelevant.

Both Owen and Nella moved out of his way instinctively. "That's me!" Nella said. "Mr. Wagner?"

"Please, call me Richard. I insist." He strode up to them and shook Nella's hand. Then he walked to the front door and went through it. "I'll see you in a few moments, I'm presuming?" he called over his shoulder. He didn't wait for an answer.

Nella had spun around to look at Owen, expecting to see that familiar look he always wore when he had something to say and knew better than to say it, but he was already backing his way down the sidewalk. She felt a twinge of disappointment—she wanted to ask Owen if she should get him a pair of Richard's striped pants in his size—but she waved and turned to enter her new place of employment, head held high.

"So," Richard said, once they'd gotten past introductory niceties and she'd accepted his offer to collapse into a leather chair that made the setting feel more like therapy than book publishing, "I suppose you're wondering how I knew who you were."

He blinked exactly twice before staring at her, rigidly, as he waited for an answer. She hadn't been wondering—that was the least of her wonders as she rode the elevator up to the thirteenth floor, her heart thrumming in her ears. But she managed to say, with a small smile, "Well, I *have* been told I look like a Nella."

Richard threw his head back and chuckled. It felt hollow, but it still shook the room—a fairly impressive feat, given the size of his office. Far bigger than Vera's, Nella noticed, the office ate up a decent chunk of one of the floor's corners, and its two large windows—one on each wall—provided more light than her and Owen's small studio apartment had ever seen at one time. Like the therapist patient chair she was sitting on, its décor was exactly what she had expected from an editor in chief, complete with a big wooden desk that looked like it had been made by an actual carpenter and not purchased at IKEA, and a grand bookshelf so substantial that she could probably free-climb her way up with little difficulty.

"So, tell me, Nella," Richard said, "what made you decide to get into publishing?"

Nella considered the rehearsed speech she'd given Vera a few days earlier about her love of reading and writing and how books could make the biggest difference in a young person's world. *Go with that speech. You know that one so well.*

"Honestly . . . I'm kind of obsessed with Kendra Rae Phillips and *Burning Heart*."

Her quick words slipped out unexpectedly. Surprise washed across Richard's face, followed by amusement. He took a sip of tea before staring wordlessly at her once more.

Nella cowered, immediately hating herself for doing so. His eyes were just too damn bright, that piercing, artificial kind of bright that belonged in science fiction movies, and she longed for some sort of distraction.

"You've heard of her?" he finally asked.

Nella nodded excitedly. "*Burning Heart* made me fall in love with reading."

"Mmm. Well, I actually turned down the opportunity to edit that book," Richard confessed. "I loved the early draft I read—I knew it was going to be huge!—but the moment I heard Kendra Rae had the slightest bit of interest in working on it herself, I stepped out. I knew Kendra Rae would be the better editor for Diana."

"Really? Wow. I always thought Kendra Rae discovered her." Nella assessed the skin on his forehead and in between his eyebrows. She'd pegged him as fiftysomething, but *Burning Heart* had been published in 1983, putting him into his mid-seventies at least. "That's pretty cool of you, stepping aside."

"Yes. I knew Kendra Rae really was something then."

He rested his gaze on a small rubber plant that was on the corner of his desk, an impression of some kind of memory splashed across his face. Her cup of tea was burning her fingers, but now that his eyes had found something else to occupy them, she felt bold enough to say, "You must really miss her."

Richard's head snapped up. He cleared his throat. Confusion looked strange on someone of his stature, but Nella was certain that yes, it was in the look he was giving her. "Yes. I mean, she's not—she's still—"

"I didn't mean—sorry, I—" Nella closed her mouth, opening it only when she knew it was useless trying to convince him she hadn't meant to imply that she believed Kendra Rae Phillips was dead. "Just the fact that she's been keeping to herself for so long . . ."

Richard lifted his tea to his lips and blew a small puff of air across the top. "Maybe for the best. The spotlight, you know. Some people can't handle it, and she . . . it was clear she was starting to snap. Even Diana, her longtime friend, vouched for that."

Nella didn't know what else to do but agree, although what Richard meant by "snap," she wasn't entirely sure. She remembered reading something about Diana saying Kendra Rae had had some kind of "break," but hadn't been able to verify it.

"Now, enough of that. We're here to talk about you. Tell me about *you.*"

Nella smiled. "I'm not sure there's too much to say," she said. "I'm from Connecticut, and I lived there for about eighteen years, until . . ."

She petered off, fully aware that Richard had grimaced when she'd said "Connecticut." The state often evoked strong reactions from people, but his weird, just-bit-down-on-a-lemon-seed look seemed a bit *too* dramatic—even for a man in navy-blue-and-kelly-green striped pants. "Is everything okay?" Nella asked.

Richard sprang up. "Yes. Yes. I'm—I'm so sorry," he said, reaching into his pocket and pulling out his cell phone, "but my phone started ringing a moment ago. I was trying to ignore it, but I think I should really take this. Will you excuse me for a moment?"

"Oh! Of course." Nella put down her cup and started to stand. "I'll just wait out in—"

"Oh, no, no. Please, you stay. I'll be back in a minute, no more than three. So sorry."

She waved him off. "It's no problem at all. Take as much time as you need." Richard bowed before ducking out of his office. A moment later, a clear and flustered "Hi, yes" floated from down the hall, but the remainder of his words were swallowed by the distance he'd put between them.

Nella exhaled. She was relieved and glad to be alone for a few moments; it meant she could finally take a good look around. She'd been able to process the furniture, but the walls had too many items peppered across them—a few dozen, at least—for her to sneak more than just a flyover glance.

But now, Richard was gone. And she was feeling emboldened. Not emboldened enough *not* to cast a glance toward the door, but emboldened enough to sidestep the coffee table and walk a few paces over to the left wall. She let her eye fall on a framed piece of paper that, judging by its typewritten text, was as old as she was. Maybe older. A closer assessment told her she was right. The letter, only two paragraphs long, was dated November 1, 1979, and was addressed *To my editor, my friend, and my brother, without whom I would be nothing.*

Nella skipped over the rest of it—with a salutation like that, what else did she need to see?—and read the signature. It belonged to a Nobel Peace Prize winner whose obituary she recalled reading only a few months ago. *Alright, Richard,* she thought, impressed. *So you really* are *a big deal. Noted.*

Not quite satisfied that she'd noticed everything worth noticing, she moved on to the next wall in front of which Richard's desk sat. The few times she'd dared let her eyes stray had suggested that this was his own personal Wall of Fame. Indeed, it was. Faces filled every single frame, some in black-and-white, others in color. Some were silly—a young woman in an evening gown putting bunny ears behind a young man in a tux; four smart-looking men in polos smiling in the middle of a lush, green forest.

It was all unnerving, really, all these body-less pairs of eyes staring down at her, and Nella was ready to walk away, return to her tea and her comfortable therapist's office chair, when the clouds shifted outside and something flashed in the corner of her eye. Just once. She looked up to see what the mid-afternoon sunlight had caught and noticed a photo framed in bronze, no larger than a postcard.

Nella moved closer so she could make out the three people in the photo. One was a younger, less gaunt version of Richard. Each of his hands was resting on the shoulders of two brown-skinned women, and he was smiling so hard that his eyes were closed—although judging from the bacchanal ruddiness of his cheeks, it was clear he wouldn't have been looking at the photographer even if they had been open.

The smiling woman in the bright white dress on Richard's left was clearly Diana Gordon. Nella paused, unsurprised at the resemblance between the Diana Gordon she'd seen in an interview a few months ago, and the Diana Gordon in this photo. Old Diana and young Diana both had permanently smooth skin and dazzling grins.

Then, her eyes shifted to the other Black woman, who was leaning—just a little bit—toward the right. Something was flitting across her face, too, but it wasn't a smile. And if anyone wanted to believe the woman *was* smiling, Nella was confident the expression could be attributed to her martini, which she held high in her right hand—not quite in proposal of a toast, but of a declaration. *I'm still here,* she seemed to be saying, and the way she looked head-on at the camera, unbothered at how apart she seemed from her two companions, confirmed this.

"I see you've found your hero," a voice behind her said.

Nella whirled around. Richard had reentered his office, but instead of returning to his desk, he was standing by the chair she'd been sitting in, the shoulder strap of her overturned tote bag trapped beneath his left polished shoe. It made her nervous, the way he was watching her.

"Happens all the time," he explained, gesturing toward the photo wall. "So many photos, so many faces. Whenever I have company, I never tire of seeing which one piques whose interest. Everyone has different . . . tastes."

"Sorry, I couldn't help it. I've just never seen this photo before, this one of Kendra Rae. And you and Diana." Nella crept back over to her chair as Richard returned to his.

"That picture is probably worth thousands. Kendra Rae hardly took photos before . . ." He shrugged. "As I said, that woman wasn't too big on being the center of attention. I'm glad I was able to get this snapshot, at least. That was taken at Antonio's the night we celebrated *Burning Heart*'s debut at number one on the *New York Times* bestseller list. My gosh, those parties back then were the best.

"Now . . ." He crossed his legs pointedly at the ankle. "What was I saying before I was so rude? Oh, yes! That we're here to talk about you. You're from Connecticut, you said?"

Desperate to do something with her hands, Nella reached for yet another cube of sugar—her third, she realized, hoping he didn't—and said, "Yes. I'm from Springville. It's a small town, about a fifteen-minute drive from—"

"New Haven. Yes, I'm familiar with Springville. I got my start at Yale University Press while I was finishing up my senior year at Yale. Great place. So rich in culture. Good food, good theater. And the art, ah . . ."

"Mmm. Yale's galleries are incredible."

Richard perked up at this. "The Center for British Art?"

Nella bobbed her head. "I've spent a lot of time there. First when I was in high school, but I like to go back whenever I'm there for the holidays."

"Oh?" Richard leaned forward in his chair, his eyes practically boggling out of his eternally youthful face. Nella matched his body language with hers. It might have sounded peculiar, but it was in seemingly mundane moments like those—when she told a white man something so basic about herself that made his eyes boggle out of his head—that she felt closest to all the Black people who were Black long before she was: all of the enslaved Black men and women who impressed white people with their reading abilities; all of the Black men and women who became doctors and lawyers and other things people said they couldn't. Garrett Morgan, Marian Anderson, Diahann Carroll. Barack Obama. Her parents. Anyone who had impressed a white person simply by existing. Which, given the number of times Black people had been lynched and raped and beaten down over the last four hundred years, should have been *every* Black person.

"It must have been very nice to have all of that New Haven culture at your disposal," Richard was saying, taking another sip.

"Oh, very."

"I thought young people didn't do art galleries these days. Not with the Internet and Instagram and whatnot."

"I'm a bit of an old soul, I guess you could say." Feeling emboldened by his approval, even though she really needn't have, Nella crossed her legs and took her first sip of her Earl Grey. At that point, of course, it was cold—she always managed to miss the narrow drinkability window of tea—but she commented on how much she liked it anyway.

"Not too sweet?" he asked, raising an eyebrow.

"I went to college in the land of sweet tea, Richard. This ain't nothin'," she quipped, using the same exaggerated sassy tone that she'd used with Owen when she joked that she'd been raised by the streets. A passing glimpse of the bronze frame behind Richard's head made Nella second-guess the daring move she'd just pulled. Pulling it out in a professional setting risked misunderstanding: One might think she was either a Black girl who actually *did* roll her neck in corporate settings and didn't know better, or a Black girl who was making fun of other Black girls who did—and Nella wasn't sure which was worse. What would Kendra Rae have thought about Nella's performance?

She had no way of knowing. But what she did know was that Richard was drinking it down with the countenance of a child who was finally about to have that eerie noise he's been hearing in the basement explained to him. Nella had delivered the perfect neck roll, apparently, and the precise amount of sass. She felt the air ease between them, felt the tension fall from her shoulders.

And so, she took another sip, set her cup down, and ventured to admit, smooth as honey, how badly she wanted to become Wagner's next great Black editor.

Nella could use a cup of warm tea now, but she settled for a deep, centering breath as she rose from her desk, trying to summon the confidence she'd had the last time she and Richard had sat down to talk. What she was about to do could very well blow up in her face. She wasn't even sure Richard knew anything about the Colin incident at all. Nella *had* double-checked Colin's Twitter to make sure he hadn't tweeted about it to his five hundred thousand followers, and Vera had always rejected the idea of reporting her business to anybody—especially a man. Chances were, Richard knew nothing, and if Richard knew nothing, she risked blowing up her own spot for no reason.

But she continued toward Richard's office anyway. The most practical thing for her to do was explain everything and apologize for the misunderstanding. She'd take control of the narrative, fall on her sword. She'd do it so beautifully, so selflessly, and he'd admire the way she did it, just as he'd admired her sassy neck roll in their first meeting. He'd be convinced that Nella was still that plucky, mature employee he'd met two years ago. He'd see she had upstanding moral character and decide he didn't want to swap her upstanding moral character for someone else's.

Nella approached Donald's desk with her head held high and her mouth open, ready to ask if Richard was free. But she abruptly closed it when she saw that Donald wasn't there. His Discman was, but he wasn't.

Nella peered across the hallway. Richard's light was on, and the door to his office was wide open. She could hear him speaking, but his voice was so low that it sounded like he might have been talking to himself.

She glanced at Donald's chair again, as though he might have suddenly materialized in the last two seconds. But he was still nowhere to be seen. So she moved closer to Richard's office, prepared to knock on his open door and ask for a few minutes of his time. But something caused her to close her mouth and swallow her words whole.

It was his tone, hushed and stern.

"—middle of the day. I can't say more right now. I told you email was better."

Silence.

"Yes, I know. But—"

Richard sighed. When he spoke again, his voice was biting.

"Look, *you* don't get to suddenly grow a conscience. Remember whose idea this was?"

An even longer silence.

"Fine. But just remember, you put the ball in motion. *You* chose to deal with Kenny the way you did, and now you—"

Something about the way he'd spat out the words "deal with" turned Nella's blood cold. But then she remembered Kenny Bridges. Of *course*. She'd heard through the grapevine that this particular author had been giving his whole publicity team trouble. His agent hadn't been keeping him in check, which explained Richard's uncharacteristically angry tone. The realization thawed Nella's thoughts as she waited impatiently for Richard to finish his call. If someone were to walk by her at this very moment, it would look pretty damn incriminating.

"Fine," she heard him say. "But do us both a favor and stop pretending you don't need a little assistance, alright? Okay. Love you, too. Bye."

There was the click of a phone, followed by the soft muttering of the word "Dammit." But Nella was fixated on the L-Word. Had she misheard Richard before? No. *Deal with Kenny,* he'd said, clear as day. She'd been so sure he was talking to Kenny's agent.

So where did "love" come from? Everyone knew Richard's wife managed a chain of candle stores that stretched from SoHo to the Hamptons. Richard's wife dealt with fragrances, not fussy authors. It didn't make sense.

Unless that hadn't been Richard's wife on the phone. And he and Kenny Bridges's agent were . . .

Nella gasped, covering her mouth. She'd clearly overheard something she wasn't supposed to, and this something had propelled Richard into a foul mood. Now was definitely not the time to barge in and start talking about how she'd fucked up with one of Wagner's most important authors—especially if he was still in the dark about all of it.

The sound of computer chair wheels rolling against wood shook Nella out of her paralysis. "Hello? Is someone there?" Richard called, his voice so singsongy that he must have seen the shadow Nella was unconsciously casting across his doorway. "Donald? Are you back?"

Nella didn't stick around long enough to see if he inquired further. She sped off, rounding the corner so quickly that she nearly stepped right out of her Keds.

9

For the next few days, Nella walked around Wagner with her head down and her mouth closed. Her eyes, however, remained open. She kept her sights upon every single writing utensil her colleagues utilized. And when anyone stopped by her desk—*anyone*—Nella jotted down the time of the interaction and what was said.

Hazel wasn't exempt from such surveillance. Nella took note of all of their interactions, benign as they were, and she took note of Hazel's interactions with Vera, too—starting right after she'd accidentally snooped on Richard outside of his office. When she'd returned to her desk that day, she'd been shocked to see they were still talking about *The Lie*. By the time Vera's door had finally reopened (*approx. 68 min. after Hazel first went in*), Nella had finished the massive bag of pretzels she kept in her emergency snack drawer. They were supposed to be that month's Sprint Snack—the snack that got her through the last hours of the day for at least four weeks—but the occasional giggle that fluttered beneath Vera's closed door, coupled with the panic that she might be fired, drove her to obliterate every single twist.

Nella had been poised to empty the bag into her mouth for that last bit of salt when Vera's door finally heaved open and a cheerful Hazel gallivanted out from behind it.

"Thank you, Vera!" she said, manuscript pages askew in her hands. "That was *such* a wonderful conversation."

"Oh, thank *you*! And thank you again for taking a look so quickly, Haze. I'd love to hear what you think when you finish—if you have the time, of course."

Vera's door was slightly ajar, but the way her head peeked around the edge of it, and the way she was looking at Hazel—fondly, giddily—had reminded Nella of the way a bride-to-be might look at her maid of honor in a department store dressing room. Nella had never received such a look from her boss before.

"Right. Just let me know if lunch works better for you tomorrow or Friday. Or coffee," Hazel added, walking backward toward her desk so as not to ruin the precious moment they'd been having. "I know we'll have even more stuff to cover then, even though we just spent . . . god, what time is it now, anyway?"

It had taken Nella a moment to realize this question had been directed at her. Hazel was peering over at her warmly, as though all three of them had been chatting like old friends in Vera's office. Vera was staring intently at Nella, too, the silver Rolex watch on her right arm glinting as she braced herself against the doorframe, but that giddiness from before had hardened.

Nella looked over at the clock in the lower-right corner of her screen. "The time is ten twenty-seven," she said stiffly.

That was all it had taken for them to scatter. Hazel shook her head and whistled in amazement as she hustled back to her seat to check her phone messages; Vera stuck her head outside of her office just far enough to ask Nella, in a more recognizable tone, to kindly ask everyone to leave her alone for the time being. An author had just delivered a manuscript that required all of her faculties to edit, she'd told Nella, and her door would be closed for the rest of the morning.

It was a fair request. Nella would have done the same thing—especially given how many times Wagner employees saw open doors as green lights, and how many times she herself had wished for a barrier to protect her cube. A more solid barrier, like a big glass floor-to-ceiling wall that she could control with her keyboard. Then, at least, she wouldn't have to feign a phone call or pretend to have to go to the bathroom to escape awkward, drawn-out conversations she didn't want to have. It would be the second-best thing to having an assistant. Maybe even better.

So, although Nella wanted some of her own time with her boss, she was patient as she waited for Vera's office door to open once more, all the while taking her messages and printing out emails she worried her boss might miss in her inbox.

But Vera's door never opened. Not that morning and not that afternoon, after lunch. She hadn't emerged a minute before four thirty, and when she did, she was wearing her raincoat and had her quilted bag slung over her shoulder.

"Oy, what a day. Nella, I'm off to an appointment. Thanks for today! See you tomorrow."

In between bites of leftover honeydew she'd found in the kitchen, Nella had no choice but to say, in what was surely the most pathetic tone she'd ever mustered, "Good luck."

That had been bad enough. But when Hazel, whom Nella had hardly spoken to all day, proclaimed, "God, Vera is *so* awesome," Nella had picked up the remaining plate of stale fruit and dropped it in the trash. She said nothing as she longingly ran a hand along the bottom of her empty emergency snack drawer.

A whoosh of air brushed her ear. Hazel was suddenly at her side, holding a bag of Bugles out to her. An offering, maybe.

Nella's stomach protested as she gestured *No, thank you.* The glass barrier she'd been imagining materialized in her head again—this time with Hazel fixed on the other side.

"Okay, tell me: Did Vera send you *The Lie* yet?"

Hazel didn't ask as though she was *trying* to taunt Nella. There seemed to be genuine concern in the way she crunched on her corn chips, wide-eyed. But the question stung so much that she almost lied and said that Vera had sent the manuscript.

Nella took a deep breath. No, she decided, Hazel wasn't the problem here. Vera *had* to be trying to pit them against one another to keep Nella on her toes.

"Vera hasn't sent it to me yet," she admitted. "Would you mind maybe . . . ?"

"For sure!" Hazel hurried back to her station. "I'm sure it just, like, slipped her mind. She has a *lot* going on."

Nella listened to Hazel's fingers rap her keyboard, feeling more than a little infantilized. Vera had never shared manuscripts with any other assistants before; in fact, she'd been one of the more private editors at Wagner. She rarely discussed books she was thinking about going after so early on in the process—not until she'd had enough time to decide how she felt about them.

It was odd to Nella, then, that she'd sent the Leslie Howard pages to a shiny new employee. It didn't seem right. Not unless Vera had been purposely trying to ostracize Nella. Not unless she was still pissed about the Colin thing.

"Just sent it!" Hazel wheeled her chair around so that she was directly facing Nella.

"Thanks." Nella checked the clock on her computer to see how much time she had before she could make an exit of her own. "Got it."

When she looked over at Hazel a few moments later, she still had her chair turned toward Nella and was waiting, patiently.

"Hey. Thought you might want to hear this."

"What?"

"While I was in there, Vera mentioned *Needles and Pins* to me."

Nella cringed.

"You know I haven't read a word of it," Hazel continued, "but I tried to back you up on the Shartricia thing as much as I could."

"Oh. You did? Thanks." Nella turned her chair just a bit, so she wasn't completely closed off by her cubicle wall. "And what did *Vera* say?"

"Well, she thanked me for weighing in. Then she emailed me the draft."

"Really?"

"Yep. For a second opinion, I guess."

"Hm." On one hand, it was irritating that Vera hadn't trusted Nella's judgment. But on the other hand, didn't it also mean that Vera *did* care, a tiny bit, about what Nella had said? Maybe Vera had reread the book and was second-guessing it. "Nice. Doesn't Maisy care that you're doing all this other stuff for another editor, though? I remember her getting super possessive of her last assistant."

Hazel shrugged. "Maisy has been busy with personal things, I think. I'm not really sure what. But she's been checked out and has pretty much left me to my own devices. I think Richard asked Vera to give me some things to do so I wouldn't get bored. I'm still new here, so I guess they don't think I can keep myself occupied."

"Ah." Nella realized for the first time how quiet it had been in their area for the last few days. Maisy had exploded into the office earlier, but had mysteriously departed no more than fifteen minutes later, a bundle of more bags than usual stuffed under her arms, her lips pursed even more tightly than usual. "I guess I didn't notice."

"Yeah. Since I have more time, I figured it wouldn't hurt to read Colin's shitty novel. And really," Hazel said, lowering her voice, "having two negative Shartricia reviews from two Black girls could do wonders. Not that your opinion isn't legit, of course, because it totally is, but . . . the more reads, the better. Right?"

Nella nodded, her make-believe glass wall sliding away as quickly as she'd put it up. "Totally."

She'd been happy to go along with this narrative for the rest of the afternoon until she printed *The Lie*, gathered all of her things, and made her way to the train, ready to leave Manhattan after what felt like days. The freshly printed five-hundred-page manuscript pulled hard at her left shoulder as she went down into the depths of the subway, but she didn't mind. It felt like a purposeful weight, like a full bag of groceries bought for a newly cleaned-out fridge. This tote bag held sustenance. She would gobble up the Leslie Howard text immediately and wow Vera with feedback she hadn't even asked for. Simple as that.

Except, it wasn't. Because as Nella stood on the train platform, resolved and ready to begin the next day on a fresh foot, she reached into her bag to pull out the manuscript—and instead pulled out an envelope she didn't remember putting there.

An envelope with her name on it. Her name, again written in all caps. Her name, again written in purple pen.

How did that saying go? *There's always something.* She wasn't sure if it was a saying as much as it was a fact of life, like gravity or indigestion. The phrase was one her father had often said, especially over the last few months, since he'd finally bought a house in Chicago after renting a place not far from her grandmother's senior care center for nearly four years. Just the week before, Nella's father had described to her in great detail how he'd just finally gotten the hole in the roof fixed when he realized that the pipe connected to the washing machine had decided to air out its grievances, too. "That's the thing when you buy a house," he'd sighed into the phone, more to himself than to her. "There's always something."

These words drifted back to Nella now as she stared at the shiny new white envelope, her heart racing. It couldn't possibly have been the envelope she'd already received a few days earlier, read, and lost sleep over; she had tucked that first one away in her closet.

No, this second note was indeed a second one—she knew that much. What she didn't know was how it had gotten there, in her bag, while she stood on a subway platform that was beginning to get a little too crowded. She looked over her left shoulder and then her right, even though she'd been wedged between the same two people for the last fifteen minutes—a man who reeked of raw meat and an older nanny who seemed ready to fight her bratty charge.

Nella sighed and, holding the envelope close to her chest for privacy that was impossible to find on a crowded subway platform during rush hour, peeled back the flap.

LEAVE. THE LONGER YOU STAY, THE HARDER IT'LL BE.
WANT PROOF? CALL 518-772-2234. NO TEXTS. CALL.

A hand suddenly graced her lower back, causing her to almost drop the envelope on the tracks. She twisted around to see who was touching her, the words *I don't* already forming helplessly on her tongue. But there wasn't a familiar face from Wagner in sight—just the energetic young child who'd been the source of the nearby nanny's anxiety.

"No, no, no! Bad Chloe!" the woman shouted, her words wrapped in an indiscernible Eastern European accent. She placed a heavy arm around the girl's shoulders and reeled her in. "Little girl—stop that. You're making every single person around here miserable. Including me."

Nella usually hated to hear adults speak to children so harshly. Her parents had sometimes yelled at her when she was a kid, but they'd been respectful when they did it. As she stood there on that crowded platform, though—elbow-to-elbow with an antsy rug rat and Smelly Meat Man—she was inclined to agree with this Eastern European woman. *No, no, no, no, no.*

Diana

November 1983
Essex, Vermont

"What do we think—yes? No?"

I held up the auburn wig and wagged it high above my head the way I'd wagged around a potentially undercooked breakfast sausage earlier at the hotel. Two hours ago, he'd laughed agreeably before taking another bite of his eggs. But now, he didn't crack. This didn't surprise me. I'd counted how many times his reflection had paced back and forth behind me in the bathroom mirror (twenty), and how many times he'd checked his watch (far more than that). I'd even offered to wet some paper towels in the sink so he could wipe up the beads of sweat that were gathering underneath his chin. But being who he was—Elroy K. Simpson, thick-necked and thirty-four; a man who never lost his cool in front of anybody, not even when he realized his hairline was beginning to recede—he politely nudged my hand away.

"Di. Hon . . ." He stroked the dark, soft beard that he'd started growing back when we first went away to school. "Don't you think it's about time we started to make our way downtown? It's already half past ten, and I thought you said they wanted us there at eleven."

I sighed as I carefully pulled at a curly tendril. The last time I'd worn this particular wig—in Vancouver, I think—it had left my scalp itchy for days afterward. I'd scratched it during dinner and on the subway and in the middle of the night, the violent swaying of the bed causing Elroy to curse my new antique furniture. I'd scratched during author interviews and watched as the amount of couch space around me seemed to grow.

I vowed I'd never wear it again. Now here it was, a contender in my beauty preparations. *The hard things we do for easy hair,* Mom always used to say.

"Makeup's done," I called to Elroy. "Clothes are done. Just need the hair. Five minutes."

"You don't *need* the hair. C'mon, now. We're going to be late."

"I tell you this every time, El—when the people running these things tell us to get there at eleven, they really mean twelve. They *say* eleven because they know we're going to be late. Traffic, gas . . . you know. All those things."

Elroy lowered himself onto the closed toilet seat lid and shook his head. "If that's the case, baby, we should have left this place half an hour ago. At *least*. Or hailed a cab."

I waved him off. "Eh. You and your perpetual earliness."

"It's not being early," said El defensively. "It's just that we don't know how long it's going to take to get to the playhouse. And we don't know how long it's going to take for me to get a cab around *here*," he added, a softer way of reminding me that we were in completely unfamiliar waters. Vermont.

"Silly. The point is, we'll get there when we get there." I repinned a section of hair behind my ear to take care of a few strays. Then I stretched the mouth of the wig open and placed it on my scalp. "After all," I continued, watching new hair swallow the old, "it's not like they're going to start the Q and A without me. No way Kenny would let that happen. She was always the headstrong one out of the two of us, you remember."

Elroy grunted. In a manner of indirect protest, he undid yet another one of the buttons on the maroon silk shirt I'd bought him last week when we were at the mall. "Shoot, Di," he said. "You know who you're starting to sound like?"

I stopped my wig adjusting long enough to meet his eye and grinned. "Who?" I asked, wrapping my voice up in as much gold glitter and cashmere as I could. "Diana Ross?"

Elroy laughed that honey-coated laugh that had made me fall in love with him back in Newark, back when he'd followed me, Kenny, and Mani around school trying to sing and dance like a Temptation; and again almost ten years later, when we were home for the holidays and freshly graduated from our respective universities. But even as the usual four crinkles bracketed his eyes, I could see something sharper than mere playfulness lay beneath. Reproach, maybe.

I didn't like it. Not even as he stood up from the toilet seat, came over, and kissed me on the cheek, contorting his body so he could get around the tall back of the wooden chair I'd dragged into the bathroom from the bedroom.

"No," he said, twirling one of my new locks of hair with his finger. "Not Diana."

"Who's more diva than Diana?"

"Your mom," he said. "And all those fancy Jack and Jill ladies she used to bring around the house. The ones we always made fun of back in the day, with the long white gloves."

Elroy must not have seen me wince, because he continued on. "What was that one lady's name? The one who had a different pastel outfit for every day of the week? Beverly Carter?"

"Uh-huh. No—*Rebekah* Carter," I said, moving the brush and the toothpaste out of the way so I could reach for the curling iron. "Wife of Herbert Carter the Fourth."

It was Elroy's turn to wince, bracing himself with my chair. "Right. Rebekah with a 'k' Carter. Always so uppity."

"'It's Re-beh-*kah*. Not Re-beh-*kuh*,'" I recalled, busting into a fit of giggles so convulsive that I almost burned my forehead. "Remember that time you called her Rebek-can't to her face?"

"I was such a terrible kid," Elroy admitted. "I'm surprised your mom still let me come by for dinner all those times."

"She didn't. Well—not really. Remember those nights I told you that you couldn't come over because I was studying Swahili at Sidney's house?"

"Yeah."

"Do you remember ever hearing me speak one word of Swahili?"

Elroy laughed. "Makes sense. We couldn't have little ole El from around the way messing up a Gordon dinner."

"Tracking brown mud up and down all of Mom's white carpets."

"Updating everybody on the latest bad news. Getting to second base on the front porch . . . with all the lights off." Elroy wiggled his eyebrows.

"Don't forget feeding Bubbles to the raccoons. And that time we almost fed Jonathan to them, too."

"Hey, hey, that was all you," he said, smiling. "Jonathan and I were always cool. He was the only Gordon who could stand to have me around. Your dad? Maybe a little bit. But your ma, though . . . lord have mercy, the daggers that woman shot me whenever I came around, all because my dad was a doorman."

I eyed Elroy again. Something had shifted beneath his ready-to-go exterior. An unsettling memory mixed with a rush of repulsion. Just like that, our reminiscing was over. His hands were still on the back of my chair, but his eyes were shut, and I could tell he was drifting somewhere else entirely. It almost always happened this way: a swift shift from perfectly okay to painfully wrong.

I returned to my reflection, feeling less confident about what I saw than I had moments before. For the first time, my blue eye shadow looked garish; my liner like a child had taken a crayon to my eyelids. My skin was too pale, much closer to the color of dry sand, much closer to the appearance of a sick person.

This was who was getting up onstage in front of three hundred people? My stomach lurched. I was going to look so washed out beneath those bright lights compared to Kenny, who would be all beautiful and brown and Harvard-polished.

I pinched my cheeks once, willing some color to come through, until I remembered that was something that really only worked for white women. Then I put my head in my hands and did the one thing you're not supposed to do before a public appearance: I started to cry.

Elroy placed his hands on my shoulders, and I knew he was back. "I just . . . this satin shirt, your being late to your own event—it all feels kind of over-the-top, you know? I just don't want you to become one of those . . ."

I blinked at him. He blinked back.

"The Rebekah Carter comparison *might* have been an exaggeration," he continued carefully, "but you know what I mean. You know how much of a self-important devil she could be."

He had a point. A "well-to-do" Black woman with café au lait skin and a heel for every occasion, Rebekah had been a fixture in my house nearly every summer morning from 1959 until 1967. Supposedly, she was lonely; supposedly, her husband's line of work sent him all over the country. All I knew was that whenever I woke up and went downstairs to have breakfast, she was almost always chatting with my mother at our claw-footed kitchen table about politics or music or the latest Jack and Jill gossip. Sometimes, she'd comment on my shape or how dehydrated I looked, as though I were supposed to roll out of bed looking like I was ready to go find a husband. But usually—mercifully—she ignored me, too tied up with proffering this or that Black person to fulfill whatever latest need my mother had: a new grass-cutter, a new hairstylist, a new dentist.

Mom always referred to her as a lifesaver. At dinner—when Rebekah wasn't present, of course, and when Mom was in a looser mood—Dad called her a life-sucker.

I reached up and squeezed one of Elroy's fingers before going back to curling again. "Well, *I* know that as of at least fifteen years ago, Rebekah never finished reading a book in her life."

Elroy stooped down and kissed me again, this time on top of my head. The feeling left much to be desired—I could barely feel the light peck through my wig. "I also know that you're far, far prettier than she ever was. And far more brilliant. And more open-minded: No way she'd let a man put his hands in her—"

"See, now," I quipped, pointing at him with the curling rod as he mock-ran out of the bathroom, "you should have stopped at 'brilliant.'"

"Open-mindedness is sexy, too!" Elroy called over his shoulder.

I snorted. "Hey, where you going? You're not leaving without me, are you? One more minute. I promise."

"Calm down, woman," he shouted from the bedroom. "I'm not going nowhere. The lighting just got unbearable in there, that's all. Felt kind of claustrophobic."

"Sixty seconds," I sang, turning another piece of hair with the curler over and over again in my right hand the way I'd seen my mother do every morning for nearly eighteen years. Except it had been her own fine hair she'd been burning, not synthetic. I was always careful to make that distinction when I looked in the mirror: that even though I was hiding my own hair, at least it would be healthy for that one day I decided to let it out in the open. It wouldn't start to fall out the way Mom's did in her last few years—although, I suppose, the sickness had had a hand in that.

"Do you think this thing is tacky, El?" I asked, reaching for the hairbrush. "This red hair?"

"I think that's a trap that I've known you too long to fall into."

"But what do you think Vermont people are going to think about it?"

"I wouldn't think too much about that, Di," Elroy called. "Those white people can't even imagine that it's not yours. And that's not what they're there to see, anyway. They're there to see the brilliant Diana Gordon and the brilliant Kendra Rae Phillips talk about their brilliant—no, *the first of what surely will be many brilliant, bestselling*—"

His voice cut out abruptly.

"El?" I glanced over at the bathroom door, craning my neck to get a look at him. "What is it?"

He didn't reply.

"I know it's been more than sixty seconds," I said, unplugging the curling iron, "but I just . . . I don't know." I tried to smile at my reflection in the mirror, but it turned into more of a grimace. "I'm just not feeling this look."

I waited. I'd given Elroy an opening to go on another one of his speeches about natural brown girl beauty and how all makeup was really made for white people, so he didn't know why I bothered so much. But the only thing I heard was the occasional drip-drop of the faulty toilet tank.

"Baby? Is everything okay?" I grabbed my lipstick, my compact mirror. "Fine, you win. We can get going now," I said, starting for the door.

I was beginning to think that maybe he'd left to see about a taxi, since he had always been the practical one. But then I saw that he was still very much in the room, hunched over the foot of his bed.

"What are you looking at?" I asked him.

Elroy crumpled up whatever it was that had had his attention over the last few moments and held it behind his back. That worried look had returned. "I'm not going to say it's nothing, because by now you can obviously see that isn't the case. But, still . . . Di . . ." He exhaled. "It really *is* nothing. Well, not really. But it *will* be. In a few days."

I eyed him suspiciously. "That looks like a newspaper," I observed.

Elroy hesitated, seeming to consider whether it was worth lying or not. "It is that," he said awkwardly.

"Let me see it."

"I . . ."

"We don't have time for this," I said.

He handed it over, facedown—the frustrating equivalent of a child chucking a tennis ball at my head after I'd asked him nicely to hand it over—but I didn't say anything as I flipped it right side up. Nor did I say anything as my eyes met the black-and-white printed face of the woman with whom I'd been rocketed into the national spotlight over the last three weeks. The woman who had been my best friend for twenty years, since we'd first met in Ms. Abraham's seventh-grade science class.

I swallowed, took a breath. "Bestselling *Burning Heart* Editor: 'If You White, You Ain't Right with Me,'" I recited clearly, like I was reading a birthday card. I paused for a moment before looking back up at Elroy. "Jesus Christ. What did Kenny *do*?"

Elroy tugged at his beard again. He had about as much of an answer as I did. "I don't know," he said, "but you'll probably want to wait until after this event is over to find out."

"But what if they ask me questions about it during the Q and A?"

Elroy shrugged. "I'm not sure people up here read the *New York Times*, baby. *I* only read it because of you." Then he snapped back into action, seizing the pair of black heels I'd left by the floor-length mirror that hung by the front door of our hotel room and handing them to me. "If I were you, I would play dumb for now," he said. "Plead the Fifth. It's the best thing you can do for yourself, and for Kenny. Then maybe you can talk some sense into her. Let's take her out after this is all over in a few hours."

I grimaced as he took the paper back from me, placing it at the foot of the bed. "Not ideal, I know. But this ain't good, Di. That's all you need to know for now. Kenny done stepped in it. Now you just gotta make sure she didn't track it all over *your* living room."

I shook my head, woozy from the thought of having to play pretend for a few hours even though I knew Elroy had a point. I needed to pack this worry away and slip on my shoes.

Just then, the phone rang.

"Don't answer it," Elroy said.

We stared at each other during the second ring and the third. On the fourth, I lunged for it, pushing Elroy's hand aside. "It could be Dick," I insisted, ignoring the way my husband wilted at the sound of this name. I put the receiver up to my ear, and waited.

And waited.

"Di," the voice on the other end finally whispered. "We need to do something. *Now*."

10

September 14, 2018

"So, I printed out the five email replies from Sam Lewis about the five proposed cover options for *Crystal Soul.* This one on top is the last note I have from Sam, dated from Tuesday." Nella sifted through the pages in her lap, tracing her finger across the body of the email. The ex–rock musician had sent her more than five emails, one of which contained nothing except an expletive for its subject line. But for the purposes of this conversation, these other replies didn't exist. "He told me on the phone this morning that he didn't like this layout as much as he liked the second one, but he *did* like it more than the fourth one."

"'*Five*'? Wow. Okay. Enough." Vera had asked Nella to print everything out in hi-res on glossy paper and bring it into her office, but that hadn't stopped her from opening each of the attachments Nella had emailed her and scrolling through them slowly.

Nella stared at the five printed covers, silently bemoaning how much ink had been wasted not with just this task, but with every single task she'd ever been asked to complete at Wagner. Nine times out of ten, the pieces of paper would end up in the garbage. How much money had she had a hand in throwing away over the last two years? Enough to pay back her college loans? Enough to buy grown-lady shoes? "And I'm not sure if you remember, but the last time we spoke to Leonard I'm pretty sure he said, 'I'm not doing any new cover designs for *Crystal Soul.*' So. Do we think he's being serious?"

"Yes. The man cornered me in the elevator last week and I'm still traumatized from it."

The mental image was just too good: five-foot-three Leonard in his trademark red-and-blue checkered shirt with a golf pencil behind his ear; five-foot-eight Vera in all black, glowering down at him. Nella had to swallow a chuckle. "That sounds terrible. I'm sorry."

"It was. You didn't forward him Sam's emails, did you? Please tell me you—"

"*Definitely* not. Nope. No. I reworded every single thing."

"Great." Vera sighed, massaging her temple. "You're so good at that. Thanks. But anyway, bottom line is, we're going to have to work to get Sam to pick from one of the ones he has already. That or outsource, which we can't afford to do. Not enough money in the budget for that."

"Right. That's what I figured. Here's what I think—and let me know if this sounds crazy, and I hope you don't mind me making this suggestion—but I think we should really try to push the second cover Leonard drew up."

Vera said nothing, but the look in her eye didn't say *stop* talking, so Nella *ahem*ed before continuing on.

"Because it fits more with the covers from Sam's last two books, and Sam's response to that one seemed a lot milder." *It's got a real smell to it,* he'd said over the phone, although what kind, he hadn't specified. Nevertheless, Nella had taken this as something of a positive appraisal. "Does that sound good?"

"What?" Vera asked. Her computer had dinged and she'd turned to see what had caused it.

"Pushing for the second cover? The one with the stars. Maybe Leonard can change the font size or something so that it's technically a 'new' version, and we can send that to Sam? Is that okay?"

"Yes! Wait. No." Vera held out a hand, her eyes still fixed on her screen. "Can you just hand it to me, please?"

Nella leaned forward and handed her the top page. She swallowed and said, with as little meekness as possible, "If you want, I'd be happy to run over to Leonard's desk and tell him that we should maybe take some of what was on the fifth cover and sort of meld it into the second one instead. Because Richard was a big fan of five, right?"

Vera stared at her screen for another thirty seconds, as though Nella hadn't just offered to stick her neck into the cage of an underfed lion. Nella seized upon this distraction, surveying her boss's office without her noticing. She peeked at Vera's collection of pens and pencils for the millionth time that week—no colors but black. The clear plastic box of stationery sitting next to the zen garden was a new addition to Vera's desk, but those were expensive and fancy, definitely not what Nella had received. Briefly, she imagined the perpetrator standing in the Papyrus store, shrouded in black, deliberating over which blank card would best convey their racist little message.

It had been a while since Nella had really felt like laughing, but she had to hold in a gasp when Vera turned to register the image Nella had handed her and said, "No, sorry—not this. Can you hand me the printout of the very first cover, please? I can't remember what it looks like."

"Oh, sure. Here." She handed Vera the first cover.

"No—thanks, but I want to see the *very* first cover Leonard proposed, side by side with these five."

"Absolutely," Nella said, although she didn't know what "very first cover" Vera was referring to. She remembered Leonard making five covers, not six. She hastened to stand, picking apart her brain for a memory she knew didn't exist. "Of course. I can try to print that for you right now. I have a quick meeting downstairs with production I have to run to, but I can—"

"That's alright, just leave it for me this afternoon, please, when you get a minute." Nella exhaled as Vera folded her hands matter-of-factly. "What the man really needs is an ultimatum. Leonard has been overworked as it is these days, and Sam should understand by now that we've got some pretty qualified folks here."

Nella had nodded. She'd known all of this—or at least, a small part of her knew—but putting her foot down with Sam hadn't ultimately felt like her decision to make. What if it had backfired in the same way the Colin Franklin meeting had? After all, the air was still thick with remnants of the Colin Incident, given Vera's tone and fickle eye contact.

Nella watched Vera return to her screen and started to leave. But before she crossed the doorway, she pivoted and said, offhandedly, "There was one more thing I wanted to mention."

"Yes?" said Vera into her computer.

I've been getting these notes from some stranger telling me to leave work. They've been freaking me out.

But she couldn't do it. "I just finished reading *The Lie*."

Vera's chair sounded like it was going to fall apart from how quickly she spun around. The radiance coming off her smile was mesmerizing. "That's *great*! And? What do you think? You loved it, right?"

"Well . . . I missed my subway stop for real while I was reading it, so if that's any indicator . . ." Nella trailed off, her eyes wide from mock awe. *The Lie* was fine, nothing she deemed worth figuring out comps for, but Vera didn't need to know she felt that way. "Want me to send you my report?"

Vera nodded. "Please! That'd be great. I'm really thinking of making an offer on it. I can't believe I forgot to send it to you—Hazel shared it, I assume?"

There it was: an apology. Kind of. "She did. It's nothing. Really."

"Goodness, I'm so embarrassed." Vera paused, clutching at her neck. "Hey . . . since you were able to get to that one so quickly, any chance you'd be able to read another one by tomorrow? I'll send it to you right now, promise. *Steeled Heart.* It's really, *really* good. It's *Pride and Prejudice* meets *I, Robot.*"

Nella nodded and said that of course she could, even as she remembered that she and Owen had plans to meet his moms, who were visiting from Denver, at the High Line that very evening. She turned to leave, praying the book was short, when Vera called out, "Nella? One more quick thing."

"Yes?"

"I know I haven't really been present lately. And I know you must be thinking it's in regards to the . . . Colin situation." Her voice was low and measured.

Nella clicked her pen open and closed awkwardly, staring at Vera from the doorway.

"And maybe it *is* about that, a little. I'm not sure. Things have just gotten really crazy . . . I'm just feeling like I'm busier than I've ever been . . . anyway, this is my own inadequate way of saying that I apologize if I made you uncomfortable at all. In any way. I asked you for your opinion, and I'm glad you gave it."

Nella smiled. "It's all good. I'm sorry, too, that it all happened the way it did."

"Great." Vera let out a deep breath. "I'm so glad we could clear the air. I've been talking to Colin almost every day, getting a sense of how he's feeling about things, and I will say that I think he feels pretty bad about the way everything happened, too."

"He does?"

"He does. But I *do* think . . ." Vera squeezed one set of fingers with the other. "I do think that it's not a bad idea to apologize to him again. Just a small apology. And then, tabula rasa."

Nella stopped clicking her pen.

"What do you think about that idea?"

I think I already apologized to him before he left the office, four times. "I have to say . . . I may need to think on it," Nella said, realizing how hollow her voice sounded. "Respectfully, that is. I'd kind of thought we'd moved past it by now."

"Well, respectfully, Nella, I'd have to say that your apology was a little . . ." Vera wobbled her head from side to side. "'I'm sorry you thought I called you a racist' is a little bit like saying 'I'm sorry you thought I ran over your puppy with my SUV.' It's . . . a bit empty. You know what I mean?"

Do you *know what* you *mean?* "I'll do some serious thinking about it," Nella repeated.

Vera said that she understood, although something in her last word turned down a bit.

Nella looked away. She realized she was crossing her arms, so she uncrossed them. "I can give him a call, I guess."

"Actually, it may be better to do it via email? He's in California now, doing film stuff for his last book. But hey, send me an email of it first, just so I can look it over?"

An apology over email was exactly what Nella didn't want to do. She preferred to do it verbally, partly because she wasn't sure how to word it, and she imagined hearing Colin's tone on the phone might help. But she also felt that it was something her mother would have found a way to resist. *Never let your boss have anything in writing,* she always said.

An image of Colin printing out her email and putting it up on his refrigerator for all his guests to see, all while wearing the multi-fabric cap, flashed through Nella's mind. But *she* could wear poker faces, too. "Got it. Will do," she said brightly.

She held this brightness in her face all the way to the bathroom. It was only when she'd latched the stall door that she let herself break.

Nella had to work hard to convince herself she was alone in the office later that evening. It was almost nine p.m., and she hadn't seen a coworker pass by her desk since seven . . .

But what was that whistling sound she'd heard at the end of the hall?

She paused her music and peered around. There was no whistling. No sounds. They were all in her dizzy, dizzy head. But those notes that had appeared in her bag and on her desk hadn't been all in her head. They were as real as the two hundred pages of *Steeled Heart* that she still had left to read. And if the person who'd sent these very real notes was indeed a coworker, they knew by now they'd have to be extra sneaky if they wanted to slip her note number three.

Still, a week had passed since she'd gotten anything else.

Nella collapsed into her seat and went back to finding a GIF to send to Owen. She wanted one that said *I'm still in the office but I'm sorry and I love you and please say hi to your parents for me,* but the best she could do was a clip from a messy dating show she'd roped him into watching a few times. She pressed Send and hoped it'd get a laugh. Then she went back to the book Vera had asked her to read, scowling at how many pages she still had left: hundred ninety-nine.

The read was slow going. The author had tried and failed to blend nineteenth-century ideals with modern-day tech speak. But Nella preferred pushing through the clunky robot dialogue over writing the Colin apology. Both tasks needed to be finished before she left the office, but the latter was so utterly demoralizing that she couldn't bear to start it. And whenever she *did* finally finish everything, she'd have to ride the train home knowing that she'd missed hanging out with Owen and his parents, and what would she have to show for it? Comments on a shitty book, and an apology to a shitty writer?

The more Nella thought about it, the angrier it made her. It made her so angry that after a few frustrating minutes of not absorbing anything she was reading, she went to YouTube and searched "Jesse Watson + apologize for what." Since the office was empty—even Donald had gone home already—she didn't bother putting her headphones in. She sat back in her chair, put her feet up on her cluttered desk, and turned the volume all the way up.

"Tell me, please, what on god's green earth do you want from us? 'I'm sorry my skin's so black, my hair's so thick'? 'I'm sorry you've been killing my people for generations—gen-er-*a*-tions, people—and the Black people you haven't killed, you've left financially debilitated, without any wealth to pass along to their children'? 'I'm sorry you brought my ancestors over on those ships and forced me to live with your people'?"

Nella watched it twice, relishing in the way Jesse's indignance radiated off her cubicle walls. Then she created a new file and started to type.

Dear Jesse Watson,

I'm sure you get many notes like these, every single day, and I'm sure that right now you'd rather do anything than read an unsolicited email from someone who wants something from you. But before you delete this, I want to assure you: I don't want anything from you. I want something for *you. For all of the young Black readers out there who don't feel like the book industry sees them.*

I think there's a book inside you that could

A light brush skittered across her leg. She yelped and thrashed, noticing a moment too late that it was just Pam, the sweet Chilean woman who cleaned the building afterhours, trying to empty her trash.

"Oh, Pam," Nella cried, clutching the woman's arm. "I am so, so, so sorry!"

Pam politely removed her hand. "It's okay, honey," she said, reaching again for Nella's trash can. "This place gives me the creeps, too."

11

September 26, 2018

The main Wagner conference room was abuzz with watercooler chit-chat as dozens of employees stocked up at the breakfast bar, then filed into their rightful seats—editors and other upper-level employees at the big stone table; everyone else in the four rows of chairs that faced the big stone table.

Nella and the other Wagner assistants were posted up in "Assistants Alley," close enough to take notes on the first marketing meeting of the season, but far enough to zone out undetected. They weren't *quite* in the nosebleeds. That was the last row, which was taken—almost out of protest—by the e-books team, an underappreciated department that was never taken as seriously as it should have been, and Leonard, the grumpy cover designer. Nevertheless, Hazel had expressed disapproval of the Assistants Alley seats Sophie had saved for her and Nella when they'd arrived a few minutes earlier. *There are seats open up front,* she seemed ready to say. But then Sophie had suddenly and very loudly praised Hazel's updo, leaving Hazel no choice but to accept her third-row seat with a smile.

Nella was happy she'd been spared from explaining that no assistant had ever sat so close to the stone table. That it just wasn't done. But that didn't stop her from wondering, as she took a bite out of her bagel, why it never actually *was*.

"So." Hazel took a bite out her cinnamon raisin mini-bagel, moving forward so she could engage Nella, Sophie, and Gina, a know-it-all assistant publicist, at the same time. "Y'all are coming to my Young, Black 'n' Lit event tonight, right?"

A muscle tightened in Nella's neck. This question felt like it had been directed at her and her alone. She pretended to be interested in testing the functionality of her ballpoint pen.

It wasn't that Nella *didn't* want to go, because she'd considered it on more than one occasion since receiving the Facebook event invite a couple of days earlier. She'd looked up Young, Black 'n' Lit, the nonprofit poetry organization that Hazel herself had founded for Black high school students in Harlem, and realized it was exactly the kind of thing that she and Malaika always talked about doing more of—being engaged in the communities in which they lived, partaking in Black extracurriculars.

She discovered that plenty of other people felt the same way, too, once she'd looked around some more. YBL had approximately fifteen thousand Instagram followers and twenty-two thousand Facebook fans. *Since 2012, our mission has been to amplify the voices of teens who have the words, but don't have the microphone,* the main home page read. *We aim to promote the next generation of Mayas, Lauryns, and Lucilles.*

Their net went far beyond New York—it extended to Chicago and LA, too, where educators had started YBL chapters in their own communities. Most impressive of all, though, was YBL's Twitter page, which had nearly thirty thousand followers and a breadth of tweets, sometimes five in a day—interviews with Black writers from all over the country and from all decades; posts dedicated to the birthdays of Black poets, many of whom Nella had never heard of. It was rife with so much rich Black content that Nella could have cozied up on her full-sized bed and settled into it for an hour. Two hours, even.

But she didn't have the time these days. Ever since their conversation about *The Lie*, Vera had been inundating Nella with manuscripts, day after day. She was thinking about which one she should start first when Sophie said, "Wait! Your reading thing's *tonight*? I totally forgot. Where is it, again?"

"It's at Curl Central. In Bed-Stuy."

Gina frowned. Nella practically heard the corners of her mouth turn down. A "what's hot and what's not" crystal ball of sorts, the redhead fell into the small but revered category of hardcore publicity employees who heard the name of a place located in the city, then joyfully told you if she deemed it literary enough to hold an author event—whether you wanted to know or not. It was a gift that Nella did not wish for, but it did impress her.

"Curl Central. Hm." Gina's mouth scrunched up into the left side of her face. After too much thought, she concluded, "We've never held anything there before."

Hazel laughed. "I didn't think you had," she said good-naturedly, but Nella could sense a glimmer of amusement in her eye—the same one she'd had when Maisy had whitesplained Harlem to her. "It's at a hair café. My boyfriend's sister's. It's her first time hosting a literary salon. She's got the space for it, so we figured, why not?"

"'Hair café,'" Gina repeated, taking a sip of her coffee as she computed once more. "*That's* different."

"I'm down, definitely," said Sophie, practically bubbling over with glee. Sophie had been coming over to Hazel's desk at least twice a day to chat, and Nella imagined she was psyched at the idea of hanging with Hazel outside of work for a change.

"Great." Hazel nodded. She shifted her focus; this time, her eyes really *were* on Nella.

"I'll come, too, if the other thing I have going on cancels," Gina said, a bit resignedly. "It'll be nice to scope it out, see if we'd want to host something there in the future."

"Sweet! Nella?"

When Nella looked up, Hazel's eyes were practically pleading with her. *Please, girl, don't leave me with these white chicks at a Black hair salon.* "How about you?"

"Um . . ." Nella ran a hand across the back of her neck. She had plans directly after work that evening, and not just the kind of plans she invented when she preferred to go home and stream reruns of *A*

Different World. *Real* plans. She was supposed to be meeting a young, established agent she'd been chasing for months; after that, she and Owen had plans to split a blunt and go see *The Blob*, one of their favorite bad-but-good sci-fi movies, downtown. They'd purchased tickets for the movie two months earlier, nearly a year in New York City time, and she was still in the doghouse after missing quality family time with his parents. She owed him.

"C'mon, it'll be fun! You've been meaning to come by Curl Central, right? You should come. You can bring Owen, too."

Something about that suggestion felt a bit odd to Nella, but she shrugged it off. "I might be able to make it. I have drinks with an agent scheduled for tonight, but that hopefully won't go for too long."

"Drinks with an agent?" Sophie practically shrieked. "Awesome!"

"Which agent?" Hazel asked.

"Lena Jordan."

"I've been thinking about how I need to meet with agents, but I just don't know how to find the time in between everything else," Sophie complained. "You know?"

Even though Kimberly had yet to return to the office post-surgery, Nella gave her a sympathetic nod. She was relieved by how much their conversation had veered considerably away from Hazel's poetry reading.

"Is this your first agent meeting?" Gina asked, her interest in the conversation renewed.

"Yep. Only took me about two years to get someone to take me seriously enough."

"That's the norm for you guys in editorial, isn't it? Really, I don't know how you all manage to hang on for so long," said Gina. "If I hadn't gotten promoted to assistant publicist last year, I would have totally gone to a different publishing house."

Everyone except Hazel nodded, even though everyone except Hazel knew that the only reason Gina had been promoted so quickly was because someone at the top had died.

"I can't believe how long it takes to move up the ladder," Hazel said, polishing off the last of her bagel. She paused so she could finish chewing. "But really . . . it's sort of case by case, right?"

"What do you mean?" Nella asked. Maybe Hazel *had* known that Gina's previous boss had died peacefully at her Wagner desk. It was, after all, still the talk of the office.

"Like, it sort of depends on the assistant? Richard was telling me that exceptions are sometimes made. Sometimes. It's not like I have my hopes up or anything," she quickly added.

Sophie's eyes widened. "He told you that? When?"

Nella searched the room for Richard and found him, easily, at the head of the meeting table. With his sweeping eye, his high-collared satin persimmon shirt, and faint trace of a smile, he looked more like Macbeth eyeing potential suspects rather than a supportive editor in chief. "Did he say that to you during your welcome tea?" Nella asked, equally thrown by this.

"No, no. Actually, I've been meaning to tell you guys . . ." Hazel leaned forward in her seat; again, she seemed to be addressing only Nella. "I invited Richard to an event we had a couple of weeks ago for donors who've supported YBL, just to see if he'd be interested in donating some money. And he bit! He'll be coming to my event tonight, too."

"That's great!" Sophie exclaimed, tugging at her braid. "We really need more young Black people in this industry. We were literally just talking about how weird it is that it took so long to get another Black assistant here at Wagner. Right, Gina?"

Gina grew very interested in her cuticles. "Yeah, I think I remember that conversation."

"Like, Hazel is so smart. And you are, too, Nella," Sophie added. She shook her head. "It just . . . it *sucks* how white it is here." For perhaps the tenth time, she cited the op-ed that had run in *BookCenter* a few months ago. This time she even said the author's full name—a new touch, Nella noticed. "Black people just *really* need to be given the chance. Period. Just because we don't see them in these spaces doesn't mean they can't thrive here. Right?"

Gina seemed to understand why "they" had been such an improper word for Sophie to use, because she shrank deeper into her seat. Hazel eyed Sophie, looking bemused.

Amy Davidson, the head of the marketing team, saved them all. "One more minute, everyone, and then we'll get started," she called out. A third of the room, including Gina and Sophie, scattered to top off their coffees and grab just one or two more bagels.

"It's really awesome that you run an organization for young Black female writers," said Nella, looking over at Hazel. "I would have totally loved to be a part of something like that when I was in high school."

"Thanks! A few girls from my old high school are reading tonight, so I'm extra hyped. Half of the food and drink proceeds are going to the group's members, by the way."

"Sweet."

"The girls are really dope, too," Hazel added, gazing into the distance. "And they're so, so talented."

"I bet." Nella took another bite out of her bagel so she didn't have to say anything else. It tasted a little like onion and a little like a flavor she hadn't asked for. "And Richard is *really* coming tonight?"

Hazel bobbed her head and looked to the front of the room, where Richard was sitting. "You know, I thought he was pretty intense at first. But he actually can be really, really chill. I think I broke him in with all of my tea knowledge. Manny's obsession really came in handy for once," she joked.

"Richard is definitely a character," Nella agreed. She looked at the front table, too, but the tall, balding man who'd been occupying the seat in front of her had returned from the coffee station, obstructing her view. She sighed, a touch of grumpiness creeping into her spine. She hadn't intended on going to Hazel's reading. She couldn't bail on Owen *again*. But now that Nella knew Richard would be there, and that exceptions might be made for promotions, she couldn't ignore it.

Nella made a mental note to email Lena Jordan about moving their drinks up to five thirty instead of six thirty. It wasn't ideal—it had taken her months to pin down this meeting—but it had to be done.

Besides, how awful would it look if one of Wagner's only Black employees wasn't supporting another's endeavors?

Amy swiftly clapped her hands to get everybody's attention. By the time her palms met a third time, a hush fit for a wake drifted throughout the room of two dozen people.

"Now that everyone's settled," Amy said, slipping off her crimson-tinted glasses, "I think we should get started." She flipped her purplish-gray hair over her shoulders, then grabbed the wire-framed reading glasses that were always not far from the crook of her left elbow.

Legend had it that Amy's tinted lenses, which she donned everywhere except meetings that required her to sit at the head of the table, had been prescribed by an optician when she was in her twenties. But Nella was almost positive that they were a bit of a power play. Hell, every person who'd been at Wagner for as long as Amy had—thirty-two years, in her case—had some sort of quirk that would have been inexcusable for someone new to the business. Or for any person of color. And when compared with other quirks, Amy's wasn't the strangest. Talking to her without seeing her eyes wasn't as bad as talking to Alexander while he was also talking to someone in his Bluetooth earpiece, or talking to Oliver, a veteran editor who peppered every conversation with quotes from authors he'd worked with.

"Lots of great plans to talk about in today's marketing meeting," Amy continued, shuffling her papers in front of her. "We're going to start with Vera's two fall titles: one from Kitty Kruegler; the other from Colin Franklin. Any preference on which of your authors we start with, Ver?"

"Yes, actually. I've got one," Nella heard Richard say. "Let's start with Colin."

"Might as well start with the cash cow, right?" Josh, ever the seconder, agreed. He'd managed to get to the meeting room early, and was separated from Richard only by Alexander—a notable feat.

Everyone laughed and nodded their heads eagerly. Nella jotted down this small joke—not the cash cow comment, but the level of confidence with which everyone at Wagner still beheld Colin Franklin. She knew it would please him the next time she and Vera sat down to give him a sales update, especially since numbers from his last few books had been fairly mediocre—and had been since 2009, actually, which was when the lead actress in the film adaptation of *Not My Priest* had sued Colin for harassment in the months following its premiere.

Who would agree to play Shartricia if his new book were adapted into a movie? No one famous, she assumed. More likely an unknown, looking for her big break. And maybe this would be it for her. Maybe the movie would blow up, lead to better roles, and she'd become an achiever of "firsts" that one would have thought another Black actress had already achieved. She'd go from acting to talk-show hosting, become the next Black Ellen—Blellen?—and then, after a few years, she'd go on to start her own Black women–run film company. Billions of dollars; millions of followers; EGOT status; a household name across the world. And once it was all said and done, perhaps nobody would remember the Shartricia role that had made it all possible.

Maybe.

But probably not. Black people wouldn't forget. Not people like Nella; not anyone else who spent more than a few moments thinking or talking about Black representation in the media.

She shook her head, again considering the apology that Vera had asked her to make, again wondering what the media would think about Colin's new book when it dropped . . . and how helpless she felt about all of it. Maybe she should have tried harder to get through to him during that meeting in Vera's office.

"What's most impressive of all about this book, though," Vera was saying, "is that Colin has been particularly proactive in his quest to get deep inside the minds of his characters. And I think what he has here is going to ring so true with readers in these damaged communities, too. Because those are the folks whom these books are truly for. The people out in rural Ohio, and all the other rural areas in the United States."

"But do they even read?" Sophie whispered into Gina's ear, a bit too loudly. Gina covered her silent laughter with a hand.

Amy cut into Vera's spiel. "I think that all sounds fabulous, Vera. I read this book and I have to say that it really is something else. It's a true departure, if you don't mind me saying, from what Colin has worked on in the past. The family scenes all really hit me. So hard, so deeply."

Amy paused, then, which meant the woman had closed her eyes the way she often did in the middle of speaking, to emphasize her point. Nella felt her own eyelids grow heavy, which wasn't an unusual response to Amy's yoga voice. "After I finished the manuscript I called my younger son up at Yale, and told him I loved him for making the choices that he made. And for the choices he didn't make."

The balding man sitting in front of Nella nodded his head in agreement.

"I do have just one question, though."

Another pause. Nella wondered if Amy was about to ask everyone to drop into downward-facing dog.

"I do wonder about *audience*, and how we're going to get this book into the hands of people in those ravaged communities."

Sophie reached over and squeezed Gina's thigh, victorious.

"I'm sorry, but I'm going to have to be that heartless old witch and ask everyone here at this table, as much as it pains me—do these people that Colin is writing about buy books? Or are they more focused on simply buying more opioids?"

Nella flinched. Hearing the phrase "these people" in reference to a mostly white group of people was strangely satisfying. She wondered if Hazel felt the same way, but she was seated too far to the left to show up in Nella's periphery.

"I think that's a fair question to ask," Josh said. "And I also wonder—and I'll happily be the warlock to your witch, Amy"—a few overly generous chuckles—"do we think the public has had enough of this story line? The opioid epidemic has come and . . . well, it hasn't gone, exactly, but frankly, it doesn't feel like the news cycle cares as much about it as it once did. This means that we'll really need to think hard about how we market this one."

Opioids still sexy? Nella jotted. She'd translate it into something less cheeky when she typed it up for Vera later.

"I agree, it will be a bit tricky," Vera said, adding a bit of bass to her voice. "And no doubt about it, Colin is aware of that, too. But he's planning to do a lot of Q and As on the process of writing this book, which media platforms will really appreciate. And he's really willing to go after young adult audiences. Maybe speak at some high schools out in middle America."

A few seats down from Vera, Maisy—a conspicuous shade of bronze—cleared her throat. Since returning to work a few days earlier, she'd told everyone that she'd "simply needed an extra-long vacation," although Nella had not forgotten the brief cameo Maisy had made, hustling in and then out of the office with all of those bags. "I'd just like to chime in here, too, if I may," said Maisy.

The right people sitting at the table nodded that yes, it was okay.

"I read some of this—" She readjusted her position so she could make eye contact with Vera. "Like Amy, I was touched, and I told my son that I love him, and to always make good decisions—although he's still figuring out how to say 'mommy,' so we'll revisit his choices in sixteen years, I guess." A few more overly generous chuckles; Nella gave Maisy half a titter. "And I think one thing that's really special about *Needles and Pins*—and stop me, Ver, if you were about to touch upon this—is that it shows various demographics that have been hit by the opioid crisis. Not just white people, but Black people, too."

"Yes," Vera said, "I was going to speak on that. Thank you."

Nella stiffened. It was one thing to talk about Shartricia in Vera's office, but to have to sit through it with two dozen of her coworkers was another thing entirely. She did not want to listen to Maisy and Vera wax poetic about how good of a job Colin had done presenting diverse characters. She did not want to watch everyone respond enthusiastically. For a fleeting moment, she considered going to the bathroom, even though it would be terribly conspicuous for her to do so.

Then, she remembered: She had an ally now. If any other coworkers happened to cast a glance in her direction to see if she'd exhibited any opinion on what was being said, it meant they would also be looking at Hazel, too. How had she forgotten she wasn't the only Black girl in the room?

Nella inhaled. The burden wasn't gone, she realized. Not by any means. But at least it could be shared and laughed about later. Maybe she'd even invite Hazel to drinks with Malaika the next time they went out, and they could hash it all out together.

She felt the tension leave her lower back again, rising through her shoulders and evaporating up to the ceiling.

But it was a mistake to let her guard down. Because it left her unprepared for what happened next.

First, Vera said Hazel's name. And then Richard did, too, venturing to turn his attention toward Assistants Alley.

"Would you mind sharing some words, Hazel?"

Nella froze. She'd never seen Richard ask any entry-level employee to speak at one of these meetings before.

"Sure. I asked Vera if I could take a look at *Needles and Pins*. I've been a big Colin Franklin reader for a while, and I was curious." Hazel's voice, an audible jolt of youth and ardor, was perfectly loud and clear and crisp. Everyone in the room had turned to get a good look at her, as though it were commonplace for an assistant to pick up the mic at a marketing meeting.

Didn't Hazel say Vera *had asked* her *to take a look?* thought Nella, as Oliver leaned over to whisper something in Alexander's ear at the big table. Alexander nodded his head in the direction of Maisy.

"And I'll say this, if I may," Hazel continued. "I think the Black protagonist and her family will really resonate with audiences of color, particularly those who are struggling with addiction. My parents came of age during the crack epidemic in the city in the 1980s, and it brought back memories of stories they've told me—and how little anybody white seemed to care."

Some people nodded. Amy hummed a note befit for a church choir.

"I'll be honest. There are a few things about Shartricia that *some* people might call attention to . . ."

If Nella had any doubts that Hazel had cast a very direct glance in her direction, the pointed gaze of the balding production editor who was sitting in front of her confirmed it. She could feel everyone else staring at her, too.

"But overall, Colin did a really good job of bringing it home in a way that I think will connect with all readers. It'll be fun to see how it all comes together."

"Thanks, Hazel, for that," said Vera. She was beaming so hard that you'd have thought her puppy had stood up on its hind legs and started composing the next great American novel. Meanwhile, the PE still hadn't taken his eyes off Nella. His eyes were narrowed in hard, indisputable distrust.

Nella fake-coughed into her elbow.

"My pleasure! Thank *you* for letting me take a peek. And for giving me the opportunity to speak today." Hazel bowed her head.

Amy bowed her head in reply. "Yes, thanks, Hazel, for your thoughts. We'll definitely keep in mind the racially diverse angle, too. Great stuff, no?" she asked the room. It was a rhetorical question, but a few people verbally agreed anyway, not wanting to be mistaken for nonbelievers. Richard clapped his hands a couple of times.

"Great!" Vera said. "Okay, next: Kruegler. When we first met Kitty, she was a no-name debut author with no partner, and no kids, with seventy-five thousand dollars of college debt. But when *Translucent Shadows* hit, all of that changed . . ."

Nella reached a forefinger up to her face and pressed on her left nostril and counted to ten. The corners of her eyes were beginning to burn, and now that the PE was finally facing forward again, all she could do was focus on the back of his shiny, bare head. The tears were about to fall, she knew, and even though no one would probably notice—everyone was infatuated with Kitty Kruegler, a college dropout who'd gone on to be a professor at Princeton—crying was not an option. Showing any feeling wasn't an option. She knew what her colleagues would say. What her *mother* would say. *Damn it, Nell, you're a twenty-six-year-old editorial assistant working at one of the best publishing houses in the country. You've got nothing to cry about.*

What Nella couldn't have possibly explained to her mother was that the tears that threatened to flow down her cheeks weren't tears of sadness. They were hot, heavy tears of anger and embarrassment. She locked her jaw, trying to keep from looking over at Hazel. She was dying to see what the girl was wearing on her face, but was scared that if she moved her head even an inch, she'd need to scramble to the exit—or, worse, spring from her chair, grab Hazel by the shoulders, and give her a shake in front of all of their colleagues.

Nella sat stock-still like this for the next forty-five minutes, focusing only on her breathing and the sounds of the editors' voices. By the time Amy launched into her usual closing remarks about the market and the social climate for books and how important the work every single person in that room was doing, the heat had left Nella's face and her jaw had relaxed. She had so many questions for Hazel, but she knew that her best option was to keep calm and quiet. Wagner was not a good place for this conversation—it would be better to wait until they were at Curl Central.

Resigned for now, Nella casually turned her head to the left, feeling the tightness that had formed on her left side unfurl. When she turned back, she was surprised to see Hazel staring right at her, brows scrunched and eyes clouded over, like she was thinking something through.

Bring Owen. Coming from Hazel, this had sounded more like a command than a suggestion. But no. That wasn't why those words had rubbed Nella the wrong way. What had confused her in that moment was the sound of Owen's name coming from Hazel's mouth. Nella hadn't ever mentioned it to Hazel. Not even in passing. She was certain of that. And Owen was nowhere on her Facebook—he didn't believe in social media, bless his free-spirited heart, and she respectfully kept him off her page. She didn't use Facebook like that anymore, anyway.

Nella held Hazel's stare, radiating as much blatant condemnation as she could. Hazel withstood all of it with an air of neutrality. Then, she slowly turned her head back toward the front of the room, the beginnings of a slow, small smile creeping across her face.

Kendra Rae

September 26, 2018
Catskill, New York

You've got to help me. I feel like I'm going insane.

I took a long, deep breath, then raised my glass and took an even longer, deeper sip of my wine. I couldn't keep running away from this voice mail. I'd done everything I could to take my mind off it. I went out on the trail for an hour; I picked up some groceries and a case of pinot noir, too. I'd even done a little writing, just to give me something to do while I drank.

But I couldn't find any peace. Not once. I just kept hearing this girl's squeaky voice instead of my own.

I sighed and hit Play, her frantic rant filling up my kitchen for the umpteenth time.

"Look, I don't know who you are, or why you keep contacting me. And, actually, I don't even know why I'm calling *you*. You . . . stupid, creeper-stalker weirdo."

There was that light, snotty snort noise—the one that told me she'd been crying.

"God, I'm a mess. My *life* is a mess. Owen's been mad at me. Vera thinks I'm an unreliable assistant, and I'm definitely gonna lose my job . . . although truthfully, I don't even know if I want it."

The caller paused again. I wiped at the drop of pinot noir that had slid off the green bottle onto the table, smearing it across the cherrywood. I licked my finger and wiped at it again, counting down the four seconds that I knew would pass before she said, "No. That's not true. I—I *do* want it. I *want* to be an editor. How many young Black female editors are there? None." The girl sighed. "You keep telling me to leave, but I can't. I can't let Hazel . . ." Another snort, this one more self-deprecating than the last. "Fuck, I'm not sure why I'm telling you . . . whoever you are . . . any of this."

I don't know why you are, either, I'd thought on my first listen, pretty peeved, *because* you're *the unhinged wackadoo who contacted* me. The only person I ever contacted was Trace. She was my lifeline, the vein connecting me to my money, my family, the life I had before. Everyone else, it was better to avoid—my ex-colleagues, the few friends I had left over from Harvard.

I'd even left Diana behind, although that part was easier than it should've been. Honestly, I thought she'd at least offer a hollow apology to Trace for leaving me out on the vine to wither all those years ago. For making me feel like I was no longer welcome. For trying to change me.

Shoot, don't get me wrong—I know the timing of what I said wasn't perfect. But it didn't give her the right to try to do what she did.

I listened as the girl rambled on a little while longer, waiting. And then it came: the reason why I hadn't been able to think straight all day.

Wagner.

Hearing it for the fourth time didn't make it any easier. It all came surging back: the decades I spent running away from his name; the threats on my life; the Black parents who wrote telling me I'd no longer be seen as a role model in their households. Years had passed since I'd changed my hair, found a new job, and settled into a small town in upstate New York where folks didn't particularly feel like bothering their new Black neighbor . . . all to get away from that name. But then I got that voice mail from that Lynn girl saying something about Wagner and the work her "team" was doing. And now here Wagner was again, invading my life.

What were the chances these two messages weren't connected?

That this girl *wasn't* one of Lynn's people, sent by Lynn to force my hand?

I downed the rest of my glass, refilled it, then hit Play again, then again, until I pieced together a hazy picture: This anonymous caller worked for Vera Parini, a mousy waif of a white woman who'd been just a humble Wagner editorial assistant when I'd met her. And now Lynn—or one of her people—had given this poor girl *my* number. Probably hoping that she'd get me to come back to the city.

Sighing, I let my eyes rest upon the blues and golds of the Jacob Lawrence print my father had sent me just weeks before he passed. His funeral had fallen on a beautiful day, one considerably warm for March, and had been so full that my mother had to turn people away. At least, that's what Trace had told me.

I didn't go.

"But it's *Dad*," Trace had implored the week before he was put to rest. Through the phone I'd felt her pulling on my arm the way she did when we were children and she wanted my attention. "You can hide your face. Wear a wig. Anything. Just don't make me do this alone, Kenny."

I'd sucked my teeth. "They've been watching everyone at home just to see if I come back. They'll figure it out."

To anyone else—*almost* anyone else—I would have sounded like a lunatic. But Trace was my own flesh and blood, my best friend. She *had* to understand. She saw me in those final days before I left. *She* saw the change, too. There was no other logical reason for all of those years she spent helping me remain out of sight from Richard, from Diana, from all of it.

I feel like I'm going insane . . . My life is a mess . . .

My phone had gone black but I kept staring at it anyway as my insides changed their tune. Suddenly, I wished she hadn't blocked her number. I wanted the girl to call back, tell me more. Her panic wasn't that evergreen twentysomething self-centeredness of a life not going according to plan, I realized. Clearly, whatever this girl was experiencing ran down to the bone.

I leaned back in my chair, painfully aware of the battle between fear and compassion that was chipping away at my senses. That I even *felt* the tug-of-war surprised me; for so long, I'd let my desire to remain hidden dictate where I lived, where I shopped, whom I spoke to. When Lynn contacted me about all of her big theories about Wagner, and her even bigger ask, I'd told her in no uncertain terms that I wasn't interested in returning to the city. *It'd be crazy to risk it all now. I've finally found peace.*

But had I, *really*? Seventy wasn't far off, and here I was, living all by myself. I had only a few friends—acquaintances—and I was two weeks late sending notes to my client. Today's excuse? I'd gotten too wine-drunk on a weekday all by myself.

As much as I wanted to ignore it, my cracks weren't just showing—they were dominating. Whatever fragments of me that *were* left were poking hopelessly out of this lost girl's soliloquy.

I moved my wineglass so I could slide my laptop over and log in to Trace's Facebook account, which she let me use whenever I was feeling particularly lonely. I didn't know the name of the caller, but I did know whom she worked for, and whom she might work *with*: someone named Owen, and Hazel. But when I typed their names into the search bar, both yielded far too many results for me to comb through.

I pinched the bridge of my nose. After some deliberation, I pulled up Google and searched "Hazel" and "Wagner Books" together, expecting another avalanche of results. But halfway down the page was a link to a Facebook event hosted by a young woman named Hazel-May McCall. That very same evening, Hazel-May McCall's organization would be holding a reading at a Black hair salon in Brooklyn.

Among the confirmed attendees: Richard Wagner.

And the cosponsor of this event? Wagner Books.

This information sat strangely in my stomach, threatening to come back up with the wine I'd had for lunch. Desperately, I clicked Hazel's photo. Her dreadlocks were her most prominent feature; next in line was how socially involved she was. But her timeline said she'd been at Wagner for barely two months.

Either Richard had experienced a massive change of heart, or, more likely, he had An Angle. Why else would he give so much money *and* publicly post that he couldn't wait "to support the importance of increasing diversity in publishing"? This was the same man who had invited me over for dinner my first week at Wagner so his fancy white wife could tell me, "woman to woman," that I'd never make it in publishing if I didn't tame my hair and talk like I was from Northampton, not Newark. The same man who told me a couple of years later that *Burning Heart* seemed "too niche" to find a real audience, but that Diana was pretty enough, and I was smart enough, and if Black people could be international pop stars, then we would certainly get some traction.

The same man who'd angled his way into our spotlight the moment it became a bestseller.

I considered this young woman's dreadlocks, her hand on her hip. Was Richard sleeping with her? It was a shameful thought, but not a far-fetched one. She didn't have that soft, easy glow he'd always gravitated toward, though. Hazel was emitting something else entirely.

He couldn't possibly. *She* wouldn't possibly. She seemed too strong for him. Too . . . *solid.*

But so had Diana.

All of a sudden, my legs went to work on their own, sweeping me into my living room and leaving me at the mahogany bookshelf I'd purchased from a tag sale shortly after moving to Catskill. I was running a finger across the worn-out spines of books I'd collected over the last fifty years when I finally realized what I'd come here for.

Ralph Ellison and Toni Morrison whispered at me to pick them up, give them another spin, but I resisted the temptation and dropped to my knees for a better view of the bottom row. There was Gordon Parks's memoir, a biography of Billie Holiday, and a collection of other books about Black creatives. I'd never understood people who alphabetized their libraries; I only believed in arranging mine by themes—and even *that* could be tricky. So, I read every spine, scanning the old issues of *JET* and *Ebony* until I found a spine too small to read.

There.

I reached for the thin slice of pages prudently, wary of keeping its fiftysomething-year-old spine intact. This was it: the old theater program from the performances of Amiri Baraka's *The Slave* and *The Toilet* that my parents had taken me to see when I was fourteen years old. I held it in my hands for a few moments, recalling how many times my father reminded me during that ride to St. Mark's Playhouse that Baraka was from Newark, too. Then I opened the program, stuck my hand in the flap, and unearthed the photo proof I hadn't looked at in years.

There we were, Diana and me, posing for a magazine cover that never was. I was in black and she in rose, and we both had shoulder pads so sharp you could've cut your finger on them. The photographer had suggested we put our fists in the air, which we both thought was too corny, so we'd agreed to stand back-to-back with our arms crossed and our eyebrows raised—because for whatever reason, that had seemed like the more natural pose at the time. At the bottom of the page, written across our brown ankles, were the words "A New Era in Publishing?"

The punctuation of the title aggravated me now as much as it did then. *Why present it as a question?* I'd asked the editor in chief. The fact that we were going to be on the cover of a prestigious magazine had made it so. To me, at least.

But then I opened my mouth. Then, they pulled the cover. And what had become of this so-called new era?

I placed the proof and the program on the couch and returned to the kitchen. Just ten minutes ago, I'd wanted to reach inside my phone and tell this stranger that being an editor *wasn't* worth it—that if she wasn't careful, she might turn into someone like me. Or worse.

At the same time, I'd wanted to smash the phone against the wall.

I didn't. Instead, I focused on the Jacob Lawrence print again, on the sturdy Black arms that would push a cart of library books for an eternity, maybe longer. And I called Lynn.

Part III

12

September 26, 2018

Malaika held a tuft of synthetic 4B hair that had been dyed powder blue up to her hairline. "You know she's trying to fuck with you, right?" she asked, leaning toward one of the mirrors that bookmarked the aisle of hair dye products. "That's all it is. She's trying to fuck with you."

Nella reached for yet another hair product, held it up to the light, and squinted. They'd walked through the front door of Curl Central almost ten minutes ago, but her eyes still hadn't adjusted enough to its low lighting to read the jar labels from a reasonable distance. "'Good Vibes,' this one is called. Supposedly, massaging this product in your scalp two times a day will make you feel 'good vibes, good fun, and have an all-around good time. Perfect for the beach, the bar, or for just bingeing Netflix in your living room.'"

Malaika snorted. "How about for the office? Because it sounds like your place needs some good vibes. Those coworkers of yours might need some, too."

Nella imagined herself handing Sophie a jar of Good Vibes hair grease, pictured her smoothing it in between her two French braids in the ladies' room. If such a carefree response had felt readily available to her, she might have laughed. But she didn't. A touch of embarrassment from the marketing meeting earlier that day—*and* her subsequent breakdown—brushed her cheeks. She hadn't told Malaika she'd actually called the anonymous person earlier that day, and she didn't plan on doing so anytime soon. Malaika would judge her if she knew, and rightfully so.

"How are things, by the way? You haven't gotten any other notes since that second one with the phone number, correct?" Malaika asked, noticing her friend had suddenly gone quiet.

"Uh, nope. No more notes since September seventh."

"That's good. But damn, after today . . . they've *gotta* be coming from Hazel. Right?"

Nella did nothing but shrug her shoulders, a gesture that Malaika either couldn't see or outright ignored.

"She knows there's only space for one Black girl, and she wants to be it. I think she wants you *out*, girl," Malaika continued, picking up a green tuft of hair next. "She's playing you. How else would she have snuck those notes to you so smoothly, without you noticing? And the way she threw you under the bus today, in front of everybody?"

"I don't know. But I plan to talk to her about it tonight. Did I tell you she brought Owen up, too? By name. Even though I'm sure I've never mentioned his name to her. Not ever."

Malaika's eyes went wide. "Never? You sure?"

"Definitely. I mentioned I had a boyfriend, but that's it. And you know how he wouldn't touch social media with a ten-foot pole. He hates it so much he has interns do that part of the job at work."

"Right. So when you say you want to 'talk' to Hazel, do you mean . . . ?" Malaika's outline mimed removing her earrings one by one.

"No," said Nella, giggling. "I mean, *actually* talk. Innocent until proven guilty." The words, acrid on Nella's tongue, came out sounding a lot more self-righteous than she meant them to.

"But you can't—"

"I wonder what kind of chemicals go into 'good vibes,'" Nella intoned, changing the subject. "Panthenol, glycerol, fructose . . ."

Malaika made a *pft* sound as she sullenly went back to fingerpicking the fake tuft of green hair.

Nella put the Good Vibes grease back and leaned closer to the shelf. She was intent on holding it together tonight. She couldn't just run into a closet at Curl Central and leave another crazy message on some stranger's machine.

"This line of hair products is crazy. How is this a thing? There's one called 'Chill Pill,' 'Turnt 'n' Free,' 'Strut Ur Stuff'—"

"What's in 'Strut Ur Stuff'?"

"Probably all of the things that are in 'Good Vibes.' And something spicy? I don't know."

"Garbage for your scalp," Malaika said dismissively. She placed the tuft of green hair back on the rack next to the mirror, dejected. "I want to do it so bad."

"Do what?"

"Put color in my hair. Something plant-based, obviously. I'm just really craving a change, you know?"

"I do," Nella said, recalling that hot summer day she'd walked by a barbershop in Bushwick and decided to finally cut all of her relaxed hair off. "Why don't you just go for it? Your hair would look bomb with some blue or green, especially when you pull it into those cornrows like you do sometimes."

"Even if I had the balls to do it, I know I'd hear about it from Igor for, like, a month. You know how he is about these kinds of things."

Nella nodded. Igor *had* had a particularly hard time adjusting to the tiny emerald-green nose piercing Malaika had whimsically had done the previous summer. He'd thrown a fit, telling Malaika in no subtle terms that "her choice in nose jewelry might come off a certain way to potential clients." Malaika had griped and groaned about it, but she'd received the message and taken out the piercing anyway. The pay was too good, and having her own place in Fort Greene was even better.

"Okay, no hair dye. But did you want to get anything else from this aisle? Like hair grease or something?"

"Girl, you know I don't believe in buying hair grease. It's like buying barbecue sauce."

"You've started making your own barbecue sauce, too?"

"Pinterest is an invaluable resource."

Nella laughed—a real laugh this time—and playfully smacked Malaika's arm. "Let's go, Mal. I want to take a peek at Iesha B.'s book before this thing starts."

"Miss Iesha B.! Oh, yes, please." Malaika hustled ahead of Nella, the neon pink swooshes of her Air Jordans the only visible part of her shadow. Nella followed giddily behind her. They'd spent an unhealthy amount of time poking fun at Miss Iesha B., wondering whether or not she ate steak or believed in the Illuminati, or if she'd be present at the reading that evening. It was this last reason that had gotten Malaika to attend the reading, since Nella's plea for Malaika to "do it for the culture" hadn't quite moved the needle. Not on a weeknight, at least.

"Do we have time before this poetry thing starts?" Malaika asked. "I want to see if the books are actually worth the ten bucks she's charging."

Nella nodded. She'd clocked both the bookshelf and the bathroom as soon as they entered, a habit she performed whenever she entered someone's home, and she led the way to the back of the store, deftly sidestepping two other young Black women who were closely eyeing a selection of bright sprays that doubled as perfumes and moisturizers. One had a mouth full of braces; the other had a teeny-weeny fro that reminded Nella of her own shortly after she'd done The Big Chop.

"This one's supposed to make you less anxious," said the girl with all the metal in her mouth, whose black cabbie hat and box braids were a clear homage to Janet circa *Poetic Justice*. "Maybe this'll help me with the SAT?"

"Nahhh," her friend replied. "Go with the Serenity Spray instead. My sister swears by it. And you know she got into Fordham Law."

Nella held back a knowing chuckle at the idea of a spray that promised serenity in a world doomed by horrific school shootings and senseless church bombings and irreversible global warming. But as she and Malaika turned a corner, her amusement at their earnest exchange deepened to envy as she thought of all those youthful years of hair she'd lost out on thanks to chemical relaxers. How *big* her fro would be now if she hadn't hated her roots so much then.

She couldn't dwell too hard on this, though, because Malaika suddenly stopped and let out one loud, ear-piercing shriek.

"Sweet lord. It's even better than I imagined it would be!"

Nella moved forward to see what Malaika was freaking out about. The squeal had been well earned. Standing tall in front of them, showered in a bright beam of white light, was a laminated, life-sized cardboard cutout of Miss Iesha B. herself. Atop each side of her head were two honey-colored buns that were the size of Cinnabon rolls. Her lips were freckled with rose-gold glitter lipstick, and she had one gloved hand on her hip while the other held a blow-dryer with its nose pointed up, Blaxploitation-style. If not for the Kente-cloth-patterned smock that was tightly tied around her waist, or the speech bubble coming out of her mouth that said "I'M HAIR TO HELP," Nella would have assumed this woman was not Miss Iesha B. at all, but a heroine from a graphic novel.

"What in the . . ." Nella said, trying to keep her giggles contained.

Malaika started to cackle with reckless abandon. "Shit, do we think they sell this apron here? I'd rather spend forty bucks on that instead of the book."

Nella's shoulders were shaking. "Shhh. One of them might hear us."

"'I'm hair to help.' What else do you think they came up with? 'I'll be hair for you'? 'Iesha B. here, your friendly neighborhood psycho-hair-apist'?"

"Mal!"

"I'm sorry. This is just too funny. I'm sorry," she repeated, her voice still at full volume. She turned around so she could position herself for a selfie. "I gotta send this to my cousin. She's studying cosmetology."

Embarrassed, but not quite enough to shush her friend again, Nella picked up a copy of *Black Hairapy: Ten Ways to Key into the Power of Your Locs*, skimming its pages for the kernels of truth that the copy on the Curl Central website had promised Miss Iesha B. would deliver. The writing wasn't bad, but judging by the font—three times too big in her opinion—it was pretty obvious that the book had been made in someone's basement. She turned it around to study its spine. It was a Wagner-inspired habit that drove Owen just a little bit bonkers every time she did it, especially when they were in someone else's home, and she felt a touch of relief that he hadn't arrived at Curl Central just yet.

Nella put the book down, ready to hop into the photo with Malaika and Miss Iesha B., when a voice trilled, "Remember, all proceeds go to the school!"

They turned around quickly, busted. It was Juanita Morejón in the flesh, looking just as she had in the photo Nella had seen of her online, high-waisted skirt and crop top and all—except this time, her ensemble was decorated with black-and-white horizontal stripes. "And all purchases come with a half-priced drink!"

"Yes, I've heard," Nella said, smiling brightly and holding out a hand. "That's awesome. Juanita, right? Nella. I work with Hazel at Wagner Books."

"Oh! *You're* Nella. It's so nice to meet you! I've heard so much about you," Juanita said. Before Nella could prepare herself, Juanita was pulling her into an unexpectedly tight embrace that she didn't think she'd earned. The hug was soft and smelled a lot like cocoa butter, and the familiarity of the scent put Nella a little more at ease. "Hazel isn't here yet. I think she was taking the Young, Black 'n' Lit girls out for dinner before they read tonight. Isn't that sweet?"

She hesitated far too long, prompting Nella to contribute a reluctant "cool."

"But we are both so glad you could make it. She mentioned that tonight you had an important meeting with an *agent*?" To accentuate this last word, Juanita held up her long, pointy fake fingernails, which glittered and twitched in full spirit-finger mode.

"We ended up rescheduling. Turned out the person I was supposed to meet with couldn't do any other time today, and I didn't want to miss this."

Malaika coughed beside her—not because she was uncomfortable with not having been formally introduced to Juanita, but because she'd been particularly vocal about Nella's sacrifice.

For a bunch of high school girls you've never met? Malaika had asked.

For the culture! Nella had repeated.

"This is my friend Malaika. She didn't want to miss this, either. She's a huge fan of poetry."

Two out of three of these statements were untruths, but in the dimmed lighting, Nella knew Juanita couldn't see the treacherous look Malaika was throwing her way. "Welcome, welcome, welcome! So glad you could come, too," Juanita said, pushing back one of her long curly tendrils with her razor of a pinky nail. For whatever reason, Malaika did not receive a bone-crushing hug; it was better this way for the both of them, Nella knew. "Please—if you have any questions about any of our products, let me know. If this is your first time here, though, I highly recommend scheduling an appointment with Miss Iesha B. before doing anything else. She'll happily tell you which products you might try in order to get through your hair ups and downs."

She stopped speaking for a moment and peered closer at Nella's hair. "And, just so you know, we have plenty of deep-conditioning moisturizers and sprays that will zip your roots right up, too."

Nella's hand flew up to her scalp, which did, now that she thought about it, feel a bit dry.

"So great to meet you both! One last thing: If you Instagram anything—please, if you can, remember to tag Curl Central. But be sure to try to leave any drinks out of the photo," she added hastily, "since we don't have a liquor license yet. You feel me? Great! See you ladies soon." Juanita clapped her hands once, then made her way over to the high school girls who were still debating on the Serenity Spray.

Nella felt her roots again, then looked over to see which face Malaika was wearing. It was hard to tell, since she wasn't quite in Miss Iesha B.'s spotlight. But before Nella could ask, Malaika snorted once and said, "She looks like a Real Housewife."

Nella snorted, too. "She doesn't have a liquor license, and she's serving alcohol in a place where high school students will be reading? No judgment, but . . . judgment."

"Judgment," Malaika said. "But I'm also just a little bit here for it."

Not altogether atypically, Owen showed up two minutes before the reading was supposed to start, after nearly every seat had been filled. Nella waved at him, first casually and then, when this method did not work, spasmodically, until he noticed the three center seats that she and Malaika had secured in the back row.

"Leave it to one of the only white people at this event to show up on CP Time," Malaika observed as Owen made his way over to them.

"Didn't Jesse tell us to give up 'CP Time'?"

"Oh god, yeah. 'Time is yet another construct that was created and upheld by people who don't look anything like me. Some constructs are valid. Other constructs are constructed just to prevent other constructs from being constructed.' Whew, he was definitely . . ." Malaika took a hit from an imaginary blunt.

Nella laughed, continuing where Malaika left off in her best old Black man impression. "'Therefore, my brothas and my sistas, we *need* to stop and think every time we use the phrase "Colored People Time." Each time we use it, we're merely reinforcing the stereotype that there is just *one* kind of "time," and that there is a problem with Black people not adhering to this particular kind of time. I show up when I show up. It's my prerogative. I make my own constructs.'"

"Man, fuck that. Talking about CP Time is as natural to Black folk as worshipping Angela Bassett. There's no denying it. Maybe *that's* why he's taking a break from social media now—because he finally accepted that all of that is a construct, too."

It was a fair point, but Nella was more interested in Owen's progress than continuing the riff. It had taken him far too long to get past a Black bookish couple who were deep in the throes of a heated debate; now, the only thing in his way was a group of four eclectically dressed Black women. As he climbed over them politely, offering apologies galore, each one of them looked up at him with curiosity, trying to figure out where this young white man—red-faced and brown-haired and one of now two white people in Curl Central that evening—was aiming to sit. When he stopped by Nella and Malaika, the woman sitting on the far end of the row said something in a voice too low for Nella to hear. Another woman responded spiritedly, using her hands to help illustrate whatever point she was trying to make, and they all nodded in consensus with raised eyebrows.

Nella tried not to wonder what their court had decided as she stood up halfway to plant a kiss on her boyfriend's cheek. "You made it!"

"Sorry. I had to go into the office because something was up with the Internet. And by the time I got to the theater, there was a long line at the ticket booth, and I just missed the first train." Nella got a faint whiff of perspiration mixed with a little bit of ire as Owen removed his messenger bag and stuffed it under his folding chair. "What's up, Mal?"

"Oh, the usual. Drinkin' wine. 'Bout to get 'cultured.'"

"Any luck getting our *Blob* tickets switched?" Nella asked him.

"Nope. The other showing is full, and even if it weren't, the guy at the booth said their return policy doesn't include swapping movie showtimes as an option."

Nella groaned. "Damn, babe. I'm sorry. We'll definitely catch the next one. And it'll be on me."

"It's fine. I just better hear some really good poetry tonight. Like, *for colored girls*–level," Owen said, a little less grumbly. "My soul better grow wings and fly away by the time this thing is over. Then, I'll forgive you. *May*be."

"I appreciate that you referenced Ntozake Shange," said Nella playfully, "and not Maya Angelou. Ntozake's kind of a deep cut."

"It shows he has depth," Malaika agreed. "Let's keep your boyfriend, shall we?"

"I think we should." Nella smiled and squeezed Owen's thigh.

Owen rolled his eyes, although their banter had visibly loosened him up some. He probably would never admit it, but Nella knew he secretly reveled in the attention she and Malaika gave him. After all, Owen had come a long way from being referred to by Malaika as just "Nella's Latest White Boy" for much of their first year together, and not always behind his back. A cross between the sister Nella had never had, and the mother that she did, Malaika had been fairly skeptical about Owen's intentions from the get-go. She'd had enough of her own experiences with white dudes to believe that Owen would inevitably unleash the douchebag entitlement that she presumed more or less every white man had within him.

Nella understood this. Her college roommates had dragged her to so many white frat parties that, when she'd first met Owen online, it'd been impossible not to be skeptical of him herself. Being one of the only Black girls at these parties often meant being noticed immediately—and if she was alone, which was fairly often, it meant being eagerly approached. She knew what these bros saw as they walked over: a long-legged Black girl wearing a tight crop top and even tighter high-waisted jeans. A long-legged Black girl on her own, drinking. An easy target. Nella would endure the bros' chitchat about what year she was, and how she'd gotten into the frat house (her roommate, Liv, usually; she practically lived in the student center). But to the bros' surprise, and often disappointment, Nella would ask real questions back—not just *where are you from* but *what are your favorite books* and *what's your favorite way to get to the quad*—and suddenly a bro who thought they'd eventually end up in a bathroom, the zipper of her high-waisted jeans between his teeth, was instead having a clean heart-to-heart about one of his favorite literary characters. He would find it baffling, but he'd play along, sometimes opening up more than he'd probably ever opened up at a frat party . . .

. . . Until he realized that Nella's zipper had no intention of coming down. That was usually about the time the bro's lights went out, his cup ran dry, and he ran off. A horse in search of easier pastures.

When Nella was a freshman and sophomore, this flip of the switch had disappointed her. In those days, she still held on to the idea that she might meet someone in college—maybe in the dining hall, when a guy asked her for the chair she wasn't using, or on the grounds, when she was deep in thought, contemplating that A-minus. Maybe even at a frat party, eighteen-year-old Nella supposed, because this was what happened to girls in movies and television shows.

Then she graduated, moved to the city, and grew up. She downloaded a few dating apps on her phone and didn't try so hard at bars. Many men still flipped that switch when they met her—not just white men—and eventually she found one who didn't. From their first exchanges on OkCupid to beers at The Jeffrey, it was clear to Nella that Owen had nothing to shift *to*. Blessedly, he had just one gear—"thoroughly interested"—and once he'd stuck around long enough to prove that their relationship was anything but just an itch he was scratching, Nella's feelings for him crystallized.

Malaika's reins had loosened, too. She didn't stop calling him Nella's Latest White Boy, but she did treat him as a worthwhile suitor, even started to joke about his blind spots as a white cis man in front of him. In return, Owen seemed—somewhat paradoxically—at ease. If people were making fun of him, he preferred to be let in on it, which was why Nella felt comfortable repeating Malaika's CP Time joke directly to him.

"Guess you're rubbing off on me," he quipped back, laughing. "Hey, how was work? And how did it go with the literary agent? Is she going to start sending you lots of cool 'commercial-but-still-literary shit'? Her words for the genre, not mine," Owen added in response to Malaika's raised eyebrow.

Nella avoided eye contact with her friend, knowing the look on Malaika's face was less about Owen's genre mash-up and more about the truth. "Work was fine," she lied. "And I'll tell you all about it on our way home."

"That's great." Owen unzipped his black bomber jacket and took a good look around the space, examining first the crowd of forty or so guests, then the row of four hair-washing sinks brimming with ice and cans of Red Stripe and PBR. "Innovative. Do you think I have time to grab a drink?"

Their three sets of eyes traveled together to the front of the room, where the line of chairs that had been reserved for Hazel and the readers sat unoccupied. Another appraisal of the white people sitting in the audience suggested that Richard hadn't arrived yet, either.

"You've got plenty of time," Nella sighed.

Owen didn't look convinced. "That's not Hazel?" he asked, bobbing his head in the direction of Juanita. She was leaning over a patron a few rows down, laughing and still poking back hair with various glittery fingernails. The pink liquid in her clear plastic cup sloshed around in her other free hand every few moments, threatening to spill over onto her outfit, but she did not seem bothered by this. Nor did she seem bothered by the fact that Hazel still hadn't arrived yet.

"No. That's the woman who owns Curl Central."

"Ah." Owen stood up. "Okay, then. I'm going to get something to drink. You ladies doing okay?"

"Another Red Stripe? Please?" Nella squeezed his thigh again, this time a bit pleadingly. If Owen felt her nails dig a bit too deeply into his leg, he didn't notice, because he said, "Got it. Mal?"

"I'm good, but thanks."

Owen climbed over Nella and then the four women again, who were far less forgiving than they were the first time around. Everyone was beginning to get antsy. The people sitting in front of them had long since run out of things to talk about with their neighbors, and they had gotten to the point at which they were tired of trying. It was a quarter after seven, and Juanita had yet to make an announcement acknowledging what everyone else seemed to know: that they were running behind.

"Does he know anything about all the stuff that's been going on at work?" Malaika asked.

"Well . . . I haven't exactly told him."

"You *haven't told him* about the notes? Or how Hazel has undermined you in every possible way? How she took that front desk lady with the scarves away from you? How she's even taken Vera—although we didn't really want her?"

"Nope."

"But why not?"

"The Hazel stuff, I'm not sure he'd understand. The notes stuff . . . I know he'll flip and tell me to do something I don't want to do." *He'd also chastise me for calling the phone number,* Nella thought, *and so would you.*

"Which is what, exactly?"

"Report it to HR."

"And that doesn't seem like a good idea to you at this point?"

"I told you already. I feel like I'm still kind of on thin ice with the higher-ups. I should probably figure this one out on my own."

Malaika crossed one leg over the other and bounced her foot—a clear sign of impatience. "You wanna know something?"

"I already know it. I'm being irresponsible."

"Wrong. Well, yes. But I was *going* to say that you still could have met that agent for a drink. See what time it is?"

"Please. Don't," Nella grumbled. She was about to check the time on her cell phone when the front door of Curl Central swung open. In clicked Hazel, looking like a literary deity in a black turtleneck, a pair of gold-rimmed glasses, and tight-fitting violet corduroy overalls. The young readers followed closely behind her, all flushed faces and guilty smiles as they quickly hurried into the four empty seats in the front row.

Just like that, the tension in the room melted into a shower of applause. Someone called out, "There you are, Hazel-May!" Another person hooted, "Yasss, you go, girl!"

Nella was slow to put her hands together.

"He's not here," she said, having to strain a bit to be heard above the cheers.

"Who's not here?"

"Richard Wagner."

Malaika stared at her blankly. Not one for clapping or for waiting, she'd stopped after a few seconds and had gone back to resting her free arm across her torso.

"My boss-boss. The real reason why I came here, instead of meeting up with that agent."

Malaika shrugged. "I thought your main mission was to confront the new Black girl. You're not going to back out of that now, are you?"

"No. And I can have *two* missions," Nella snapped, sounding a bit like a child as Owen passed in front of her once again to get to his seat. He looked at her quizzically as he handed her a Red Stripe, but said nothing.

"Y'all, I am *so* sorry!" Someone had handed Hazel a headset and now she was walking, TED Talk–style, across the front of the room. "I was just grabbing some food with these amazing girls and we got held up by the buses. MTA, my people, amirite?"

The crowd murmured collectively in agreement.

"Alright, before I get started, I'd just like to tell y'all a little something. Is that okay? Do any of you mind if I tell y'all a little something first?"

"Tell it, sis," a woman—probably the same woman who'd told Hazel to *Go, girl!*—cried out.

"We were over at Peaches before we got here. Y'all know Peaches, right?" A cheer from a few of the audience members. "And we had a damn good meal, let me tell you. Fried green tomatoes, catfish, you name it . . . all the fixins. I swear, when someone asks me which has better cuisine—Harlem or Bed-Stuy—I have to betray my grandmama, God rest her soul, and say Bed-Stuy does it better."

A few more cheers and a *No she didn't*. Nella's stomach gurgled. The cubes of cheese Juanita had set out for the event were no hush puppies, but she was beginning to regret not popping a few pieces into a napkin the way that Malaika had upon their arrival. She'd resisted because she didn't want to have bad breath when she spoke to Richard. But now, with Richard nowhere in sight, she felt like she could eat an entire fistful of pepper jack and cheddar cheeses, toothpicks and all.

"I bet he's not coming," Nella grumbled, leaning over so she could whisper in Malaika's ear.

Malaika put her hands up as if to say *What can you do?*

"—Peaches, with a gentleman I started working for nearly two months ago," Hazel continued. "Richard Wagner: Do any of you know him? Maybe you don't, specifically. But you do know his books, and you know his authors, I'm sure. You know *Blue Sky* and you know *Going, Gone.* You know *Leaving Jimmy Crow.* And I know you all know Diana Gordon's *Burning Heart*, too."

Someone sitting behind Nella let out a whoop. Hearing this, Hazel held up the drink that someone had handed to her at some point during her soliloquy. A smattering of others lifted their own cups in solidarity.

"*Burning Heart* was a shining light in a valley of darkness. Or should I say, *white*ness," Hazel continued, and a few people nodded their heads. "It took on some very difficult topics, and we are all the better for it now. So, when I finally found myself at Wagner, I took a chance and asked him how he'd feel about helping sponsor our girls. A small piece of trivia that some of you may know: Ms. Gordon *and* her editor, Kendra Rae Phillips, were both teenagers when they discovered their passion for the written word. It's *such* an impressionable time, you feel me?

"Anyway, it felt big, what I was asking of Richard. But to my surprise, not only was he enthusiastic about it, he donated ten thousand dollars."

The audience hollered. "Sweet Baby Jesus," a bald-headed woman sitting in front of Nella said, to nobody in particular. Malaika tried to catch Nella's eye, but Nella didn't latch on.

"I am also thrilled to say that for every dollar we make tonight on hair product sales, Richard plans to match it! And—" Another round of applause befell the crowd. Hazel waited for it to peter out, smiling and closing her eyes contentedly, seasoned politician–style. Once the noise finally ceased, she continued on.

"I know, it's great. Money is great. But there's one more thing. Something even more lasting, and more valuable. Richard Wagner has also pledged to rethink the way editors at his company hire new candidates. He's going to do this by focusing on new criteria. By using a more holistic approach. And he'll be doing a full analysis of every book Wagner has bought in the last ten years to see how it compares with the demographics of our country.

"Y'all—for those who aren't aware of just how much the publishing industry has struggled to address its diversity problem, this is huge. *Huge*. Wagner has been predominantly white for some time, and, well . . . we all know we've been waiting for our next *Burning Heart* for far too long.

"And since Wagner is at the front of the curve, it will no doubt impact the way other publishing houses think about publishing, too! My people—this is *Just. The. Beginning*."

"Wow." The lilt of surprise in Owen's voice was barely audible over the thunderous ovation that had seized the audience. He grabbed Nella's knee as he said, "That's a pretty big deal, isn't it?"

Nella nodded, even as her blood turned cold. For the second time that day, she felt her eyes start to burn as people clapped their hands high above their heads. Those with plastic cups smacked their thighs wildly, cheering Hazel on. Even Malaika was smiling and snapping her fingers the way she did whenever she listened to *The Read*.

Nella was supposed to be ecstatic, too. No, not just ecstatic—she should have given Hazel a standing ovation, complete with foot-stomping and hip-shaking and one of those two-fingered mouth-whistles that she didn't know how to do but always wished she did. *Or* she could have really made a statement by strolling up to the front of the room, grabbing the mic from Hazel, and spilling all the sweet tea. She could tell everyone all about how she'd tried and failed to start a diversity committee at Wagner, about how the one time her coworkers were particularly attentive toward the notion of diversity was during Black History Month, when they'd asked her to blackify Wagner's Twitter and Instagram accounts during the month of February. She could tell them all about the small group of people who were making big decisions about which books were and weren't worth publishing, and how this, in turn, affected which kinds of books the public would see on bookshelves for years to come. She could tell them all about which titles hadn't made it through the front gate, simply because that small group of decision-makers could not foresee a certain demographic buying it.

She could tell them about Shartricia.

A few times—mostly when Nella first started working at Wagner—she'd tried to advocate for books written by Black writers about Black people. Kindly, she'd been overruled. White voices of dissent came not just from Vera, but also from other editors, as well as Amy. Their reasons were vaguely specific enough to quiet her qualms—at least, they were until the next time she met up with Malaika to rehash the latest. Over drinks, she'd deliver her best imitation of these white voices—which, for some reason, often meant putting on a posh British accent, even though none of her coworkers were British. *From a financial standpoint, this book just doesn't seem worth the gamble. I just didn't connect with the characters. The writing just wasn't strong enough.*

Nella found this last excuse particularly amusing, since it was a phrase that could be and often was said by literally anyone who read anything, ever, at Wagner. As if all writing *weren't* subjective; as if anyone who read an early draft of any book could be 100 percent sure that it would become a bestseller. The way her colleagues would "run numbers" had surprised her—how they compared books they were thinking of buying with books that had already been published, as though culture were something static and predictable, as though one set of past numbers could dictate any future success.

But Nella had kept her mouth shut. Slowly but surely, in the hopes of making the ride a bit smoother—in the hopes of getting a promotion—she'd accepted every excuse. She'd picked her battles, if she dared pick any, wisely. After all, that was what she had been taught: to stand still for so long that when you started to run, they'd be so dumbfounded that they wouldn't even follow. Well, that was what Nella had been doing. Standing still.

And now here was Hazel, miles ahead.

In that moment, it didn't matter that her new coworker had single-handedly discovered how to turn the status quo upside down in just a couple of months. Nor did it matter that Hazel had found a way to open the door for other people of color at Wagner. All Nella could think was that she felt redundant.

Utterly and painfully redundant.

It was impossible to get Hazel alone after the reading. Nella tried twice.

The first time, Hazel had waved a silent *hello* to her before continuing her conversation with a woman who appeared to be one of the students' parents. Nella let her be.

The second time, about fifteen minutes later, she saw Hazel head toward the bathroom in the back corner of the shop. She excused herself from Malaika and Owen and claimed she had to go to the ladies' as well. She thought she'd wait in line for Hazel and then pounce. But a tug on her arm when she was a mere five steps away from the bathroom deterred her from this mission, and she suddenly found herself in a conversation with Juanita and a young light-skinned Black man she'd seen putting out the folding chairs before the event started. He had a case of straight-up baby face, capped with a high-top fade and rounded out by what appeared to be a grill on his bottom set of teeth.

"Hey, girl! I thought maybe you'd be able to offer Andre some pointers," Juanita said to the space above Nella's head. She was clearly drunk, maybe even a bit coked out, and the pink liquid that had been in her hand earlier was replaced by a Miller High Life. "Andre, this is Stella. She works with Hazel-May at Wagner. Nicole, this is Andre—he's one of my best sweepers here. He's a freshman at Brooklyn College and he's trying to get his novel published."

"Sophomore," Andre said, at the same time Nella said, "Nella." They both stared at each other blankly, unsure of what the other had just said, but not in any particular need of clarification.

"Perfect! So how about you two chat. Talk! Converse! Parlez! I have a feeling this will be very productive." Juanita patted them each on the back and wandered off.

Nella had liked Andre's calm vibe—he reminded her of her baby cousin a little bit—and so she gave him fifteen minutes. It was long enough for him to tell her the synopsis of his book—"sort of like *Do the Right Thing*, but it's a sequel, and it's like, what would happen if Mookie killed Sal after Radio Raheem was killed by the cops, instead of helping him, and if it took place in Baltimore"—and long enough for her to tell him what she told any writer who pitched his or her novel to her, which was to get an agent first, before he paid some rando on the Internet eight hundred dollars to design a "dope-ass" cover.

Nella wished him luck and started to walk away, still unsure if that glint in his mouth was a grill or just a few golden teeth. But then he asked her if she'd take a look at his writing. When she said yes and gave him her work email, he grinned. She went back over to Malaika and Owen feeling vindicated, and much calmer than she had fifteen minutes earlier.

"Cool," Malaika said flatly, when Nella told her about *Mookie's Revenge* and, more importantly, Andre's grill. "But have you talked to homegirl yet? It's getting late and I want to start thinking about how I'm going to get home."

Nella reached over for Owen's arm to check his watch. It was getting close to ten and the trains were all rerouted thanks to late-night construction. With every passing minute, their way home was becoming less of a trip and more of an odyssey. "I need to talk to Hazel. Just give me ten minutes, okay? Owen, is that okay for you?"

Owen ran a hand across his jaw. "Aw, Nell. I'm so tired . . . and you know I have to wake up early tomorrow morning . . ."

"Ten minutes," promised Nella. "If I'm a minute longer, I'll pay for the car. Alright?"

Malaika raised her eyebrows.

"For *all* of us," Nella clarified.

"Fine," said Malaika. "But *only* ten. I have an early morning tomorrow, too, with Igor." Malaika scanned the crowd, which didn't take too much time since it had thinned out to about one-third of its original size. Many had started to trickle out roughly half an hour earlier, once they'd walked up to Hazel to give her a hug and wish her well. "Snake's over there."

Nella turned. Hazel and Juanita were standing by the windows that faced out onto the street, giggling into tightly wound fists about something. "Thanks. I'll be back."

"Let me know if you need anything, girl," Malaika said, pretending to take off her earrings again. "What?" she asked, when Owen made a face.

"Why is she a 'snake'? Do you have a problem with her or something, Nell?"

"I'll tell you all about it in the car," Nella said, an echo of herself. Again, this was a part truth. She would tell Owen about how Hazel had screwed her over with Shartricia, but not about the letters.

He was still eyeing Nella closely, like he could sense that she was lying. Because of *course* he could. They did live together, after all. "I feel like there's something else I'm missing here," Owen said, slowly.

Poor Owen: a man whom Nella loved, but who would almost always be one half step behind. "She's just been a little shady lately, babe," she said as soothingly as she could. "I just want to talk to her about a couple of things at work and then we'll go."

She started to walk away, but Owen spoke again. "Shady? That seems hard to believe. She seems pretty . . ." He trailed off, his eyes fixed on Hazel and Juanita.

That stopped Nella in her tracks. She didn't like the irritation that tinged every single part of her being, and she especially didn't like the way Owen was looking at the two Black women by the window. It was her own fault. She'd created this anxiety—not tonight, but weeks ago, when she'd first met Hazel and felt envious of Hazel's clothes and Hazel's sense of self-confidence.

And then there were Hazel's locs. About a year into dating, as Nella and Owen stood in line for hot dogs at Coney Island, he had asked her if she'd ever considered locking her hair. *You'd look pretty sexy with them,* he'd reasoned.

It hadn't been out of the blue: Standing in front of them had been a slightly older woman in a tight body-con dress with long, thick locs that went all the way down to her butt.

Nella had been impressed by her hair, too. Before Owen had commented on it, she'd even considered asking the woman if she did them all herself. But this comment—somewhat mitigated by Owen's loving hand on the small of her waist—had made her feel self-conscious about her own hair, her own sexiness. She'd been free from relaxers for only so long at that point, and her hair, all two inches of it, was still deciding on a curl pattern. The last thing Nella needed was the possibility of her boyfriend imagining her with long hair—whether it was Black natural hair he was imagining or not.

"'She seems pretty' what?" asked Nella. "How would you know?"

"We chatted for a bit. When you were off . . . I don't know what you were doing . . . she mentioned maybe joining forces between YBL and App-terschool Learning on a future project, and I thought—"

"'Joining forces,'" Nella parroted again, incredulous.

"She just seems really chill. And she seems really optimistic about being at Wagner, too—"

"Unlike me, right? Because I complain about my job all the time. *Right?*"

She crossed her arms. She hated the way she sounded—short, curt, one of those obsessive girlfriends Owen's friends always complained about—but she didn't appreciate the way her boyfriend was talking about Hazel right now.

Owen tore his eyes away from her just a little too quickly. "I'm just saying she seems nice. That's all. Never mind. Go."

That broke the spell. "I'm sorry, O," she said, stepping toward him so she could grab his hand. "I shouldn't have . . . I . . ."

"It's all good. Just go," he repeated, but this time the command was much gentler. He looked down at his watch. "The countdown begins."

Nella nodded. She'd have to be kinder to him later on. Then, she turned and made a beeline to where she'd seen Hazel and Juanita standing a moment before. Except now it was just Hazel, her arms resting loosely at her sides. She stared straight at Nella as she came closer, a statue of tranquility, as though she'd expected this very thing to happen at the exact moment it did.

"Nella! You made it."

Hazel always seemed so calm and composed, but it still stunned Nella how excruciatingly even her voice was. She tried to think of the right thing to say, suddenly feeling stupid for not having planned it on her way over. Nothing came to her.

"I'm glad at least *one* of my colleagues could be here tonight," Hazel continued. "Damn. Gina and Sophie had both sent me *sorry can't make it after all* texts, like, the minute they left the office this afternoon. Pretty whack, right? I think they were too scared to come out to Bed-Stuy after dark."

Nella had forgotten about them. They'd seemed so excited to come earlier. The three of them had even exchanged phone numbers, something she'd never considered doing with Gina or Sophie before.

"What did you think of the reading?" Hazel asked. For the first time, Nella noticed she had switched out her eyebrow stud piercing for a tiny hoop. "And the space? Pretty great, right?"

Nella took a half step forward and whispered, before she could lose her nerve, "What the *fuck* is your deal?"

"Sorry?"

"What the fuck is your deal? With Richard, and those notes, and with Colin's book . . ." Nella was shaking now; she couldn't help it. It upset her that her embarrassment had taken precedent over all of her other emotions, tenfold, and she wanted to start this interaction all over again. She was supposed to go through every one of her grievances calmly, one by one. She was not supposed to say "fuck." It was just that she and Hazel weren't in the kitchen or at their cubicles, and the expletive had flowed out of her mouth so easily, so fluidly.

"What? I'm sorry, girl, but you need to break it down for me a bit more." The gleam in Hazel's eye was too knowing, too deliciously pleased, to suggest that any explanation was necessary.

But Nella continued on. "And all that stuff about Richard. Is that true? Is he really going to try making Wagner more diverse?"

"Yes! We've already started talking about ways we can recruit for people of color."

There. Her presumptions had been right. That list she'd found on the printer *had* been a list of Black young women Richard was thinking of hiring.

Hazel squinted at her. "What? I didn't hear you."

Nella hadn't realized she'd spoken her thoughts aloud. "I said," she repeated, "I don't get it."

"Don't get what?" A trace of a grin hovered just beneath the surface of Hazel's nonplussed demeanor. "Let's slow down here. You must be referring to the marketing meeting thing today."

"I looked like an idiot," Nella said. "What made you change your tune so soon?"

Hazel laughed. "That wasn't about you at all. I finally finished *Needles and Pins* this morning, and guess what? I didn't hate it. Here, let's sit and talk for a minute. Is that cool? You got a minute?"

She gestured toward the folding chairs that had been set up for the reading. Andre had started to put away a few of them, but had been thrown off his task by the only Young, Black 'n' Lit Girl who'd stuck around after the main event. The two of them shared sips of something pink that was almost certainly not lemonade in the corner, moving closer to one another by the minute. Against Nella's better judgment, she sat down in the chair across from Hazel.

The only other person still in earshot was the woman who'd said something about Jesus during Hazel's speech. She glanced over her shoulder for just a second to see who had joined her in the seating area, then went back to looking at her phone. On the right side of her closely shaved head, Nella was able to make out a medium-sized pink scar. It was the shape of a small crescent, as though someone had taken their gel-manicured fingernail and dug it deep into the back of her head. The thought alone made Nella's own scalp hurt.

Hazel looked over at the girl, too. She frowned for a second, perhaps taking in the pink scar, too, before taking a seat. "Nella, I'm gonna be real with you, okay?" she said, her voice softening. "Black girl to

Black girl. That Shartricia book isn't great. Real talk, it's pretty badly written. Contrived. Caricature. You know that. *I* know that. And I'm pretty sure anybody outside this place who has any sense will pick up on that, too. That shit's offensive. It's embarrassing."

Nella swallowed. After the marketing meeting, a handful of colleagues had poked their heads into Vera's office so they could talk to her about how much they loved Colin's books. These same colleagues had then poked their heads into Hazel's cubicle, asking her personal questions about herself and her parents' lives growing up in the '80s in Harlem—questions that seemed invasive to Nella, but ones that Hazel had seemed more than happy to answer.

Nella had eavesdropped awkwardly from a few feet away. She'd tried to remember the last time anyone had asked her about her own personal life and decided it had probably been when she herself was the new girl—but even then, those questions hadn't really gone beyond *Where are you coming from?*

"So, wait," she said, confused. "What you said in the marketing meeting was—"

"An act?" Hazel said. "No, not quite."

"Then why do it?"

"Fine." Hazel looked around. Satisfied with how far out of earshot they were from anyone, she lowered her voice. "I'll tell you everything. But you can't tell anyone about this."

"Fine."

"Not even your friend. *Or* Owen."

Nella bit her lip. Hearing his name in Hazel's mouth wasn't any more normal now than it had been at the marketing meeting earlier.

"I mean it . . ." said Hazel.

"Fine. Just go ahead and say it."

"Okay. This is going to sound crazy, so just hear me out, okay?" Hazel twisted one of her locs and looked up at the ceiling. After about five seconds of this, she said, apprehensively, "There's this thing. I'm not sure if you've heard of it."

Hazel peeked over at the back of the girl sitting nearby. The scar was still facing them, her face now deep in her cell phone. "This thing—it's a kind of social phenomenon. It's called . . ." She inhaled deeply, then exhaled through pursed lips and leaned forward. " 'Code-switching.' "

The tips of Nella's ears started to burn as Hazel dissolved into a bout of giggles. "Never mind," she grumbled, starting to stand.

Hazel wiped at a tear. "Sorry, sorry. C'mon, you gotta admit that was funny. It was just too easy." Seeming to notice Nella wasn't smiling, she added, "So, what? You have regrets about saying how you felt about Colin Franklin's book now? Is that what's going on?"

"No," Nella said. At least, she didn't think she did. What was really bothering her, when she thought long and hard about it, was the feeling that Hazel not hating the Colin Franklin book—and actively looking at Nella while not hating it—had broken some sort of unspoken, inherent promise. Inherent should have been Hazel's hate for the Colin Franklin book. And the unspoken promise was that Hazel would more or less publicly back Nella up on all racial matters that arose in the office—or at least, would confer with her about it first. Wasn't that what Black people were generally supposed to do: stick together? Hadn't *Hazel* implied such loyalties when she'd first asked Nella for the scoop on Maisy?

Nella didn't know what to say. "I just wish I had known you were going to talk it up so much."

"I didn't realize it would mess things up *that* badly with Vera," Hazel said with a sigh. "I'm sorry. And don't worry. I'm going to definitely tell Vera which Shartricia places Colin can do a bit better on. I'm just going to be a little gentler with him, that's all. That's the only way he'll listen."

Nella stared at Hazel impassively.

"If you want, you can send me your notes and I'll incorporate them into mine before I share them. What do you think? I won't tell Vera they're yours."

Nella didn't like the idea of not getting credit for all of the time she spent reading the manuscript, even if Hazel was trying to be a bit helpful. She was also still feeling uneasy about Hazel in general. Was it possible that Hazel was so good at code-switching that she could switch herself into someone who wrote hate mail to her fellow Black coworker? Nella wasn't sure.

She *was* sure that it was getting late, and she needed to go home. "I have to go," she said simply, getting up from her seat. "My friends are waiting."

"I understand. But Dick is here now, in case you wanted to pop over and say goodbye to him on your way out."

"Who?"

"Ack, sorry . . ." Hazel mimed a facepalm as she stood, too. "I meant Richard."

"He's here?" Nella spun around. Sure enough, Richard Wagner had just strolled in, a dark denim jacket casually thrown over his right shoulder. He was walking steadily toward them, as though he hadn't shown up three hours late to the main event, as though it didn't matter, since he had donated ten thousand dollars to the organization.

"Richard! What's going on?"

"Hazel, hello!" he said cheerfully, his eyes never quite making it over to Nella. "So sorry to miss this. I made the mistake of getting into a long conversation with an author about the pros and cons of including the word 'the' in the beginning of the title of his next novel. Needless to say, it lasted for over an hour, and then I had a few other legitimate things to take care of and . . . well, time just flew away from me."

"Wow!" exclaimed Nella, just as Hazel said, at the same exact time, "Was it Joshua Edwards?"

Richard laughed and patted Hazel's shoulder. "You guessed it."

"Joshua Edwards? What a piece of work!" Nella heard herself say, a bit too loudly, her tone brightening considerably.

Richard looked over at her—for the first time, really—and smiled wanly. "Nella! What a pleasant surprise." Then he turned to face Hazel once more, his eyes two polished sapphires. "Please tell me you recorded a video of these girls reading. I think I'd like to include them on our website at Wagner somehow, maybe incorporate them into our social media."

"That sounds great! I think Juanita recorded everything. I'll introduce you to her soon."

Richard clapped his hands again. "Great. By the way, this place? Even better than you made it sound. You know . . . being here kind of reminded me of that film. What was that film that came out in the nineties, with the young African American man who's a poet, and the woman he falls for is a photographer?"

"Love Jones?" Hazel guessed.

Richard slapped his thigh. "Indeed! This feels quite like that movie."

Hazel supported his claim while Nella studied him through watchful eyes. The man looked downright *moved.* Like he might cry. *What do* you *know about* Love Jones*?* a vexed Angela Davis asked in Nella's head. *Not a damn thing.*

But Nella didn't dare utter a word. Maybe he had a soft spot for '90s rom-coms, or for Nia Long.

Or . . . maybe Richard was dating his *own* Nia Long. Maybe Kenny's agent—his mistress—was of the melanin persuasion. Nella grinned in spite of herself as Hazel said to Richard, "Isn't this space great? I've been compiling a mental list of all of the authors we could have here for readings and stuff, if you'd like to talk about it."

"Let's plan on it. How about before the week ends?"

Nella breathed out a loud, fake yawn, made a show of buttoning her jacket. "Well, it's getting late."

Richard nodded as he turned his attention to something on the wall behind her.

Curious, Nella turned to see what was so important. It was a large poster of a beautiful woman with bone-straight, just-blow-dried hair. A beautiful *ebony* woman.

"Um . . . I'm going to head home now," Nella said. "Nice to see you both."

She lingered as long as her dignity would let her, which happened to be the same amount of time it took Richard to point to the poster, turn to Hazel, and ask, "Does this woman work here?"

Nella ambled away, queasy. The snub stung more than Vera's or even India's had, because it hadn't just been a snub. It was a slap on the wrist, a punishment, an answer to the question that had been bugging her for weeks: Yes, Richard *had* heard about her problems with Colin's book—maybe from Vera, but also quite possibly from Hazel, too. *I wish all of our editorial assistants worked as hard as you,* he used to say to her in that first year, a glow in his eye whenever he saw her burning the midnight oil at her desk. *Vera's very lucky to have you.*

The sentiment seemed to have blown away in the wind.

Feeling a bit out of whack, Nella scanned the room until she spotted her boyfriend and best friend. They waved at her, thrilled at the prospect of leaving, before abruptly lowering their hands. Owen leaned over and murmured something to Malaika, who shook her head and closed her eyes.

Nella felt a tap on her shoulder.

"Hey—girl?"

Nella spun around. It was Hazel again. She was holding a small, bright blue jar in her hands that hadn't been there before. "I meant to give this to you before you left," she said, handing it over. "Remember how you were talking about how dry your ends get in the fall? This will help with that."

Nella accepted it, turning it around in her hands beneath the overhead light closest to her. There was no label, no ingredients listed. Just the blue of the plastic. "What's this?" she asked, unscrewing the cap and sniffing the jar's contents. It smelled a little like Brown Buttah, but a tad bit sweeter. A deeper inhale granted her a syrupy whiff of molasses.

"It's called Smooth'd Out. I swear by this stuff. Juanita uses it, too."

So *this* was the hair grease that Hazel was always wearing. More pomade than grease, Nella realized, as she dipped the tip of her pinky nail into the substance. "It's a leave-in conditioner?"

"Yep. Use it twice a day, or just once if you want. It's pretty great."

"Thanks." Nella wiped the bit of grease she'd accrued on her nail onto the napkin she still had scrunched in her hand. "Maybe I'll try it when my Brown Buttah runs out."

"You really should. Honestly, if I were you, I would start integrating it into your regimen now. Lock in that moisture, prep for the dryness of winter, you know? And this stuff is *way* better than Brown Buttah. Maybe you can start off by using half-and-half?"

It was Hazel's version of an olive branch, but Nella didn't say a word as she dropped the jar in her bag. When she looked up again, she noticed the nearly bald woman had moved toward the door of Curl Central. Their eyes met briefly before Hazel started speaking again.

"I know things just got kind of weird between us, but I just wanted to say that they don't have to be."

"I—"

"Wait," said Hazel, holding up a finger. "Let me finish." She sighed, casting a glance over her shoulder at Richard. Then she lowered her voice. "It's just . . . it's really so damn un*fair*. White people never have to be as hyperaware of themselves as we do. When they walk into a room, they don't have to instantly clock the demographics and analyze what they see. They don't have to worry about having to represent however many million Black perspectives there are in this country just because hiring managers were too lazy to bring in a few others. They can enter a small store without worrying about being followed around. They never have to worry about having car troubles in the South when they're driving around back roads at night. Or any time of day, really. You know?"

Nella nodded.

"Half the time, I don't even think about any of these things," Hazel continued, lifting her chin. "Not consciously. But that stress, that anxiety—that underlying weight is there. Right?"

"I feel that," said Nella, "I really do. But going back to the Shartricia thing . . . you *must* get why I feel like you turned me into the bad cop at work. Everyone is talking about—"

"I *do*, trust," said Hazel, "but forget them. The bottom line is, at the end of day, Colin's book is going to be better. Because of you and me. *We* did that, sis. Together.

"Anyway . . . I guess this is all my way of saying we don't need to see each other as competition. We already have enough stress being two young Black women in a crazy white environment. And so . . ." Hazel put her hand on Nella's shoulder. "What are you doing on October twenty-fifth?"

The question came from way far out of left field. "October twenty-fifth? Um. I'm not sure."

"I'm having some girlfriends over for a natural hair party at my place. Just a small get-together. Some wine, some cheese. A little Maxwell. Juanita is going to come and show us some new products from Curl Central, and my cousin Tanya is going to braid some hair for free. I could even have Juanita bring some scarves over, too, if you wanted to learn how to tie one."

"That sounds fun," said Nella. And it did, even if it did hurt her some to admit it.

"Great. We'll chat more about it tomorrow at work. You can bring your friend, too. What's her name, again? Something with an 'M'?"

"Malaika."

"Malaika. Right." Hazel patted her on the shoulder. Nella took this as a gesture that their conversation was finished, but before she could wish her a good night again, Hazel was speaking once more. "By the way," she said, tugging at one of her locs, "you mentioned something about 'notes,' and I was wondering—what did you mean by that?"

"Notes?"

"You said something like, 'What the fuck is your deal with Richard, and the notes . . .'"

"Oh. Right." Nella hadn't meant to let that slip, but the words had already escaped her lips and made it into Hazel's cognizance. "I've just been getting some weird notes from some anonymous person," she said as nonchalantly as she could.

"Weird notes? What kind of weird?"

"Essentially, they've been notes telling me to leave."

"Leave *Wagner*?"

Nella studied Hazel. The girl had gone pale, her face shifting from a healthy shade of hickory to an uneasy walnut. For the first time during their interaction that evening, Nella noticed that the deep red lipstick on her upper lip, which was almost always impossibly perfect, had faded.

"Yes," said Nella. "One told me to leave Wagner."

Hazel stared at her. Then, unexpectedly, she laughed—deep, resounding belly laughs that were louder than any sound Nella had ever heard her make. "And you thought *I* did that?" she practically yelled. "That's crazy! I definitely didn't do any of that. You know that, right? Definitely by now, you must."

Nella stared at her for a moment. "Yes. I do," she finally said, even though she really didn't.

"That's some crazy, hate-crime stuff, you know," said Hazel, putting her hands in the pockets of her corduroy overalls.

Nella shrugged and said the only thing she could think to say: "There was no mention of the n-word."

"But . . . still."

In that moment, Nella remembered Hazel's grandfather, the one who'd died in the protest in '61. *But still,* indeed.

"And *you* haven't gotten any notes like that, right?"

"Nope. But you know what? Now that I think about it, I *did* recently overhear some people in the ladies' room talking about your whole thing with Colin. They sounded pretty upset by it."

"News travels pretty fast at Wagner."

"Yeah. I get the feeling, though, that if you maybe just apologized to Colin, it would all fizzle out. Just think of it as an exercise in code-switching."

Nella prickled. "I'm thinking about it."

"Good. You know what? Forget HR. You should just go straight to Richard about the notes. Just so he knows what's going on. Maybe," Hazel said, her voice growing with excitement, "he could even incorporate what you're going through into some sort of diversity discussion among all of Wagner's employees. Turn it into a teaching moment, kind of. The Colin thing, too."

Nella was going to shake her head and say that no, that sounded like an absolutely terrible idea, but she now had no clue what was and wasn't a terrible idea anymore.

"Alright . . . well, I know it's getting late, so have a good night." Hazel looked over her shoulder to track Richard down again. Once she found him, though, she didn't budge.

Nella didn't, either. She was too busy taking stock of Hazel's movements. Something hadn't felt quite right about this exchange—the whole night, really. But then she heard her name called behind her, followed by the sucking of teeth.

"See you tomorrow," Nella said, turning to join her friends. "And thanks for the grease."

Shani

September 27, 2018
Joe's Barbershop

Rules. The Resistance had so many rules. But none were drilled as deeply into us as the two most important ones: *Stay off the grid,* and *Don't tell anybody anything.*

Right after I told Lynn I'd come to New York, she spent the better part of an hour telling me why I had to promise her I'd adhere to these two fundamental rules. Maybe longer. However long it was, by the time she finally finished, I'd started to wonder if I really *did* want to fuck with the Resistance, if they were gonna be so uptight about everything.

But then she sent me the list of Eva's ever-changing identities, the map documenting her wild trajectory, and the destruction she always somehow managed to leave in her wake. That was enough for me. I deleted Twitter and Facebook and Instagram. I cut off years' worth of hair. *Years.* And I told Ma my reason for leaving Boston as quickly as I did was because I'd experienced something "unspeakably racist" at work. *I want to start over,* I told her, *and what better place to start over than New York?*

Ma was surprisingly chill when I gave her the news. I figured she would be—she had "started over" her own share of times, one of them being when she moved to Detroit shortly after getting pregnant with me. She always said when I was a kid that New York had been her number one option. "We would've ended up in Queens with your aunt Whitney, tried to make a life out there," she'd said. "But I couldn't do it."

Ma didn't ask me too many questions when I told her not just that I *could* do it, but that I was going to. I already had a ticket. And when it came time for my aunt Whitney to pick me up from Penn Station, her eyes flickering from mine to my shaved head then back to my eyes without a word, she didn't ask me any questions, either.

I was glad for that. I didn't know how long I could stay quiet if Aunt Whit had asked me why my long, beautiful hair could no longer be woven into a braid that went down to my butt. Or—if our Skype connection had been less fuzzy—if Ma had caught on to the remnants of something awful in my eyes. Just one little "what's wrong" would have ended me then, because my exit from Cooper's was still hot and fresh in my mind. The betrayal. The shame. The underhandedness of Eva sneakily emailing that article to everyone at Cooper's right when I was on the most important phone call of my career . . . which explained why I didn't see it, which explained why when Anna yanked me into her office, I had no clue what she was so mad about.

God. What an idiot I must've seemed like, sitting in her expansive glass office with a goofy, uneasy smile on my face after she'd told me to pack my things. "But I just now got someone from the Boston Housing Authority on the phone," I'd told Anna. "Four different people living in public housing signed on to talk to me. What's going to happen to that piece? We were going to position it as being *the* Feature of February."

But you need me, I was saying in no uncertain terms, *because who else will write the Black Stories? Who else will bring in Boston's Black Voices for you?*

"We'll find someone else for that article," Anna had said. "Besides, I can't imagine you'd be happy here one more day, working for a bunch of—what was it you called us? 'Vampiric, self-important white saviors whose definition of diversity is writing about Black and brown people who do nothing but hurt and heal?'"

She'd thrown this last sentence at me so fast that I could feel it in the back of my throat, obstructing my windpipe. It was a direct quote, one I'd said just the evening before. At Pepper's. To Eva.

Eva.

I'd looked left, then right, searching for her in the sea of faces that had quickly accumulated outside of Anna's office. I was the zoo animal on display, and people I'd worked with for nearly two years—people I'd publicly called friends but had also privately called 'self-important vampires' because in corporate life, these things weren't mutually exclusive—had their noses pressed against the walls as they merrily watched me eat my own shit.

The only thing worse than that was knowing that dozens, maybe even hundreds, of other young Black women were experiencing this same kind of humiliation, too . . . and young Black women were the cause of it. Hundreds of young Black women, probably more, were undergoing severe personality changes all over the world. The degree to which they were changing varied from person to person. Some spoke differently, others dressed differently. But the most important thing was that the change wasn't superficial. It went down to each and every one of their souls.

OBGs. "Other Black Girls," Lynn had dubbed them, "because they're not *our* kind." They were something else entirely. Something close to alien, although Lynn wasn't out-there enough to suspect that these OBGs—or whatever it was that was changing them—had landed here from outer space. She just knew there was a deeper explanation for why these young women were suddenly no longer beholden to anyone but themselves and the white people they worked for. Why they were so obsessed with success—and with taking down any Black women who got in their way.

Twice a month, Lynn held early morning meetings at Joe's so she could tell us what she heard from her people who were keeping tabs on other parts of the country. The verdict was that the OBGs were spreading far, and they were spreading fast. When Lynn first learned about these OBGs five years ago, they'd been contained to just a few northeastern cities: New York, Boston, Philly. But now, they were being sighted as far south as Miami, as far north as Portland, and as far west as Los Angeles.

Joe himself confirmed it at our last meeting, after visiting his daughter out in California. There'd been a wetness in his eyes as he'd stood in Lynn's usual spot at the front of the room and explained how it was as though a layer of his baby girl had been peeled away and replaced by a fake, transparent sheen that bore no resemblance to the person he'd raised. "And I know it ain't just that basic Hollywood bullshit that's gotten her, either," Joe had promised us vehemently. "Her goddamn agent got her auditioning for three slave parts this month alone. *Three.*"

Pen poised above her signature orange notebook, Lynn had pressed Joe about the symptoms his daughter was exhibiting. The smile-and-nod? The helpless shrug? The glassy-eyed stare?

"There was some of the glassy-eyed stare. But when I asked her if she knew what she was doing, my daughter actually said that she didn't like the idea of playing a slave. And she started explaining it all to me . . . justifying it. Spouted all this crap about 'playing the game' until she didn't need to play no more. Said she letting *them* think they pulling the strings, when really *she* is."

This got to Lynn. To all of us. This meant OBGs were blending in easier with non-OBGs. Blending in meant they were advancing in numbers. They were radically different now than they were twenty years ago, which was when Lynn suspected OBGs—or some form of them—had first come into existence. But at least they were keeping to themselves back then. Heads down, eyes on the top spot. Now, anyone who got in their way to the top got stepped on.

Or worse, if you weren't careful.

When I'd searched for Eva in that crowd outside Anna's office, I'd found her toward the back, her arms tight across her body, her eyes two hard spheres of onyx. I'd heard the screeching sound of life as I knew it coming to a halt; the words, narrated softly but certainly, of the woman I'd met on the train hours earlier: *You said too much. You're fucked.* Only then did I realize far, far too late, that something was wrong with Eva. No Black woman would ever do that to another Black woman. Not without being deeply, deeply disturbed. Not while seeming so down. So human.

We'd have to come up with more complex ways to separate ourselves from them, said Lynn. And we'd have to be even more vigilant of my least favorite Resistance Rule: *Never confront an OBG or potential OBG unless directed.*

Such a rule kept me from going in on Eva when I saw her with Nella at Nico's in August, and then last night, when I listened to her preach about solidarity and diversity to everybody at Curl Central. In fact, I'd had to restrain myself to keep from jumping out of my seat, grabbing her by a loc, and asking her to run that smug shit about solidarity by me one more time.

I was still envisioning how good it would have felt to wield a piece of Eva's hair above my head like a captured flag when Lynn called over to me from my desk, asking me for an update.

I swallowed my grin and brought my legs up to my chest. It was a rare occasion for me to have the couch all to myself, but I'd gotten so used to scrunching myself up to make room that it came naturally now. "So far, still good. I was sitting in the front row and Ev—sorry, *Hazel*, barely even looked at me. You know how it is. Paranoid people don't see what's standing right there in the light. They only see what's in the shadows."

Lynn did know. "And Nella?"

"Nella's not compromised. I saw them having a pretty intense-looking exchange at the end of the night. But I'm pretty sure she's fine."

She made a noise, but she didn't look up from her notes.

"So," I said, trying to sound neutral, "Pam says that ever since she left those notes for her, Nella's been staying late in the office practically every evening. Nella's apparently been trying to get Jesse Watson to write a book for Wagner. I doubt that'll happen, but he's a loose cannon, so who knows *what* he's willing to do . . ."

Lynn motioned for me to get to the point.

"I'm wondering if maybe next week we should finally make contact? Maybe I can pretend to be an up-and-coming writer and try to schedule a meeting with Nella? I doubt she'd take too well to being approached on the train, because she looks flighty as hell, but if we set up the publishing pretext, maybe she'll—"

"No," Lynn interrupted.

"Why not?"

"Because 'I'm pretty sure she's fine' isn't enough. Unless you noticed any other signs that I should know about?"

I shrugged. "Nella's still dating the white boyfriend. Owen."

"That means nothing. What if she's finished already, but he just hasn't picked up on it yet? A lot of young white men are *into* OBGs," Lynn said, making a face.

I bit my lip and started fussing with the scraggly trim of one of the pillows nearest to me. Noticing my silence, Lynn finally peered up at me and asked, hopefully, "Did you see the white boyfriend and Hazel talking at any point last night?"

"For a few minutes. But it looked harmless."

"Hm. Okay. Let's go back to Nella and Hazel. Did you hear anything they said?"

"No. But Nella *looked* like she wanted to strangle her for most of that conversation." I'd seen it all in bits—all out of the corner of my eye, of course, so as not to be too obvious.

I was still playing with the pillow when something else popped into my mind. "Oh!"

"What?"

"When I was leaving, I saw Hazel hand her something. It looked like hair products, something like that."

"Did you see her hand things to anyone else?"

"I did. If I'd been close enough to her she probably would've handed me one, too."

"Those were probably just favors promoting her organization. Or the shop." Lynn sighed as she jotted this down. "Shani, we can't just assume Nella's good yet. She's still at Wagner. She even showed up to Hazel's event. We've seen enough to know that we have to be extra careful, haven't we? Remember what happened to you at that magazine? And do I need to remind you about my med school program? That OBG is still there reaping all of the benefits from research *I* did. All the money I wasted on *not* getting a degree—"

"I know," I said, gritting my teeth. I knew this speech by heart. "But what I'm saying is . . . she did that to you *five years ago*. And here we are. Hiding in the shadows. We *still* don't know anything new, Lynn, beyond the fact that they're wreaking havoc in Hollywood. We don't know how Black girls are being changed. We only know that they're selfish *monsters* who are getting better at putting on award-winning performances."

"We also know why they're so good at changing other Black women when they want to," Lynn added, "which is why we need to stick to keeping her at arm's length."

"Look." I put the pillows aside and sat up some. "Being part of this whole spy thing with you guys has been . . . an experience. I loved sneaking those notes to Pam—she's the sweetest woman ever. And I respect what you all are trying to do. I just want to know why I came all the way to New York if we aren't gonna make any moves on this whole Nella-Hazel situation. I might as well focus on something else. Some*one* else. Like me. Not Nella, and definitely not Hazel. I don't even want to be in the same room with her anymore after what she did to me."

I didn't mean to make it sound like Lynn and the Resistance hadn't been doing enough to stop the OBGs. But it must've sounded like that, because Lynn said, in a low, cold voice, "I respect that. But there's more to this Nella situation than you could possibly understand." Then, she closed her notebook and put it back in the bookcase.

The next day, she asked me to come by Joe's Barbershop as soon as I got off work. "We need to talk." Nothing more, nothing less. I agreed.

By the time I'd clocked out of Rise & Grind, waved hello to Joe and his customers, and flown up the creaky back stairs, I'd already gotten it into my head that Lynn was going to tell me that my time in the Resistance was over.

But when I opened the door, I didn't see Lynn. I saw a woman who, judging by the halo of silvery curls that cascaded down her shoulders, looked much older than the usual demographic that rolled through Joe's. She was standing in front of the bookshelf with her back to me, looking up at one of the room's crowded purple-gray walls.

I lingered by the door for a moment, hesitant to interrupt. I'd been captivated by the walls, too, when I first saw them. Each was filled nearly to capacity with photo upon photo of various Black activists—some familiar to me, some unfamiliar. Of the ones I knew, Malcolm X stood out the most; at least 30 percent of the photos plastered all over the walls were of him. Many were black-and-white images that I'd grown up seeing in history books and newspapers, but a few were contemporary renderings of Malcolm X that I couldn't remember ever seeing before: Malcolm through a pop-art lens, in neon shades of blue and orange; Malcolm through a comic-book superhero lens.

The most eye-catching piece of all depicted Malcolm with his hand placed pensively on his temple, painted in shades of red, white, and blue. In case one didn't know to what it was paying homage, a small, postcard-sized rendering of the Obama HOPE posters that were big during his first presidential campaign was tacked right next to it, a period next to a very long, very powerful sentence.

"You know, he's still one of my heroes. I miss him. I still remember that day . . ."

The words came soft and low, but perfectly enunciated. It took me a second to realize that it was the silver-haired woman speaking, and that she was speaking to me. Really, I didn't truly realize it until she turned around to face me.

My first thought was how she reminded me of someone—a family member, maybe. The kind of family you see only once every three years or so, at family reunions. My second was how good she looked. Her skin was almost completely wrinkle-free, and her build looked slim—fit, even—in a pair of black skinny jeans layered beneath a black sleeveless tunic.

"Obama?" I managed, when I realized I had waited far too long to respond. "Yeah. I miss him, too."

"No." She cut me off as she walked over to the couch nearest to her and had a seat. "Malcolm."

I could only nod.

"Oh, Shani—great. You guys finally met."

Lynn had entered the room. There was something resembling a smile on her face, but she didn't look particularly happy—an expression, I noticed, that the silver-haired woman had also been wearing when she first turned and looked at me.

"We actually haven't," she admitted.

I moved to remedy the situation, reaching my hand out for hers. "Shani Edmonds."

The woman reached out, too. "Kendra Rae. Kendra Rae Phillips."

She watched as recognition lit up my eyes, filling the rest of my face with a blaze of embarrassment. "Oh my god," I said, shaking her hand slowly. "Ms. . . . Phillips. Hi. I didn't know you were . . . in the city?"

Or anywhere, for that matter, I thought.

"No one does," Kendra Rae said, as firmly as her fingers were clasping mine, "and we intend to keep it that way. Don't we?"

"Sure."

"Good."

"So, um . . ." I gestured around the room. "How long are you . . . have you . . . ?"

I stopped, then started again as Kendra Rae continued to stare at me intently. She wasn't wearing any makeup, but she was still gorgeous—ageless, even—with eyes as rich and deep brown as Karo corn syrup.

"What are you doing . . . *here*?" I finally managed.

At that, Kendra Rae's impassive demeanor collapsed into a small, dazzling grin. I grinned right back, relieved. I'd barely been able to keep my eyes from bugging out of my head, but this woman didn't seem put off by it. She seemed to be thriving off it, like a daisy turned toward the sun for the first time in who knew how long.

Kendra Rae extracted a newspaper article and a notebook from a small patchwork bag I hadn't noticed she'd been carrying. "Lynn reached out to me not long ago with some very interesting information," she explained, flattening the article across her lap. "So, I'm here to tell you both a little bit about my time at Wagner Books. But first . . . Shani?"

She paused and looked me in the eye.

"Yes?"

"You need to tell me what you saw Hazel give to Nella at Curl Central."

13

October 17, 2018

Hey, Nellie!

First things first—my deepest, sincerest apologies for such a late reply! Promise to let you know some upcoming dates for our drinks as soon as I have them.

In the meantime, would you mind sending me Hazel-May McCall's contact info? (Do you know her? She works with Maisy, right???) Just saw that wonderful article about her mentoring program in BookCenter and thought I'd give her a little shout. I'd be forever grateful!

Thanks so much! xx Lena

Nella looked over her shoulder one more time before taking another violent whack at the Keurig with her fist, but the damn thing didn't babble or sputter the way it was supposed to. It just kept hissing.

Crossing her arms, she stared at it for a moment, contemplating other ways to beat the Keurig into submission. It certainly wasn't how Jocelyn would have done it, but since Jocelyn wouldn't be returning to Wagner—rumor had it, Germany had taken her back—Nella saw any method of fixing the Keurig as fair game.

She'd already used her fist on the machine, but she wondered what would happen if she used her head. This method sounded particularly appealing, given how well she'd memorized Lena Jordan's rather irritating email. *Sincerest apologies,* Lena had said. *Thought I'd give Hazel a little shout.*

And, perhaps the worst part of it all: *Hey, Nellie!*

Nella had made the mistake of reading and then rereading Lena's note before she had a chance to do anything reasonable that morning, like grab a coffee or get a bagel from the café. Lena's words had been running through her mind on loop like a bright bodega marquee sign, punctuated every now and then by two meaningless X's.

Had it *really* been that difficult for Lena to give her one or two dates she was available? And was Nella's name *really* that hard?

Nella glanced over at the microwave clock to assess the damage. It was a quarter after ten, which meant she had no time to run downstairs and buy a coffee across the street. Defeated, she filled her mug with hot water and reached for a box of green tea. She would simply have to sit through the ten thirty cover meeting with Vera, Leonard, and Amy undercaffeinated. It would suck, but it would suck less than walking into the room five minutes late.

Nella tried to keep her hands steady as she poured a slow stream of honey into her steaming mug. Cover meetings had been the highlight of her week when she'd first started working at Wagner. She usually arrived a few minutes early so she could snag that one corner seat by the window with the best view of Leonard's cover mock-ups for Amy, Richard, and the editors. Back then, those meetings had seemed like the most magical part of publishing. She got tipsy comparing the designer's artistic renderings of a book with the hypotheses she'd come up with during her own read, and high off the anticipation leading up to the big cover reveal.

She would even sit in on discussions of covers of books she wasn't working on, listening closely to Amy and the designers discuss color and balance and font size and kerning. And she took copious notes—notes she planned to internalize for that day when *she* was the one sitting in The Editor's Seat. Sure, there was an author here and there who quashed a tiny bit of the magic, but this never precluded how humbling it was to be just a few feet away from the inception of an image that would adorn thousands of copies of books and be distributed all over the world. Being able to provide her opinion on covers made her feel powerful, even if—at the end of the day—Vera had the final say.

But this cover meeting coming up in nine minutes was different. *This* meeting was for *Needles and Pins*.

Nella swiped at the steam on her face with the back of her hand, getting a nostrilful of cocoa butter in the process. She winced, unprepared for it. She hadn't planned to use the hair grease Hazel had given her until she ran out of all of the other products she had at home, but on the elevator ride up to the office that morning, it had dawned on her that she hadn't put any kind of moisturizer on her scalp in more than a week. When she happened to reach deep into her bag and find, to her delight, that the small jar of grease was still there, she went ahead and massaged a pea-sized portion through her hair.

It's so pungent, though, she'd murmured to her reflection in the bathroom mirror, and now again in the kitchen as she took three slow, deep breaths—a habit she'd developed in the weeks that had passed since Hazel had sung Colin's praises at the marketing meeting. Thanks partially to her, *Needles and Pins* was swimming in a sea of buzz so deep that the title was now known around the company as a "surefire bestseller" that Oprah might even tweet about "if we get the packaging just right."

Nella poked at the tea bag with the thin wooden stirrer, her fourth poke so hard that a part of it split open. She watched, annoyed, as tiny flecks of jasmine broke free and swam out into her cup. The Keurig hissed on behind her, a sweet, mocking reminder of how little control she had over anything these days.

Nella had received this message in other ways—for starters, in the absence of invitations to have lunch with Gina and Sophie. They'd stopped asking Nella to eat with them after she declined five lunch offers in the span of two weeks—she simply had too much work to do—and they'd opted to try Hazel instead. Something magical had to have happened during their first lunch together; after that, they started hanging around her cube, gushing about her boyfriend's latest art project or her favorite thing she was reading that week. Even Gina—dubious, uninterested, "That Don't Impress Me Much" Gina—had walked away from one of their chat sessions on a particularly cool day saying that she wanted a pair of platform Timberlands like Hazel's. All the while, Hazel had gobbled up the attention like a pro. Of course.

Nella didn't know what to make of any of it. The kind of celebrity status that Hazel had achieved in such a short span of time rubbed her in a way that bothered her, and it bothered her that she was bothered at all—especially since she and Hazel were supposed to be on the same team. She hated how disappointed she felt when editors suddenly started asking Hazel for sensitivity reads, but not her. Nella had never been given even just an iota of the attention everyone had paid Hazel. If she were being honest, she would say that she hadn't thought she'd ever receive it. And if she were lying, she would say that she'd never wanted it in the first place.

But the validation was important to Nella, and watching Hazel move through Wagner like a knife through whipped cream made her begin to question her own presence there. *Maybe I should have listened to those anonymous notes I received last month,* she sometimes thought, and once, in a bout of desperation, she'd even tried calling that phone number again. But to her relief—and her chagrin—it had been disconnected.

In a way, she felt like she was already gone, anyway. Her coworkers were certainly treating her like she was. They were floating by Hazel's desk to chat more and more frequently, and Nella was beginning to understand exactly what Hazel had meant when she'd brought up code-switching. She'd known what the phrase meant, obviously; how else was she able to read about the latest incident of police brutality on the news, then clock into work at nine a.m. with a smile on her face?

But, Hazel . . . something was off with her. A vibe. Nella didn't completely trust the way she took code-switching to an entirely new level, or the way she constantly asked Vera about the books she was editing and always charming the plaid-patterned slacks off Josh. Once, while Nella was microwaving some leftover dinner in the kitchen, she'd even caught Hazel talking to Amy about her grandparents. "They met at a march? And he died at a march? My, my," Amy had crooned, taking a rare moment to remove her crimson-tinted glasses and dab at her eyes. "Talk about a character arc."

Nella, who'd feigned deep involvement with something on her cell phone, had found this pretty distasteful. But to Nella's surprise, Hazel had agreed. "I've actually been thinking of commissioning a writer to take their diaries and their correspondence and write a love story around their lives dedicated to activism."

Then there was C. J.: so dazzled by Hazel, so consumed. He would hang on to the edge of her cube and flirt with her for five, ten minutes at a time, smiling at her with those big old eyes he'd once used only on Nella, and Hazel—good-natured, affable Hazel—would smile back. Together, they made a beautiful twosome that belonged in a Black nineties rom-com instead of the thirteenth floor of a Midtown office building.

Meanwhile, Nella would sit quietly across the aisle trying to tune out their conversations. But bits of autobiographical information leaked into her cube anyway, juicy bits that C. J. had never told Nella in the two years he'd known her. She couldn't help but wonder why this was. She'd been far friendlier with him than she'd ever been with India. Had she not asked him the right questions? Or had he simply figured Nella, raised in a middle-class suburb by two parents—parents with a dysfunctional marriage, but two parents nonetheless—would never truly "get it"?

Whatever the reason, it didn't matter. What had preoccupied her more was the alien sensation she felt overhearing them reminisce about growing up in Black neighborhoods. It brought her back to her high school days, when Black kids would see her holding hands with her white boyfriend in the hallway or eating lunch with her white friends in a café and whisper to one another, not very discreetly, *there go the Oreo.* It wasn't *her* fault that her honors classes had been overwhelmingly filled with white and Asian students—that they were all she'd really known—and so she'd just pretend she hadn't heard. Pretend she didn't worry at least once every day that she wasn't "Black enough."

Her primary source of comfort had been the belief that this feeling would go away once she went to college. But now it was back to rear its ugly head, spewing all of the insecurities she thought she'd gotten over.

Nella leaned forward so she could scrutinize the specks of jasmine that were floating around her mug. Then she checked the clock again: ten twenty-four. There was still time to fish out a few of the pieces.

She was reaching for a metal spoon from the drying rack when the sizzling of the Keurig was overpowered by the sound of footsteps behind her.

"Hey, Hazel! How's it going?"

Nella spun around and saw Sophie, red-cheeked and now highly embarrassed.

"Oh, shit," she said. "*Nella*. I am *so* sorry. I thought you were—"

"Yeah," said Nella, glaring at her. "I think I know exactly what you thought." She dipped her spoon into her mug, grabbed some jasmine, and tossed it into the sink.

"It's just that . . ." Sophie stopped. "Well, did you realize you two are wearing the same color today?"

"Are we?" Nella looked down at the eggplant sweater that she'd pulled over her head a few hours earlier. She hated this particular sweater; it was too small and too itchy and the tag always stood up in the back. But she'd barely had time to pick anything else. Lately, her body had been waking her up at all sorts of irregular times in the middle of the night, and when sleep did come back to her, it was usually half an hour or so before she needed to actually get out of bed.

"Hazel's sweater is purple, too," Sophie pointed out, even though Nella's question had been rhetorical.

"It's a very different purple."

"Yeah? I remember them being pretty similar, actually."

"No," said Nella, a bit more forcefully. "I'm pretty sure Hazel is wearing lilac."

She was sure of this because she'd caught herself eyeing the girl's bell-sleeved sweater enviously earlier in the morning, when Hazel had wheeled her chair over to ask her how to set up a conference call. Nella had helped her, delivering the same spiel she gave new assistants, but it had been hard. Her spiraling sense of self-worth had started to encroach upon her sanity; her sanity, upon her sleep; and her sleep, upon her ability to be a functioning human being at work. A functioning human being who was able to forgive and forget the fact that a colleague had mistaken her for a dreadlocked girl who was four inches taller than her.

There's this social phenomenon. It's called code-switching . . .

Weeks had passed since Hazel said those words to her, but a pang of fury dug into Nella's side nonetheless. Yes, she knew all about code-switching and being flexible and easygoing and not taking anything too personally, but as Sophie continued to tap-dance around her faux pas, waxing poetic about an article she'd read about how the eye saw hues, Nella felt too tired to play along. She didn't bother to nod or laugh at Sophie's half jokes. She simply stood there, stone-faced, picking jasmine out of her mug piece by piece, waiting for the girl to stop speaking—or, at least, to finally stop tripping over herself long enough to realize that she wasn't going to undo what she'd done.

At last, Sophie stopped to take a breath. She looked to her left, appearing to notice that the Keurig had been making strange noises beneath her own strange noises over the last couple of minutes.

"Is the Keurig broken again?" asked Sophie, clearly still uncomfortable. "Damn thing. I have a friend over at J. F. Publishing and she told me their Nespresso machine never craps out, not like this one. Maybe we can petition to get Richard to make the switch."

Nella grunted. Then she dropped the spoon in the sink and made a break for it down the hallway.

"Nella, hey—I'm so sorry, again, for the mix-up," Sophie called out from behind her.

Nella didn't turn around and she didn't miss a beat. "All good, *Gina*," she replied curtly, and after delivering this final blow, she moved faster, indifferent to the drops of hot tea that splashed on her hand with each step.

When she walked into the cover meeting a few minutes later, she wasn't at all surprised to find Hazel sitting in what was supposed to be her seat, swiping through Vera's phone.

"That paintbrush! Vera, he's so cute. And how old did you say little Brenner is turning tomorrow?"

"Five." Vera leaned over so that she could see which photo Hazel was looking at, as though she hadn't been the one who'd taken it in the first place, and grinned.

"He's such a precious size! And how long have you had him for?"

Vera beamed. "Three years. And every new day is a new adventure with him, even still."

Nella assessed the lousy seating situation. She hadn't arrived early enough. Amy, Josh, and Richard had already taken their usual places at or near the head of the table; to the left of Amy sat Vera; on the other side of Vera, Hazel. The only empty seat close enough to the action was on the other side of the table—across from Hazel, and beside Grumpy Leonard.

Nella reached for the chair while Leonard remained hunched over his notepad, one hand covering half of his face, the other squeezing a golf pencil. He didn't seem like he wanted to be bothered; he might have even been asleep. Even still, Nella softballed a *How's it going, Len* as she slid into the chair beside him. She was desperate for some kind of normal human contact, and damn it, she was going to get it.

Leonard glared up at her. She swallowed, taking in his bloodshot eyes, the furious black scribble on the paper in front of him. "How do you *think* it's going?" he snapped. "This place has been running me into the ground as usual. That's how it's going."

Nella nodded in commiseration.

Vera looked up. "Oh, Nella! Hi!"

"Hey, Vera," Nella said as cheerfully as she could, studying her boss.

Today's outfit was a long, baggy burlap sleeveless dress layered over an eggshell-white sweater. Her dress was super cute—very cozy-looking, very 1993, very something Nella would buy if she thought she could afford it, though she was almost certain she couldn't. But Nella was quite positive that, just like the freshly cut blunt bangs that stopped halfway down her forehead, it was yet another Hazel influence. The last time Vera had worn something that didn't perfectly fit her tiny waist, she'd had pneumonia.

Vera herself had seemed aware of this fact, too; she kept running her hands up and down the burlap straps as though checking to make sure the fabric was still there. "I'm so glad you could make it. You weren't at your desk a couple of minutes ago, so I decided to be a little selfish and ask Hazel if I could steal some of her time for this meeting."

Nella had heard this particular song before. She and Vera had been passing ships in the night for weeks, communicating mostly via email and telephone, always just barely missing each other in person. Whenever Nella did happen upon Vera sans closed door, she was either asking Nella to do something, talking to Hazel, or talking about Hazel to another colleague. Compliments on her new wardrobe, which had gradually shifted from black and navy to include a few earthy tones and even some patterns that bordered on "whimsical," were due to Hazel. Those deep burgundy highlights in her hair, visible only in very particular types of lighting, but still visible? Hazel's doing, too.

Never before had Nella seen her boss open up to any lower-level employee at Wagner.

"Selfish?" Hazel asked Vera, her eyes still trained on a photo of Brenner. "Not selfish at all. I'm absolutely thrilled to be sitting in on this."

"Me too," Nella said, through gritted teeth.

Vera smacked the table with her palm. "That's the spirit! I remember when I was first starting out here, I always sat in on every cover meeting I could."

"That's true. Every single one," Amy chimed in from the head of the table. "She started a couple of years after me, and I remember how she always used to steal my chair. Frankly, I wanted to kill her."

Richard snickered, tossing back his head. "That's true, too," he said, less to Hazel and Nella and more to Amy and Vera. "I still remember when Amy marched right into my office and asked, 'Where did you find that Velma chick? Wherever you found her, you can send her right back.'"

"Agh, yes," Amy said, coloring a little bit. "Not my finest moment. But now look at us! We're the *best* of friends."

"The *best* of friends," Vera agreed coolly.

"Mmm." Hazel set Vera's phone down on the table. "Seems like a little bit of competition can be a good thing, huh?"

"You're right," said Amy.

Josh finally stopped checking his teeth for stray flecks of granola in his front-facing phone camera. "Probably wouldn't be here without it."

Nella glanced up at the clock as Amy clapped her hands, then slid off her tinted glasses. "Okay everybody, ready to get started? This is going to be a quickie—Len, you got Alexander's note about having to reschedule his cover meeting today, right?"

Leonard ventured to catch Amy's eye and bow his head, but he said nothing. A member of the old guard of senior-level employees at Wagner, Leonard had headed the design department for nearly four decades, even won numerous awards for his innovative work on covers for books that would become classics. But he seemed truly, deeply unhappy, carried a limited number of smiles around in his pocket—at least when he was at the office—and only whipped them out at very particular occasions. Nella was quite positive he kept the majority of his smiles to himself, when he was alone in his office, door closed, creative gears turning.

Nella studied Leonard for a bit longer, taking in his unassuming checkered shirt, the golf pencil behind his ear, the gray hair that would have grown in patches on his scalp if he didn't shave it regularly. His head, which almost always hung low. She was quite certain that he made three times what she made, probably more than that. She was also pretty sure that he didn't have any children. Why *didn't* he just retire? Was he simply holding on until he could physically hold on no longer? How could someone be so settled, but so clearly miserable?

Amy broke the awkward silence that had befallen the meeting since she posed her question. "Great. Vera, we've got some really awesome cover proposals for you this morning! You're going to love them all, I promise. Len, hon, want to show us what you came up with for *Needles and Pins*?"

"Yes! Show me what ya got, Leonard!" Vera gave him a forceful wink, a peace offering after all the Sam Lewis drama she'd thrown his way. Nella found it unnatural, but there was an ever-so-slight decrease in Leonard's hunch.

"Sure." He unearthed a manila folder that had been sitting in his lap and showily pulled out three glossy pieces of paper. He stood and placed each page on the table, spinning them around so that they were facing Vera, with a slight tilt toward Richard.

"So, I've done up a few different approaches here," Leonard said, swaying just a tiny bit left and a tiny bit right. "These first two are along a similar vein of his last few books: minimalistic, striking color dichotomies, sans serif. If we want to keep with the branding we started doing for him in 2011, we may want to go this route. I think readers who are used to his books looking a certain way—and readers who like having books that look like they belong together—will flock to something simple like this: melon-red words against a black backdrop."

Should've made the words chartreuse, thought Nella sourly.

"Nice," said Vera.

"The black background definitely works well with this topic. It's desolate. It's despair. It's *the opioid crisis*," added Josh.

Nella rolled her eyes at her lap.

"And then we have one other option, in case he decides he wants to completely dismantle the format that worked for his last few books. Here. This one isn't even a little bit close to the route we've traditionally taken with Colin's books, but I think it might be worth exploring."

Nella looked at the piece of paper that Leonard was pointing at. Its background was a watercolor rendering of the American flag, with illustrations of various faces weaved among the red and white stripes so that only pieces of faces were visible.

Immediately, Nella was drawn to the third one—how fragmented, how disjointed it looked. She leaned forward to examine the faces more closely, a decent indicator, she recognized, that someone might be inclined to do this in a bookstore. But suddenly she felt herself recoil, moving backward in her seat as quickly as she'd moved forward.

That was when she really saw it: The dark brown face. The wide nose. The thick lips. The wide-open, almost frightened eyes. The wild tufts of black hair pulled into Bantu knots. All presented in pieces, scattered among the stripes, but placed front and center.

Shartricia.

Hesitant, Nella peered over at the cover again to confirm that her gut had been right. No other character in the novel had been featured quite as prominently as the Black one. Shartricia was the most realized, the loudest on the page.

Nella glanced up across the table at Hazel, who raised her pierced eyebrow in reply.

"We're thinking it could be smart to go for a new approach here," Amy explained as Vera took in the two nontraditional covers with some hesitation. "This opioid crisis has been so debilitating to this country. It has painted so many Americans as being less than human. We thought that if consumers picked up this book and saw the array of people Colin writes about on the cover itself, they'd be inclined to spend more time with it."

"I see." Vera nodded, although she still didn't seem too convinced. Her eyes were still trained on the cover. "Well, I will say, it really is a . . . different approach. Much more artistic than the others."

"And with artsy covers, it can sometimes be a risk," Josh said. "But I really dig this—from a marketing perspective at least. Did anyone see that recent article in *BookCenter* about how few books have characters of color on the cover?" Nella held her hand up directly in Josh's line of vision, but he ignored it. "This is going to stand out from the pack. It'll definitely be a draw for broader audiences of today—sort of like we discussed at our marketing meeting. But it also looks back unflinchingly on the past, forcing us to reckon with our country's racist roots."

You think so? Nella thought, scratching at an itch that had been set off by Josh's showboating speech. She glanced across the table at Hazel again. But this time, Hazel was looking at Amy.

"Actually, if I may?"

Everyone's eyes shifted to Hazel. *Yes,* Nella thought. *Please, just do it. Expose this pickaninny for what it is.*

"I think this is kind of brilliant," Hazel said.

"Really?" Vera seemed as surprised as Nella did by this declaration.

"Yup. I think you hit the nail on the head, Leonard."

"So, you would pick this book up if you saw it on a table out in the wild?"

It was Richard speaking now, his piqued interest rendering his blue eyes that much sharper.

"Definitely. It's striking. Leonard, I think you did a phenomenal job, as Amy said."

Richard nodded. Vera noticeably brightened. Even Leonard, ever the Eeyore, looked like Hazel's claim had set him free of his self-made prison.

Nella shuddered as she stared down at the cover, searching for some subversive element that she might have missed, like a conversation starter that might get people talking about race and colorism and class. But all that was there was Colin's caricature. Live and in living color. *You can't just do this,* she thought, fuming. *You can't just put an image like this on a book cover without providing any context.* She saw little Black and brown and white children walking up to the New Releases table at Barnes & Noble and picking it up, attracted by the bright colors. Saw the little gears turning in these kids' heads for two seconds, or however long it took for images to imprint upon their young, impressionable brains. And she saw these same kids running back to their families, forever touched by the troubling racist image of Shartricia without even being aware of it.

The Bantu knots. Those eyes. Those lips.

These people.

"Any other thoughts?" Amy asked.

"You people are un-*fucking*-believable."

Nella didn't realize she'd been thinking this, let alone that she'd said it. But she had, judging from the current of attention that had suddenly surged in her direction.

"Did you say something, Nella?"

Amy's top lip was quivering. Leonard looked appalled. Vera loosely clasped her hands around the back of her neck as embarrassment colored her cheeks. Even the never-fazed Hazel seemed caught off guard.

Richard, though, had his hands folded on the table in front of him as he waited for Nella to answer Amy's question.

"I—no." Had it always been this hot in this room? She began fanning herself with her hand distractedly. "I was just saying, your work is un-fucking-believable. This is going to make all those top-ten cover lists, Leonard. You really knocked it out of the park with this one."

"He really did." Vera cleared her throat, ready to move on. "Well, I'll think this over some more. Len, can you send me the highest-res version of these covers that you've got when you have a moment? All of them, please."

"Certainly." Leonard's feathers still seemed ruffled as he collected the sample covers, clipped them, and handed them off.

"Ver, let us know what Colin thinks. I can have Hilary send him sales figures for books that have covers with similar renderings on them, if you think it would ease his mind a little?"

"You know him so well," Vera said, with a small smile.

"Oh, we *all* do," Richard said. Everyone except for Nella chuckled knowingly. All was right with the world again.

"Alright, terrific. Great stuff, people!" Amy put on her glasses, adjourning the meeting. Everyone readily collected their things. A couple of feet away, Hazel was asking Vera how she and her husband were planning to celebrate Brenner's fifth birthday.

Nella kept her gaze downward, pretending to write in her blank notebook. She wanted everyone to leave the room before she did, lest she have to awkwardly eavesdrop on Vera and Hazel's discussion about the best places to buy cupcakes for dogs, or listen to Josh explain that *BookCenter* article in great detail. Plus, she'd always found something deeply soothing about sitting in the quiet of a meeting room after everybody had left, even if it was only for a moment.

After about thirty seconds, she felt ready to return to her desk and maybe even call building services to see if someone could come and fix the Keurig. But when she looked up, she realized Richard was still sitting at the head of the table, typing away on his cell phone.

"Oh," Nella murmured, deeply embarrassed. "Sorry. I'll just—"

She placed her palms on the table, preparing to hoist herself up and out. But before she could make a swift exit, Richard had placed his phone facedown and shifted his attention directly toward the space between her eyes. "No, *I'm* sorry. Please, have a seat, Nella. Do you have a few moments to chat? Yes? I was hoping we could discuss a few things, especially since we wrapped this meeting up so quickly."

"Um . . ." Nella looked over at the door. Someone had closed it without her noticing. "Sure. I have plenty of time to chat."

"Great!" Richard slipped his phone into the front pocket of his pants. "I just wanted to have a quick check-in. See how things are going."

"Things are going pretty well," she said, not sure what he meant by "things." She searched her brain for something new to share. "You've probably heard this already, but we finally got Sam Lewis to agree to a cover. Big relief. Thanks for steering that ship. I know how he can be; his agent lets him get away with far too much.

"Oh, speaking of—I'm sure you've heard about this, but Darrin sent us a new project this morning that he's positive is going to go fast. It's about this tiny town in northern North Dakota that doesn't believe in using—"

"That's great. Listen, Nella, I'm going to cut to the chase."

Nella blinked. Had he found out that she'd been creeping outside of his door—and therefore, that she knew he was cheating on his wife? Or had he heard what she had *really* said in the meeting?

Richard pushed his chair a couple of inches away from the table so that he could cross his long, left leg over his right thigh. "Hazel mentioned something to me in private recently. Something that has been happening to you here that is, I must say, deeply disturbing. And I wanted to know if you'd like to talk about it. The floor is yours."

Nella sat up in her chair. "Disturbing?"

"Yes. Now, I know this might make you uncomfortable, which is why I didn't want to get Vera involved. Not unless you explicitly tell me that you want me to."

"I'm not sure what you're . . ." Nella stopped herself. Relief washed over her, followed by trepidation, then anger. Hazel had opened her mouth again. "You mean the notes."

Richard rested his elbow on his thigh, cupping his face with the palm of his hand. He stared at her expectantly in this position for an unbearable amount of time without saying a word. "Can you tell me what those notes said, exactly? Do you remember?"

Nella closed her eyes. It had been a little while since she'd read them—since she'd even had time to really think about them. But how could she forget? "The first one said 'Leave Wagner now.' And the other said something like 'The longer you stay, the harder it is. Leave.'" She'd left out the bit about the phone number on purpose, aware of how poor it looked that she had an actual phone number but hadn't reported it to the police.

Richard shook his head. "And they weren't signed?"

"Nope," she said, surprised and a little pleased by how disgusted he sounded. "Not signed. Just left by my desk."

"My god!" Richard said, banging his fist on the table. "Cowardly fuckers."

Nella stared at his pink, pinched face, intrigued at this new and unfamiliar version of Wagner's editor in chief. She had never heard the man swear before, and the expletive didn't quite mesh with his avocado-colored cashmere sweater.

"Have you told anybody about these letters?" he asked. "Besides Hazel, of course."

She shook her head.

"No? Have you tweeted about it, or anything? Or told any of your friends who might have written about it?"

"Sorry—what?" asked Nella, genuinely confused. "No, I haven't told anyone. What did Hazel tell you?"

"Never mind. Don't worry about it," Richard said quickly. He visibly softened. "Can I see them?"

"See what?"

"The letters. I'd like to see them."

"Well, they're more 'notes' than they are 'letters.'"

Richard peered at her, curious. It seemed as though he wanted to comment on the distinction, or at her need to make the distinction, but he said nothing.

"It's been almost two months since I got the last one, and I got rid of them, actually," Nella added, sliding one of her own legs over the other as the lie slipped seamlessly between her teeth. She'd actually put the notes in the pocket of a raincoat that hung in the back of her closet. This explanation just felt much easier.

"Well, in any event, I want you to know that we have zero tolerance for that kind of behavior here at Wagner. Do you understand?"

"Yes."

"Natalie is looking into it as we speak. Starting tomorrow, she'll begin talking to the mail staff one by one."

"Oh. Thanks, Richard. I really appreciate that." Nella put her pen down, which she realized she'd been clicking and unclicking nervously in her lap. She thought of C. J., with his wide, unassuming smile and disarming velvety charm. The mailroom was filled with C. J.s—kind, helpful people who kept their heads down and their eyes averted. They all had different origin stories, but almost every mailroom staff member had skin that fell somewhere in the brown portion of the color wheel. They all knew her, too. Maybe not as well as C. J., but well enough to greet her. "But, with all due respect, I don't think anyone on the mail staff is responsible for those letters."

Richard shrugged. "Maybe not. But they might recall someone handing them those envelopes to give to you."

"I guess that's possible."

"Well, then." Richard paused to remove his tortoiseshell glasses and hold them up to the light. He rubbed at something on his lenses with his thumb before putting them back on. "I'm glad we had this chat, and that you're aware we're on it. Sounds good?"

"Sounds good," agreed Nella. "Thanks."

"Of course. And, one more thing, between you and me: There are going to be some changes around here."

Nella stiffened. "Changes?" she asked, her mind immediately going to that list of Black names she'd found on the printer.

"Changes. In the next month or so, Natalie will be sending out an email to everyone on the Wagner staff reintroducing a series of Diversity Town Halls. They will be mandatory for all employees."

Hazel's doing. "That's wonderful," she said robotically, trying to suppress her annoyance, even though it really *was* wonderful.

"Isn't it? It'll be an excellent way for us to . . . to *talk* to one another." Richard put his hands on the table and pushed himself onto his feet. "Do you see what I mean? I feel like there's not enough talking happening here. We're talking. Sure. But we're not *talking*. If we were *talking*, I don't think you'd be receiving notes like the ones you've been receiving. You see?"

Nella shrugged. Something about his fixation on the notes and the talking was making her feel restless. His fixation on getting her to agree with him didn't sit too well, either. "Got it."

"I have another change for you, too. It's an even bigger piece of news that I'd like you to keep private. Do you promise me?"

"Sure." A cramp was settling into her neck from all of the nodding she was doing, but she kept at it anyway.

"The profound, inimitable Jesse Watson is coming in to the office to meet with a few of us next week. And I'd like you to be one of the folks who meets him."

For the teeniest amount of time, Nella forgot to inhale and exhale at a reasonable rate. The "profound" Jesse Watson? "He's . . . he's coming *here*?"

"Indeed. You have heard of him, yes?"

Nella nodded. "I have. I just thought he was . . . um . . . taking a break from the spotlight."

"He was. He has been. He and Hazel happen to share a mutual acquaintance, though—small world, isn't it?—and she gleaned that this hiatus has come from his desire to finally write a book. He's been wanting to for quite some time, and, well . . . one thing led to another, and now we have a meeting with him before all the other publishing houses have even had the chance to think about contacting him."

Of fucking course Hazel knows him, thought Nella petulantly, childishly. For a moment, that was the only piece of information she'd gleaned from Richard's statement. "Small world, indeed."

Richard studied her for a few moments, trying to read her blank expression. "If you don't mind me being so blunt, I'd say you seem absolutely stupefied, Nella. You'd like to meet him, wouldn't you? Surely, a man like that, of his caliber—"

"Of course. I'd love to meet him. Jesse just seems like . . . how do I put this . . ."

"I know exactly what you're thinking," said Richard, a small, knowing smile playing across his face. "You think he's too young and hip for us. I get that."

More like too Black, she thought, recalling the time Vera had called Jesse an "emotional terrorist." She was surprised Richard didn't feel the same way; then again, his interest in Jesse *did* support her Black mistress theory.

"I know—this whole thing is unconventional. All the controversies surrounding this young man . . ." Richard shook his head. "He's so young. So outspoken. But like I said: There are going to be lots of changes occurring around here. And who knows—we could have our own bestseller on our hands with this guy. And you . . ." Richard pointed at Nella. "*You,* Nella Rogers, have an opportunity to be a part of that. You'll join us, yes?"

"Of course," Nella said warmly. She was feeling far more revitalized by this conversation than she'd expected to. "Would I be able to work on this book myself? As in . . . be the editor?"

Richard nodded. "Vera and I have talked about it as an option. And we both agree you've done more than enough to prove yourself."

Finally! He hadn't *told* her she was being promoted, but she could already see herself logging into her LinkedIn page and updating her title to "Assistant Editor." She only had about twenty contacts on it, but she could change that. Maybe she'd add Lena just to remind her she existed—and to remind her how to spell her name.

She beamed. "I'm—wow. I would be honored. Thank you, Richard!"

"How*ever,*" Richard said, straightening his collar, "we would be remiss not to give Hazel an opportunity, too. Since she introduced us to him in the first place, of course."

Nella's smile vanished. She wouldn't have been more surprised if Richard had picked up one of the chairs and thrown it at her. *But Hazel practically just got here!* she wanted to scream. *I took the initiative and emailed Jesse, and I've been wanting this forever!*

For a fleeting, rage-filled instant, she envisioned picking up the chair herself. But she pushed the fantasy away, scared it might come to fruition the way her outburst minutes earlier had.

"So, then . . . what? We'll be coeditors?"

"Let's not concern ourselves too much with 'editor this' and 'editor that,'" Richard said. "We'll see how the meeting goes, alright? See how Jesse feels us out. There's a chance he might even want a more seasoned editor—maybe myself, maybe Vera. Maybe he'll go with another publishing house. Or, there's a chance he's not ready to do a book at all. You know how it is with these kinds of things. Always unpredictable."

Nella tried to keep her face as impartial as possible, even though his lackadaisical tone about something as career-making as this irked her. Nothing needed to be that unpredictable. Richard had the power to pick her or Hazel; it was that simple.

Richard pushed himself back from the table with a self-satisfied sense of finality. "Well—I have to run into another meeting," he said, standing, "but I hope this time has been useful to you. I wanted to let you know everything that's been happening behind the scenes, one-on-one."

Nella clenched her fists in her lap as she watched Richard stride toward the door, willing him to move faster. He needed to be gone, now, so she could fume in peace. His hand was on the doorknob when he paused and turned to address her once more. "Oh. And one last thing, Nella. I still remember when you told me about how you wanted to be the next Kendra Rae all those moons ago—and I think that you're well on your way."

She swallowed. "You do?"

"I can't help but think of her when I see how hard you've been working," said Richard. "How attentive you've been to detail. And I'll say that . . ." He shook his head thoughtfully, closing his eyes. "I had a chat with Vera the other day about giving you a promotion in the next few weeks or so."

"You did?" Nella asked, unable to conceal her astonishment. Between Richard's putting Hazel on an equal pedestal to her, and her last few weeks at Wagner, she hadn't felt like anyone thought she'd been doing a good job at all, despite how much of her social life she'd given up, and despite how quickly she answered the phone (an impressive 90 percent mid-first-ring rate). She'd even quietly fixed a few catastrophic production issues, then prevented the knowledge of their existence from ever reaching Vera at all. She felt—if she could be so proud—like the unsung hero of publishing at the moment.

But these measures hardly compared with her surrendering a typed-up apology to Colin Franklin. Such an act had taken an extreme amount of willpower, since it still didn't feel necessary to Nella—but she'd done it. Simply because Vera had asked her to.

Except Vera had barely batted an eye at the extension of an olive branch. It wasn't like Nella expected to get points for putting her tail between her legs—no *Yay! You've put your pride aside to make this project more bearable for everyone, except for you*—but she *had* expected some kind of proverbial pat on the back; at the very least, a thank-you. Instead, Vera had said, "Great," then handed her yet another four-hundred-page manuscript to read in under forty-eight hours.

After months of giving everything to this job, she still felt as though she were doomed, stuck in assistant purgatory forever, like Donald. She could see her future spreading out right there in front of her—blotchy and precarious and filled with *While You Were Out* slips—and she hated how little control she felt like she had over any of it.

But now, here was Richard, smiling that dazzling smile, telling her he thought that yes, she was deserving of a promotion. And also deserving—possibly—of working with Jesse. If not directly, then at least *meeting* him.

She was still searching for something to say when Richard spoke again.

"You know, we see a great deal of amazing things in your future, Nella. We *value* you as part of the team, too, and it would be a shame for you to leave us just because we have one bad apple."

Nella frowned, confused. "What? Leave?"

"I mean—I'm not saying we *want* you to leave," said Richard, quickly. "I was just saying that getting letters—*notes* like those—might make you want to. That's all."

"Oh . . . but I'm not—"

"Just promise you'll let me know if you get any other threatening letters. Alright?"

"Um . . ." Nella squirmed uncomfortably in her seat. "Alright."

"And please—if you do get more, don't throw them out. Give them to me instead. And if she—sorry, *this person* contacts you in any other way—email, text, what have you—we might be able to use them in our investigation." Richard chuckled to himself. "'Investigation.' Listen to me. Mr. *Murder, She Wrote* over here. But you know what I mean. Right?"

"Sure. I know what you mean." Nella stood up, too.

"Good." Richard strode over to her and gave her hand a shake. "We'll be in touch soon about all that promotion business; we just need to get all our ducks in a row before we go forward with the official title change."

Nella brightened, even as Richard's cold, damp hand squeezed the life out of her own. "Sounds great."

"Nice chatting with you, as always, Nella. And do remember: this whole conversation—Jesse, the letters, the promotion—"

"Between us."

Richard bowed. "Until next time."

Nella was still nodding even after she'd been left alone with her thoughts. She caught herself mid-bob, mildly embarrassed and majorly in pain as she pawed a few times at the cramp that now stretched beyond her neck and down to her right shoulder blade. Then she pulled out her phone to Google "Wagner Books." Thankfully, no op-eds about her employer came up, only a few social media posts about books that had been published recently.

Nella exhaled slowly, the wave of relief washing over her like a ray of sunshine. But such light, she knew, could be fleeting—so she set a Google alert for her name right then and there. Just in case.

14

October 20, 2018

"Nala?" The barista stared at her, wide-eyed beneath his bangs, his marker poised tentatively over a white paper cup. "Like *The Lion King*? Cool!"

Nella shifted her weight to her other boot. "Not quite. *Nel*la."

"Bella? Sorry." He started to write.

"No. Sort of like Bella. But with an 'N.'"

He blinked at her. "Okay. So, *Mella*," he said, crossing out the "B." "That's a cool name, too. I guess."

"Actually . . ." Nella paused. Hardly anyone could be heard over the sound of Christmas music that—in Nella's opinion—had no business playing in mid-October. Behind her, a double-decker stroller continued to bump against the back of her legs, pressing her closer to the counter. She wasn't sure why she was spending so much time putting the poor guy through this name thing when he had already taken her order. His only job was to defend that particular Midtown Starbucks from tourist riffraff and the crazy people who went into work on Saturdays.

Nella, a member of the latter camp, conceded. "Mella works. Thanks."

She scurried out of the way of another potential stroller hit, scouring for a safe place to wait for her latte. Nella couldn't remember the last time she'd seen the coffee shop so crowded . . . but then again, it was a particularly chilly day, the holidays were rapidly approaching, and the Herald Square Macy's was a mere six blocks away. She supposed that this was what she deserved for leaving Brooklyn on a Saturday.

"Logan! Venti chai tea latte no foam on the bar for Logan!"

A petite blonde woman in a beige fur coat stepped forward to claim the cup. Her trappings swished vigorously as she stormed out, apparently miffed that she'd had to wait at all for anything in Midtown on a weekend.

Nella pulled out her tablet and started to read, so that she wouldn't become one of those people who felt their important time had been wasted. She hadn't finished a full page when she felt a tap on her shoulder.

"Excuse me, miss?"

Nella turned around. A tall, broad-shouldered Black man in a green parka holding an iced coffee was looking down at her. She decided in a matter of seconds that he was probably in his late thirties and, as she took in his kind eyes and his bearded face, fairly attractive. An added plus was that he'd elected to pull his black sock cap all the way down over his ears, rather than let it hang off his head like a careless hipster. She wasn't sure if she knew him from somewhere, although he did look an awful lot like Marvin Gaye in his *What's Going On* phase.

When it became clear he wasn't going to say anything, she smiled and asked, tepidly, "Yes?"

"Sorry," he said shyly, running a hand along the back of his neck. "You're just . . . *so* beautiful. Wow."

A flash of heat flared beneath Nella's turtleneck. "Oh," she said, as though people told her this in coffee shops all the time. "Thanks?"

He cocked his head at her and stopped smiling only long enough to take a sip of his iced coffee. His pearly white teeth resurfaced as soon as the straw left his mouth. "You are *very* welcome. So, uh. Anyway, I just wanted to say . . . well, that you're beautiful. And also—I think you dropped this."

She held out her hand. He dropped a Starbucks napkin in it.

"You have a good day, now," the man said with a wink. Then he turned and pushed his way toward the door.

"Thanks?" Nella repeated. She looked down at the paper napkin, prepared to crumble it up and throw it in the trash. But then she noticed nine digits and three dashes.

Did that guy just ask me out on a Starbucks napkin? She felt both a little bit horrified and a little bit thrilled at the thought of it. She tried to find the tall Black man again. He was now walking to the door, pulling it open, squeezing his way not impolitely through a family of tourists. Malaika would love this story, she knew. She'd tell Owen, too—except maybe she'd downplay his attractiveness. Just a little bit.

Nella looked at the napkin again, expecting to get one last laugh before she went back to her reading, but what she saw turned her blood cold. Somehow, before, she'd missed the words that had been written above the phone number in all caps:

WAGNER'S DANGEROUS. YOU'RE RUNNING OUT OF TIME.

Nella stared at the first three digits of the phone number, prepared to see the number that she'd called up last month. But the area code was different: 617. This was a Massachusetts area code, a fact she'd involuntarily committed to memory after a brief fling with an MIT grad back in her early NYC days.

So, this *wasn't* the same person she'd spilled her soul out to last month. Presumably, anyway.

Unless whoever had been following her had simply changed phone numbers.

She craned her neck to see if Marvin Gaye's doppelganger was still outside, watching her. Was *he* the person who'd been following her this entire time? But all she could see were streams of bundled-up tourists moving down the sidewalk, holding hands, swinging shopping bags, staring down at cell phone screens. The Black man was nowhere in sight.

Nella turned back around, awash with relief that almost instantly ebbed into fear. She *wanted* to see someone watching her. She *wanted* answers. It had been weeks since she'd received a note, and she'd been naive enough to think that calling that number last time meant the letters would cease. But now that she'd received another one—no, not received, it had practically been *thrown* in her face—she felt like a stone-cold fool.

This was getting ridiculous. That guy was no racist stalker. He was the guy you called when you needed protection *from* a racist stalker. He really seemed to be . . . *warning* her.

Nella pulled out her cell phone and quickly typed out a new text message. She had to outrun her other self—the Nella who had sense; the Nella who would remind her that she'd seen far too many horror films and episodes of *Dateline* with girl-being-stalked plotlines to let herself walk willingly into a trap.

Who are you?

The message turned blue. Three gray dots signaling a response appeared almost immediately beneath it.

I'll tell you if you meet me in forty-five. 100th & Broadway.

You couldn't just talk to me at Starbucks? Nella wrote back.

There were too many eyes and ears there. And that was my friend, not me. So, 100th & Broadway. Cool?

Stupid. It would be stupid to go. Nella couldn't believe she'd even texted this stranger without trying to figure out how to block her own number first. Whoever was following her now had gone through all this trouble to get her phone number, and now they had it. Whatever upper hand Nella'd had was gone. Going to meet this person wouldn't just be stupid; it would be *idiotic*.

And yet.

She bit her lip. Typed a few letters, deleted those, then typed some more. *Can you at least tell me what this is about?!* she finally typed.

Once more, the gray dots materialized instantly. But then they were gone.

"Come on," whispered Nella. She gave her phone one violent shake, as though that might help eke out an answer. But no dots. No luck.

Nella threw her phone in her bag, ready to step out onto the sidewalk and inhale some necessary breaths of sweet fall air. Her fingers were on the handle when she felt the small pulse of a new message:

Her name's not Hazel.

Shani

October 20, 2018

As I turned onto Broadway, trying to scrape my way through droves of zigzagging tourists, a turbulent succession of thoughts popped to the surface of my brain: *I don't need to be a hero. I don't need Nella's side of things, either. I can go home right now, disappear from everybody, and still write an entire fucking exposé.*

I should've been grateful. I *owed* Lynn. The only thing that had made Boston bearable was Cooper's; without that job, I would have holed myself up in my apartment with a bottle of Jack and a bowl of Reese's Puffs.

But I'd had enough. How could I sit back and let Nella make the same mistake so many other Black girls had made, especially now that I'd met Kendra Rae?

I watched the red hand stop blinking, paused at the edge of the crosswalk, and recalled that pleading look I'd seen on Kendra Rae's face hours earlier. It had been enough to convince me not to leave New York. Not yet.

But it was this same look—the look that pushed me to go rogue and text Nella this morning, despite Lynn's orders—that made me likewise want to hop on the next bus back to Boston: Troubled brown eyes turned down at the edges. Corners of her lips turned down, too. No doubt about it, Kendra Rae still looked good—no, *great*—for her age. But there'd been a light missing. Something was off inside her, and this something had caused her to spend more than thirty-five years in hiding.

I could see the headline trending now—something clever about the river of Uncle Toms flowing beneath the shiny, plastic surface of corporate white America. That article could be my gateway to telling Kendra Rae's story next—a story of betrayal not just by a friend, but by an entire industry.

The symbol above changed to a white man. I forced myself to keep walking, but my legs felt like lead. Behind me, a young Hispanic woman who thought I'd been moving too slowly muttered something profane under her breath as she passed me by. I'd committed the ultimate New York City sin.

The thought made me laugh out loud—to myself, to no one. Sins. What did I know about sins? Nothing.

Now, Kendra Rae—*that* woman knew about sins. She'd committed one of the real ultimate sins by trying to be herself: Black. Unapologetic. Someone who told it like it was. Someone who rejected what was expected of her as a Black woman in a predominantly white industry.

The thought of it still got me. What a *boss*. Who else tells an interviewer that she'll never work with another white writer, right when her star is starting to rise?

She was grinning when she'd handed me the article clipping. Like she was proud. I couldn't help but smile a little, too, as I'd started reading aloud: "'I'm tired of working with white writers. I hate it. We've had enough of them. No offense to any of them, but I don't need a white scholar telling me about the Great Migration. I don't need a Jewish man telling me why Miles was the greatest jazz musician ever alive, or why Black people eat black-eyed peas and corn bread and collard greens on New Year's Day. I don't need any of that.'"

I'd looked up at Kendra Rae once I'd finished reading, the brown, faded piece of newspaper threatening to disintegrate in my hands. While I'd been reading, she'd grabbed a copy of *Burning Heart* from the shelf and started going through it, turning its pages with one neat, short, unpainted index fingernail. She'd become so engrossed that she hadn't noticed I was ready to speak again, so I'd taken a breath and said, quietly so as not to startle her, "Was this taken out of context?"

"Not really." Kendra Rae hadn't looked up.

"Oh. Well . . . this seems pretty mild by today's standards . . . but I'm presuming readers weren't too crazy about it back then?"

Lynn had scoffed. "They weren't. No one at Wagner Books appreciated it, either." She'd walked over to the couch with two steaming mugs and set them down on the small coffee table. "Tell her about Diana, if you're feeling up to it?"

"Wait. *Diana Gordon* is involved in this, too?" I couldn't imagine the beautiful, enigmatic author from the billboards advertising her latest bestseller-turned-feature film being involved in such a nefarious operation.

"We go back. Friends since we were younger than you ladies are. But the night I left, I heard Diana talking on the phone about something Imani said."

"Imani's another childhood friend of theirs," Lynn had said.

"So you think she . . . ?"

Kendra Rae had pursed her lips and shaken her head. "That change you've all been seeing happen to our kind? I think someone changed *her*, too." She'd taken a quick sip of her coffee. "I think it was Richard—he's the man Diana was talking to on the phone. That's the only explanation I can think of for why she would try to do that to me. And why she wouldn't be seen with me in public after what I said."

"Richard Wagner was Kenny's boss," Lynn had said, before I could ask. "And he's Nella's boss now. I'd been sensing there was something behind the connection between Diana and Richard—he's always at her functions and shows up in her acknowledgments far too frequently."

I'd blinked. Hazel was toxic; that much I'd known. But I hadn't known Richard Wagner and Diana were, too. What about my bosses?

Had Anna had a hand in what happened at Cooper's? Had everyone been in on it except me? "Why didn't you tell me about any of this before?"

"Because I wasn't one hundred percent sure before Kendra Rae confirmed the connection. Plus, I didn't want you to go off and tell Nella something only for us to find out Nella *is* working on the other side. And she *still* can't know anything," Lynn had rushed to say.

"You didn't trust me," I'd said, hurt.

"Don't do that, Shani. You knew what this was: a need-to-know-basis. I'm telling you now because you need to know."

I'd turned back to Kendra Rae. This wasn't the time. "And you guys think he's the one who's been behind all of this?"

"It wouldn't surprise me in the least," Kendra Rae had said.

I'd thought of Diana again. I'd only read an earlier novel of hers, since most people agreed her story lines were becoming more contrived with each new book she put out. But the one I'd read—a coming-of-age story about Black friendship that spanned forty years—had been so raw and so moving that it had made me cry on a bus.

My voice had been hopeful when I'd used it again, more like a child's than my own. "But why would Diana do that?" I'd asked her. "Didn't you say she was your best friend?"

The ultimate sin.

She hadn't used those words to describe what Diana had tried to do to her, but I didn't need to know all that to know what I'd seen in her eyes. That her best friend, bestselling author Diana Gordon, had committed the ultimate sin.

A truck blared its horn at a Seamless delivery person who'd strayed out of the bike lane. I looked up at the nearest street sign, those three words reverberating in my brain. Somehow, I'd managed to get to 100th Street without noticing. It was too late to turn back now, even if I did feel sick. And afraid. What if, one day, I showed up to Joe's and Lynn had been turned? *Then* what would I do? Would I even know right away?

I couldn't sit back and watch this happen to another person. I *had* to tell Nella. Besides, Lynn had already said herself that she didn't trust me.

I surveyed the sidewalk, but she was nowhere in sight, so I moved to the side, pushing myself up against the glass window of a store on the corner so I wouldn't be in the way. Then I unbuttoned my black trench coat, a feeble attempt to cool things down a bit. But it was too late for that. The space between my breasts had grown sweaty to the point of no return. My insides felt as though they were swallowing themselves.

I'm losing it, I thought, but I realized instantly that that wasn't true. I'd finally *found* it. This was the clearest I'd seen in months.

I was planning out my article pitch to Nella when my phone started to buzz. Thinking it was Nella, I pulled it out immediately, prepared to say *I'll be there soon.* But it wasn't Nella. It was Lynn. Calling me.

Her voice sounded far away. "Shani! What the hell are you doing?"

Fuck.

"Nothing. I'm just . . ."

"You're trying to meet Nella, after everything we told you? What the *hell,*" she repeated.

I whirled around the street, disoriented. "What? How do you know that?" I said, even though I knew immediately Will had talked. Never in a million years would he side with me over Lynn. Lynn was blood. "Do you have someone following me or something?"

"Yes," Lynn hissed, "and you're lucky I do. You need to go black now. I repeat, *go black.* You're on your own."

Shit. "No!" I said, a sob clawing its way through my throat. "You can't just leave me out here like this, Lynn. C'mon!"

"Go black!" Lynn shouted again. "Kenny's around the corner. Just—"

Reluctant, but with no other choice, I slipped my cell into a nearby open garbage can, pivoting to run. But at some point during the call, a car had pulled up. I hadn't noticed the soft click of a car door opening, or the subtle steps of shoes against the pavement. I only felt the firm hand take hold of my arm and yank me hard into the backseat.

15

October 20, 2018

Nella knew she was about ten minutes early when she arrived at the meeting spot, but she checked her phone again anyway. Nervous habit. So, too, was the way she kept pacing on the sidewalk, spending ten seconds over here, then fifteen over there. Facing south, then north as an icy wind whipped pieces of her afro into her eyes.

Those bored enough to notice Nella from the restaurant window behind her probably assumed she was up to no good, or maybe just a little bit off. And Nella wouldn't have argued with any of them. She *felt* like a madwoman. People were bustling by her and she kept looking every single one of them in the eye, desperately. Many of them ignored her. Most gave her dirty looks. One man wearing a seemingly innocuous tie-dyed bandanna spat on the sidewalk in front of her and growled, *"Get the fuck out of my face, bitch."*

Nella took this last interaction as a sign. She texted Malaika to let her know that the mystery person hadn't shown up yet.

Good!!! Now go the fuck home. Seriously. You're acting crazy.

Nella stared at Malaika's words for a few moments, letting them sink in. Crazy. Yes. What was she going to do—fight whoever had been terrorizing her these last few weeks? She remembered C. J.'s bewildered expression when he'd asked her this very question that morning she told him about the notes. She wasn't thinking logically. Out here, she was a sitting duck. If it *was* a manipulative monster who'd been sending her notes, wouldn't she be screwed?

Nella looked around, eyeing the conveyor belt of people next to her. Then she turned and quickly ducked into the restaurant she'd been pacing in front of.

The restaurant's bright yellow walls and the smell of hamburger meat didn't especially put her at ease, but she pulled out one of the high stools facing the window anyway and took a seat. To her right, a couple of guys who'd been watching her conspicuously shifted their attention back to their hamburgers and whether or not Rob had heard back from his landlord yet.

Nella sighed and braced herself for at least eight more minutes of this conversation, keeping her eyes trained on the spot where she herself had just been standing.

But it wouldn't be that long. Less than a minute had passed when she noticed a young Black woman ambling up to the corner of 100th and Broadway. She was tall, close to six feet, and her skin was an unusual shade of copper.

An uncanny bolt of familiarity struck Nella square between the eyes. This was the woman she had been texting. It *had* to be. It wasn't just the fact that she'd stopped exactly where Nella had been standing mere moments ago, or that she looked more determined than any of the other people who were milling around her. It was all that, paired with a long, black calf-length coat that hid everything except for two black pant legs and a pair of black Doc Martens. The girl looked like she was on her way to meet Bobby Seale.

She also looked like she could have easily kicked Nella's ass if she wanted to.

"Hi there, ma'am. How are you today?"

Nella tore her eyes away from the sidewalk. An older white man in an apron was wiping down the empty seat next to her, giving her a big *Why haven't you bought anything yet?* grin. "Hi," she said, after she'd secured her sights once more on the girl outside. "I'm fine, thanks."

"Just wanted to let you know right now we have a Saturday special going until four p.m.," he said, "so you've got about twenty more minutes until that ends."

"Thanks. I'm just waiting for a friend. She should be here before then."

"Of course. Would you like to see a menu in the meantime?"

"I—" Nella glanced over at the sidewalk again to make sure that the girl was still there. Her brain seized with frustration, then relief, when she saw that she was. "Sure," she said, exhaling.

"Great. I'll be right back. You order up at the counter when you're ready."

The moment he disappeared, she looked through the window again and nearly fell off her stool. The girl had moved farther back onto the sidewalk—away from the street, and closer to Nella. Close enough that, if there weren't any glass between them, she would have been able to reach out and touch the pink scar that ran along the back of this stranger's head.

Nella eased forward a bit to get a closer look. This scar, the shape of a small moon . . . she'd seen it before.

They stayed like this for a little while longer: Nella staring at the back of this stranger's head; the stranger staring out into the street. Finally, after what felt like forever, the girl pulled out her cell phone. Nella reached for her own phone, expecting to receive an annoyed text. But to her surprise, it stayed quiet.

"Sorry for the delay, ma'am." The aproned man had suddenly reappeared, a few menus in hand. He placed them in front of Nella so gingerly that it made her heart hurt. "For you."

Nella tipped her head graciously. Still, she kept her eyes forward, trying to place the scar on the back of this girl's head, trying to imagine who this person could be talking to. An accomplice? Hazel herself? Reenergized and finally ready for some answers, she descended her stool and strode toward the door. She kept her eyes trained on the scar—until, all of a sudden, the scar was on the move.

Nella paused just inside the doorway of the restaurant, shocked, as she watched the young woman quickly drop her phone into a trash can.

Then, out of nowhere, there was a hand.

A Black hand, attached to what looked like a Black woman, wearing what appeared to be workout clothes.

A Black hand, grabbing the girl's arm and pulling her from the sidewalk to the street, then, into the backseat of a black sedan.

And then, just like that, the hand, the scar, and the girl were all gone.

Part IV

Diana

October 22, 2018
Locke Hall, Howard University
Washington, DC

For a while, I thought she'd killed herself.

Whether I believed this for her sake or mine, I don't know. I just know that for months after she disappeared in December of '83, I had dreams of her doing it wherever she went—off the coast of Connecticut, where Dick was sure she'd gone, or the coast of South Carolina, where she'd always wanted to live. Wherever she'd ended up, it didn't matter. I imagined water being involved. And I imagined her gone.

My mother would disown me if she heard this, God rest her soul, but I truly believe it would have been easier that way. If she *had* done it, that would mean she hadn't seen how much I've given up. It would mean she hadn't read the fluff I've been writing, simply because I want to stay not just fed, but *well* fed. It would mean she hadn't suffered through that *Burning Heart* made-for-TV movie that I never should've signed off on.

I bent my head backward, considering the news Dick had just given me. So, Kenny was alive and well this whole time. She'd seen me dilute myself and my career. Even worse, she'd read what I'd told that interviewer in '84, the year after she vanished: *"I've known Kendra Rae Phillips as a friend—and sister—for years. And while I love her dearly, I truly believe she has severe mental stability issues. Please forgive my friend for any pain or hurt she has caused you all. All writers matter. All stories matter."*

Dick could've been wrong. *I should call him back to make sure,* I thought. But he'd *sounded* so sure. I might've had it in the back of my mind that Kenny had been dead over the last thirtysomething years, but Dick and I *had* been trying to track her down. It was only natural that we'd eventually find her.

The question was—now what?

A bell rang through my computer speakers. Imani had sent me an email with the subject line *LOL have you seen this?*

I opened it, in need of a laugh, and snorted when the page fully loaded: *Longtime Editor in Chief of Wagner Books Donates Hefty Chunk of Change to Diversity Initiative.* Dick was at it again. He had always been concerned about optics. That was the only reason he'd been so insistent upon keeping an eye out for Kendra Rae all this time. She knew too much. She was a liability.

I studied the photo of Dick and that Lead Conditioner we'd redirected from Cooper's to Wagner not long ago. The two of them looked pretty cozy, and for a selfish second, I regretted not going up to New York for the event even though Dick had begged me to come. He missed the smell of my skin, he'd told me, but what I really heard him say was, *Now that your husband finally left you, we don't have to hide anymore.* That was Dick—seizing any opening he could.

I pulled at one of the dry, tiny coils of hair near my ear as I continued to dissect the picture. Dick's shirt was unbuttoned a third of the way down in the picture, the way I'd told him he should have it whenever he went to social functions because it made him look less like a yuppie. When I first met Dick in the early eighties, he'd had it buttoned so tight he looked like his head might pop off.

Still, I'd felt a tingle when that yuppie told me he thought *Burning Heart* was incredible, and I'd practically passed out when he said he believed my book—*my* book—could change the world. Beneath the table, one of his black and positively expensive shoes had rubbed against my bare ankle.

I hadn't minded it. I'd only pulled away when he'd added, in between sips of his cognac, *However, I think it would be better for both of us if you went with Kendra Rae on this one.*

Sensing my discouragement, he'd gone on to say how "in" Black authors were. He'd cited Alex Haley and Alice Walker. "Black *everything* is in. Look what Michael and Quincy did. So why don't we put you with a Black editor, too?"

It wasn't just any Black editor they were going to put me with. It was my very best friend—someone I'd known and trusted for years. Still, I'd been skeptical, because *I'd* cared about optics, too. That was why I had tried so hard to get Dick to change his mind. It wasn't anything personal against Kenny; it was just that she'd still been so *new* to the publishing world. Only three books under her belt, none of whose names I remember now. Why wouldn't I want to go all the way to the top with someone like Dick, someone who became a legend by thirty and knew all the bells and whistles of publishing? Once I got there, I knew I'd be able to bring Kenny right on up with me.

That wasn't how it quite happened, though. To my surprise, Dick had been right. Kenny and I were perfectly fine on our own. Not perfectly fine—perfectly incredible. Everything started to come together: the story, the publicity, the positioning. Kenny took *Burning Heart* and elevated it to new, fantastic heights—heights I hadn't even imagined when I'd first started writing it back at Howard. "You're playing the short game with this draft, Di," Kenny had written in her first set of notes back to me. "You need to be playing the long game. Write for yourself, nobody else. Pull no punches with Evie. Give her more breath."

I did. And after a few more revisions, we were able to come up with a book that readers devoured. It was hard to find a copy of *Burning Heart* in any library or bookstore after it came out, and when high schools started banning it for its explicit, occasionally gruesome content—it was the time of Reagan, after all—its comparisons to *Native Son* caused book clubs to spring up in unexpected places: white suburban homes, but also Black lower- and middle-class homes, too.

Apparently, something about two Black women—one light, one dark, both college graduates—had captured the heart of America.

I clicked out of the article and clicked open the latest spreadsheet of young Black women who needed fixing. Teachers at a women's college in Atlanta, I noticed. The thought was unappealing—women's colleges were new territory for us, and we didn't have as much experience working with fortysomethings as we did with twenty- and thirty-year-olds—but if Dick hadn't told the dean no, I couldn't, either.

I hit Print, spun my chair around, and glanced out the window, comforted by the mechanical sounds of hidden gears and shifting paper. But rather than the cool, sparkling blue water of the McMillan Reservoir, I saw Kenny the last time I'd seen her: her sickly brown face held in place by flat, glassy eyes. A dull, monotonous voice. The effect was supposed to be a purely temperamental one; Imani had promised me that. But we were both frighteningly optimistic then, I suppose. Neither of us could know it would take her years to fashion a less harsh formula.

A ding signaled a finished print job—the most recent of many. Sometimes, when Dick gave me assignments that seemed particularly difficult, I contemplated getting out. Telling Dick that he'd have to find himself a new connect—something he'd never be able to do because Imani had always been good about keeping her lab affairs on lock. But how could I do that to him? Dick took care of me after Kenny disappeared. He'd connected me with a new publisher so I could have a clean slate. He'd helped me land the talk shows, the television adaptations, the movie deals.

Most importantly, he'd funded the whole thing. Once I got him to believe it would work.

"I know, I know," I'd said into the phone that winter night in 1983, keeping one ear attuned to Elroy's snores in the next room. "The whole thing sounds unlikely."

"More like impossible. What Kendra Rae needs to do is just suck it up. Apologize for what she said and be grateful for what we've all been able to achieve here so that we can get back to business as usual. I've got four—no, *five* authors who've told me they're holding on to their work until Kendra Rae gets with the program. One of them is Black, too, you may be interested to know."

"But Kenny's not going to *say* she's sorry," I'd said, not taking the bait. I hadn't wanted to know who the sellout author was. "She'd literally do anything else on this earth instead of say sorry, even if it means being blackballed from the entire industry. We both know that. And we both know where she's coming from, right? You've said it yourself how suffocating this place can be. If *you* were in her shoes—"

"I wouldn't be. I'd never shit where I eat, and it serves the damn bitch right."

"*Je*sus, Dick. She's been getting death threats. Everybody's been putting her through the ringer, and—"

"Oh, *she's* being put through the ringer? After all the crap she told people about the 'frigid racial climate' here, you think *she's* the one being put through the ringer?"

This was why I'd approached him about this topic over the phone: I knew just the mention of her name would set him off, and I knew that his explosion would make me want to hit him, hard. It wasn't that he didn't have empathy. No. It was that he used it as a weapon whenever it benefited him. I knew this firsthand.

But could I judge him for that? Just because I'd spent so many of those days whispering into his neck about how guilty I felt leaving Kenny to fend for herself didn't excuse me from the fact that I had. I hadn't spoken out against her, but I hadn't defended her, either, because I'd known it was in everyone's best interest not to get involved.

"Alright," Dick said. "If she's not going to apologize, then you know what you need to do."

"We've been over this. I'm not denouncing her, either."

"Why not?"

"That'd never work. Some Black people will see me as a traitor and they won't buy my book if I do that. Look," I'd said practically, "do you want to end the media circus or not?"

I'd imagined Dick sticking his pinky in his ear and giving it a little turn, a tick I'd never gotten used to, not even after watching him come so many different ways, so many times, with the most inscrutable of expressions.

"Fine," he'd finally said, after a long, drawn-out pause. "What the hell do you want to do?"

I'd proceeded to tell him how I'd recently returned to Newark and run into Imani, a childhood friend I'd also attended Howard with, in the freezer aisle of Wegmans. How I'd asked her what she'd been up to since the two of us had fallen out of touch after graduating, and she'd told me that she'd recently received her PhD in chemistry from George Washington University. She'd started working at a cosmetics company just a few months earlier.

That had been her dream, and her parents' dream for her, back when we'd talked future plans on Kenny's stoop. I was so proud of her. *So* proud. I congratulated her on it all, and she congratulated me, too, on *Burning Heart*—my own professed stoop dream.

I'd started to cry then. Right there in the freezer aisle.

Then, I'd handed her an article about the Kenny controversy. It was news to Imani, but not extraordinary news. *And here I was thinking that the* science *world had all the problems,* she'd said.

And then—after looking down the aisle to make sure we were alone—she'd told me all about the pet project she'd started working on afterhours. A project that could make the lives of Black women all over the country just a little bit easier.

"But I don't get why any Black person would want to do that," Dick had said. "Isn't Black Pride still in?"

"Of *course* it's still '*in*,'" I'd snapped. "And Imani's creation isn't going to change any ounce of that. It's just supposed to . . . help keep that pride intact. Help us Black women wade a little easier through the waves of racism without feeling like we have to swim so hard."

"'Waves of racism'? Sounds like something—"

"Kendra Rae would say. Yeah. I know." I was beginning to regret bringing this up to Dick. I was about to tell him to forget it when he took a deep breath and slowly released it.

"And this is supposed to fix everything?" he asked softly.

"That's my hope."

"Hm. I don't know, Di . . . that's a tall order for a chemical that might not work. On one of the most stubborn women to walk this earth, especially," Dick had added, his voice cloaked in bitterness. But I knew I had him. I'd have the check in hand within a week; maybe sooner, if Elroy ended up going to visit his folks like he'd been planning to.

"I'm not saying I want her shucking and jiving. I'm just going to help her chill out a bit, that's all," I'd whispered. "Help her find her footing again. Trust me—she's better relaxed than uptight."

Relaxed. Help her. That's what I'd told Imani I wanted to do, too. That's what I'd planned on doing all along. Smooth Kenny's kinks out for a little, just long enough to make everyone happy so that everything could go back to normal. We'd play the long game, just as Kenny had told me to do. We'd eventually shoot to the top, maybe create our own imprint. Maybe even our own Black publishing house. I owed Kenny that much.

But then she'd disappeared. A few weeks later, Dick told me about a friend of a friend who was having some problems with a Black writer who was spreading rumors about his white boss at a magazine in Tulsa. A few days after that, a Black adjunct professor at Wash U claimed she'd been called the n-word multiple times at a Christmas party. I refused both of Dick's asks, only to learn later that both of these individuals had been fired and left unemployed, with families to feed and no one to hire them.

So, when the next ask came . . . well, I hadn't been able to save Kenny. But maybe I could save others.

I grabbed the pages off the printer, cringing through the names of the women's college instructors: "'Quinnasha,' 'Rayquelle,' 'Kasselia,'" I read, shaking my head. "My goodness. We people keep naming our kids these names and yet we still wonder why we're not getting any of the jobs?"

"Aw, shoot. Who we got now? Involuntaries?"

I looked up and registered Imani's tall frame standing just inside the door. "Seems like that's all we get these days," I said.

"Mmm." Imani crossed her arms. "Well, if you asked *me*—and I know you didn't—I'd sleep a lot better at night if they weren't Involuntaries."

"And *I'd* sleep a lot better if that last big batch you concocted didn't make these girls so darn competitive against their own," I snapped. "I'm very concerned about how often our Lead Conditioners end up being the Last Black Girl Standing at the office. That's not what this grease is for."

"I know, I know, I know. How many times do I need to tell you, I'm sorry? It's an unfortunate side effect. But I've been working on it, and I think I got the right balance on my newest batch. Less *Terminator* this time."

"Good. Thank you." I handed her the list I'd printed. "Here's the latest."

"'Quinnasha'?" Imani's tone rose higher than her eyebrows. "What the hell happened to 'Mavis' and 'Cheryl' and 'Estelle'?"

We both giggled. "So, what do we think? Who's the closest Lead Conditioner that can get into that college?"

Imani tapped her long, narrow chin with a long, narrow, peach-colored fingernail. "I'll reach out to my Spelman contacts. See what they say."

I nodded. "Great. Let me know, will you?"

"Mm-hmm. Oh, before I forget—" Imani reached into her pocket and pulled out two Ziploc baggies half-filled with a white, greasy substance. "For you. Freshly made. I'll buy you lunch if you can guess which flower I added to this batch." She dropped it on my desk and started for the door.

"You're a goddess." I wasted no time opening the bag and inhaling its contents. "Ugh, yes, *please*. Honeysuckle?"

"Bingo!" Imani chuckled. "God, I've come a long way since the first one, haven't I? Remember how awful that stuff smelled?"

Suddenly, Kenny flashed through my mind again. But this time, it wasn't her face I was seeing. It was her thick, dark hair divided into eight vulnerable parts, my right gloved hand smothered in the cool, creamy formula. *I'm positive* this *batch won't burn,* Imani had promised when she'd dropped the jar off the day before.

I'd done a test run with just my pinky, anyway. Just to see.

"Feel okay?" I'd asked her, hoping she didn't complain about the smell.

"Mmm. Just, whatever you plan to do up there—braids, curlers—don't make me look like a fool, Di. I'm trusting you."

I'd promised not to. Then, I'd reached a gloved hand into her hair, grabbed a piece by the root, and said a little prayer.

16

October 22, 2018

Nella had never particularly enjoyed listening to Pitbull. Not at her senior prom, and certainly not on those nights she'd spent in frat houses, glugging up party juice and bobbing her head to "I Know You Want Me" like it was delivering a vital life force into her system.

Now, huffing and puffing beside Malaika in Bop It Out Fitness, Nella despised it with every burning ounce of her being. But she *did* have a lot to bop out: the notes, her cover meeting outburst, the pickaninny cover that had inspired the outburst . . .

And then there was that possible crime she'd witnessed just two days earlier. Even if the music was terrible, struggling to straighten her back and hoist her knees in time with the beat provided a much-needed temporary distraction from her bizarre reality. It also made her feel better that Malaika, who spent most of her day breathing the same air as fitness freaks, was struggling just as much as she was.

"Before you . . . say anything," her friend huffed, power-jacking with little power on number fourteen, "let me just say . . . I'm sorry about this."

Nella scowled as sweat dripped into her eyes.

"I'll also say . . . you owe me," Malaika gasped. "I feel like . . . I haven't seen . . . you in years."

"I . . . know . . . time flies . . . when you're being stalked . . . at work," said Nella. "Not so much . . . when you're listening . . . to Pitbull."

Malaika eked out an apology. "Beyoncé Cardio . . . was filled by . . . the time . . . I looked at . . . the schedule . . . this morning. This was . . . the only open class."

"I wonder . . . why!" Nella said, although, she supposed, as she took stock of the burning sensation in her thighs and the prominent sheet of sweat that had already accumulated around her waist, a Beyoncé class probably would be even harder. The woman *did* have thighs of steel, after all.

So did Isaac, their perfectly tanned fitness instructor, who was now pumping his fist twice to the beat and bending his knees. "And now . . . SQUAT! IT! OUT!"

Nella obeyed. She lowered her torso, albeit delicately, and took a "break" so she could check out the rest of their class. The forty-by-twenty-foot room was hardly full; eight or nine women and one extremely serious-looking old man had decided to spend their Monday evening exercising with a demonic workout instructor in the Flatiron District, rather than doing something sensible, like restocking their wine supply or doing a crossword. Maybe *that* was what Nella should've been doing instead. What if the kidnapper on the loose stormed into the gym while she was mid-squat, looking to snatch Nella next? What if the kidnapper was waiting outside for her, prepared to pounce the moment she and Malaika went their separate ways?

What if it *wasn't* a kidnapper, though?

Nella had never seen a kidnapping in real life before—at least, not that she knew of. Through the glass door of the burger restaurant, she hadn't been able to see the look on the bald-headed girl's face. Nor could she see how tightly that hand had been grabbing her arm. Nella just knew that the hand had been one of their own. Black. And she also knew that, apparently, none of the passersby had felt moved enough by what was happening to say or do anything. Which meant maybe the bald-headed woman *hadn't* been screaming . . . which meant maybe she'd known she wasn't *really* in danger?

Nella put an end to this line of thinking very quickly. No, of course passersby wouldn't say anything. This was New York City. And she was a Black girl.

Whatever had happened, the girl's name was still a mystery—so she couldn't report much of anything to anybody. She was sure of this; she'd practiced calling an anonymous tip line enough times while she was in the shower. "Here's what I know: A bald-headed young woman sent me these strange notes in September. Then she started texting me strange things about my coworker who, by the way, is also really strange. And that bald-headed girl and I were supposed to meet up, but then she got put into a car . . . but not before she threw her phone into a garbage can. Moments after said car drove away, another strange, hooded person dug the cell phone out of the trash can and ran away." In this hypothetical explanation, she'd leave it there.

But there was more.

Hours after the kidnapping, as she lay on her bed replaying what she'd just seen, she got a call from the cell phone she'd watched get picked up.

She thought about declining it, but Owen wouldn't be home for another hour—she had time.

She held it up to her ear, thinking it might be the Marvin Gaye doppelganger from Starbucks. But the fraught voice that filled her ear sounded like it belonged to someone's grandmother. "Nella. You answered. Thank you."

There was a pause.

"I'm sorry you had to see all of that. We weren't really prepared for . . . There have been some people watching you, trying to look out for you. But I guess not closely enough. I told them to be more careful," she added, more to herself than to Nella.

"Who's 'they'? Who are you? And what happened to that girl who got shoved into that car? Do you know anything about that? And what about her friend—that Black bearded guy? Where is he?"

"I can't answer any of that. Just know that we're trying to help you. I'm working on it. I need you to know that, and I need you to keep this conversation between us, okay? Don't tell anyone at work about it."

"You're *working on it*?" A bang had clattered from somewhere out in the hallway—likely the neighbor bringing his bike up the stairs. "How do I know you're not the person I was told to watch out for? And what's Hazel's real name?"

The line went silent. "You aren't supposed to know that yet," the voice said, exasperated. "Hm. Okay . . . you have two options. You can write me off as a lunatic, or you can find out who Hazel really is."

"But—"

"Do some more digging."

The call ended.

With this, Nella had contemplated smashing her phone with a saucepan and hiding under her favorite blanket. But before she could go anywhere, it pinged. The woman had sent her an image and the words, "Taken this past summer. Keep digging."

When Nella enlarged the photo, she'd made out a young, short-haired Black woman wearing a sweatshirt imprinted with the words COOPER'S MAG, and when she increased her screen to full brightness, she could see the girl's shining brown eyes clearly. They were filled with mirth and a sparkle of something else—ambition—and although she didn't have an eyebrow piercing or long, flowing locs, Nella recognized that Lena Horne nose and that go-getter glint.

Nella's fingertips had gone numb from gripping the phone too tightly. The call, the photo . . . it was all too much and yet still not enough to quell a small, sneaking feeling of curiosity. What had happened to that bald-headed, Black Pantheresque woman? Who was looking out for Nella, and why?

And who the hell was Hazel-May McCall, *really*?

"It's hard out there, right?" Isaac barked, pointing at the room's one tiny window. "Isn't it hard out there? It may be hard in here, but it's even *harder* out there. I want you to give me everything you've got. Squat. It. OUT!"

"Oh lord." Malaika squatted down low once, and then a second time. "I had no idea this was going to turn into a therapy session."

Nella squeezed out an otherworldly groan of protest that she herself didn't altogether recognize.

"Although maybe you *do* need one," Malaika continued. "Especially after what happened to you Saturday."

Nella tried to scoff, but her lack of breath made it sound more like regurgitation. She asked, weakly, "What do you mean, 'after what happened' to me?"

"You know, when you froze. When you were this close to finding out who's been creeping on you—like, literally, *this* close—but you let her go."

Nella rolled her eyes. "Do we have to do this again? Now? While we're listening to shitty top-forty music? I came here to bop it out, not in."

Malaika's squats had depreciated; now she just looked like she had to go to the bathroom. "*Yes,* we have to do this again. Shit, Nella . . . you were supposed to get the license plate of that car. You were *supposed* to get into another car and follow the bald chick's car. But you didn't follow the bald chick, and now you're back at square one."

"Well . . . not exactly."

Keep this conversation between us, the woman on the phone had said, but what did she *expect* Nella to do? Sit with this new knowledge on her own? "Before the bald-headed girl disappeared, she told me that Hazel's name isn't really Hazel. And after that girl disappeared, I got a call from the phone she ditched."

Malaika froze. "Wait. What?"

"I *know.*"

"Why didn't you tell me before? What did the caller say?"

"That I needed to find out about Hazel for myself. Do some digging."

"And that was it?"

"No . . . she also said that she and some people have been following me, too. But that they're looking out for me."

"What the *fuck*?" Malaika panted.

"I know, I know. But this woman sounded like she was being for real."

"I don't even know what to say anymore, Nella. This whole thing is getting scarier and scarier."

"How do you think *I* feel?! I'm being fucking followed!"

Malaika ignored this. "I just think you should be careful, that's all," she said. "What if these people who've been watching you are on the bad side? What if it's someone who's in this class right now?"

Nella glanced around the gym again, her eyes falling on the convulsing man at the front of the room. "I doubt it. And we don't know which side *is* the bad side," she reminded her.

"All I'm saying is, you need to take everything this new person is texting you with a pound of salt. Why is she suddenly telling you all of this stuff now? Why wouldn't these people have said something before, instead of sending you these cryptic notes?"

"I don't know. I wasn't able to ask her," Nella admitted, irritated by Malaika's questions. She was confused enough by the worries bubbling in her own head without having to add Malaika's to the brew. "But I feel like I'm finally starting to get somewhere here. Can't we agree that's a good thing?"

"But were you able to find anything about pink crescent scars online? Because it sounds a lot like a cult," Malaika pressed, but then she must have finally heard herself, because she quickly added, "Okay, okay, fine. It's a good thing. I'm just worried about you, that's all. And I don't appreciate these people fucking with my best friend."

Nella felt a pang that was so sharp and so shameful that it had to have been that of guilt rather than a charley horse. The weirdness that had arisen between her and Vera since Hazel's arrival was really taking a hit on Nella's personal life, and the worst part of it all was that she'd barely noticed how much of an impact it had had on Malaika—not until now, when Nella had no work emails to entrap her, no new manuscripts to distract her. These days, Nella barely had time to see anybody anymore; she felt an ongoing obligation to say no to all non-work-related activities and yes to all the work she could be doing instead—because there was always work to be done. So much work, in fact, that she would sometimes get so tied up that she'd forget to say anything at all in response to Malaika's texts.

Then there was Owen, with whom Nella hadn't spent any meaningful time in weeks. The dinners they did eat in tandem often consisted of her turning pages over takeout Chinese or Indian or Thai as Owen scrolled through his phone, reading email after email. Nella hadn't thought he'd noticed. Earlier in their relationship, she was the one who'd had to fight for *his* attention—the one who'd had to wrench his cell phone or the newspaper out of his hands as she'd set the table. Owen had always been an avid reader; this had attracted her to him in the first place, and once his startup really began to take off a few months after they started dating, this quality stepped up considerably. "You know social justice doesn't take breaks for dinner," he'd joked after she'd picked up his tablet, hurled it onto the couch across the room, and asked him to grab a couple of beers from the fridge.

Owen hadn't done this when Nella had gone into aggressive assistant mode. He'd let her read her manuscripts in peace during their meals, had said *no worries* when she'd decided to forego an episode of *The Sopranos* because she had to finish something for Vera. He'd even forgiven her for missing family time with his moms. But Owen wasn't dense. He was good at reading the room—another quality Nella had admired in him—and the week prior, as he'd popped the greasy plastic cover off the basil fried rice one evening, he was finally ready to say something about it.

"It's the new girl, isn't it?" he'd asked, rather plainly.

Nella had already impolitely started in on the steamed bok choy, had already even more impolitely opened up her tablet so she could continue reading the contemporized, queer reinterpretation of *Lord of the Flies* that Vera had asked her to take a look at that evening. It had been as good as the agent had promised it would be, maybe even better, so she couldn't help but feel the tiniest bit ruffled when Owen pulled her out of it.

"I'm not sure what you mean," Nella had said, reaching her fork out so she could snag a rogue green bean that had fallen onto the table. She'd skipped lunch that day—again—and rued the notion of any vegetable getting left behind.

"What I *mean* is, you're busting your ass at work because of the new girl. Am I right?" Owen finally handed her the container of fried rice and started to push his food around his plate with his plastic fork.

It was an act that produced a loud, scratchy sound that Nella could feel in her gut. But instead of calling him out for it, she'd just clenched her teeth and spooned rice onto her own plate, waiting for the scraping noise to cease.

"Hazel has nothing to do with any of this. I've just realized I've been slacking. I've gotten too comfortable in my position at Wagner, and I really need to step it up."

"*Bull*shit. Come on. This new Black girl's gotchu *shook*."

She'd had to keep herself from smiling. "First of all, you can't use my own people's slang against me," she'd joked. "And second of all, Hazel isn't new anymore, not really. She's been at Wagner for three months."

"Didn't you say that you felt like 'the new girl' for the first six?"

"That was different. I was the only Black girl then. The only Black *person*," she'd corrected herself, "never mind the only Black girl."

"That's what I'm saying. She blew up your spot."

"I'm pretty sure no one says 'blow up your spot' anymore."

"The guys that I work with do."

Nella gave him the chuckle that she knew he'd been fishing for. Most of Owen's coworkers thought "Hey Ya!" was Outkast's best song.

"Admit it, though," said Owen, his lips flattening into one horizontal line. "You sort of liked being the only Black girl at Wagner. Right?"

Nella had gnawed on a piece of baby corn and eyed him silently.

"Hey, don't worry, baby. You can be honest with me, because I get it. I totally get it. Okay, so I don't *get it* get it," he added self-consciously, feeling the force of her raised eyebrow. "But you know what I mean.

It's not awful being the only minority. Whenever I'm the only straight guy at brunch with all of your friends—"

"Which happens pretty rarely . . ."

"—I always feel kind of . . . I don't know, exceptional, maybe? Because everybody always wants me to weigh in on everything. 'What does *this* text mean?' 'Why'd he use two exclamation points?'" He'd pinched his nose so he could mimic Alexandra, an online-dating-obsessive Nella had met through Malaika a few years prior.

"I get what you're saying. But, babe . . . are you *really* comparing you being a 'minority' in certain situations to me being a minority in certain situations? Really? Because, just . . . no."

Owen had put his fork down at this. "What I *mean* is, I—"

"It's astronomically different from what I'm talking about."

He held up his hands, visibly hurt and clearly wondering how this conversation—which had started as harmless speculation—could have taken such a turn. "Whoa, Nell. No. Who said anything about comparing? You know that's not what I was trying to—I was just trying to—"

Nella cut him off. "Babe, it's fine. I know what you meant."

"Are you sure? Because I would *never*—"

"I'm positive," she'd said, although it had taken her a moment to realize that she was looking not at her boyfriend but at her plate of food, which was getting cold. She caught herself, reached out a tentative hand, and squeezed Owen's as affectionately as she could. She'd done this dozens of times in the past, times when they'd suddenly looked down and found themselves knee-deep in an uncomfortable conversation about race, and it always eased any tensions that had risen between them.

Those other conversations had felt different, though. Those conversations had been composed of much sweeter tones; equipped with alcohol or pot or the dim backseat of a late-night Uber, Nella had no problem telling Owen that she sometimes felt guilty for missing out on "Black love," and Owen could admit that his maternal Missourian grandparents were die-hard MAGA supporters.

In the bright lighting of their painfully cramped kitchen, this conversation about being a minority and a 'minority' felt like too much. "I love you," she'd said, so that she didn't have to say anything else. Then she'd reached for her tablet once more.

"What? Are we done here? Seriously?"

"Was there something else you wanted to say?"

Owen had stared at her. "No," he'd finally said, picking up his own phone. "Never mind."

They'd sat like that for nearly half an hour, until Owen had risen to his feet, picked up his plate, and thrown it in the trash.

"O. I'm sorry." Nella had spun around in her chair so she could face him. "I just really want that promotion. And I'm so close. I told you about what Richard said to me last week, right?"

"Oh, something about you having a 'bright future,' and how you're 'well on your way to being the next Kendra Rae' . . . yes, I think I remember," Owen had said. He hadn't returned her gaze, but she could see the small smile that had cut across his face.

"And maybe it *is* Hazel that's driving me a little crazy," she'd continued. "I don't know. I just . . . it's hard."

Owen had swiped his hands on his Adidas shorts, which served as his loungewear whether it was seventeen or seventy degrees outside, and walked over to where Nella sat. He'd reached out and begun to work her neck with his blessed, blessed fingers, a white flag of sorts. "Have you tried to get to know her? Like, *really* tried?"

"We got lunch when she first started. And I went to the Curl Central thing."

"That's not the same thing. Invite her out with you and Malaika. Get to know her." He'd shrugged. "I don't know, it seems to me like you might want her on your side. All the connections she probably has . . ."

Nella had looked up at him. "How do you know about all of her connections?"

Owen had frowned. "From when we met at Curl Central; I just got the impression that she knew a lot of people." He'd stepped back a few inches, as though taking her in for the first time. "Are you feeling okay?"

"I'm feeling fine. But can I ask you something?"

He'd nodded, looking concerned about where this was going.

"I can't believe I'm saying this, but . . . Curl Central *was* the first time you met Hazel, right?"

Owen had blinked at her. "What?"

"You didn't know her before that evening? She's not someone you were talking to online before you met me?"

"What are you saying?"

"I'm saying that there was this one time when she referenced you by name—'bring Owen to Curl Central!'—but I'd never told her your name before. So, I wondered if—"

"I've never met Hazel in my life," Owen had said, his blue eyes ablaze with defensiveness. "You probably just mentioned it to her in passing and forgot."

"I know I didn't. I've hardly told her anything about you."

Owen had flinched.

"It just never came up," Nella had said, as though this would make it better.

His arms had left her neck. "Have you considered that most of your other coworkers know me from all of your whack holiday parties? That they could've said something to Hazel about me at any given time, since you've somehow always been too busy to mention me?"

Any chance of Nella telling Owen about everything that had happened at work had walked out of the kitchen with him. She hadn't followed. She'd just sat there and thought about how impressed Owen was by Hazel's connections. How *together* Owen thought Hazel's shit was, and how untogether her own shit was.

Owen had a point, Nella thought now, copying Isaac's jumping jacks even though she felt like she'd been beaten by a human-sized tenderizer mallet. Receiving mysterious notes at work and not telling anyone about them; agreeing to meet the stranger who'd been sending them; and now doing this crazy workout class so she could . . . what, be ready to run from someone at the drop of a dime? Her shit wasn't together at all. Not lately. Lately, it felt like it had been scattered across all seven continents. And all Owen knew was that she was having a weird time adjusting to the new Black coworker at the office.

Nella promised herself that the moment she started to get answers, she'd explain exactly why she'd been so strung up.

"On a more positive note," she said to Malaika now, jogging in place after she'd thrown herself down onto the floor for a burpee, then decided she wasn't going to do that again, "Richard told me that I'm going to be getting a promotion soon."

"No shit! I'd say 'way to bury the lede,' but that kidnapping you saw definitely took precedence."

"True. Guess what else might be coming with this promotion, though?"

"I'm incapable of guessing anything in this current state of being, so please just tell me."

"The opportunity to work with Jesse Watson."

Malaika abruptly stopped moving, this time from elation rather than exhaustion. "What?!"

"He's thinking about doing a book with Wagner."

"With *you* guys?" Malaika snorted. "No offense, but Jesse Watson being published by Wagner Books is akin to putting mayo on corn bread."

Nella gagged, partly from the metaphor, but also from the fact that they'd now switched to push-ups, and the late-afternoon latte she'd had at her desk had come back to haunt her. "Well, for some reason—cough, *Hazel*—we've finally made our way into the twenty-first century."

"Yes! Welcome," Malaika said, bemused. She took her time rolling onto her stomach, unbothered by the fact that Isaac had already done ten push-ups on one hand. "It contains lots of woke white people. And a whole lot of Pitbull."

Nella laughed.

"So, let me guess: They want you to do a nice little song and dance when he arrives, telling him 'dat Wagner is one of the best places to work on earf, and dat you just couldn't 'magine working no-whea' else . . .'"

Nella had heard Malaika's slave affectation plenty of times before, but never had it made her as uncomfortable as it did now. She wasn't sure if it was the worry that other exercisers might overhear, or the fact that the slave in question here—theoretically—was Nella herself. But she clenched her jaw, waiting for her friend to finish her little soliloquy.

"Oh, c'mon," Malaika said when she noticed Nella hadn't found her minstrel impression particularly amusing, "we both know that's really the reason why they asked you to meet Jesse. Not that you're not qualified," she added quickly, "but when have they ever let you meet someone as high-profile as him in the last two-plus years you've been working there?

"And he's not even that high-profile anymore, either, since he dipped out.

"God, I wish I could hear him weigh in on that shooting that happened in the Bronx last month. And all that KKK shit happening in Indiana. Just . . . all the shit."

Nella nodded, oblivious to whatever incidents Malaika was talking about.

"So, I have to ask: Have they enlisted the services of you-know-who for this Jesse thing, too?"

Nella snorted. "Yep. Richard said he may even let *her* edit it."

"What? She just got there! And didn't *you* write Jesse that email? Did you tell Richard about that?"

"I thought maybe he wouldn't appreciate that I'd gone behind his back."

"Bureaucratic bullshit."

"Yeah, I know. It's fucked up."

"Ugh. Weren't you saying Hazel's been, like, best friends with the boss, though?" asked Malaika. "They were all buddy-buddy at Curl Central. So bizarre. Do we think they're . . . ?"

"I'm still not unconvinced his mistress *isn't* a Black woman . . . but *Hazel*? Ugh, I'm feeling nauseous enough without even discussing that." Nella sighed as visions from the *Needles and Pins* cover meeting shuffled across her brain. "*Every*body at Wagner's obsessed with her. Not just him."

"Well, on the bright side . . . you're gonna meet Jesse, and maybe even work on his maybe-book, right? That's pretty exciting. Even if it *does* mean you have to collaborate with Hazel. Maybe he'll even want to discuss that book idea you sent him."

"Something like that. Although Richard didn't *exactly* say that I'd get to work on it. But it is looking pretty promising."

"Promising," said Malaika, trying to appear convinced, even though she clearly wasn't. "Nice. And if it *does* become your book . . . you're still gonna do it, right?"

"Why wouldn't I?"

"I *do* remember a certain person talking about how she was going to quit after a certain author went batshit on her. And how everybody at Wagner seems to be drinking the Kool-Aid. Or should I say Crystal Light?" she self-corrected, finding enough breath to laugh at her own joke.

"True. But now that I have this opportunity, it—"

Isaac clapped his hands. For the first time, the sound of his palms didn't cause Nella to flinch. She was actually relieved she had more time to think about a response. "Now, planks. Keep those arms straight and those cores engaged!"

"Alright, it's official," Nella huffed, relieved that she could stop moving even if it meant more muscle burn. "This guy is a fucking monster."

"Looking good, guys!" Isaac called.

Beside her, Malaika whispered a faint obscenity, her arms shaking precariously. Thirty seconds later, when she spoke again, they were still planking. "You *do* have a choice," she said. "The way I see it, you have two. I think it's obvious what you *should* do. Or at least, what you should *want* to do. Weren't you thinking about quitting? Don't you hate this place? You should want to go to the meeting and fuck it all the way up. Tell Jesse about how you dropped his name to Vera centuries ago, but everyone there thought he was too Black to drop him a line. Tell him all about Shartricia and how Hazel's been stepping all over you to get everyone to like her. And then pull out your boom box, jump up on that conference table, and give everyone the finger to the reeling sounds of 'Fight the Power.'"

Malaika had always said that she didn't mind being a soundboard for Nella and her many Wagner grievances, and for that, Nella was grateful. Owen could only withstand so much talk about microaggressions; his eyes would glaze over after fifteen minutes of conjecture around what this or that unsigned email from Vera meant. Her own boss could be just as frustrating, so Malaika was almost always "here for it," offering Nella words of wisdom that she considered as good as gold.

Thus, Malaika's advice about sticking it to the Man shouldn't have caught Nella by surprise. It was exactly what her friend had been saying since day one, ever since Nella first started complaining about her job: *If you're so unhappy, then fuck all of it. Leave.* Every time, Nella would agree that yes, she should leave—and that she would, one day. That she wouldn't turn into Leonard or Maisy or even Vera. But every time, after she'd laughed over all the different ways she could quit with Malaika, she would say that she hadn't reached her breaking point. That it hadn't gotten that bad yet.

But in this instance, Malaika's advice seemed way off base. The thought of jeopardizing her career by burning all of her bridges at Wagner, after Richard had told her just days earlier that she was close to getting a promotion, seemed downright absurd. It unnerved her so much that she spent the next sixty seconds trying to keep pace with the fiftysomething-year-old woman who was showing everybody up in the row directly in front of them, rather than saying what she felt in her heart: that, Hazel or no Hazel, Shartricia or no Shartricia, she wasn't ready to give up. There had to be another way.

Malaika appeared to have noticed Nella's trepidation. Because after the next set of planks, she was clearing her throat so loudly that Nella could hear it over Pitbull. "That was option one," she clarified, her tone more sober than Nella had heard her friend speak in a while. "But we both know that's not viable. So, what you really should do is prepare like crazy, then go to that meeting and wow the pants off Jesse Watson and your boss and your boss's boss. Make Jesse want to work with you and *only* you. And then, find out if he's really dating that purple-haired chick who was in his profile picture a few months ago. If not, give him my phone number."

Nella brightened.

"But really," Malaika continued, once she'd dug deep enough to find another wind from within, "sit in that meeting and be nice to Jesse. Connect with him. Do it so well that by the time the meeting ends, he's begging *you* to work with *him*. And if it's not you—if Richard tries to put another editor on it—then Jesse won't accept a deal with Wagner."

"But Hazel—"

"Ms. Hazel-Shit-Don't-Stink-May has built her reputation of being the 'good Black girl' at Wagner, right? How do you think your bosses would feel if she suddenly got super . . . Black?"

"Ladies in the back!" Isaac screeched. "Get with it!"

Nella glowered at the floor before spinning onto her back. She hadn't thought about it before, but she supposed it *would* be especially hard for Hazel to be two-faced in front of both Vera *and* Jesse. Jesse would be able to smell her bullshit as soon as he landed on the tarmac at JFK, would be able to take one look at Hazel comparing hair notes with Vera and call her out for exactly what she was.

Nella flipped to her stomach, then up on her hands. "You think I should go to this Jesse meeting, then?"

"I think you've worked too hard not to go to this thing. But go ready. Hold on until you get what you want. Black it up and get Jesse to love you. Or, at least, like you more than Hazel."

Nella's shoulders started to burn as she tried to keep her back flat and abs tight. "But what if this whole Jesse Watson thing is just another carrot? And there's nothing on the other side of it but, like . . . more carrots?"

"If that's the case," Malaika said, remaining where she'd fallen, "then at least you have your carrot. Maybe start thinking about making some moves. Take that carrot to a different publishing house. Don't publishing people do that all the time? Weren't you just telling me about that disgruntled assistant who'd been so helpful with one of his boss's authors that when he changed jobs, the author followed him?"

Joey Ragowski. Judging from the way Vera had told her this story once—her voice dripping with caution—it was widely viewed as the ultimate assistant betrayal. Close, Nella presumed, to calling an author racist to his or her face.

"It's not really that appealing of an option," she said, "but definitely better than the first."

"I know. I can't imagine having to start over with a new Igor. But at least you'd have a sexy little Jesse Watson carrot on your arm." Malaika chuckled. "Go get what's yours. We all know you deserve it, but first you gotta do the work."

17

October 25, 2018

Malaika stomped her foot. "I said 'you have to do the work,'" she groaned. "I didn't say '*you and I* have to do the work.'"

"What can I say? You inspired me." Nella leaned forward and squinted at the list of silver buttons that were attached to Hazel's front door. "Which number did I say it was?"

"Number two."

Nella pushed the number once, waited a second, then pushed it again. "She told me to buzz this one, even though the whole place is hers. I think."

She knew this for a fact, but she couldn't bring herself to say it. She was too engrossed in envying Hazel's home. It was exactly what she'd expected—which is to say, it was exactly what Nella would probably never be able to afford, but would almost always yearn for: a tall, beautiful brownstone, occupied by Hazel, her boyfriend, and Juanita, located a convenient five-minute walk away from the Classon stop on the G train, a three-minute walk from Curl Central, and a one-minute walk from a hip, Black-owned hybrid vintage store and bar that Nella had always meant to check out.

A year earlier, when Owen and Nella had found themselves strolling through Clinton Hill arm in arm, more than a little buzzed off overpriced apple juice spritzers, she had jokingly asked him how many app downloads it would take for them to be able to afford to buy in that neighborhood. "Let's just say we'd need to make a YouTube channel, and I'd need to learn how to braid," Owen had replied. Nella had laughed and squeezed his arm, admittedly giddy with delight—partly from the overpriced spritzers, but also from the realization that Owen was in fact watching those cheesy interracial couple videos she sent him. They were intended as gags, but they were also ways of saying *Hey, look at this—aren't you glad we're not these people?*

But now, as Nella made her way up the steep steps of Hazel's Huxtable-inspired brownstone, hoisting her long, flowing skirt above her ankles so that she didn't trip, fall, and bust her face on the way up, she remembered why people wanted to become "those people" in the first place. She wanted a vestibule to put a coat rack and a bike in. Neither of these things were something she particularly needed to own, but she liked the notion of at least having the option.

"Well, what are you waiting for?" Malaika leaned against the railing. "The sooner we get up in here, the sooner we can confirm this bitch's real name, pull out her fake dreadlocks, and then get the fuck out."

"The abridged version of the plan. I like it," Nella joked, even though she was starting to wonder if bringing her friend had been a mistake. It had taken her much longer to convince Malaika to come along to this natural hair party than it had taken to drag her to the Young, Black 'n' Lit Girls reading, and her resistance was palpable. When they'd met up for a quick dinner beforehand, a Puerto Rican kid no older than eight had entered the burrito spot wearing a navy-blue Adidas tracksuit and a gold chain; Malaika hadn't said one word about it when she normally would've given him a high five for his outfit. And when a white guy passed by them on the street rapping "99 Problems," Malaika hadn't lingered to see if he rapped the n-word, either.

Nella nudged her playfully. "He-ey. You owe me for all that Pitbull, remember?"

"Pretty sure you'd already owed me at that point. Which means now you're going to owe me again. But this is going to count double, I think. Yeah. So, now you double-owe me."

"This is going to suck as much for me as it will for you. But just remember what we discussed: We pretend we don't have any problems with Hazel, so we can get rid of the problem that *is* Hazel."

"That's exactly what I just said, but fine."

"Right. Whatever. Okay." Nella reached up and pressed both buzzers. Hazel materialized in front of them, locs posted high atop her head.

The muscles in the back of Nella's neck slackened. She didn't know what she would've done if a maid had answered. Probably gone home and cried into yet another sad meal of cheap Chinese takeout. "Haze! Hey."

"Nell! You made it!" Hazel rushed to hug her, as though they hadn't been seated across from each other a mere three hours earlier. Meanwhile, Nella could feel the chill coming off her friend a few feet away as she waited to be greeted. Even still, she made an effort to grab Malaika's arm and tell Hazel how excited they were to be in this very vestibule.

"It's lovely," Malaika added flatly.

"Thank you! Melanie, right?"

"Close, but a little Blacker. Malaika."

"Right. You work for that big exercise guy, right?"

"Igor Ivanov."

"Right. I just love his IG," Hazel said, straightening the hem of her black T-shirt. It was the most casual Nella had ever seen her dressed, she realized, taking in the girl's purple leggings and her lime-green pair of fuzzy socks. She felt overdressed. It had been silly, really, for her to have worn the same cream-colored lacy blouse that she'd worn to work to a natural hair party, where she would most likely be shedding bits of hair and hair grease all over it. But it was too late to worry about that now.

"It's a shame we couldn't properly meet at Curl Central a few weeks back," Hazel added.

"Yeah. Well." Malaika cleared her throat. Nella did, too, feeling a bit like a child who had stupidly rounded up her divorced parents for a dreaded school function. She craned her neck over Hazel's shoulder. At the end of the hallway, she saw a sheer yellow curtain that seemed to serve as a door for another room. "That must be where the party is. And where Anita Baker is, it sounds like?"

Hazel perked up. "Mm-hmm. That's the foyer. I've told Manny this has to be one of the first songs we play at our wedding," she said, starting toward the music.

Nella practically felt the air change as Malaika sucked her teeth. "Such a good choice. Is Manny going to be here tonight?" she asked, hopeful.

"Nah, I told him girls only. He's out with the boys."

Damn. Manny was supposed to be her way in. She considered excusing herself to the bathroom and texting the person she'd spoken to on the phone to say that things were already taking a turn from the plan. But she didn't trust that Malaika wouldn't get into trouble without her.

Plus, it wasn't like Nella wouldn't be meeting a handful of other women that she could size up. She could already hear bits of their laughter bubbling beneath Anita's crooning. "Girls' nights are what I'm all about," she said.

"He was disappointed, of course," Hazel added, leading them first past a huge rubber tree plant, then past a small vintage wooden table that was home to three framed photos. Nella peered closely at the largest one: a six-by-nine black-and-white picture of four smiling Black folks who appeared to be no older than twenty-five or so. She was able to steal only a brief glance at the other two photos, although it was obvious from their faded condition that those, too, had been captured in another time. Hazel was in neither of them. "He has long, curly hair that he takes really great care of. Better care than I do of mine, actually."

"Better care than you do? Now, *I* find that hard to believe," Malaika piped up from somewhere behind them.

Nella froze. There it was: nudge-nudge number one. It had

been stupid of her to show that photo of non-dreadlocked Hazel to Malaika, she decided, but it was too late to change that. Once she was positive Hazel was too busy leading them toward the living room to notice, Nella turned and shot Malaika a look. *Stop it,* she mouthed.

Malaika pretended not to see, feigning interest in an antique-looking mirror that was hanging on the left side of the hallway.

"What was that?"

Nella felt a touch of whiplash as she spun to look forward once more. Hazel had paused and was looking back at the two of them curiously. Anita finished and a livelier En Vogue song started up.

"I was just admiring this intricate bronze frame. This mirror is *so* lovely."

"Oh, that old thing? Thanks, Mal. That was Manny's grandma's. This was her home since the seventies; her daughter gave us this place when she passed."

Malaika nodded solemnly. "How nice. 'Malaika,' please. Not 'Mal.' Thanks."

"Um, *wow*—look at that! Are these Manny's grandparents here?" Nella practically shouted, pointing at the old black-and-white photo of the smiling couple she'd been eyeing a few seconds before.

"No, those are mine," she said. "This was taken the day before they rode down to Washington for King's march. All four of my grandparents marched together, which I think is pretty cool."

For just a split second, Nella forgot to breathe. "Very cool."

Hazel cocked her head slightly. Nella could practically see the gears turning in the girl's head as they turned in her own. What year had Hazel said her grandfather died protesting busing when they were at Nico's all those months ago? 1961?

And the year of the march . . . 1963. Her father had quizzed her on such facts when she was a teenager, around the same time he'd given her that copy of *Burning Heart.*

"My grandmother remarried," Hazel said, almost instantly. "He's my stepgrandfather, but the word 'step' gets so messy . . ."

But it was too late. "Yes," Nella said, nodding satisfactorily. "It's so admirable that she was able to move on."

Malaika looked from her friend to the enemy, confused. But Hazel ignored her and continued walking.

Nella exhaled a puff of air she hadn't realized that she'd been holding in. "So, how many are you expecting tonight?"

"There'll be seven of us, total."

"Great. Friends from college, or—?"

"A real mix," said Hazel. "I know them from all over the place. You know how you pick up friends along the way—at college, different jobs, different places in life . . . all that."

"Mmm. It's really something that you still keep in touch with them all, even after you've moved around so much."

"Yeah, it is. You know, I prefer when the number for these things is a bit lower, at about three," said Hazel, at last leading them through a prewar awning. "It means everybody can get a little more attention. But when I put out the bait, everybody bit. And speaking of everybody . . ." She paused in the doorway so she could make an announcement to the women who were already sitting in the yellow-orange glow of the living room. "Ladies, I'd like you to meet Nella and Malaika. Nell, Mal—" She moved out of the way so they could enter the foyer, too. "This is everybody."

"It's Mal*aika*," she said sternly. At the same time, Nella heard a cackle come from the green paisley armchair in the right corner of the room, which was all but swallowing a brown girl with an Elaine Brown–sized afro who had been flipping through a magazine before they walked in. On the floor, a curvier Black girl with skin the color of Nella's palms rolled her eyes and nudged Juanita, who was sitting behind her on the big sofa, hands in her hair. Juanita just shook her head and continued to grease the girl's scalp.

Nella bit her lip anxiously. She put up her hand and flicked her wrist in that awkward, beauty pageant way that she always did when she felt out of place and didn't know what to do with her appendages. "Hi, everybody."

The girl in the paisley armchair was still snickering when Juanita spoke. "Dang, Hazel. We don't even get names? Sheesh."

"She said, 'There go everybody,'" the girl on the floor added, before gently pulling away from Juanita so she could stand up and shake Nella's hand, then Malaika's. "I'm Ebonee."

"Kiara," Elaine Brown's hair heir said, waving her magazine. That it was an issue of *Harper's* didn't escape Nella, nor did the fact that she had a pen in her hand, as though she were marking it up.

"And you remember Juanita, right?"

"Of course. Good to see you again," said Nella. Malaika bobbed her head and managed a weak *hello*.

Hazel looked around the room as Nella and Malaika moved to take seats on the two empty cushions that had been placed on either side of Ebonee. "Where's Camille?"

"She had to step out," said Juanita. "Something about having to call her boo because he was getting off work and he likes to talk to her for at least half of his commute home."

Malaika helped herself to a handful of blue corn tortilla chips that were sitting on what appeared to be a small square IKEA-looking table in the middle of the room—the only piece of furniture, Nella noted with interest, that actually seemed to be from IKEA. Everything else around them looked like it had been owned and cherished for some time. The green-and-beige cushion she'd chosen to sit on was just as squishy as Kiara's armchair looked, and the artwork on the walls—lots of black figures that were supposed to represent humans in various states of joy painted against miscellaneous bright backdrops—were reminiscent of another time. Between two of these paintings, standing tall at maybe six feet or so, was a dusty yet obstinate money tree plant that had to have been around when Bush was in office. Maybe even the first Bush.

"Camille's boyfriend gets off work at eight thirty p.m.?" asked Malaika, incredulous, as though she'd known Camille her entire life. "What does he do?"

"He works at an insurance company." Hazel lowered herself onto the open seat next to Manny's sister. "But he lives in . . . where does he live again, Eb?"

"Somewhere out West. Colorado, I think."

"Doesn't he live in Montana?" asked Juanita.

Ebonee snorted. "Like I remember. Aren't they basically the same?"

"He lives in Missoula," Kiara interjected, flipping a page in her magazine.

Nella nearly choked on her potato chip. "Missoula?"

"Uh-huh. At least, that fine snack she was showing me pictures of on her phone lives in Missoula. And he looked fresh out of a Patagonia ad, so." Kiara shrugged her bare shoulders, two muscular knobs beneath a periwinkle wifebeater.

"You been there?" Hazel asked Nella, surprised.

Nella shook her head. "No, I just—is that where Camille is from, too?"

"Believe it or not, yes. She's part of that small point-five percent of Black people who grew up there."

"Now *that's* something," Malaika said.

Nella regarded her friend, who appeared at ease now that she'd seen Hazel's friends really did have mouths instead of the multiple rows of leech teeth she'd presumed before arriving. But when Malaika caught her eye, that ease quickly transformed into concern. She wrinkled her eyebrow, as though to ask, *You good?*

Nella wasn't good. Far from it.

She swallowed and glanced over at Hazel, who had grabbed a satchel from behind the couch and was now starting to take out long, vibrant pieces of fabric. "I picked up a bunch of these last weekend—you know, from that African fabric store I got India's scarf at," Hazel said, holding up a black scarf with rows and rows of tiny white and red diamonds. "They were having a sale, two for twenty-five. Take a look and see which one you want?"

"Those are gorgeous," said Malaika, taking the satchel from Hazel so she could pass it to Nella. "Nell, that black-and-red one would look great on you."

Nella accepted the bag awkwardly, still hung up on Missoula, and still getting weird eyes from Malaika. She considered pulling her friend aside to tell her that maybe coming here wasn't such a good idea after all, but she knew how it would look for the two of them to go off and have a private conversation at an intimate party such as this one: rude at best; suspicious at worst.

Nella plucked the scarf Malaika had pointed out and held it up to the light. "I think this one's the winner," she said, setting the satchel on the ground between her feet.

"Nice choice. Wanna slide on over here? I can try a few different scarf styles on you and then you can pick which ones you want to learn how to do."

"Sounds great." Nella removed the large black elastic from her hair and slid her cushion over so that her shoulders rested against Hazel's knees. The act alone sent a jolt of memory up her back muscles. As Hazel stuck her hands in Nella's hair, giving it a superficial feel and then roaming her way around, Nella couldn't help but recall how many times she'd done this exact same thing with her mother back when she was a kid, and her grandmother, too, whenever her father took her out there to visit and she wanted her grandbaby girl to have freshly done braids. In almost every instance, she'd hated it: when she was getting cornrows; when she was getting DIY relaxers (the year that Nella's mother said they needed to start "cutting back"); when she had to sit through her mother's tedious soap operas; when her grandmother insisted on pressing the curler so close to her forehead that she could feel her skin sizzling, even if "it's not touching!" like Grandma always promised. Nella was tender-headed; always had been. Restless, too.

But there'd also been something profound in those moments. Something intangible. This something was in the look that her friends gave her when she told them how many hours she'd spent sitting between her mother's legs watching the *227* marathon that had been on TV One that weekend (then, explaining what *227* was); it was in the nature of this elongated physical contact that most non-Black teenagers didn't have with their mothers, but she did. And it was in the little things such contact—however many hours of time she'd spent with hands in her hair—taught her about the women in her family. Hair-care regimens, passed down from both sides. Patience, until the fine line of impatience settled over the whole scene like a bad odor. Perfectionism.

Nella had adapted and incorporated a few of these elements into her own hair-care routines as she'd gotten older. But the one that she didn't consciously remember holding on to was the one that drew her to getting her hair done in the first place. Wasn't that part of what had attracted her to the idea of going natural, anyway? Being able to do it herself?

Even still, she relaxed her shoulders as she felt the poking of a comb, and when she felt a few bobby pins here and there, she let every hint of apprehension go. She forgot about being mistaken for the other Black girl in the office. She forgot about that girl who'd gotten shoved into the backseat of a car. And she forgot about that awful pickaninny cover. She relaxed so much, really, that she didn't flinch when she felt the shocking coolness of something creamy touch her scalp. In fact, she leaned into it, welcomed it, as though the substance had been a part of her body all along.

"What's that?"

Nella jumped at the sound of Malaika's voice so close to her ear. Opening her eyes—had she closed them? She didn't recall doing so—she watched wordlessly as her friend dipped her nose close to her scalp so she could smell it.

"Just some hair grease that I've been using for a while. It's called Smooth'd Out. I think I gave Nella a jar of this back when you guys came to Curl Central."

"Oh yeah," Nella murmured, as her eyes locked on the open blue jar Hazel was holding. "That's the stuff that kind of smells like Brown Buttah."

"Yep. I always like to prepare my scalp before I put scarves on,"

Hazel explained. "More moisture to lock in. You've been using the stuff I gave you, right, Nell?"

"Of *course* I have."

The lie didn't get past Malaika, who shot her an inquiring look. "Well, it smells incredible," she said, reaching for it. "Can I see the label? Nella didn't tell me she found something new."

Kiara's eyes snapped up from her magazine and locked on Malaika, then on Nella, but she didn't say a word.

A beat passed. Finally, Hazel picked up the jar and handed it over. "Sure. Only thing is, there's no label to see."

"Are you one of those people who loves to read labels, Malaika?" asked Ebonee.

"As a matter of fact, I am."

"Kiara does that, too. I practically have to drag her out of the grocery store; it can get so bad sometimes. We're roommates," Ebonee explained.

"Hey," said Kiara, putting her magazine down in protest. "I like to know what I'm putting in my body. Nothing wrong with that."

"That's fair," said Nella. "Hey—kind of random, but do you get *Harper's* on the regular? I've been thinking of getting a subscription."

Kiara shook her head. "Whole Foods checkout aisle. I've thought about it, too, because that's what my creative writing teacher suggested to do during my last semester, but it's too rich for my blood. Besides, I already get the *New Yorker*, *New York* magazine, the *Atlantic*—" She paused, staring at the fingers upon which she'd been ticking off her subscriptions as she tried to remember the others. "There are a couple more. But I can't remember which. Most were gifts from family."

"I hear that. That stuff adds up," said Nella. "I work in book publishing and I've been blessed enough to get a discount on *Publishers Weekly*. One of the many perks to compensate for the low pay," she added, rolling her eyes.

"Hey—the pay could be worse," said Hazel, rubbing a bit more grease on a part she'd just created. "The magazine I was working at before paid me a tiny bit less to do almost twice as much."

"You were in Boston, though, weren't you? Cost of living is different there versus here."

"Not necessarily better, though."

"Which publishing house do you work at?" asked Kiara, putting the magazine down at her feet.

"I'm at Wagner," Nella said, at exactly the same time that Hazel said, "We work together."

"Ohhhh," said Kiara, nodding slowly as she gestured for Ebonee to pass the small ramekin of Wheat Thins. "Makes sense. God, they publish the best books there. You must love it. And Richard Wagner is, like, a god."

"He's pretty decent."

Malaika raised an eyebrow. "Really? Weren't you just telling me that—"

"You must be *brilliant*," Ebonee interjected, staring at Nella. "It's harder than hard to get a job there, from what I've heard."

"Even just getting an internship seems harder than getting Lauryn Hill to show up on time," Kiara agreed, slipping a cracker in her mouth. "Congratulations! That's a pretty big deal. You should be proud."

"Thanks." Nella grinned. A tide of pride started to roll over her as she resisted telling them what Richard had said: *I see how hard you've been working. We value you.* "I've been there for more than two years now, and it seems like I may be getting a little more responsibility soon. Maybe even editing my own book!"

Nella felt a light tug on one of her strands of hair, but when she looked up, Hazel's hands were in her lap, not on Nella's head. "So, um, what do you do guys do? If you don't mind me asking, of course," she added quickly, remembering that she was at a natural hair party, not a networking event.

"It's all good. I just finished my bachelor's in English," said Kiara.

She *did* seem young, not just because of her baby face, but because she appeared to have spent maybe forty-five minutes in front of the mirror getting ready, judging by the heaps of eyeliner encircling her top and bottom lashes, her foundation, and her perfectly done matte lips. "But I'm looking at jobs right now. That's how I met Hazel."

"Same," said Ebonee, gesturing to have the Wheat Thins back. "We went to NYU together, although I graduated a couple of years ago. I've been interning at the *Paris Review* the past year."

"But we're almost *positive* they're going to offer her a full-time assistant position before the year ends," Hazel boasted. "Sorry, I can't help but brag, Eb—you're a badass."

"Whoa, okay. Tons of literary people here," observed Malaika lightly. "Nell, aren't you always telling me how white the literary world is?"

Nella raised an eyebrow. She'd been thinking the same thing. "Very white," she said stiffly. "It would be great to have you guys in this world, too."

"*So* great," Hazel agreed. "The two of us can only do so much."

"Well, I'm not into books or writing or any of that," Juanita said proudly. "I'm working on getting my hair technician degree."

"Nice!" Malaika looked down once again at the jar she'd been handed. "Since you know hair—tell me what the deal is with that goop Hazel's slathering into Nella's hair. Is it homemade or something? Is *that* why there isn't a label?"

"That's exactly why," Juanita said. "And hey, I can do your hair next, after I finish with Eb. Any idea of what you want to have done tonight?"

Malaika spun the jar around in her hand, searching for answers she wouldn't be able to find on unlabeled plastic. "Cool! Thanks, but no thanks to the grease. Maybe some braids, since it *is* starting to get cold out . . ."

"'Nita does a fierce protective style," said Ebonee.

"I do, it's true."

Nella heard a mutter of assent come from above the back of her head, followed by, "And the Smooth'd Out really locks the moisture in, too. I recommend it."

Malaika shrugged, handed the jar back. "Thanks for the offer, but I'm gonna pass."

"How come?" asked Juanita.

"I'm not too big on using hair products that don't have their ingredients listed. Any products, really—but especially hair products."

"Yeah, Malaika is *really* obsessive about those kinds of things."

Hazel started wrapping the fabric around Nella's head when she said this, and she didn't have to look up at her friend's face to know she was giving her That Look again. Malaika had a point about only using hair products she trusted. Still, Nella couldn't muster the courage to agree with her.

Juanita tutted as Ebonee leaned over to examine Malaika's hair. "That must be a pretty hard rule to live by. Does that mean you shop at, like . . . Target?"

Nearly everyone in the room visibly shuddered. "SheaMoisture really fucked up *my* hair," Kiara said. "Fucked up all my ends. I ended up quitting Target entirely."

"Hey, I used SheaMoisture for years before I started using Brown Buttah," Nella finally mustered. "It's not *that* bad."

"Look, everyone's hair is different. I just know mine is sensitive," Malaika said coolly. "When I bought some unlabeled product once at a natural hair care fair in the Bronx a few years ago, that fucked up *my* hair and that was it for me. I knew I'd never to do that again. But I *can* trust what's in my own homemade hair grease." She turned to Hazel. "Unless you can tell me what's in yours? Maybe then I'd change my mind."

The pieces of the scarf tightened around Nella's hairline—too tight. But she didn't say anything. "It's a secret recipe," Hazel said, grinning. "A friend of a friend of a friend's mom made it, and she hasn't told anybody what's in it. Ever. Sorry."

Malaika handed the jar back. "No worries." She still seemed as calm and as light as summer rain, but Nella sensed a thunderstorm brewing under her eyes after that exchange. "Nell—that scarf looks incredible on you."

"Yeah?"

Kiara put down her magazine. "It *does* look dope. You have a great-shaped face for scarves."

"Really? I've never worn one," said Nella, feeling—against all of her smarter instincts—flattered by the compliment. "Never for fashion, anyway. Just for bed."

"Let me see?"

Nella turned around so Hazel could take a look at her work. She nodded. "You should wear them all the time," she said. "And just think, you're deep-conditioning right at this very minute. 'Nita, you got a hand mirror?"

"Ah." Juanita punched her thigh. "I *knew* I forgot something. I think I left it in the car. Can I get it when I'm done with Ebonee?"

"I can take a photo for now," Malaika said, reaching into her purse to grab her phone. But Nella stopped her before she could get it.

"No," she said, a bit curtly, keeping her eyes on Malaika's long enough to spark cognizance. "I actually have to use the bathroom, so can I just use the mirror in there?"

"Definitely. It's upstairs on the left," said Hazel, pointing at the doorway through which they'd come.

Nella thanked her and, ignoring Malaika's pleading gaze for her not to leave, lifted herself up from the cushion. Then she slipped out of the room just as Kiara made a joke about what Camille and her boyfriend were probably doing on the phone.

Camille, from Missoula.

This couldn't be a coincidence. That list of names she'd found on the printer a few weeks ago couldn't have just been a guest list, or an author list.

You know how you pick up friends in different places along the way, Hazel had said. As though she'd collected each of them, like a handful of Black girl Tamagotchis.

Nella quickened her pace, taking the stairs two at a time. When she reached the top of the landing she saw three doors. The one on the left was cracked, the faint light of a candle just barely visible through the sliver. The other two doors were shut tight.

Time was ticking. She already estimated she had about five minutes left to explore—seven, if Malaika distracted them successfully. Nella regarded the glow one last time. Then, without one more thought, she reached for the doorknob on the right side of the landing and turned.

18

Nella had to practically fling herself into Hazel's room. She'd never been the type to explore spaces that weren't hers. To be fair, she rarely had the opportunity. Being an only child meant pretty much every room in the house was fair game, since her parents would let her watch movies in their room all the time when she was little. But even when she was older and more curious, she refrained from purposely going to a room that wasn't the bathroom, held herself back from opening cabinet doors above sinks that didn't belong to her.

Her reason for this wasn't because she had a strong moral code. It was because she'd seen *The Texas Chainsaw Massacre* far too young. She knew what could happen while exploring a place that wasn't your own: At worst, a big dude in a mask came and dragged you into a back room so he could slaughter you. At best, you were off on a thirty-minute chase, quite literally running for your life.

Nella wasn't exactly sure what she expected to pop out at her when she pushed open Hazel's door—not some man with a cleaver, but maybe something just as unsettling, like photos of her taken from a stalker's distance. She had no reason to believe that Hazel actually gave a shit about her. Maybe everybody else at Wagner had been fooled, but Nella was able to see through the bullshit.

She stepped through the doorway quickly, making sure to turn the knob before she shut it behind her. She didn't think the sound of metal clicking against metal would be heard above Sade's "Smooth Operator," but, again: Hazel had somehow always managed to be one step ahead of her on everything since the day they'd met. What made this any different?

She fumbled around the wall for a minute, her hand finally landing on a light switch. She flicked it, thoughts of chainsaw-wielding psychos still dancing around her brain. The shift from dark to light revealed not a torture chamber, but what seemed to be an ordinary bedroom that belonged to two twentysomethings: a Samsung smart TV was perched at the front of the room, along with a Sonos speaker, a Wii, and a WiFi router. Facing the television in the center of the room was a queen-sized bed with a maroon comforter that Nella recognized from Target—one she'd almost purchased before Owen found a black-and-gray option in the clearance section.

Nella moved toward the bed so she could get a better view of the room. She estimated that she had about five minutes before people started asking questions—maybe fewer if Malaika lost her cool and started in on Hazel's dreadlocks.

No. She needed to stop thinking about all the things that could go wrong and think instead about where in this room she would hide something. It depended, she supposed, on how much Manny knew. If he knew her name wasn't Hazel, maybe she wouldn't need to search too deeply. If he didn't, well—she hoped she'd have the time to dig deep enough.

Nella threw back the maroon curtain that was set up on the far side of the room. Waiting behind it were rows and rows of clothes, all varying pieces of fabric, all quasi-foreign, obscure patterns that had to have been thought up in another decade. Nella reached out and grabbed the arm of a powder-blue blazer, then the pocket of a burlap Afropunk Festival kind of thing that just kept going and going. Romper or maxi-peasant dress, Nella wasn't too sure, although the thought of it being the former caused a phantom itchiness to grow between her thighs.

She let it go so she could check the other side of the closet, where she found a pair of forest-green men's sweatpants, then a kelly-green pair of running shorts, then a Green Bay Packers T-shirt. *Your boo thang might have "good" hair and might be a dope AF artist,* she thought to herself, shining a light to see whether or not the footwear on the ground was actually just footwear (which it was), *but it seems like he has one fashion setting: basic.*

Nevertheless, she counted the pairs of Nikes and Adidas before deciding she'd finally seen enough. She pulled back and contemplated other obvious hiding places, looking for some kind of work desk or a haphazardly left laptop. There wasn't a ton of furniture. And then she realized—for the first time—that there weren't a hell of a lot of things in Hazel and Manny's room at all. There weren't any books scattered around. No photobooth snapshots from so-and-so's wedding. No overflowing dirty clothes hampers. Just the bare minimum: a bottle of perfume lined up next to a bottle of lotion next to a blue tube of deodorant, some of her unlabeled hair grease, and a small cup of bobby pins. Tidiness devoid of any personality, not unlike her cubicle desk.

Strange.

Stumped, Nella looked to the bed again. It was worth a try. She fell to her knees, the plush burgundy carpeting cool beneath her fingertips as she slid her head beneath the frame. When nothing of note jumped out at her, she used her phone as a flashlight. Still nothing.

Okay, fine, she thought, pushing herself up off the floor. *I suppose that would have been too easy.*

She felt herself beginning to panic, and then waver. Time was running out. Was any of this worth it? What had she expected to find?

She looked around the room again, hoping for a Hail Mary. Then she noticed the two glass doors beneath the television screen, clocked a few bottles of what looked like hair grease, and—more notably—a manila folder lying next to them.

Boom.

Nella had begun making her way over to the glass doors when her phone began to vibrate. *Please be Owen calling. Please let him be asking where I am. Did I tell him where I was? Anybody but Malaika. Anybody but—*

Two coming up for bathroom. Code Kente.

Two . . . at once? Why two? This wasn't the club. This was a hair party.

Nella sent back a simple *K* and tried to stay relaxed. She knew that the two girls coming upstairs would return downstairs with the news that she had not been in the bathroom. But she also knew that "Code Kente" meant that nobody suspected anything yet—or, at least, it *seemed* like no one suspected anything. It simply meant that she might have company.

A bead of sweat trickled out from beneath Nella's scarf and down her forehead. Then, like a certified prowler, she lunged for the light switch so that whoever it was didn't tell Hazel that she'd forgotten to turn her bedroom light off—or worse, went to turn it off themselves. *I needed to take an impromptu phone call in a private area,* she could say, if caught, and if they needed extra convincing: *It's my mother. She's sick.*

Aided now by nothing but her flashlight and roughly two-thirds of the courage she'd felt when she first crossed this threshold moments earlier, Nella returned to the cabinet and grabbed onto one of its knobs, making sure she left not one fingerprint on the glass. Then, she extracted the manila folder and began to leaf through it, turning over what seemed to be various magazine clippings.

But just as she was about to put the folder back, close the cabinet door, and figure out an exit strategy, her fingers found a non-glossy page. And then another. A little more careful concentration of the beam on the stack of pages revealed that one-quarter of the folder's contents were regular pieces of paper, eight and a half by elevens.

Nella refrained from letting loose a hysterical cheer, but when she came across the rows of wallet-sized faces—all familiar, all in varying shades of brown—she allowed herself a soft one. There they were: Kiara, Ebonee, and according to the name next to the photo, Camille. Next to each of their faces were a city, a three-digit number—a labeling system?—and countless handwritten notes.

She'd been right.

Nella's first instinct was to run and tell Malaika. Malaika could distract Hazel, and then Nella could tell all the other girls downstairs . . .

Tell them what? She didn't know *what* to tell them, really—and she knew she didn't have time to read any of the notes. Not now. So she listened to her second instinct and took a photo to save for later. Then, not nearly satisfied, she continued to leaf through the pages, speeding up when she heard the vague sound of a toilet flushing a few feet away.

She'd hit the jackpot. There were more and more pages just like this one, each filled with Black girls. She didn't recognize any of the faces besides the ones downstairs, but she continued to flip anyway, feeling more and more validated that she'd thrown caution—and the Dumb Fool Playbook—to the wind. Because here she was, sitting on Hazel's floor, sifting through a folder of documents in the dark, finding answers to questions that seemed insane.

And then, to her horror, she found another answer.

The curtains caught her eye first. Aquamarine—her mother's. And the bright-eyed, wine-tipsy girl standing in front of these curtains . . .

It was her.

Nella stared down at herself, transfixed. The photo had been taken on her twenty-fourth birthday, when she'd gone up to Connecticut to celebrate with her family. She looked so happy and anxiety-free that she'd made it her profile picture for all of her social media accounts immediately after leaving her party. She'd never taken a photo quite as good as that one, which was why it was the last photo she'd ever publicly posted of herself.

Nella couldn't escape the message the woman had texted her days earlier, minutes after she'd implored Nella to keep digging.

She's coming for you, too.

There was one more photo behind hers. Nella waited about a tenth of a second before finally flipping over the page—she'd come this far; how could she not?—and caught an unmistakable glimpse of Kendra Rae Phillips.

Terror and confusion filled her chest as she quickly snapped a photo of the woman. Then, without thinking, she turned back to the photo of herself and snapped a picture of that, too, the flash of her phone temporarily illuminating her chocolate-lipsticked lips and sprouts of a teeny-weeny fro that was still trying to find its wings. But before she put it back in the folder, she skimmed the rest of the page. Nella swallowed, as desperate to sit on the floor and read every single word as she was to throw it all into the nearest garbage can and set the whole thing ablaze.

She'd been allotted an entire page—not a row, like the other girls had gotten. Stuck beneath her photo was a hot pink sticky note with handwritten words on it: *Seems complacent enough; but more efforts won't hurt—order of 8 jars coming in 10/20.*

That was enough. Nella slid the folder back where it belonged and closed the cabinet. Then she tiptoed over to the door. She was prepared to let herself out when she heard a toilet flush, followed by the sound of voices.

"Do you think Nella, like, left or something?"

Nella froze.

"No clue. She's an Involuntary, right?"

"Mm-hmm."

"So funny. Why *wouldn't* you want it? My mother would have *killed* for this stuff when she was my age."

"She's probably one of those uppity Black girls who thinks she can get by on her charm alone."

"Ew, those are the *worst.* Good for Hazel for trying to help her out."

Help me? Nella bit her lip. These girls weren't Hazel's victims. They were her comrades.

Nella waited, listening to the sound of running water. For a moment, she thought they might've already gone back downstairs, but then she heard one of the girls—Kiara, she realized—say, "Dang, Juanita hooked you *up*."

"It looks good?"

"Yeah, but stop fussing with it, now—let it be."

"I just—it's so tight. I told her to make it a little bit loose."

Nella didn't have a chance to hear whether or not Kiara told her to stop complaining, because their footsteps were already winding down the stairs. Only when she heard nothing did she count to ten once, then a second time, before slipping out of Hazel's room as quickly as she'd entered.

"That was *terrible*," Malaika complained. "Even worse than I thought it would be."

Nella remained silent as she took a seat next to Malaika on the row of cold, dirty benches to wait for the train.

"They don't care about anything other than getting jobs and working in 'this' industry and 'that' industry," Malaika continued. "And hair . . . like, do they not have any other concerns? I love being natural, too, but you don't hear me talking about it every two minutes. Do you?"

Nella still didn't say a word.

"And, speaking of hair—you should have *seen* homegirl's face when I leaned forward and tried to touch one of her dreadlocks! She practically—"

"Please, Mal. Stop," Nella snapped, the sound of her voice startling herself. The entire walk from Hazel's front door to the subway, she'd been too stunned to speak. She'd even had a hard time walking. She didn't feel like she could trust her mind or her body.

Nella scanned every face on the train platform. Once she was sure none of Hazel's girls had followed them, she pulled out her cell phone. "And you're *sure* nobody suspected anything?"

"I showed them some dumb hair video on my phone the minute you went upstairs. C'mon, now—tell me what you sleuthed! You were up there for, like, days."

Nella narrowed her eyes.

"What?"

"I just . . ." Could she trust Malaika? She studied her best friend, wondering if Hazel had somehow managed to get to her, too. Malaika studied her right back, visibly concerned. "You good, Nell? You looking like you took a trip to the Sunken Place and back."

Nella nodded once. Malaika, she could still trust. She *had* to.

"What did you find?" her friend pressed.

"I took as many photos as I could." Nella pulled up the pictures, then handed her phone to Malaika. "These pieces of paper were in her room."

"Jeez." Malaika pinched the screen for a closer look. "Is that Ebonee?"

"It's Ebonee and Camille and Kiara. It's all of them. Mal," Nella said, her voice shaking, "I didn't have a chance to tell you this before, but those girls—all of those girls at the party—I'd seen their names before."

"You had? Where?"

Nella told her about finding them on the printer one morning, all the while keeping her eyes trained on passersby.

"And you think—"

"Well, I *thought* they were candidates in the running to replace me at work. 'Diversity hires.' But now—now I don't know what their deal is. I overheard them call me 'an Involuntary.' As though I'm being, like . . . *converted* to something."

Malaika looked at the photos again before answering her own question. "Well, see, that explains a *lot*. They're sipping that Crystal Light, too, right? Hold up. What are these words next to their faces? They look like bios."

She was about to say more when she abruptly cut herself off. Nella looked around to see what had brought on the heavy silence. A brown-skinned girl with locs that had been rubbed with pink hair chalk wheeled a bicycle by them, humming softly to herself.

Nella watched her, too, until she was a good fifteen feet away. Just to be safe. When she was out of earshot, Malaika began to read. "'Kiara is an amazing writer and great at picking up social cues. Pretty shy, though, with a lower-than-usual understanding about the classics.'" She scrolled down. "'Ebonee's blaccent is so thick you can hardly understand every other word that comes out of her mouth.' 'Camille brought such great vibes to the workplace. But word got around that she was feeling less than pleased with how we were "treating her." Good attitude, but overall ungrateful.'

"What the fuck—what *is* this?"

Nella snatched her phone back, did some scrolling of her own. "This page is dated as having been printed on March 4, 2017—which makes sense, because Ebonee doesn't have a blaccent at all now. Not to me, at least."

Malaika shook her head as Nella pulled back from that photo and started swiping to the right, skipping over the other photos she'd taken until she got to the page with her face on it. "Here's the worst part of it all, though. *I'm* in here, too. With entries dating back to my first few months at Wagner. Way before Hazel got there."

Malaika's eyes widened. "What? Lemme see!"

Nella held up a solitary finger and cleared her throat. "'June 2016. NR seems smart, quirky. Has white boyfriend, Owen, which could be useful. Is from CT and proud of it.'"

She flinched, but read on.

9/3/16. NR sent Jesse Watson link to external email. Apparently subscribed to his channel.

1/4/17. Cop shooting. Temporary Diversity Town Halls put in place; NR seems complacent.

"Seriously, what?" Malaika said. "'Complacent'? What kind of bullshit—"

Nella continued on, trying her hardest to separate herself from the person she was reading about.

7/14/18. BookCenter article about black grief in a white space published. NR sent article from SK: according to emails back & forth, this was NR's first time seeing it (said she agreed w/ article's content but said she did not write).

8/21/18. NR noticeably happy with Hazel. Seems like perfect match. Estimated time until cycle completion: ~4 months.

"'Completion'? Complete what?!" Malaika spat, causing the lady who was emptying the garbage a few feet away to pause her activities long enough to eye them questioningly.

But Nella lowered her voice and continued on. "'9/26. Accepted grease, no questions.' And here, in smaller letters, 'Mystery note seems to have her on edge—is it KP? Consider alt plan.'"

Malaika scrunched her eyebrows. "That's the same night we went to Curl Central, isn't it? And wait, who's KP?"

"I'll show you in a moment," Nella said, reading faster and faster with each new line.

10/16/18. Still concerned about notes. NR may know more about Hazel than she's letting on. Working with KP?
10/17/18. Note-sender discovered to be Shani (Cooper's). Confirmed NR still in the dark—more time bought w/ Jesse book & promotion talk.

"Hazel wrote all of this?"

That was the most unsettling part. She knew this handwriting, and it wasn't Hazel's.

Nella closed her eyes, picturing this cursive she'd seen a hundred times—the signature on every contract, every thoughtful holiday card written to Wagner's authors. "Richard. This is Richard's handwriting."

"Richard, as in your *boss*?! I *knew* that man had skeletons," Malaika breathed. "But why does Hazel have this?"

Nella covered her face. "Because she's clearly helping him do . . . whatever it is that she's doing. Maybe that's why she's at Wagner—to convince me to be 'complacent.' To . . . hypnotize me? I have no fucking clue. Whatever's happening here, it's terrible, and it's big. Bigger than me, and probably even bigger than Hazel. Whoever she is."

Nella stared out into the dark abyss of the train tracks to clear her mind. But she saw the bald-headed girl, the Black hand. The black sedan. If she'd spent more time looking through those files, she would have probably learned her name, too.

"Four months," Malaika repeated. "That was written what—three months ago? What's supposed to happen to you next month?"

"I don't know. But if that's not confusing enough . . . meet KP."

Nella scrolled to the very last photo in her camera roll—the one she'd snapped of the Kendra Rae Phillips page. Judging by the quality of her wallet-sized picture, Nella guessed it had been taken around the time *Burning Heart* was published. It was maybe one of the last public photos the editor had ever taken. Beside it were more notes, also in Richard's handwriting, with dates that went from the eighties all the way up to present day. Nella read a few of them out loud—*Possible sighting upstate, 1/5/86. 1992—moved to Paris???*—but the last one captured her attention and kept it there.

10/20/18, confirmed sighting of KP near 100th and Broadway. Took Shani's phone, then went underground.

Something ice-cold shot through Nella's veins. Adrenaline. Fear. Awareness. It was Shani who had been put in the black sedan.

So, then, the new nameless texter—the person who'd told Nella someone was coming for her . . .

You chose to deal with Kenny the way you did.

The words clipped Nella in the jaw, suddenly, as though she'd been socked. She tried desperately to remember where she'd heard them. Outside of Richard's office, when she'd suspected he was speaking to his Black mistress.

"What does Kendra Rae Phillips have to do with *you*? Isn't she basically, like, gone?"

Nella looked over at Malaika, who was sitting thoughtfully beside her, nibbling at her thumbnail. She wanted desperately to tell Malaika everything she was feeling—about how scared she was to go to work; about how she'd been talking to someone who was supposed to have been "dealt with." And how she might soon be "dealt with" herself.

But she didn't. She simply kept her eyes trained on the turnstiles through which they'd swiped, mulling it all over. Hazel might have pretended she didn't suspect a thing, but Nella was fully aware that she'd disappeared for just a minute too long. Hazel was Hazel: If there was anything she was perfectly attuned to, it was timing.

"So, now what? You *are* going to quit, right? Or blow the whistle on the fact that Richard Wagner has been keeping tabs on you like this? You *should* write an article about this," Malaika huffed, growing more and more indignant. "Would serve his guilty ass right. Maybe then he'd *have* to explain everything else here."

Nella sat as still as stone. She inhaled slowly, then exhaled even more slowly, trying to think of a way to put what she was feeling into words. Something rotten resided within Wagner's walls, and she'd been tracking that rotten something around on her shoe since Day Damn One. How many people had known? Everyone—it *had* to be all of them. Vera, Maisy, Amy . . . they *all* had to be in on it. How else would Richard have such copious notes?

Far down the track and into the tunnel, Nella could make out the lights of a slow-approaching train coming to take her away from Clinton Hill. After a few stops, she would transfer to another train and be swept into a different, less attractive part of Brooklyn, where few businesses were Black-owned, and brownstones became boxy, medium-sized apartments. Where there were no fancy vestibules to put her imaginary bike and coat rack in.

"Whoever that phone belongs to has had your back since day one. Presumably," Malaika finally said. "And you're gonna send those photos to that person who's been texting you. Right?"

Nella nodded. She started to stand, the red-and-black scarf Hazel had gifted her suddenly pulling uncomfortably at her eyebrows.

Malaika stood, too. "Good. Because you *know* that's the right thing to do. Maybe it seems like the *crazy* thing to do, but what have you got to lose, right?"

"Right." Nella's eyes were still trained on the lights in the tunnel.

"Great! So . . ." Malaika pointed at Nella's phone, which Nella was clutching tightly to her torso. "Wanna do that, like . . . right now?"

"I think I just want to handle this when I get home," Nella replied. "The train is coming."

"We have plenty of time," said Malaika. "Here—you must be really freaked out. I can just do it for you. Pass it."

She reached for the phone, but got Nella's arm and a withering glance instead.

"I *said* I'll *handle* it, Mal. I just want to do it when I get home. My head's spinning right now, I'm tired, and I'd rather talk about something else for the rest of this trip. Let's drop it for now. Please?"

Malaika looked hurt. "Okay, okay, sorry. I just figured . . ."

The arriving train rattled so loudly, Nella didn't hear the rest.

19

October 26, 2018
Wagner Books

Eleven forty-three a.m. Still no new messages, and still no missed calls.

Nella slipped her phone into her pocket and sighed. Had she dreamed the last few months? Maybe. Maybe there was some explanation for all of this—one that was hiding in plain sight, right under her nose.

The morning was as normal as any other one. Hazel had greeted her with her usual *What's going on?* when she'd first entered the office that morning, and Nella somehow managed a lukewarm greeting in return. Vera'd asked her if she could read two new manuscripts by the end of next week. And just a few minutes earlier, she'd received an email from Donald reminding her that the Jesse meeting was at noon, and that it would take place in the small conference room. "The most *intimate* Wagner room," everyone always called it.

Nella pushed herself up from her desk, smoothed her Prince-purple blazer, and started the fifteen-second walk over to the conference room. She was going to be fifteen minutes early—more than early enough, since she was sure Jesse would be at least thirty minutes late. Like he'd said in his CP Time segment: *I show up when I show up*.

Nella was checking her phone a third time, setting her first foot in the conference room, when she was proved wrong.

There was Jesse Watson, sitting at the far end of the table with a blue fortieth-anniversary Wagner mug in his right hand and a ballpoint pen in the other. "Oh!" she exclaimed.

He looked up from his notepad and over at her, his mouth articulating words that sounded even smoother in person than they had in her headphones, and in a flash, he was moving to greet her. "You must be Nella," he said. "It's so nice to finally meet you. I've heard *so* much about you."

"Um . . . yeah. Yes. Hi!" He hadn't said he'd read her email and loved it, but he didn't need to. She was starstruck: Jesse was even cuter in person than he'd been on her computer screen. He smelled good, too, like autumnal potpourri. "It is so, so nice to meet *you*! Thanks for taking the time to come to Wagner."

"Oh, it's no trouble at all. I'm always traveling, and New York is one of my favorite places."

Nella looked around at the empty seats as Jesse sat back down. Seeing her hesitation, he gestured at the one closest to him. "Have a seat?"

She smiled. "Thanks. I wish I could," she apologized, picking a seat three chairs down, "but I think my bosses will want those seats."

Fuck that. White people have been arriving late to the party for centuries, and they still *get priority seats.*

But Jesse didn't say this. He just shrugged. "Oh. Got it."

"And you know how it is: probably better for us Black folk to spread out. Be evenly distributed, you know what I mean?"

She was sure she'd used the perfect amount of sarcasm, had verbally wink-wink-nudge-nudged without actually wink-wink-nudge-nudging. But Jesse was staring at her like she'd suggested they blow up the entire building . . . while they were still in it.

Nella swallowed, suddenly aware of the tightening in her throat and the dryness on her tongue. She'd felt more at ease speaking to Richard about the notes than she did at this very moment.

Richard.

Just the thought of his name stripped away any chance of her speaking again. Fortuitously, Vera whirled into the room at exactly that moment, pink-cheeked and positively cheery. "Mr. Watson! You've arrived! Vera Parini. I hope you found us okay. Can we get you any coffee? Tea? Water?" With this last question, she regarded Nella.

"I'm good, thank you," Jesse said, shaking the hand she had stuck in his face. "Donald beat you to it."

"Great guy, isn't he?" Vera asked.

"Yep. He's a hoot, too."

"A riot," said Richard, who'd quietly entered the room without Nella noticing. She wrapped her arms around herself, a chill burrowing into her bones as he and Jesse greeted one another. The feeling lessened only when Amy and her new high school intern filed in next. Nella couldn't remember his name, but he appeared to have a drop of something nonwhite in him, which was why—she imagined—he'd been invited to this high-profile meeting.

Vera asked about Hazel. Nella shrugged. "She wasn't at her desk when I walked over here. Maybe she came down with something?"

Maybe she decided not to come in today. Maybe she's too busy mixing up new batches of hypnotic hair grease. Maybe she—

"Hazë! Girl, how you doing?" Jesse popped up so fast to give Hazel a fierce embrace that he practically knocked over his chair. "It's been a minute."

"Been *too* long. I'm great! Better now that we've got you here."

"Didn't take too much to do that," he said, casting an arm toward the chair Nella had turned down. Hazel took it without a second thought as Richard smiled at her from across the table. "Thanks for hooking me up."

"Yes, and for hooking *us* up, too!" Vera said forcefully. "What a great meeting of minds this is going to be."

"Indeed!" Amy said, clapping her hands. "Let's get started, shall we?"

"Let's. But first, Jesse, have you met Nella yet?" Richard asked emphatically. "She's one of our finest assistants here. She has a *really* sharp eye."

Nella swallowed and forced a smile. The warning nature of his tone hadn't been lost on her. "Thanks, Richard. We did meet, briefly."

"Indeed!" Jesse said, beaming. He was practically vibrating now, he seemed so happy. Much happier than he had been ten minutes earlier, Nella noticed, as though a light had just turned on inside of him.

Nella shook off the thought, trying not to let it faze her from the task at hand: *Win Jesse over. Make him want to work with you. Leave Wagner.*

"Jesse, we normally start off these kinds of meetings by telling potential authors a bit about what each of us does here at Wagner," Amy began, folding her hands in front of her, "but Richard and I spoke earlier, and we think that it's best that you start us off. Would you like to tell us a little bit about why you're here today?"

Jesse nodded and licked his lips in the way that Nella had seen him do countless times onscreen. "Absolutely. As you all may know, I've been avoiding the spotlight for the last year or so—everything became too overwhelming. The news, the politics, the tweets—all of it was just too much. It seemed appropriate for me to take a break."

"Was there any particular reason you did this?" asked Nella, curious. "Like a breaking point, or anything?"

"Nell—maybe we should let him finish first. No?"

When Nella looked over at her boss, she noticed that Vera was smiling a bit too hard.

"Yes, you're right," she said, embarrassed. She averted her eyes to the scribblings on her notepad. "Of course. Sorry."

"It's all good. Um, anyway—where was I?"

"You wanting to take a break," Richard reminded him, quick-firing daggers at Nella out of the corner of his eye.

"Right. So, I thought I'd take a break. And then I was sitting in the park, not really doing anything, and an idea for a book came to me. A graphic novel, actually."

The thought seemed so out of left field that even Raúl, Amy's intern, sat up in his seat. "A graphic novel?" he asked quizzically.

Jesse nodded. "A graphic novel."

Noticing that no one had reprimanded Raúl for speaking out of turn, Nella said, hopefully, "That sounds great! As in, like, a socially conscious *Persepolis* kind of thing that shows the rise of the Black Lives Matter movement?"

The social media mogul blinked at her a couple of times. "No," he said finally. "Not that."

Nella regarded her notepad again, this time reading the terms she'd written down. "Police brutality, maybe. Or bussing, housing projects, healthcare—"

"I wasn't thinking about writing about any of those things, either. I want to do something more positive. Something with two main characters who come from different worlds. Different backgrounds. One's super chill; the other's, like, super uptight. But they're brought together for a particular reason—maybe they're cops? And they teach each other things, despite their differences."

"So, let me get this straight. You want to write something like . . . a graphic novel adaptation of *Lethal Weapon*."

Jesse grinned. "Mel Gibson is kind of my hero."

"*Real*ly?" Nella asked, too baffled to hide her disappointment.

Richard cleared his throat. "Nella . . ."

"It's just so *strange*, that's all."

"What's wrong with Mel Gibson?" Vera asked, at the same time that Hazel said, "Nella, I don't think we want to push him into something he doesn't want to do. Right, Jess?"

"Thank you," Jesse said.

Nella cocked her head. "But, like—are you . . . are you sure? Is it because you don't think we have the right tools here at Wagner to help you put into words what you'd really like to write? Because we're fully equipped to help you write a really hard-hitting, award-winning—"

"I mean, believe me, we can discuss *some* political stuff today," Jesse said, holding up his hands. "But I don't want that to be the focus of my book."

"Oh. Okay." Nella squinted down at her notepad, unsure of what to make of this. She'd spent the last few weeks imagining what it would be like to actually meet Jesse Watson. She'd flipped through every possible scenario like a deck of tarot cards: snotty diva; Black hippie; total space cadet. But none of these personalities were visible in the person seated in front of her. Jesse seemed washed out. Different. And not just because of his new pair of clear plastic glasses frames, which Nella had never seen him wear in any other photos or videos. He seemed cleaner; tidier. His beard, which she remembered being less reserved and more Rastafarian, was now closely cropped; the tiny twists he used to wear were no longer. His hair now lay flat across his head, smooth and just a little bit shiny. Greased.

Nella swallowed, suddenly understanding, suddenly aware of that magnetic force that was turning her head toward Hazel. It was the last thing she wanted to do. But she had no choice. She took three slow, deep breaths. Then, she lifted her eyes up from the table to meet Hazel's. What she saw was exactly what she'd expected: a look of smug, unbridled triumph.

Nella started to cough, the dryness starting up again. "Um," she said, standing, "will you all just . . . excuse me for a moment? I have to . . ."

"Go ahead, Nella," said Richard.

Vera was already asking about Jesse's favorite books as Nella hustled out the door. She paused long enough to hear him say, almost indignantly, "*Infinite Jest.*"

There was a whoop of approval. Richard. That was all it took to propel everyone into a feverish frenzy of agreement, the echoes of their high-pitched squawks hounding Nella all the way down the hall.

Nella stared at her reflection in the bathroom mirror above the sink, taking inventory of what stared back at her. The melatonin she'd swallowed the night before left her feeling more rested than she had in weeks. Her blazer worked well with the opal earrings her father had sent her as a congratulations for getting a job at Wagner in the first place. Even her curls were looking extra springy, darting out every which way from her head in an orderly, moisturized fashion.

But everything felt wrong.

Nella reached for the faucet and began filling her palms up with cool water. Cold showers weren't normally her thing, but today her clammy forehead found comfort in the splash of the liquid. It felt good the second time, so she did it a third, too. She was reaching for the paper towel dispenser, drops of water still blurring her vision, when she felt something nudge her hip. "I got you."

Nella blinked a few times. When she opened them, she was presented with Hazel, wide-eyed and grinning and clutching a bunch of paper towels in her hand.

Nella looked from the towels to the knowing gleam in Hazel's eye to the towels again.

"Take them. Your face is dripping wet, girl."

Nella regarded the paper towels warily. "Thanks," she finally said, taking the paper towels and wiping her face.

"You're welcome." Hazel walked over to the counter and inspected it for wet spots before leaning back against it. "What's going on, Nell? You seemed really jittery in there."

"I'm fine."

Hazel gave her a once-over. Nella returned the gesture, noticing Hazel had also decided to pick a blazer for their Jesse meeting—the same powder-blue one that Nella had run her fingers over just the night before.

"You know . . . I've been looking forward to this meeting for a while. And I know you have, too. That's the only reason why I can imagine you're still here."

Nella's body went rigid. "What do you mean?"

"I mean that you wouldn't have come to work today if you didn't want to take a stab at Jesse Watson."

"What?" Nella asked, feigning ignorance, because of *course* that had been the plan she and Malaika had come up with the night before: Meet Jesse. Show Jesse everything Nella had on her phone. Then leave Wagner with Jesse, and never look back. "Why wouldn't I have come to work today?"

"I think I'm being too nice here. Let me put it this way." Hazel crossed her arms. "You shouldn't have come to work today, Nella. You should've quit. We don't need to keep you around anymore."

Nella opened her mouth to protest, but Hazel added, "And no, Richard doesn't really value you. That was bullshit. He was just saying what you wanted to hear. He's only been keeping you here to keep an eye on you.

"Plus, now that he knows that you know . . ."

"He knows I know what?"

"Stop it," Hazel barked. "Don't play dumb. Don't act like you don't know. You were snooping in my bedroom. Do you think I'm that stupid? Seriously—after *all* this time?" She snorted. "I *wanted* you to find those files. I wanted you to find them, because I wanted to see what you would do. I wanted to see what choice you would make. And now, here you are."

Nella felt humiliated. Her stomach took a trip to her toes as she contemplated her next move. But she didn't have time to actually make one. Suddenly, Hazel was right up in her face, jabbing a fingernail into her clavicle. The strong, overpowering smell of her cocoa butter hair grease burned Nella's nostrils. "I know it was a pretty big gamble on my part, because you could have opened your mouth and blabbed about it to Shani. But we handled that.

"And before you even *think* about telling anyone," Hazel snarled, her smooth, buttery-nougat voice shape-shifting into something completely unrecognizable, "nobody would believe you. Everyone would think you're insane."

"And I would agree with them," Nella shot back, putting a hand to her temple. There were so many things spinning around in her head; there was so much she wanted to know. But she was too stunned to ask anything other than "Did those girls agree to this on their own?"

Hazel still hadn't backed off, so Nella could see the tiny twitch of incomprehension work its way into her eyebrow piercing.

"The girls. The ones on your lists. They all asked to be a part of this—whatever it is?"

Hazel studied Nella so hard, and so hatefully, that Nella was quite positive she was going to be slapped. But after a long, long second, Hazel blinked. "How sad," she said thoughtfully.

"What?"

Hazel laughed. "How sad that Shani wasn't able to fill you in."

Nella resisted the urge to shield herself as Hazel reached for her purse and pulled out two jars: one bright blue; the other, hot pink.

Hair grease.

"This stuff is *every*thing," Hazel said. Her movements suddenly had a certain showman quality to them; it was as though someone had picked up a remote and switched her channel from Bravo to the Home Shopping Network. Which was strange, since Nella could still feel her nail on her clavicle. "Let's call these . . . social lubricants. You remember this one, right? Smooth'd Out? Of course, you've been using this stuff since Curl Central . . . but not enough, I don't think. Luckily, I applied a lot of it to your hair last night. Looking good today, by the way." She winked.

Nella eyed it curiously, but didn't reach for it.

"And this pink one—Kink Free—actually, maybe I'll just give this to you. You only use a dab of this one. Just a dab. This one helps you hold on to your essence. Your Blackness. It's optional—not all the girls worry as much about using it—but it's good to have in situations like this Jesse meeting."

"Slow down," Nella said, finding her voice at last. "'Social lubricants'?"

"Yep. The contents within these jars are clutch," Hazel was saying. "They'll make you more amenable when it comes to working for and with white folks. But the best part is that they'll preclude any guilt you may feel from doing so. You won't feel like you're compromising anything. No 'selling out.' No 'public versus private' disposition.

"It's gonna numb your ventromedial prefrontal cortex. But it'll also help you to do more with your time than you've ever been able to do before. Don't stress! You won't feel the numbing too much. Could be worse, too—I heard the original formula itched like a motherfucker and turned you into a babbling idiot."

"None of this makes any sense," said Nella bluntly.

"I was able to curry favor more quickly at work in a couple of weeks than most people—Black or not—are able to do in one year. That way, I didn't need to spend all of my time going the extra mile when I wasn't at work. *And* I've still been able to run YBL."

"But even if that somehow all comes from a hair product—you're still compromising who you are," Nella pointed out weakly. At the same time, though, she was thinking about how she wasn't even sure who *she* was. There were so many things she never had enough energy for—so many social interactions she'd gotten so incredibly wrong—because Wagner had sucked her dry of her confidence and her sense of self.

"What's the difference if you don't know who you are? What's that saying—'if a tree falls in a forest, but you're not around to see it, does it count?' Something like that."

"*'What's the difference'?*" Nella laughed. "You're kidding, right? Your grandfather—"

She stopped herself when Hazel tittered, but pressed on. "*Any*one older than us would be disappointed to know that you exist. That something like *this* exists."

"No. They'd be *envious*. Think how much further *they* could've gotten, Nella. Not having to feel all the pain . . ."

"You never answered my question about Camille and Ebonee and them. Whether or not they really know what's happening."

"Ebonee would've been an intern at the *Paris Review* for another year, maybe two. She needed this. So she does. A few others know, too. But a lot were referred to Dick, who then refers them to me—and a few other Black girls—to fix. As time passes, though, they start to love it. Believe me."

"So that's a no. You don't think that's just a tiny bit fucked up? Changing these girls without their consent? Their . . . *sober* consent?" Nella asked, for lack of a better word.

Hazel shrugged. "What they don't know won't hurt them."

"What they don't know will hurt all the Black people who *aren't* doing what you do. And it'll hurt the rest of the world, too, if everyone starts thinking that we're all happy compliant mammies who ask 'how high' when we're told to—"

"They already *believe* we're all 'Strong Black Women,' though," Hazel interrupted. "If they're going to believe that stereotype, and if we're going to continue to feed them that stereotype, then we might as well—"

But Nella did the interrupting this time. "How can we truly fix *any* of those stereotypes—those problems—if we're not truly *feeling* all of the real things the world is throwing at us? Who are we as a people if we're not . . . if we're not . . ."

Hazel was giving Nella another once-over, but this time it was clear she didn't like what she was hearing. "If we're not *what*, Nella? Suffering? Is that what you want? To feel overextended? To feel worn down by every microaggression you experience in the office, and every injustice you see on the news? Are those the kinds of things that make you feel like *you*?

"What I'm offering you here," Hazel said, "is an opportunity to be a part of something that will allow you to let go, and go further."

Nella scoffed. "Well, I don't want it."

"But you *do*. I *know* you, Nella."

"No, you don't."

"I do. I *get* it."

Nella knew those three words and that earnest stare that Hazel was giving her were all simply fluff. A ploy. But when she tried to wrestle away this lilt of Black-girl solidarity, she felt a pounding in the front of her brain, like she was trying to drive a car up a brick wall, ramming into this same wall over and over and over again.

"You think you're above what I do. But I see that drive you have," Hazel continued, adamant. "Everything I did, I did because I have that drive, too. I always have. Look at yourself, Nella. You know it's true."

Nella refused to regard herself in the mirror. "We're not the same," she said, glaring at Hazel. "*I* have convictions. I speak out. I don't ostracize other Black people. You're just an—" Nella stopped herself, not because she wasn't comfortable saying it to the girl's face, but because that ramming feeling had returned—except this time, the car that had been repeatedly backing up and moving forward had transformed into a tractor trailer. It hurt so much that everything in her line of vision turned a bright, blinding shade of red.

"Just a what?" Hazel asked, a grin in her voice. "An 'Uncle Tom'?"

Nella put a hand to her head, trying desperately to collect her thoughts. It didn't work. "Your words. Not mine," she said hazily.

"Sometimes we have to be in order to get what we want. Shit. *Look*." She gestured abstractedly at the white tiled wall that Nella was now using to keep herself upright, but it was clear that she was also casting a hand at all of the time that had passed Nella by without so much as a promotion. All this time without her own title to edit. All this time, just to be surpassed by a cooler, shinier, and seemingly Blacker version in a matter of months.

"You've been working so hard for so long," Hazel continued. "Don't you want to just lean in? Make it easier?" She started rummaging in the black purse slung over her shoulder.

"I'm not . . ." The pain in Nella's head was getting worse now; she could hear every thump of every artery pumping blood into her brain, louder than a bass drum. But even though she could feel the blood moving, pulsing around in her veins, something felt wrong. *Standing upright* felt wrong. She suddenly became very aware of how far away the ground felt—too far away, really, for her to feel comfortable collapsing on it. "I . . . I can't . . ."

Hazel extended her hand. It seemed to take ages for it to land on Nella's shoulder, but when it finally did it felt as though it were burning through to her marrow. "You can. Stop fighting the tide, Nella. Once you stop fighting—once you let this wave wash over you—you'll see. It'll wash over you so quickly, you won't even feel it. You won't feel the pain, the white supremacy. You'll read those articles, watch the police footage, then go to work the next morning without feeling like another part of you has died. That heavy anvil of genetic trauma that's been strapped to your ankle for all these years . . . gone. You'll swim to the top and be free. You'll be *you.* This is Black Girl Magic in its purest form.

"Just tell me yes. That's all you have to do."

Gasping for air, Nella mouthed a silent *no.*

"Don't you want to be successful, too, Nella? Don't you want to swim free?"

Yes, a voice inside of her said. But this woman's voice sounded too tiny, too muffled, to be Angela's. When *was* the last time she'd heard Angela's voice, anyway?

"I . . ."

"Just a yes. That's all I need. Just a yes, and it'll stop. I promise."

"Yes," Nella finally whispered. "Yes."

She felt weary to the bone, as though someone had picked her up and wrung her out from bottom to top. Even still, she felt better the moment the air finished traveling through her two top front teeth.

"Good." Hazel cocked her head at Nella. "Now, don't you feel so much better?"

Nella surrendered a small nod. She felt vulnerable, like she'd just gotten her first Pap smear and didn't know how invasive it would feel.

"Wait," said Nella, just now playing back the words that Hazel had said a minute earlier. "What did you mean before by 'You've been using this stuff since Curl Central'?"

"I gave you that jar of Smooth'd Out at the YBL reading a month ago, and you've been using it. I mean . . . isn't that why you apologized to Colin Franklin? You've already been converted."

A slow-moving wooziness began to creep in. Nella tried to steady herself by placing a hand on the sink, straining to recall when she'd used Smooth'd Out on her own. Then she remembered that pea-sized bit she'd applied here in Wagner's ladies' room, and how much she hadn't liked it. She'd much preferred the way Brown Buttah had melted into her roots. Ironically, she'd found Smooth'd Out a bit too clumpy; it had left specks of white in her hairline that she couldn't massage out no matter how much she tried. Brown Buttah smelled better, too: Subtle. Less sharp, less chemical.

These thoughts must have been dancing across Nella's face. Because a victorious grin was settling across Hazel's.

"Wait. You *haven't* been using it, have you?" She laughed. "Whoo-hoo-*hoo*! The fight *is* in Nella Rogers, after all. How thrilling."

"I . . . no. I'm still—"

"Face it, Nell. You gave up on your convictions a long time ago," Hazel whispered. She pointed at Nella's reflection in the mirror. "Look at yourself, and think about it. Have you *really* been yourself over the last couple of months?"

This time, Nella did venture to see what was staring back at her in the mirror. What she saw was someone who hadn't checked Facebook in weeks—a feat that wasn't too unusual. But she also saw a girl who couldn't remember the last time she'd shared a link on Twitter about any Black issues. It'd been weeks. Months, maybe. She saw a girl who'd declined her boyfriend's proposal to go see a documentary about wrongful incarceration at BAM, citing too much work as an excuse.

She moved away from the wall, approaching the sink once more. A closer look at herself revealed someone who barely saw her best friend anymore, and the few times she did, they talked about her job—not about the video of the Puerto Rican teenager who'd been shot in the face eight times by a shop owner who'd wrongfully accused him of stealing; not about that Fortune 500 CEO who'd been outed just the week before after it was revealed he'd worn blackface to a party while Obama had still been in office. Just her job.

But perhaps the most telling thing she saw—the nail in her coffin of irresponsible Blackness—was a girl who hadn't sent Kendra Rae Phillips one iota of proof that Hazel and Richard Wagner were up to foul play, even though she had all of the evidence at her fingertips. Even though, she suspected, she held the key to freeing Kendra Rae from hiding.

Nella looked over at Hazel. She was still staring at her expectantly through slitted eyes, as though she were seeing all of the things Nella was seeing.

"I don't know," Nella whimpered, wiping away a tear.

At this, Hazel knitted her eyebrows together in pity. Her mien possessed not just a sadness, but a knowledge that she could rescue Nella from the hole she'd found herself in, if only she were allowed to. Shivering, Nella held her gaze right back. She should have been thinking about herself—*What was she going to do? Who was she going to be?*—but instead, she was thinking about the years Hazel had spent doing what she'd been doing. Had Hazel chosen to convert herself, or had she been manipulated the way that she'd manipulated Nella?

She didn't remember asking this out loud, but she must have, because Hazel was nodding confidently. "I was an Involuntary, too. Why do you think they pulled me out of Boston and assigned me to *you*, Nell? We're alike, I said. I *know* you. You wanted to get along to get along, just like I did. Even when I publicly annihilated you, you didn't crack. They told me you were tough and smart, and I saw that. I see it now, too. You understand where I'm coming from. You hear me. I can tell."

It was difficult to decide whether the confidence that had always emanated off Hazel was manufactured, something that the Smooth'd Out had instilled within her. Or if it was a push she'd always had within, from the day she'd first learned that it would not be enough for her to simply go to college, get good grades, and get the interview. That it wouldn't be enough to simply show up to work; to simply wear the right clothes. You had to wear the right mentality. You had to *live* the mentality. Be everyone's best friend. Be sassy. Be confident, but also be deferential. Be spiritual, but also be down-to-earth. Be woke, but still keep some of that sleep in your eyes, too.

"Breathe in, Nell," Hazel cooed. "Breathe in."

Nella nodded. She hadn't taken a breath in some time.

"Good, good. Now take this. It'll be helpful for when you start at a new publishing house."

"But, why do I have to *leave*?" Nella heard herself whimper.

Hazel shrugged. "Because there can only be one of us per office. One per office guarantees maximum results, obviously." She pulled at one of her loose locs. "Now, where was I? Oh, yes. I also recommend using these greases for a week or two before your first day. It'll take a little bit of time to really settle in. Especially since you haven't been using it," she added.

Nella must have hummed some tune of assent, because Hazel had clapped her hands once and was now bowing her head, Amy-style. Unrestrained satisfaction danced across her face. "It won't be an easy transition . . . although it won't be as bad as it could be, either. But we should really get back to the meeting." Hazel smiled, a throwback to the Hazel she was when they'd first met. "We'll talk more after. Does that sound good? Maybe we can even ask Jesse to give you some pointers, too."

Jesse.

I've already won this one, Hazel had all but said just minutes earlier, at the table. *And there's nothing you can do about it.* Nella had thought it meant what she'd already suspected: that there was no way the social media mogul would pick any other editor over Hazel. His shiny scalp, his sweet new demeanor. He was gone.

But he'd seemed happier. He'd even seemed . . . freer.

When was the last time Nella had felt free? Really, truly, wholly free? She couldn't remember. Was it when she chopped off all her relaxed hair? When she moved to Brooklyn? When she graduated from college and realized she never had to return to the South again?

No. It was none of these times.

As Nella regarded herself in the mirror one last time, she realized—with great despair—that the answer was *never*.

Epilogue

January 2019
Scope Magazine
Portland, Oregon

> *What does this mean for the rest of us? For those of us who are fighting fair, showing up first, and clocking out last? For those of us who are doing the heavy lifting, providing domestic and/or emotional labor, armed with nothing but our dignity?*
>
> *It means, my sisters, we must stay focused. We must come together. And we must continue to resist.*

I hit Save and leaned back in my chair. It looked good—not just the last paragraph, but all of it. I'd scraped out my soul and grafted it to every sentence of this article over the last few days. Finally, it felt ready for fresh eyes.

I opened a new email, eyeing first the clock, then the dark patch of glass above Gwen's door. I still had time to send this OBG piece to her and take a short reading break before researching my next article. *Or,* I imagined, my fingers flying across the keyboard, *Gwen will prioritize this piece and reassign that basic coffee bean article to some other newbie*. As long as Gwen came in during the next hour, I'd have edits by four, we'd do another round or two of revisions by six, Ralph in legal would review my evidence, and once we got the okay, it'd be online by five a.m. the next morning—just in time for East Coast commuters in need of reading material to gobble it down on their way to work.

I grinned as I attached the file to the email in a couple of smooth clicks. Black Twitter would go *crazy* when this got out. The NAACP would probably hold a press conference; CNN, a primetime special. Jesse Watson would have a field day; this was probably enough to pull him out of his hiatus. And every workplace in America would go into crisis mode. For a while, maybe years, Black people wouldn't know which Black people to trust. It would be hard. But things would right themselves out in time. And in the meantime, maybe my career would *really* right itself. No more newbie shit, no more having to prove myself. After this article went viral, I'd be a household name, go on all sorts of television shows and podcasts, and—

A household name. *Shit.*

My cursor lingered over the Send button, a slow, steady sense of impending world annihilation rolling into my wrist. Once I hit Send, there would be no turning back. It would all be out there, whether Gwen decided to publish it or not: Screenshots of conversations; a log of Nella sightings. Photos, even—a selfie I'd posted to my Instagram story just seconds before Eva hugged me goodbye at Pepper's, cropped to fit next to the photo I'd taken of her at Rise & Grind. A point-by-point account of how I'd been able to slip away from the entire OBG mess without either side, Lynn or Hazel, knowing where I'd gone. The piece was thoroughly seasoned with undeniable evidence that was supposed to stay hidden because, as Lynn often reminded us, "Premature sharing is risky. We need to have absolute, definite proof. Otherwise they'll think we're delusional."

Lynn had had a point. But she wasn't why I didn't immediately hit Send. Kendra Rae was. *She* was the one who'd talked one of them into letting me go. *If you let us be, then we let you be,* she'd promised. *Everything stays quiet.* I owed it to her to keep my mouth shut and wait for further instruction.

But that had been three months ago. Where *was* she?

I closed my eyes. A lot could happen in three months. For Kendra Rae, a lot had happened in less time than that. When I last saw her, she seemed ready to pull away from Lynn's mission. "It's too late to stop Diana," she'd said, after our Uber driver had asked me which airline he should be looking for. "She's been compromised for far too long, and I just don't see the Resistance getting ahead of this anymore. Pandora's box done been busted wide open."

"We'll show the world what's flown out of it, then," I said. "You *were* lying to the OBGs about keeping quiet. Weren't you?"

"No," Kendra Rae had said. "Well . . . not really. We do need to keep quiet for a little while. Let this unfold. We'll keep an eye on the Hazels of the country, watch them rise to the top of their fields. Once that's happened . . . we'll cut these OBGs off from their supply."

It sounded too obvious. Too *easy*. "Really? What does Lynn think?"

"Lynn isn't a part of this plan," Kendra Rae said firmly. "She could have done more sooner to prevent Nella from going under, but she didn't."

I wasn't sure I agreed with that. I'd shifted uncomfortably in my seat as we entered the exit that would take us to Departures, an ascending plane visible through the dirty glass window. "Cut them off how, if Diana's compromised? And there's no way Richard Wagner is going to—"

"I know someone else. Just trust me."

"But Lynn . . ."

Lynn was going to leave you there, she'd said, *and speaking candidly, I wouldn't have blamed her. What you did was stupid.*

My eyes popped open and found the email. I tapped my finger lightly on the mouse. Clicking Send could blow it all open. It could get us some real detectives so that we wouldn't have to keep playing Carmen Sandiego. This could close the book on everything.

Or it could open a new chapter—one involving me. This article could spoil not just whatever Kendra Rae was supposedly planning, but my fresh start, too. Was I *really* going to jeopardize my new job, my new life, for something that wasn't 100 percent guaranteed to work?

Was I really going to take orders from someone who didn't have my best interests at heart, *again*?

My weight shifted into my index finger—by my own doing or by divine intervention, I didn't know. But it didn't matter.

The message was out.

And it felt good. Damn good. Speeding-down-an-empty-highway-blasting-TLC-with-my-windows-down good.

I'd just opened a search browser and typed in Hazel's name to confirm that she was still in New York and still working at Wagner when I heard the familiar ping of an email notification: *Delivery Status Notification Failure.*

"What?" I murmured, rechecking the email address. I'd responded to an enthusiastic note that Gwen had sent in response to my pitch just a few days earlier: *Whoa! Wild. Be ready to provide a few more materials for cross-reference, but I 100000.00% believe this happened to you. (#BelieveBlackWomen!) Can't wait to see what you do with it. xo.*

I lifted my chin once more. Gwen's light was still off. She hadn't slipped in soundlessly, the way she sometimes did when she wasn't ready to speak to anybody yet. I was considering other reasons she might have been held up when Reagan, a sprightly woman with dermal piercings in her right cheek, cruised by. Looking from me to Gwen's office, she yelped, delighted, "You haven't heard! *Have* you?"

When Gwen had taken me around to meet everyone a few months earlier, Reagan had given me a vise-grip hug and squealed, "Finally! It's about time we changed our image." She seemed even more thrilled now than she had then.

"Heard what?" I asked, chewing on the inside of my cheek.

"River told me this morning that Gwen got a crazy opportunity from one of those brainy magazines to study the effect of mass food hysteria upon the American public," Reagan explained haughtily, as though she herself had been presented the opportunity. "You saw the article about that murder in Alabama over a fried chicken sandwich, right?"

A flare of heat wound up my lower back and wrapped around my neck. "What? When?"

"Hard to say; I get all the sandwich casualties mixed up. I think the Alabama one happened in—"

"*No*. When did Gwen find out about this?"

"Friday night, apparently. She packed up all her things over the weekend and word has it she's already in Missouri."

I sat with this explanation for some time. Gently, I asked, "When is she coming back?"

"Unclear when. Or even *if*. She's been trying to work at a national publication for years now. And she's not getting any younger," Reagan loud-whispered.

I groaned. "*Fuck*. Great timing. I just finished a really important piece and I want her to take a look at it, like . . . now."

"Aw, yeah—that sucks. But don't worry!" Reagan said, patting my arm. "River says they've already hired an interim editor to take Gwen's place. Actually . . . that *might* be her?"

My eyes followed Reagan's. A young Black woman appeared to have entered from the parking garage side of the office. Holding a tote bag in one hand and a coffee cup in another, she'd already passed the potted ficus and the politics editor's empty desk; now she was strutting past Printer Row, her hair cropped and glistening, and her sights set on me and Reagan.

"Sick! Another . . ." Reagan glanced at me, caught herself. ". . . *young* person."

I didn't speak. I was too concerned with this woman's long, pronounced strides. She was making too confident of a beeline toward us for someone on her first day. Like she already belonged. Like it wasn't a big deal that her shoes were four-inch heels, shoes that I'd never seen her wear before.

And her hair . . . oh, her *hair*. Wispy, fine, the color of a roasted almond. Fashioned into a chic, asymmetrical bob that was perfectly, painfully, straight.

"Ladies," she said, casually running her fingers through the back of what could only be a full lace weave. "Hello. How are you this morning? I'm Delilah Henson—Gwen's interim replacement."

Reagan responded convivially. I only muttered my own response as I examined her painted-on eyebrows, her heavily contoured skin. When she waved, she brought a nauseating, syrupy odor with her.

"Could one of you please tell me where Gwen's office is?"

She was looking at me, but I'd already returned my attention to that bounce-back email. It was the only thing keeping me anchored to my chair. *Your email was not delivered because the email address you entered could not be found.*

Reagan pointed at the small metal slab into which Gwen's name had been engraved. "You've come to the right place! It's right here."

"Perfect." The woman held up her coffee cup in gratitude. "And now, sorry, one more ask—can one of you tell me where Shani Edmonds sits?"

Reagan pointed me out before I could tell her not to. "*She's* right here, too!"

"Stellar! Shani, we have *so* much to talk about. Gwen mentioned you've been working on a *very* important article that you're planning on finishing today? I would *hate* for it to get lost in the transition."

"Look at *you*, already hard at work!" Reagan said admiringly. "I'll leave so you two can get acquainted, but Delilah, let's do lunch? I'd love to chat more!"

"Yes! I'd love that, too. Name the time and the date and the place and I'll be there with bells on, honey."

And then we were two.

I swallowed as I slowly looked up at the Black woman again. Her teeth shone an impossible shade of white; her eyes, which were as dark and flat as her hair, were too glossy to reveal the veracity of her smile. But then she spoke, her polished, practiced tone striking an all-too-familiar chord within.

"Now, Shani, tell me . . ." Nella came closer, put a cool hand to my shoulder. "What's it *really* like here? You can be real with me, sis."

Acknowledgments

There are so many people without whom this book wouldn't be possible. First, a big, big thank-you to the amazing team of people who helped me turn my childhood dream into a reality. Stephanie Delman, my lovely agent who believed in this project from the very beginning: thank you for your dedication, your faith, and for always being just one text message away. I couldn't have asked for a sharper or more thoughtful agent than you, and I couldn't have asked for a more supportive agency than Sanford J. Greenburger. A special thanks, too, to my two fierce foreign rights agents, Stefanie Diaz at Greenburger and Vanessa Kerr at Abner Stein, who both helped transport *The Other Black Girl* to lands I'd only dreamed my novel would see.

Lindsay Sagnette, my brilliant editor and champion: Our hours-long chats and your insightful notes exceeded all of my wildest dreams. Thank you, always, for your endless encouragement and your invigorating spirit. Fiora Elbers-Tibbitts: Your diligence—and all of the instrumental work you put into keeping the gears of this book turning smoothly and efficiently, even during a pandemic—have been essential. Milena Brown and Ariele Fredman: To say you are the *best* hype women is an understatement. Thank you times a million for spreading the word about this book near and far, and in such meaningful ways. So many thanks, also, to Libby McGuire, Dana Trocker, Gary Urda, and the phenomenal Simon & Schuster sales team for pulling out all the stops when it came to publishing *The Other Black Girl*, and to Jimmy Iacobelli, Jill Putorti, Tamara Arellano, and Carla Benton for the care and time you spent making it beautiful inside and out.

I am so grateful to everyone at Atria for being so careful and considerate when it came to every detail and decision of how this book was published, including licensing an iconic work of art by Temi Coker for the cover. And I am so grateful to you, Temi, for entrusting us with your work.

Additionally, I'd be remiss not to say that I was granted the utmost good fortune of having two additional editors help me push this book to new heights: Chelcee Johns and my UK editor, Alexis Kirschbaum. Chelcee, thank you for taking each and every single sentence of this novel to heart, and for being so generous with your time and your talents. I can't thank you enough for your help. Alexis, your enthusiasm was palpable all the way across the pond, as was that of Amy Donegan, Emilie Chambeyron, Jasmine Horsey, and everyone at Bloomsbury. It has been such a pleasure working with you all, and I feel so lucky to have you on my team.

In addition to crossing continents, *The Other Black Girl* has also been given the opportunity to cross mediums. Thank you so much to my very helpful film/TV agents at UTA, Addison Duffy and Jasmine Lake, and to Tara Duncan and my entire team at Temple Hill, for showing me the ropes and believing in this story's potential to reach even wider audiences.

Bits (okay, maybe really large chunks) of my own experiences are woven throughout this book, and the writing I submitted in my nonfiction MFA workshops, as well as to my steadfast thesis adviser, Zia Jaffrey, helped me work through many of these experiences. Thank you to everyone in the New School creative writing program who read these often raw and very personal essays. Having your eyes and your ears was invaluable, as were the friendships I made there. Alison: Your notes on my early draft were instrumental. You are one of the most generous writers and friends I have ever known. Sincere: Your enthusiastic response when I first messaged you the embryo of this idea on Google Chat while I should have been working was clutch. Thank you for helping me spot OBGs, and for giving me the space to be my unabashed, Blackity-Black self.

Genevieve, my former work wife and dear friend: I don't know what I would have done if I didn't have you to laugh and kvetch and make bad Nespresso coffee with during my publishing days. Thank you for your incredible support then and now. And thank you, too, to all of my former colleagues and authors who cheered me on when I left publishing to write this book. I printed out your kind words and still have them to this day.

Grisha, my wonderful partner: It's not always easy living with your partner in a studio apartment, and I imagine it's less easy while there's a pandemic raging outside and your partner is a self-conscious writer like me. This book could not have happened without you. Thank you for talking me through tricky plot points and pulling me through moments of wondering if someone would actually want to read this book. You were right. Meow.

Last but certainly not least, all of the gratitude in the world goes to my mother and father, who nourished my love of reading and writing when I was a kid and have been nothing but encouraging—even when I quit a good job with good insurance so I could see this book through. Thank you, Dad, for all those car rides to and from karate that we spent making up scary stories together, and for showing me how important it was to write characters who looked like us. Thank you, Mom, for all those games we played on that fiftieth anniversary edition Scrabble set, and for always being there for me whenever I needed to vent or cry about life.

This is for both of you.

Additional Content Exclusively for Barnes & Noble

Diana

November 1983
Essex Theater
Essex, Vermont

My mother always told me there were two things a colored woman shouldn't be: Easy. And late.

"Neither look good on *any* kind of woman, believe me," she would add, gesturing at me with whatever was in reach—a hot comb, usually. "But they *especially* don't look good on us."

Other things on that list of Colored Girl No-Can-Dos, according to my mother and her posse of Jack and Jill friends: pleather, pink lipstick, sweatpants, grief. And sweat—sweat like the kind that was pooling at my temples when I hopped out of the cab and click-clacked through the parking lot as quickly as possible. *If Mom could only see me now,* I thought, *dodging cars and running through a parking lot in heels.*

My final obstacle before climbing the stairs leading up to the theater doors was a gaggle of elderly white ladies dressed in purple and red. I breezed past them, minding the tiny strip of sidewalk they'd left open, my purse just barely grazing one of the women's elbows by mistake.

"Hey, you!" one of her friends called after me. "You gonna pay for a new hip if she needs one? Be careful, will you?"

The contact had been so fleeting that I didn't think the lady had even felt it. But I paused and turned around. "My mistake, ma'am," I said with a sparkling smile. "It's just that I'm running a little behind, is all."

The ladies all let out a gasp; the loudest, rather predictably, came from the woman who'd so fervently called me out. "It's *you*! Diana Gordon!" she cried, digging her hand into her leather purse. "Would you mind terribly waiting for just a second? I know we'd all love to have your autograph, ma'am. Your book changed my *life.* The way you brought the Black Panther Party—no, the entire Black *cause*, to *life* . . . it just really spoke to me."

The stout woman I'd accidentally nudged had already unearthed her crinkly copy of *Burning Heart* and was spiritedly waving it above her head. "I read *Burning Heart* in a day. I couldn't move one single limb until I found out what happened to Evie. Then, I got my grandson to read it. You are so brilliant. Will you sign?"

She took a few steps forward, her buddies close on her heels. Reasons to say no popped into my brain: I didn't have time; Kenny and Cindy were probably wondering where the hell I was. But these white ladies' faces were so earnest that my hand started to reach for the Montblanc pen I kept in the breast pocket of my coat for occasions such as this.

I remembered myself only when a bright flash bloomed before my eyes, a tape recorder suddenly thrust toward my lips.

"Diana Gordon. How do you feel about your lifelong friend and colleague's disparaging, and many are saying, *racist* comments about white writers?"

I blinked into the reporter's beady little eyes without a word. He seemed young enough to be one of Elroy's students, but old enough to know better than to shove a tape recorder in a woman's face.

"I'm unable to talk right now," I said politely, starting up the stairs. But he tried again.

"Diana, are you aware of the article that was published about Kendra Rae Phillips in the *New York Times* this morning?"

"Article? What article is he talking about?" one of the elderly women asked. The other women shook their heads.

"Kendra Rae Phillips stated, and I quote," the reporter said, his voice growing louder, "'We've had enough of them'—'them' meaning 'white writers.' Do you agree with those words, Diana?"

I'd spent the entire ride from the hotel mulling over exactly that question. It had been easy to answer when Dick was droning on and on in my ear about how much of a mess Kenny had created. "She's made a mockery out of Wagner Books, and a fool out of you. You need to talk to her."

It was funny. People had been saying that to me for years, going all the way back to when we were kids. As if I'd ever had any power over what Kenny said, or what she did.

The way Kenny told it, you'd think *she'd* been *my* protector when we were growing up. And in a lot of ways, she was. She got the Black kids in grammar school to stop making fun of me for the way I spoke and the way I dressed—usually with threats, although there was that one field trip when Geoffrey Harrison just wouldn't stop calling me "High-Yellow Di" and Kenny socked him in the jaw.

It wasn't a particularly hard hit. "I could've hit him harder," Kenny had promised the principal when we were back at school thirty minutes later, and we all knew that wasn't just talk. Staring across the principal's office at Geoffrey, a homemade cold compress on his jaw, I saw more fear in his eyes than I probably would have seen if she'd had one of her uncles jump him. Not once during any of his little teasing sessions had it occurred to him that a girl might hit him the way Kenny did. It freaked him out, and the suggestion that the Kendra Rae who'd socked him was merely Level *Two* Kendra Rae freaked him out even more. We all wondered—me and Geoffrey and the principal, but also my parents, who were concerned about my being friends with a child who so boldly broke all the Colored Girl No-Can-Dos—if *this* was Level Two Kenny, what could happen at Level Three?

We never had to find out. Kids stopped calling me names as we got older. But Kenny couldn't always be around, so I'd still get a sporadic comment about my light-bright skin or my loose curls in the hallways, or at lunch. I'd be asked which one of my parents had fooled around with a white person, and if I proudly said neither, they'd tell me one of my parents was a liar. If I didn't say anything at all, they called me uppity.

What stung the most was that they all knew exactly who my parents were. Most people in town knew. I just didn't jibe with the narrative they'd written for Black people—the narrative that said you couldn't have light skin and money and superfine hair without having at *least* one white mommy or daddy.

Kenny didn't jibe with anybody else's narrative, either. Marched to the beat of her own "very loud, very annoying drum," our teacher told her once, in front of our entire sophomore science class. She did her own thing and didn't give a shit about anybody else doing their own thing, either, and I *loved* that about her. It meant I could complain to her about all the preparation that went into my Jack and Jill coming-out ball without her calling me spoiled. It meant I could tell her why my father had three jobs: to keep us not just afloat, but *comfortable*, because he himself had been raised dirt-poor in Louisiana and had been homeless for a few years of his life. Kenny would listen intently to each and every unfiltered detail of my personal life with no judgment and a lot of advice. In turn, she'd sneak me into her older friends' college parties and take me to civil rights rallies I would have never otherwise attended.

The thing was . . . that drum that our sophomore science teacher was talking about? It *was* pretty loud, and it *could* get pretty annoying. And dangerous. Especially as we got older, and we had more to lose. To put it frankly, sometimes she just didn't know when to shut up. Like that time we nearly got brought down to the police station because Kenny dumped her milkshake all over a pair of shoes after the shop owner had followed us around the store. Or the time we went with Imani to a concert and Kenny spent ten minutes cursing out a white security guard for frisking her a little too thoroughly, walking away only once he threatened to call the police.

I don't know when it became clear to me that Kenny would always be Kenny and that there would always be some kind of ado with her, something to fuss about. Kenny had the right to feel the way she felt . . . she just didn't have any concept of *tact*.

Still—Dick had been so insistent on the phone when he called the hotel, so convinced that this blunder could be fixed, that I started to think that maybe I *could* get through to Kenny somehow. Get her to walk things back just a tiny bit.

But then there was the taxi ride: a jerky stop-and-start ordeal thanks to a three-car accident right by the theater's exit. I'd planned to leave the article alone per Elroy's suggestion, but the page had been burning such a big hole in the seat between us that when the cabbie estimated we'd probably be stuck there for another twenty minutes, I opened it right up.

"Do you think the interviewer set her up?" Elroy asked, grabbing the newspaper out of my hands before I could read it aloud a fourth time.

"Honestly, El . . . I don't." I moved to cross my legs, but the driver's seat was pushed so far back I couldn't. "Kenny's life mission is to tell it like it is."

Elroy nodded vigorously. "We know that. But—"

"It's not like she said white writers are bad because they're white, or that white writers are even *bad.* God, she didn't even say she hates white people, period."

He bobbed his head again, this time with a little less confidence. "But . . . wouldn't you say that she maybe does hate white people? Just a *wee* bit?"

"No, she's just tired of it all," I insisted. "We're going to be chatting with Cindy Murphy, aren't we? And she signed off on that."

For months, Kenny had been adamant in asserting to whoever would listen that we needed to be in conversation with other Black writers and intellectuals. And yet, when Dick told us only Cindy Murphy had been available, Kenny had seemed comfortable, even positive, about the decision. Cindy *did* have four bestsellers, not to mention the trust and respect of nearly every white American woman between the ages of forty and seventy-five—an essential audience, Dick had added. Kenny had raised her eyebrows, said okay, and hadn't uttered a word of complaint about it since.

"And Kenny's never been rude to any of the white writers she's met at Wagner," I added, rolling my window down a bit. "She has a pretty clean history with the public as far as I'm concerned. So . . . why should anyone get bent out of shape over what she said?"

"*Right*. Because ain't *no* way would *Black* people get bent out of shape if they heard a *white* editor say exactly what she said," Elroy said sarcastically.

I glared at him. "Seriously, El?"

"As serious as the people who are gonna come after her for this."

"But it's not the same. Black people don't have the same kind of platforms white people do. Kenny's isn't stealing one blink of sleep from any white writer. Kenny's words won't do them an ounce of harm. It is *us* who will or won't be affected. It's us who will or won't be fine."

"And it's *you* who needs to be worried *now*, Di, is all I'm saying," said El, reaching out to catch himself as the car abruptly stopped for about the tenth time in three minutes. "Listen—*I* know what Kenny meant, and so do you. But don't sell all those racist wackos out there short. People are gonna come after her for this. And you know that means they're gonna come after you, too. Some white folks were already unhappy seeing you two wrapped up in all this success, all these television appearances. They've been waiting to see you fail."

The loud Afro-Cuban beats the cab driver had been blasting when we first got into the car abruptly ceased as he searched for another radio station. "Can we talk about this later?" I asked quietly.

"We could. But I just want you to be prepared for what could happen when we roll on up to this theater. There might not be a red carpet out there waiting for you, or crowds of white ladies screaming and handing you roses like there were back in Texas. You need to know what you're going to do once you get up onstage, Di."

"Dick seems hopeful that the damage hasn't spread to Vermont just yet. Maybe no one will even bring it up."

"And what if someone *does*?"

"Aw, El . . . I don't know. Dick says I should try to get Kenny to take it back. Talk to her before the show."

Elroy laughed one of his slow, long laughs into his open palm.

"Kenny? Kenny wouldn't take back a sweater four sizes too small once she got it in her head that it was *her* sweater."

"Of course she wouldn't," I said, glancing at my watch. We were going to be at least thirty-five minutes late. "But Dick says that—"

"Dick says, Dick says. What do *you* say, baby?"

I hadn't had an answer for him then, just as I didn't have an answer for the reporter who was accosting me on the steps, asking me if I was part of the "we" that hated white writers. His tape recorder was closer to my mouth than it'd been before. A curious crowd of latecomers was starting to form on the steps below me.

"W-well . . . I . . ." *Don't turn this into something it's not. Kenny isn't a racist. She's just seen so much. Worked so hard. And gotten so little. We all have.* "I don't—"

I didn't see the fist coming, just the reporter's widening eyes as Elroy knocked his tape recorder clean to the ground. "Sorry," my husband said. "My fault."

"Son of a *bitch*!" the reporter cried, bending down. But by the time he reached the ground, Elroy's dress shoe had already done its work.

One of the elderly ladies gasped. "Goodness gracious!"

"You can't just do that, you know," the reporter said, holding the pieces of tape recorder in his fingers like shattered diamonds. "All of these people just saw what you did, and I promise you—"

"I promise *all* of you that this is just the preshow! C'mon, everybody—ignore this fool and come check out the real show inside."

I was too stunned to do anything but take Elroy's hand. Only after we'd hustled up the rest of the stairs and reached the doors to the lobby did I turn to see if the crowd was following. Many were. But the women who'd asked for my autograph stayed behind, their heads bowed around the incensed reporter.

Kenny wasn't waiting for me when I arrived backstage. Nor was she in the dressing room that Jessica, Cindy's personal assistant, said she would be in.

When I told her as much, she pushed past me as though I might be lying, only to realize my eyes were just as reliable as her own. "This is just peachy. We get one and then we lose the other."

I stiffened at the girl's unbridled lack of respect. I could get her fired if I really wanted to—and I could tell her that, if I really wanted to. But Elroy had already lost his cool once today, and one lost cool was one too many. Especially over someone who meant so little. The only thing I could do was offer Jessica an apologetic smile and ruffle my hair. "I'm *so* sorry. It's been . . . a morning. A lot of traffic, and then I got stopped by a—a group of older women. Fans. I can't shirk my audience."

Jessica pursed her lips. "Mm. Well. It's too bad Kendra Rae doesn't have the same self-respect you do. Such a shame, just like Cindy said. All that *raw* potential, wasted." She turned on her heel.

I couldn't help myself; I followed after her. "What did you just say?" I shouted, seeing Elroy's swooping fist, the falling tape recorder, the disappointed reporter. Seeing red.

Jessica didn't bother stopping. "You don't think I know what Kendra Rae Phillips said? Really? No way Richard would let this Q and A move forward without taking precautions."

She pointed to a vague shadow up ahead as she said this last sentence. I had to adjust my eyes a little bit, but in a matter of seconds I discerned a beefy Black dude standing in front of a closed dressing room door, an open copy of *Burning Heart* in his hands. *He's probably the only other living, breathing Black man in the whole town besides Elroy,* I thought, yearning to find Kenny so I could share my little joke with her. If she hadn't met him already, I knew she'd want to. She was always fond of getting to know any other Black people she could find in the room; she often found them far more interesting than the people we were actually supposed to be interacting with.

Brother or not, though, his presence made me even more nervous than I'd been before.

"Cindy feels better, knowing he's close by," Jessica added, reading my mind. "Now, I suggest you go try to find Kendra Rae instead of me. 'Cause Cin told me to tell *you* that if you and Kendra Rae aren't onstage in the next fifteen minutes, she's going back to her hotel. And that means no Q and A."

From the outside, Essex Theater didn't seem like the kind of place any Black person could get lost in—unless they had a broom in their hands or an apron around their waist. But somehow, Kenny had found a way to do it, and after seven minutes of fruitless searching, it dawned on me that she might have left the theater entirely. Maybe even the state.

I couldn't think of what to do next, but maybe Elroy could.

The low rumble of impatience in the auditorium was audible from the lobby when I approached an usher who'd been especially kind to me when I first arrived. "Excuse me," I said softly. "I need to talk to my husband, but I'm a little hesitant to go in there and find him myself. Would you mind asking him to come meet me out here, please?"

"Sure, Ms. Gordon!" she said cheerily, her hand already reaching for the auditorium door. "Which one is your husband?"

I hesitated. "Um . . . the Black guy."

She found him at once. I pulled him down the hallway as far as I thought I needed to before saying helplessly, "I can't find Kenny *anywhere.*"

"What do you mean you can't find her?"

"I mean she's nowhere. I've looked everywhere."

"She's not backstage? Not in her dressing room?"

"Everywhere," I repeated, pacing back and forth. "Do you think she left because she was worried about something happening to her?"

"I'm not sure Kenny is *that* sensible," said Elroy gravely.

I closed my eyes and covered them with my hands. "I am so fucked."

Elroy put his hands on my shoulders, tried to pull me into some kind of hug, but his body heat did more harm than good. I was sweating again, although maybe the sweating had never stopped to begin with, and bile was beginning to rise in the back of my throat. "This is *so* unprofessional. Cindy is *never* going to want to have anything to do with me ever again. And Dick . . . *god.* I bet he's going to fire Kenny, and then what's going to happen to me? No editor at Wagner is going to want to be associated with me. I'm a disease. All because some *New York Times* reporter caught her on a bad day."

"Excuse me, Ms. Diana?"

I spun around, expecting to see another reporter with a camera or tape recorder. But it was the Black security guard, still holding a copy of my book.

"Hey, man. Julius. Security." He reached out a hand and Elroy shook it. "I'm sorry to interrupt you guys, but . . . I know where you can find Kendra Rae."

Kenny was looking down at something when I found her leaning against a dumpster, a stream of smoke trailing away from her face. Her back was to me, but as far as I could tell, she didn't have anything with her—not her purse, not even a coat, despite how chilly it was outside. Just a light gray blouse and the pair of black boot-cut jeans she usually wore to daytime book events.

I was staring at the trees a few feet in front of us, parsing out what on earth I could possibly say, when she suddenly turned around and beat me to it. "Jesus." She flinched, nearly dropping her cigarette. "I thought you were Cindy's wigged-out assistant."

Too drained to laugh, I opted for a chuckle. "Quite the delightful little sociopath, isn't she?" I said. For the first time, I saw the wrinkled piece of white paper Kenny was holding in her hands, smelled the faint trace of marijuana. I'd told her before that I hated when she smoked weed in public, especially when we were so far away from home. But judging from the circles under her eyes, she obviously needed it.

"What's that?" I asked, pointing.

"This?" Kenny held up the joint and dispensed a big, sleepy-eyed smile. "*This* is a very kind gift from Brotha Julius. And this—" Kenny held out the piece of paper and I accepted it. The handwriting was recognizable on sight. "That is . . . an apology that Dick faxed over to Cindy first thing this morning, apparently."

"An apology . . . ?"

"From 'me.'"

We didn't have a lot of time left before Cindy called it quits, so I skimmed through it quickly. But a few of Dick's words were too loud to ignore:

. . . *severely mistaken* . . .

. . . *wasn't thinking* . . .

. . . *compromised not only my integrity, but that of Wagner Books* . . .

"Wow," I said, handing it back. "When exactly are you supposed to say all of this?"

"Jessica didn't say. But you saw the reporters outside, right? And a few in the lobby? I think they paid some attendees to give up their seats."

"Damn. I almost got trapped on the way in, but Elroy scared him off."

Kenny grinned. "We could have used him backstage about an hour ago, before Julius got here." She took a few steps away from the dumpster so she could take a peek at the door behind me before taking another long hit from her joint.

"Ah. So that's why Cindy is holed up in her dressing room?"

Kenny pushed the air out between her lips. "I guess."

"Have you seen her at all, by the way? I just want to know how she's taking everything. And how *you're* taking everything," I added quickly.

"I'm fine as wine. Cindy hasn't said boo to me or to anyone else, as far as I know. But if Jessica is any indication . . . I'd say Cindy's not too happy about the whole thing."

She pulled on her joint again, blew air out. "I *knew* getting that woman for this was a horrible idea."

I couldn't believe what I was hearing. "What do you mean? You were okay with Cindy, remember? You said that you were excited at the possibility of even more white women wanting to learn more about the Black Panthers, given how vilified they've always been."

Kenny had also said, *If Dick really wants a Black author to be in con-*

versation with us, he needs to stop sending us to Bumblefuck, USA. Ain't no Black people want to travel to Vermont. But that didn't seem like it would help the situation.

"I agreed because I knew we didn't have much of a choice. But you know if it were a Black author up here with us, they'd be standing by us right now. Not hiding in their dressing room."

Us. The word felt so wrong to me that I took a step backward. "If it were a Black author up there with us, half of the audience wouldn't be here right now. Maybe even more than that."

"Well, then . . ." Kenny exhaled and put out the dwindled nub. "Good riddance to them. Right?"

The nausea was setting in again. No—anger. I'd thought she'd be a little more introspective than this. But her blasé tone, paired with a complete disregard for anybody else but herself, was pushing me over the edge.

"'Good riddance to them,'" I repeated. "Right. Okay." I put a hand to my forehead the way my mother used to whenever she heard about the latest predicament Kenny had pulled me into. "Okay. So, Kenny, that photo shoot we just did last week—the one of us for the cover of a *national* magazine—good riddance to that, too, I suppose? Good riddance to our white fans? And good riddance to either of us publishing anything again, ever?"

"Ha!" Kenny spat on the ground. "That cover was all just posturing, Di, and you know that. If publishing were really entering a 'new era,' Julius wouldn't be here. And neither would Cindy."

I pointed at her. "I know you can be dense sometimes, but you *must* know how important Cindy is to all of this. Her presence legitimizes your apology. She can help us move on. Because we need . . . to move . . . on."

"My *apology*? You mean *this* load of crap?" Kenny began to tear up Dick's fax bit by bit, letting the pieces fly away in the cold breeze despite the dumpster being only a few feet away. When just one scrap remained in her hands, she fished something out of her left jeans pocket. A lighter.

"Kenny, what are you—?" I managed, horrified, but as the spark grew into a flame, swallowing the last piece beyond recognition, I knew exactly what she was doing.

"Well!" Cindy smoothed her long gingham skirt once before taking a seat on the brown armchair that faced our couch. "Let's get started, shall we?"

The round of applause the audience gave us sounded just as sparse as the round they'd given us when we'd first walked onstage. I snuck a glance over to the left to see if Kenny noticed this, too, but her small, perfunctory smile remained unchanged.

"Now. I know you want to hear these incredibly talented women discuss *Burning Heart*, and I promise that I'm going to ask them so many of the fabulous questions you wrote down for our ushers when you first arrived at the auditorium, oh, when was it? A few days ago?" she joked.

The audience chuckled as Cindy leaned forward in her chair. Her long, straight, sandy-colored hair moved with her, and I did, too. I was still a little starstruck whenever our paths crossed, just as all of her fans were.

The secret to being a public figure, Cindy had told me very intensely at one of Dick's author dinners a few months ago, *is making your listeners believe you're telling them something only they get to hear. Even when it's an audience of a thousand, you have the power to make each and every person feel like they're the only one who knows your truth.*

She'd proceeded to take my hand and squeeze it the way she was known to do while speaking with both fans and friends, and while I knew that I was still straddling both of those categories, I felt honored all the same. So, when Cindy reached for the copy of *Burning Heart* on the table beside her and cleared her throat, I held my breath.

"And I promise you that in just a few moments, we're going to dive deep into the lives of Evie and Walter, and the lives of Diana and Kendra Rae. Diana will share the inspiration behind her bestselling novel, and maybe we can even get Kendra Rae to share some embarrassing anecdotes about the time they spent growing up in Newark!"

Kenny and I exchanged a perfectly timed look of mock panic. The audience chuckled again. I could hear Elroy clap his hands wholeheartedly a few rows away.

Okay, I thought, sitting up straighter. *This is going to be fine.*

"See? I know *you* all want to know more, too!" Cindy winked. "But before we get to the fun part of all of this . . ." She passed the mic from one hand to the other, and her playful smile vanished. ". . . Let's talk about that not-so-fun article that has set the literary world on fire in today's *New York Times*: 'If You White, You Ain't Right with Me.'"

A man gasped.

"Quite the title, isn't it? It's one we imagine you'll be hearing a lot over the next few days."

The couch shifted beneath me as Kenny recrossed her legs. The two of us exchanged another look. But this time, the panic was genuine.

"I'm sure many of you have questions," Cindy continued, "and we will get to them. But since we have the distinct opportunity to hear directly from the 'women of the hour'—long before anybody else—let's just get right to it. Shall we, ladies?"

Cindy stared at the both of us expectantly. Waiting.

I regarded the audience. Kenny on my left. Then Cindy on my right. Where was that author solidarity she'd shown me not just at Dick's home, but along nearly every step of my publishing journey? She'd read and raved about my book long before any other author. She'd made sure to mention it during her last radio interview, causing a spike in sales. She'd even promised to introduce me to a few other writers whenever I was ready to expand my circle.

Cindy nodded at me once. Relieved, I released the small breath I'd been holding. There it was. I could see it in her face—the solidarity was still there. But I also saw every single one of her promises hanging in the balance. They would hang there, I knew, until one of us backed her up.

This was our second chance. *Burning Heart's* second chance.

"What do you think, ladies?" Cindy asked, with an edge of stoniness this time. "Should we clear up the misunderstanding?"

The silence was insufferable. Crushing. I couldn't do it anymore. Holding my microphone up to my lips, I swiveled my body to face Kenny. I intimated the best possible apology I could. And I began to speak. "You are *so*, so right, Cindy. Thank you for carving time out for this. And thank you in advance, everyone, for your compassion. I think Kendra Rae is really happy that everyone will get to hear from her mouth—and her mouth only—*exactly* what she meant."

Elroy would later tell me that the moment of utter silence that followed lasted five seconds, not fifty-five. But it felt like a whole minute, an entire hour really, before Kenny signaled to me what looked a lot like a wordless apology of her own. And for a brief moment, when she opened her mouth, I thought we'd be okay. Surely, she *had* to understand what was at stake here—here, in front of all of these white people; here, in front of Cindy Murphy, one of Wagner's most influential authors. This was Kenny's chance to get ahead of whatever would undoubtedly be coming once the TV and radio stations got ahold of the interview. She could drive the conversation away from us and back to where it needed to be: *Burning Heart* itself, and its literary and cultural significance. She could get the country to focus on how the book might change the way people saw us, and even more important, the way we saw ourselves. She could say how it would empower Black girls who dreamed of not only seeing themselves in literature, but of creating it. She had the chance to build up instead of tear down.

But rather than speaking, Kenny stood. "I can't do this. I won't," she said, her gaze still locked on my own. "Sorry, Di. I just can't afford their price for my redemption."

She dropped her microphone on the couch behind her. And with that deep, impenetrable line in the sand, she was gone.

Book Club Questions for *The Other Black Girl*

Topics & Questions for Discussion

1. Zakiya Dalila Harris worked in publishing before writing *The Other Black Girl.* How do you think this might have affected her writing of the publishing world? Do you think it would've changed anything if *The Other Black Girl* had taken place in a different industry, such as tech or entertainment?

2. At what point did you realize there was something suspicious about Hazel-May? What do you think her motive is in getting closer to Nella?

3. Why do you think the book went back and forth in time? What do you think we've learned by experiencing these different eras? Has anything actually changed between then and now?

4. Who did you think originally placed the ominous Post-it note? Was this the point you realized Nella was in danger? Did you ever feel like Nella was being paranoid, or were you suspicious of Hazel-May (or others) from the start?

5. While Nella's relationship with Hazel-May is complicated, female friendships play a large role in the novel. Did you relate to Nella's friendship with Malaika, or Kendra Rae's friendship with Diana? How do you think these women supported one another—or tore each other down?

6. Were you expecting a different ending? What do you think happened at the end? How do you think they got to her? What do you think happens next?